GIRL LOVE HAPPENS

SEASON ONE

TB MARKINSON

Published by T. B. Markinson

Visit T. B. Markinson's official website at lesbianromancesbytbm.com for the latest news, book details, and other information.

Copyright © T. B. Markinson, 2016

Cover Design by Erin Dameron-Hill / EDHGraphics

Edited by Jeri Walker and Kelly Hashway

This book is a work of fiction. Names, characters, businesses, places, events, and incidents are the product of the author's imagination or are used fictitiously. Any resemblance to actual persons, living or dead, events, or locales is entirely coincidental.

LET'S KEEP IN TOUCH

One of the best parts of publishing is getting to know *you*, the reader.

My favorite method of keeping in touch is via my newsletter, where I share about my writing life, my cat (whom I lovingly call the Demon Cat since she hissed at me for the first forty-eight hours after I adopted her), upcoming new releases, promotions, and giveaways.

And, I give away two e-books to two newsletter subscribers every month. The winners will be able to choose from my backlist or an upcoming release.

I love giving back to you, which is why if you join my newsletter, I'll send you a free e-copy of *A Woman Lost*, book 1 of the A Woman Lost series, and bonus chapters you can't get anywhere else.

Also, you'll receive a free e-copy of *Tropical Heat*, a short story that lives up to the "heat" in its name.

If you want to keep in touch, sign up here: http://eepurl.com/hhBhXX

PREQUEL

CHAPTER ONE

"Tegan?"

I wheeled about with a pillow tucked under my chin, yanking up the pink rose Laura Ashley case from the bottom. The timid voice and soft expression of the dorm roommate I'd met only hours ago were no match for the energy emanating from her glorious red hair. "Yes, Gemma?"

"I've heard about this place called The Soda Jerk. Apparently, they have the best shakes on the planet." She smiled shyly, her hands shoved into her jeans pockets as she stood in the corner by the window. Sunlight made her purple and silver "Class of 1992" tassel hanging on the desk lamp dazzle like a disco ball.

"On the planet?" I quirked an eyebrow.

Her smile became bolder. "Now that the parental units have left, why don't we go find out? My treat."

"Right now?" I glanced at all the boxes and overall moving chaos with one eye closed as if soaking it in with both would send me into a nervous tizzy.

She shrugged. "It's just an idea."

I hurled the pillow onto my unmade bed. "It's the *best* idea. Get me out of this pandemonium!" I held up my hand, emphasizing the exclamation point.

She nodded. "My pleasure. These boxes will be here when we get back."

"Ugh! Don't remind me. Shall we drive?"

"Oh, I don't have a car." She took a step back, nearly stumbling over one of my boxes. "I hear it's not far, though." From her skinny frame, I gathered she wasn't averse to exercise.

"I have a car." I motioned for her to walk ahead of me. "Our chariot awaits, Gemma Mahoney," I said with a flourish.

In the hallway, I realized I had forgotten my car keys. "Hold on a sec." I dashed into the room, plucked them off my desk, and then sprinted back out, colliding with a stack of flimsy containers.

"Oomph."

Moving boxes toppled off a dolly, scattering onto the shabby beige carpet in the hallway. It seemed to show the faint outlines of footprints from students dating back to before I was born.

"I'm so sorry. Did I hurt you?" I searched for a body among the confusion.

"It'd take more than an itty-bitty thing like you to

hurt me." A plain, muscular girl popped off the floor and put her hand out, grinning. "I'm Jenny. And who do I have the honor of meeting in such an historic fashion?"

"Tegan." I shook her hand. "This is Gemma." I waved to my roommate, who was failing miserably to contain an *I can't believe you did that* smirk.

"Where's the fire?" Jenny made a show of checking out the room and hallway.

I laughed. "No fire. Milkshakes."

"Milkshakes?" Jenny cupped a hand to her ear, giving me her full attention. "Downstairs in the cafeteria?"

"No, unfortunately. But why don't I buy you one? I mean, it's the least I can do after smashing into you and your boxes." I bent over and crammed a backpack and some shirts that had spilled onto the floor back into a box, while Gemma busied herself salvaging towels and sheets. "We can help you get this stuff in your room."

"That's awfully kind of you. My parents had to bail early. Their social calendar is more impressive than mine." She smiled mischievously, making me wonder what kind of things she got up to. "Maybe our meeting was fate." Jenny, with Gemma's assistance, righted the boxes on the dolly. "I'm only a couple doors down from you."

We tagged along. Jenny's room was in disarray—even more so than Gemma's and mine. A blonde girl in a white tank top and Mom jeans straight off the set of *Beverly Hills 90210* sat on a bed rifling through a box in a lackadaisical *I wish I had servants* manner.

"April," Jenny's voiced bounced off the walls in the tiny room. "Meet Tegan and Gemma. They live on our floor. Watch out for Tegan. She packs a wallop." Jenny smirked at me.

"What happened to me being an itty-bitty thing?" I jutted out my lower lip.

"You are, Tiny T—that's my new name for you." She winked.

April hopped off the bed, plastering a smile on her face that made my skin crawl. "Hi!"

"We're going for milkshakes. Come along." Jenny's enthusiasm was contagious, and I almost forgot April's presence until the blonde met my eyes with an icy glare that conjured up an image of a scorpion with its tail raised. Girls like April should have to wear signs that read: *I take what I want by any means necessary.*

———

"OH MY GOD, this place is a trip." I scouted the fifties-style ice cream shop, half expecting Elvis Presley to appear in the corner, crooning "Blue Suede Shoes."

"Reminds me of home." Gemma studiously scanned the milkshake options on the board behind the counter.

"Can I help you lovely ladies?" An older, plump

man smiled from behind the counter and tugged on his red suspenders.

"What's good here?" Jenny gaped at the seemingly endless menu options.

"Everything." He chuckled. "But I own the place, so I may be biased. I'm Wilbur." He snapped his suspenders.

"Nice to meet ya, Wilbur. I'll have the peanut butter and chocolate shake." Gemma stepped to the side, motioning for me to order.

"That's what I was going to get," I whispered out of the corner of my mouth.

"You still can. Great minds—"

"And roommates." I laughed and turned to order. "Ditto for me, Wilbur."

"Heck, I can't argue with shake logic. Same for me," Jenny said much to Wilbur's amusement even if the statement wasn't exactly logical.

April pursed her lips. "Do you have frozen yogurt?"

Wilbur's smile dimmed somewhat. "Only chocolate and vanilla, miss."

"Vanilla, please." April smiled sweetly, but I wasn't buying her act. Everything about her, from her perfect makeup, bleached hair, and tanned skin came across as someone trying way too hard.

"Chocolate sauce on top?" Wilbur asked, widening his eyes.

She shook her head.

"Okey-dokey. Find a table, ladies, and I'll bring

your shakes out to you." Wilbur barked our order to his shake prep team, which consisted of one scrawny teenage boy with acne.

After taking seats at a table near the entrance, I turned to Jenny and April. "Did you two know each other before today?"

"Nope. Hopefully the computer system didn't royally screw up." Jenny grinned from ear to ear, her perfect white teeth nearly blinding me.

It was odd, comparing roommates who were sitting next to each other. Jenny the jock and April the beauty queen. Gemma wasn't exactly my twin, either. Her Cornhusker football fan T-shirt was testament to that. However, from the short time I'd known her, I sensed we'd become great friends.

"We didn't know each other either." I scootched back for Wilbur to set our milkshakes down.

"There you go, ladies. Give me a holler if you need anything." The older-than-dirt owner tottered to the table of two next to us and dished their ice cream concoctions from a tray.

I raised my glass. "To making new friends."

Gemma and Jenny clinked their glasses to mine, while April squished her nose in a way that suggested someone had once told her—probably when she was five—that expression was adorable. Unfortunately, this particular spoiled brat expression had an expiration date and didn't suit an eighteen-year-old.

"Where are you from, Gemma?" Jenny spooned a bite of swirled peanut butter into her mouth.

"Nebraska. You?"

"Denver."

Gemma studied April. I was sure she was going to ask her where she was from, but April's pinched face stopped Gemma cold.

Jenny swiveled in her chair and faced the girl she was now living with. "What about you, April? Seems silly I didn't ask earlier."

"Littleton." Her clipped one-word answer somehow made Jenny smile.

"Ah, we're neighbors," I said. "I'm just west of you, behind the hogback."

"Odd, most people want to be on top of me." April's face confused me since it contained the leer I was used to seeing on dudes. Before I could give it more thought, she spun toward Gemma. "Looks like you're the odd man out," she said with a cold blaze of victory in her face. From my experience, people like April were always seeking ways to exclude somebody to make themselves feel powerful. Picking on the quiet one in the group was a natural fit.

Gemma's face pinked, and the only word that came to my mind was adorable—maybe a result of the ice cream freezing my brain.

Jenny laughed. "Ouch, April. This is college; we're expanding our minds as we speak." She stretched her arms outward as if willing to embrace every new experience on the horizon.

"And our waistlines." To emphasize my point, I crammed a fully loaded spoon into my mouth.

"Another perk to college. No parents telling us what we can and should eat." Jenny clapped a hand on my shoulder. "And now for the question we'll be asked over and over for the next four years. What are you studying? You first, Tegan."

"Nursing."

"Right on. You'll come in handy, I think." She rubbed her chin thoughtfully as if weighing how my future nursing skills would help. "Gemma?"

"Economics."

Jenny slapped her thigh. "Awesome. I can never balance my checkbook. April?"

April blinked. "I haven't declared my major yet."

Jenny bobbed her head thoughtfully. "That's good. I like someone who prefers to sample different things before settling down." She whispered something in April's ear that warranted another seductive grin from the she-devil, making my head spin. Jenny patted her chest. "Me, I'm thinking of sports marketing."

Gemma perked up in her seat. "I would love to do that."

And Gemma and Jenny were off. They huddled their heads together, dropping names of teams, players, and places so fast my head spun. It was the first time I had witnessed Gemma without a trace of nervousness since meeting her earlier in the morning. I wasn't a sports nut, but their excitement was catchier than a cold in a preschool, which I knew from first-hand experience. April, though, chewed on a fingernail as if she hadn't eaten anything for days. She'd only taken a few bites of her plain frozen yogurt before abandoning it.

"Would you like to try my shake?" I offered in hopes of getting her to soften her bitchy face. It was giving me a headache; I couldn't imagine how it affected her.

Her face lit up, and she pounced on my shake with a vengeance. *Whoa, Nelly! Stay out of this one's way when there is chocolate involved.*

Gemma met my eye as if to communicate, *You weren't done with your shake, were you?* I shook my head. She casually shoved her half-full glass toward me, whispering, "I'm done if you want some."

I did want some, and I loved that she got me within hours of meeting me. This was, hopefully, the start to a beautiful friendship.

CHAPTER TWO

THAT NIGHT, THE FOUR OF US DECIDED TO hit the town. First up, dinner at Applebee's. The town of Alfrid was much smaller than what I was used to, and Applebee's was the best option, unless a person wanted Taco Bell, which I secretly did but didn't have the cojones to admit. Not with prom queen April in the group.

As I hummed along to "Save the Best for Last," Jenny snatched a fry off my plate.

"Hey! Hands off my fries." I laughed.

"Or what?" Jenny playfully crossed her arms and cocked her head.

"Or—" I brandished my spoon instead of my knife.

"You'll spoon me to death? Most pretty girls want to spoon with me, not kill me with one." She crinkled her nose.

Spoon with her? What did she mean by that?

Jenny bumped her arm into Gemma, who turned paler than a sacrificial virgin about to be flung into a volcano.

I attempted to get Gemma's attention to furtively ask if she was okay, but she kept her eyes downcast on her half-eaten chicken tenders, her face turning greener than Kermit the Frog's. A few drops of perspiration dotted her forehead. Had the fried goodness made her ill? I glanced at my plate that contained remnants of the same thing. Fingers crossed I didn't get the skitters, as my grandpa was fond of saying. Unlike Gemma, I hadn't touched the honey mustard dipping sauce. Honey and mustard—blech! Maybe my aversion for the abomination would save me from worshipping the white throne on my first night of parental freedom.

April jolted up in her seat and asked, "What's the plan tonight?"

Jenny tossed an arm over the back of her chair. "One of my school buddies who graduated the year before me is hosting a welcome to college bash at her house. I should warn you her shindigs are epic. Back in high school, she threw a party, and I woke up the next morning on a golf course with a lawn sprinkler spraying my face." She acted out getting sporadically hit in the face.

I gazed at Jenny to determine if she was serious or not. If that really happened, I didn't want to miss out. "I'm in."

"Ha!" Jenny waggled her finger. "I knew from the moment you crashed into me we'd be soul mates."

"Just as long as you don't steal my fries."

Jenny made a move, but I blocked her with my spoon, which I still had a firm grip on.

"Is that Brad Pitt?" she said in a careless way, making it clear she didn't give two shits but thought I'd be interested.

I glanced over my shoulder. "Where?"

Gemma's laughter clued me into the fact that I'd fallen for the most obvious trick in the book.

By the time I whipped my head back to defend my fries, only three remained. The rest of the approximate dozen I'd had were now dangling out of Jenny's mouth.

"You owe me dessert now." I gave her the stink eye.

She swallowed forcefully. "For what?"

"Eating my dinner!"

"Phooey. I was helping so you would have room for free beer." Jenny smiled.

"Uh-huh. Do people really fall for that?" I scowled at her, folding my arms over my chest.

"You mean like, 'Oh look, there's Harrison Ford?'"

"Where?" April's eyes panned the restaurant.

Did she used to ride the short bus to school? Apparently I did but didn't know it.

"He does look like Harrison Ford." April was practically drooling.

I hugged my arms tighter over my double Ds. "Nope. I'm not falling for it again."

"Your loss." Jenny craned her neck. "He's gone now, anyway."

I laughed. "You think I'm an idiot."

Jenny squeezed my shoulder. "Not at all."

The contact and words weren't comforting.

Gemma raised her finger to get the waitress's attention. "Can we get the triple chocolate meltdown?"

"Sure thing, hon. And four spoons?"

Gem nodded.

The waitress spun on her heel and nearly smacked into a herd of five dudes on their way out.

"At least Gemma understands me," I said, ignoring the leer of one of the guys. My boobs were a magnet for these types of stares that made me want to disappear.

Gemma smiled broadly. Jenny excused herself to talk to a guy she went to high school with, who had just breezed into the restaurant, and April fled to the bathroom.

I leaned over to Gemma, her scent blanketing me with a sense of tranquility. "It wasn't really Harrison Ford, right?"

Gemma's smile widened. "No, it wasn't, although, the guy looked a lot like him."

"Good. That'd be my luck."

She tilted her head, allowing me complete access to

her stunning emerald eyes and making me ashamed of my plain blues. "How so?"

"Missing out on an opportunity of a lifetime because of my stubborn pride."

"Meeting Harrison Ford is an opportunity of a lifetime?" Gemma said, in an inhibited sort of voice, as if her tongue was too large for her mouth.

My cheeks tingled. "Maybe I overstated it." I leaned even closer, feeling some type of pull to her, like the sun has on the moon. "Don't you think he's hot, though?"

She laughed nervously.

Unsure why she seemed ill at ease, I confided, "I'm a huge fan of *Indiana Jones*. You?"

"I prefer him in *Star Wars*. No question."

"*Star Wars*? You've got to be joking." I slapped her arm lightly.

"I never joke about *Star Wars*. Have you seen all three?"

I tapped my index finger against my front teeth, regretting calling attention to the prominent gap. "I saw the one with the furry things."

"Furry things?" She scrunched her eyebrows, shaking her head. "You mean Ewoks. Jesus, how can you be a freshman in college if you've never seen *Star Wars*? All of them?"

"Did someone say *Star Wars*?" Jenny slid back into her seat, her easygoing smile still affixed. "Who can forget the scene with Jabba the Hut and Princess Leia?"

Gemma's face tinged cherry red. Her creamy skin allowed for every emotion she experienced to be put on display. I wondered what color she turned during the heat of the moment. I furrowed my brow, questioning why that particular thought came to mind. Jenny eyed me intently. Surely she didn't suspect I was wondering what Gemma's face looked like in the throes of passion. That would be completely weird, right?

I opted for a smokescreen, just in case. "Maybe I'll dress up as Leia for Halloween. Would you two like that?"

"Which outfit?" Jenny asked in all seriousness.

"I'll let you choose, as long as you two dress up like characters from the movie." I wielded my spoon toward Jenny and then Gemma, punctuating the pact.

"Are you serious?" Jenny inched closer and said in an almost seductive way, "You're not being a tease, are you?"

"I never tease about Halloween. It's holier to me than Christmas."

Jenny's jaw dropped, and she bobbled her head like a child let loose in a 7-Eleven candy aisle with a hundred-dollar bill. Gemma avoided my eyes completely, not lending much insight if she was excited or not about dressing up in ridiculous *Star*

Wars costumes for Halloween. I needed to find a way to help Gemma loosen up some.

That made me giggle, drawing off some of the discomfort clouding my brain. *Indiana Jones* was clearly the better movie franchise, not that these two *Star Wars* bozos would ever see it my way. Or maybe I could wrest them from the dark side, at least Gemma, whose kind eyes watched me intently even though she went to great lengths not to be noticed.

April returned and rubbed her mitts together when she spied the waitress twirling her way through the rambunctious crowd as she carried the dessert to our table. She clawed her spoon with a look in her eye that brought to mind images of the Donner Party. Had she starved herself all summer in preparation to combat the freshman fifteen?

Jenny fixed serious eyes on April and motioned for her not to take a bite yet. "Are you a fan of *Star Wars?*"

April visibly flinched before looking to Gemma and then me. "Uh, is that the one with Captain Kirk?"

Jenny massaged her eyes before clopping her hand on April's shoulder, giving it a squeeze. "I need to talk to admissions. Clearly they're letting the wrong people into Hill University."

I kicked her shins under the table. "Take that back."

April's smile indicated she thought I was taking her side, and I didn't have the heart to tell her I was on Indiana's side.

Jenny leaned on her forearms and met my eyes. "Don't worry. Gem and I will convert you. May the force be with you."

"Yeah, right. The day you two convert me is the day I'll eat my own shoe."

Jenny glommed onto the table with one hand and swung her head under the table. "Those LA Gears don't look very tasty."

By the time I was able to focus on the matter at hand, the dessert was half gone. April didn't even have the decency to look ashamed.

"Shall we get another?" Gemma asked.

April nodded vigorously.

I raised my spoon. "Here's to an interesting year." I then plunged it into the remaining dessert, swiping a third of it into my mouth.

AN OBNOXIOUS SQUAWK and streaming sunlight interrupted my slumber. Rolling onto my back, I opened my eyes, confused as to my whereabouts. To my right was a battered cardboard box, and to my left was a skinny bed. My bed at home was queen-size, meaning I wasn't in Kansas anymore.

"You okay?"

I cranked my head to the right and peered over the box. "What the hell happened?"

My redheaded roommate smiled broadly. "What's the last thing you remember?"

Pinching my eyes shut, I concentrated. "Chocolate of some kind."

Gemma nodded. "We ate at Applebee's and had dessert." She raked a hand through her hair. "Although, it could have been the chocolate cake shots."

"What was in them?"

"Vanilla vodka and Frangelico hazelnut liqueur."

I smacked my lips. "My mouth tastes like fungus, and my brain feels like it's five times too large for my head."

"You need water." Gemma flipped open the door of the beat-up mini fridge crammed between the two beds.

That was when it dawned on me I wasn't in a bed. "Why am I on the floor?"

"You refused to sleep on your bed." Gemma twisted the lid off a water bottle. "You didn't want to spoil your outfit." She was trying hard not to laugh, but I could hear it in her tone.

I sat up—or tried to. The room swirled as Gemma eased me upright.

"Seriously, you need to drink water." She thrust the bottle into my hand.

Gulping the water, I had a chance to eye my outfit, if one could call it that. I wore a harmless white long sleeve shirt that didn't belong to me, a flamingo pink tutu, and had a yellow, green, and black Hula-Hoop around my waist. I rattled the hoop, and the sand inside swished. "No wonder my side hurts. I slept on this." I shook it again.

"Insisted on it. You even threatened my life if I took it away."

I smothered my eyes both out of shame and because the light was making me ill. "It must have been some night." Uncovering my eyes, I said, "I'm sorry I threatened your life."

Gemma chuckled. "I think threatening to kill someone is the perfect way to start a friendship, don't you?" Her smile was genuine and warm.

Even though it hurt like hell, I laughed. "If you say so."

CHAPTER THREE

MONDAY MORNING ARRIVED MUCH TOO SOON, along with my mother's annoying voice once again plaguing my mind in moments of weakness. If there was one thing my mother excelled at, it was to instill the seed of doubt that no matter what, I would never be good enough. I'd received better than average grades in high school, graduating in the top ten percent of my class, but my mother had been reminding me since receiving my diploma that college was a different kettle of fish entirely, where I'd be swimming in a larger pond with bigger and more intelligent fish.

"It's nothing to be ashamed of," she'd say. "Some have *it* and some don't."

Mom never explained what *it* was, exactly. And she never explicitly said I didn't have it, but she also never said that I did. Usually I was able to shove these thoughts out of my head.

"You feeling okay?" Gemma stood in front of the bathroom mirror, her thumb hovering over the on switch of the hair dryer.

"Never better." I mustered up the courage to smile and headed to the shower. Attending my first class without showering would be tantamount to riding a horse bareback. Imagining my mother's reaction, though, did put a smile on my face.

When I stepped out of the bathroom, fully clothed, Gemma had left for her calculus class. Math had been my nemesis since junior high, and living with someone who was enrolled in Calc 101 reinforced the idea that some have it and some don't.

"Get a grip, Tegan," I chastised myself. Math skills didn't define a person's self-worth. What did, though?

"TEGAN!"

I flipped around on the quad outside the student union and spied Jenny, April, Gemma, and some girl that looked vaguely familiar, sitting at a plastic white table. I waved, relieved not only that I had survived my first week of classes, but I had friends to celebrate the victory with. Of course, I wouldn't admit to them how intimidated I had been for the past five days. I had nearly hyperventilated when my American history professor went around the room asking each of us why we enrolled in the class. He called on me first, and my initial brilliant response was "Do you need an ego boost or something?" Unsure how the elbow-patched old dude would respond, I scratched it and blurted, "My advisor told me to." Several in the class laughed, but I sincerely doubted I scored any points with the prof.

Gemma pulled out the empty chair between her and the mystery girl. "You remember Michelle, Jenny's friend from high school."

I didn't, and I suspected Gemma knew that, considering how wrecked I was the morning after Michelle's party. Still, the only recollection I had was chocolate. However, I said, "Of course. How are you?"

The brunette with oodles of curly hair, big smile, and kind eyes tamped out her cigarette in a makeshift ashtray, which I think was once a coffee cup lid. "You survived your first week. It only gets easier from here. I remember how I felt when I was in your shoes last year. I nearly puked in the shower the first morning."

I could have given her a hug for verbalizing the emotions roiling inside.

"Ah, Tegan's tough. Aren't you?" Jenny walloped my shoulder.

Michelle shook her head and leaned closer to me, but said loud enough for everyone to hear, "Don't let her façade fool ya. I know Jenny better than most, and she was quaking in her boots before her first class. She even lugged all of her books every day this week, even though I'd told her not to bother."

Jenny blushed. "What are you trying to do? Ruin my rep?"

Michelle reached behind Jenny and yanked on her backpack, which hung on the back of her chair, demonstrating its weight. "Just keeping it real."

We all laughed, but April's was difficult to decipher, considering her menacing eyes were soaking in Jenny's mortification.

"I'm not excited about my geology class." April did her best to sound sincere, but my gut told me nothing about her was real, not even her too perfect, never bouncy boobs.

"Rocks for jocks. I took that last semester. Whenever I went to the lab, I had to fill out sheets about how each rock was different." Michelle laughed. "They all looked like rocks. I squeaked by with a C. Have fun with that one."

"I'm sure you'll be fine." Jenny tried to soothe April.

"Now that all of you've survived the first week, it's time to share one of the best parts of Alfrid." Michelle lit a cigarette, obviously not in a hurry. She exhaled over her shoulder. "Swimming at the reservoir on a gorgeous Friday afternoon."

Without looking in a mirror, I knew all color had drained from my face.

Besides math, bikinis were my nemesis.

ONE HOUR LATER, the five of us claimed a rocky ledge that provided a semblance of privacy about twenty feet above the water's surface. Music drifted up from other students dotting the shore below.

Aside from Gemma and me, everyone in our group wore a bikini. I went a step further and kept a tank top on over my one-piece.

Fluffy cotton candy clouds hung in the deep-blue sky as if tacked there by a child. The temperature hovered in the low nineties. The surface of the water rippled slightly with the breeze. A cluster of aspen trees off to the right had the beginning speckles of autumn color, reminding me to enjoy the day's warmth before the chill of the evening descended like a curtain on a stage.

Jenny lifted the lid of Michelle's beat-up cooler, initiating a creaking sound straight out of a B-horror flick. "Keystone Light, anyone?"

Michelle and April indicated they wanted one.

"Tegan?" Jenny held a blue and silver can as if offering me a precious gift.

"No thanks. I'm driving."

"I can drive home if you want one," Gemma offered.

"You don't mind?" I asked, unsure if that was a good idea.

"Not at all." To prove her point, she reached into the cooler for a Coke and popped the top.

Jenny tossed me the beer. "Now this is living." She stood at the edge, staring out over the reservoir, guzzling a quarter of her drink. Craning her head to take in the surface below, she asked Michelle, "How deep is the water?"

"Deep enough to jump in." Michelle inserted a tape into her boom box. I strained to hear the opening of "Walking in Memphis." After adjusting the volume, she stood at Jenny's side and said, "On three."

The two of them counted, "One, two, threeeeeeee!" They jumped, with their feet pointing down and arms tucked against their sides, from a rocky outcropping that I imagined many students had used as a diving board of sorts. I laughed when I heard the splash and Jenny shout, "Damn, that's cold."

April peered down, uncertainty nibbling at the corners of her confident smile. Gemma laid on her back on a towel, giving the vibe that she had zero intention of budging. I followed suit on my towel.

"You two staying?" April asked needlessly.

"Yep," I answered for both of us, slipping on my sunglasses.

April shrugged and then jumped. Her squeal when she hit the water was ear-piercing, followed by splashing and something that sounded like *hiya hiya hiya*, even though I was fairly confident she wasn't saying hi to the fish.

Covering my ears, I whispered to Gemma, "She's never subtle, is she?"

Gemma laughed. "You need sunscreen?"

"What did my mom do, pull you aside and instruct you never to let my skin see the sun without a thick layer of protection?" I rolled my head to face her, shielding my eyes, glad to see a smile.

She rummaged in her bag and pulled out Coppertone with thirty SPF. "Sorry, but I don't really tan, and with anything lower, I turn into a lobster."

"It's true, then, what they say about redheads?"

She blushed, making me wonder what she thought I meant, and then I'd remembered overhearing a guy in high school ask a visiting cheerleader with red hair if the carpet matched the drapes. It was hard to forget the look of scorn on her face.

Wanting to cover my tracks quickly, I said, "Redheads burn easily."

She laughed, relieved—I think.

I stuck my hand out, and Gemma squeezed sunscreen into my palm. After smearing the lotion onto my front side, I asked, "Would you mind getting the back of my neck and shoulders?"

"Uh, sure." Again she sat up. "Do you want to take your tank off?"

"Nah. I've learned the hard way." I shook my tits. "These are less subtle than April and bring unwanted attention, if you know what I mean." It was my stock answer as to why I never went without at least a tank top, and it was truthful to a point. "Your hands are soft, unlike my boyfriend's. And you're gentler. His idea of rubbing sunscreen makes me feel like an Easter egg being dunked in and out of the dye and ending up only half-covered."

When I eyed her over my shoulder, even through my sunglasses, I noticed Gemma's cheeks matched the Coke can sitting between us. "Don't forget your face," I said. "I think it's already starting to burn." I squinted at the sky, sucking in a mouthful of fresh air.

She mumbled thanks.

I stood and stretched my arms over my shoulder at the foot of Gemma's towel. Then I jabbed my elbows behind my back, sticking my chest out to relieve the backache from my boobs. "It's hot, isn't it?"

Again, Gemma reddened as if the mere suggestion of the sun scorched her skin.

The three returned sooner than I'd expected, shivering slightly.

"Hey wimps, you two should try it out." Jenny shook her hair, sprinkling water over Gemma and me.

"Jenny!" I shouted.

She laughed and grabbed her beer.

It took April several minutes to arrange herself on her towel. I wanted to say, "It's a rock; there's bound to be pokey things." I caught Jenny eyeing her with interest. There was always one prima donna in every group of girls.

Noticing me, Jenny widened her eyes as if mocking April's antics. "So, Tegan, you dating anyone?"

"Yeah, but he's going to school in Texas." I tried shrugging like it wasn't a big deal, but I didn't think I was all that convincing.

"That's rough. Not sure I'm cut out for the long-distance thing."

Michelle rolled her eyes. "Since when were you cut out for any type of relationship?"

Jenny raised her eyebrows in a mocking way. "I'm not a fan of routine, unlike you and Seb, who are practically married."

"Please." Michelle ripped the lid off a Pringle's can and chomped into a chip. She offered the can to the group and then dipped into the cooler to retrieve red grapes, setting out the container for the group after plucking a handful for herself. "We're only living together because it saves on rent. Not all of us have Mommy and Daddy paying our bills."

Jenny, unperturbed by the last comment, snatched a chip. "Let me see your ring finger. Got the circle of death on it yet?"

Michelle proudly displayed her middle finger. "Not everyone can be a player like you."

Jenny thumped her chest like Tarzan. "Damn right and proud of it."

"Although I'm getting some, and your vibe screams sex deprived."

Laughing, Jenny shook a fist at Michelle. "Whatever."

I nibbled on a chip, pondering Jenny's words since I hadn't pegged her as a player. Not once in the past week had I seen her flirt with a dude. I wasn't throwing myself at the hotties on campus, but I had a reason, namely my boyfriend. What was holding her back? "Have you ever dated anyone?"

Jenny hitched a shoulder, avoiding my eyes. "Not for long. A couple of weeks here and there."

"I've had colds that lasted longer." Laughing, I covered my mouth so I wouldn't spray chunks of chips on Gemma. "That doesn't count. Not at all!"

"I'm with Jenny. Relationships are for suckers. With all the items on the menu, why limit yourself?" April grabbed a handful of Pringles.

Jenny placed a finger on her nose and stretched out her other hand toward April. "There's a reason we're roommates."

Sophie B. Hawkins's song "Damn I Wish I Was Your Lover" played softly over the speakers.

"I love this song." Michelle cranked the volume.

Singing the lyrics, Jenny seized her beer can. April joined in, looking like Marilyn Monroe singing to the president, giving the word "provocative" a whole new meaning. Michelle egged them on, cheering like a foolish roadie. Gemma squirmed on her towel with an uncomfortable smile. When the song ended, Jenny waggled her eyebrows at April, who giggled like she thought Jenny was actually making a play for her.

"What about you, Gemma? Got someone back home?" Michelle lit an American Spirit, handing it off to Jenny, who took a drag and passed it back.

"Nah. Slim pickings in a town of only four hundred." Gemma blinked excessively, straightening the corners of her towel. The sun had reemerged from behind a cloud, but I wondered if there was another reason why Gemma looked... ashamed.

"Four hundred?" Michelle held her cigarette in front of her face as if too stunned to take a drag.

"Four hundred and seven according to the last census. Minus one now."

"That's a quarter of the size of my high school." Jenny whistled and grabbed another beer from the cooler. "I can't even imagine. Alfrid must seem like a metropolis to you." She held her arms out wide. "And as the saying goes, the world is my oyster. That's my motto."

"God, you're such a dork." Michelle motioned for a beer.

"I may be a dork, but I'm a free dork. Not like you and Tegan, tied down before you're even twenty." She turned to April. "What do you say, April? Want to take a splash with me?"

The two of them jumped over the ledge, disappearing from sight, although I could hear April's scream all the way down.

Michelle met my eye. "Jenny's always been crazy. I like that about her, but I don't believe her for one bit. She acts tough, but Jenny wishes she was in a relationship. Not that she would admit that and... She's too easily influenced." Michelle stared at the ledge. "I worry about her."

Before I could ask why, she dove off and hit the water seconds later, leaving Gemma and I alone on the rock. I turned to the redhead. "It's just you and me, kid, against the world," I said in what my mother always claimed was my over-the-top voice.

"I got your back."

"Speaking of, I should sunscreen yours." I shook the Coppertone.

"Nah, it'll be fine." She settled back onto the towel as if to prove her point.

"You sure? You don't want to be *tan* on only one side, and it wouldn't say much as a future nurse if I sat by why you turned into half a lobster."

Gemma shielded her eyes, studying me for a second before she said, "I wouldn't want you to slip up because of me."

CHAPTER FOUR

"GEMMA AND TEGAN, YOU TWO BELONG together, like gin and tonic." Michelle took a drag from her cigarette and then blew smoke upward into the haze clinging to the low-hanging popcorn ceiling. Torn and wrinkled posters ranging from Nirvana to Pearl Jam to Alice in Chains to Stone Temple Pilots were taped to the drywall in the unfinished basement. The wall on the other side was cement. The previous owners must have started renovating the space but then abandoned the job halfway through, opting to rent out the three-bedroom house to college kids who wouldn't give a rat's ass about the state of things. The worse shape the house was in, the cheaper the rent.

Gemma and I were squeezed into a rattan hanging swing chair for one, but we made it work.

Jenny bolted upright in the vinyl navy beanbag held

together with duct tape. Her movement caused a handful of beads to spill onto the concrete floor. "Dude, you're so right. Gemma is totally the gin: quietly confident and dependable, and TR is the spazzy fizz."

"I'm not a spaz!" I sloped forward in the hanging chair, shaking a fist at Jenny.

The egg-shaped chair, attached to a wooden stand, wobbled precariously to the left and then to the right.

"Whoa!" I clapped a hand over my red Solo cup, swaying with the chair.

Gem placed a foot on the threadbare area rug to save us from careening into the paint-splattered concrete off to the side.

"You see. Steady Gemmy saved your ass again while your gut reaction was to save your drink." Jenny giggled, twisting her face into the crook of her arm as if she had said the most hilarious thing in human history.

I giggled with her, rolling my eyes. "Whatever." Then her words sank into my gin-foozled brain. "What do you mean *again*?"

Sebastian held up a scratched-to-hell plastic Coors Light pitcher he had "procured" from O'Neil's sports bar one town over last year when he was a freshman. "Refill?" A chain was clipped to a belt loop in the front and draped halfway down his thigh, loosely connected to the wallet in his back pocket. Maybe O'Neil's should chain down their pitchers the first weekend of the semester since it was a rite of passage for many Hill University newbies to nab one. Unfortunately, I hadn't learned about this rule until the second week, seriously damaging my street cred. Now that we were well over a month, practically two, into the semester, it was seriously too late to pilfer my own pitcher, and I'd never be a freshman again. As mom liked to say, "There are no do-overs in life."

"Please." I thrust my plastic cup for him to refill with gin and tonic, heavy on the gin. Then he plopped a lime wedge into my glass, making the concoction fizz.

Gemma nodded her head for another round. "Thanks, Seb."

Early in September, our group had initiated the first G&T Thursday after listening to "Hey Jealousy" by the Gin Blossoms. Jenny had said she'd never sampled a gin and tonic, and before any of us knew it, a tradition had been born. Over five weeks and still going strong. If a person didn't like gin and tonic, there was no need to show up on Thursdays. That was until the gin ran out and we switched to Bud Light.

"Yoo-hoo, Seb. I need more." April batted her eyes seductively and smiled at Sebastian, Michelle's boyfriend of two years.

Michelle met my gaze, chomping on her bottom lip. The only reason any of us still tolerated April was because she was Jenny's roommate.

Sebastian's unbuttoned shirt flapped to the side, revealing a Red Hot Chili Peppers T-shirt. "Right. Sorry about that, Apes."

April's lips puckered. I hadn't been brave enough to use the nickname. I rubbed the top of my head, wondering if anyone else had or just Sebastian. He had a look of innocence with the right amount of cluelessness and could get away with it. However, I suspected he knew what he was doing and used his naïveté to his utmost advantage. It was always best to keep an eye on the quiet ones.

Gemma glanced at me with her emerald eyes, eliciting a sensation in my chest that I couldn't put a name to. We'd morphed into best friends almost instantly after our first day in the dorm.

There wasn't anything I wouldn't do for the shy redhead from Nebraska. I nestled against her shoulder, smelling her just showered fresh scent and fruity shampoo. I was on my fourth gin and tonic while steady Gemmy nursed her second. Maybe that was one of the reasons why people thought her more confident —she'd rarely got as drunk as the rest of us.

I nuzzled into her shoulder, thinking how good it felt to have her so close. I slurred, "I-I like this," and then took a sip of my drink. To strip away the bad taste in my mouth, I ran my teeth over my tongue, which was coated with a layer of booze funk.

Gemma winced, but her only response was to guzzle half of her drink.

"Tegan." Michelle snapped her fingers to get my full attention. "When's your boyfriend visiting? I have to meet the man who tamed you."

I sprung upright. "No one's tamed me!"

Once again, Gemma made sure we didn't tumble onto the floor.

"Methinks you hit a sore spot," Jenny said, raising her glass toward Michelle who did the same. She turned her head to me. "What's the matter?"

I took a nip of my drink, stalling, which did not escape their notice. Both motioned for me to come out with it.

"I don't know. I just don't miss Josh. Shouldn't I miss my boyfriend who lives in Texas while I'm in Colorado? We're 600 miles apart, but it feels more like 6,000." I shrugged, settling back against Gemma's comforting shoulder. My feelings for Josh, or lack thereof, had been weighing heavily on my mind. I peered out the tiny basement window and glimpsed the auburn, yellow, and orange leaves.

"Why did he go to school in Texas?" Jenny asked. Coloradoans weren't known to be partial to Texas or Texans.

"All the men in his family have gone to school in Lubbock."

Michelle lit an American Spirit by using the red tip of her nearly extinguished cigarette and circled back to what I'd said. "Hmmm. In the beginning, was your relationship hot and heavy?"

"What do you mean?"

"Passionate. Like Heathcliff and Catherine."

"Who are they?" My voice cracked.

Gemma placed a hand on my thigh, smiling. "You know, *Wuthering Heights.*"

"Oh, I know the Kate Bush song," I confessed sheepishly.

Michelle leaned forward on the tattered brown and orange plaid couch she and Seb had claimed after a neighbor three streets over set it on the curb. This was another tradition in Alfrid—college students who lived off campus scoured the streets for abandoned couches to put on their front decks and in their basements. Older residents appreciated the scavengers saving them a trip to the dump. "Is your relationship like that?"

"God no! Josh is mellow. So mellow sometimes it's hard to know what he's thinking, let alone that he's breathing." Not that many of the boys I went to high school with had dazzled me with their charm. There wasn't an Indiana Jones in the bunch. As far as I could tell, only one thing got Josh excited, and it was the thing I'd been taught never to discuss in public. Or private for that matter. "At least, that's how I remember him. It feels like ages since I've seen him."

Michelle and Jenny exchanged a look that said, "Where do we go from here?"

"What attracted you to him in the first place?" Michelle asked into her cracked Solo cup.

When Josh had first shown an interest, my initial thought had been whether or not he was available. My second was whether or not he was non-threatening. My third was I better latch onto him or my mother would keep trying to set me up with sons of her friends. And let's be honest, if their moms had to set them up, there was a reason. After a painful incident with a boyfriend I had been crazy about, I wasn't too keen on the idea of dating another boy from my high school. How to explain, though? "He wasn't on the football team and didn't want to be." That was true. After dating a few jocks, I had realized I should steer clear. Their massive egos and my double D boobs made for many uncomfortable nights shoving a big galoot, who only was interested in S-E-X and nothing more, off of me. The word that came to mind when I thought of Josh was *safe*.

Michelle crinkled her nose like she did when presented with a mental conundrum. "Huh, so more of an artsy type?"

"Not really. He's the type that likes to sit on a deck with a twelve-pack and only utter ten words all day. It's easy being around him. Takes zero effort." After living with my mother, who ruthlessly henpecked everyone in the family, including my father, I desired a drama-free life.

"Sounds like a real wiener." April theatrically covered her mouth. "I mean winner."

Whenever April contributed to any conversation, it was the equivalent of slinging ice water into everyone's face.

"You like easy?" Michelle adjusted on the couch, tossing an arm along the back, looking completely at ease.

I raked my blonde hair. "I don't know. With Josh, yes. He's extremely uncomplicated, but..."

"But what?" Jenny peered at me.

The thought vanished before it had to chance to take root. "I don't know. Too many of these today." I raised my half-empty cup.

"How's the sex?" Michelle asked.

My face went up in flames, and I gasped. "Who are you? Dr. Ruth?"

"In training." She waggled her eyebrows.

"You want to be a sex therapist? Not your typical headshrinker?" My voice was practically operatic.

"I haven't decided on my specialty, but I am drawn to sex—"

"Who isn't?" purred April with a smile bordering on lecherous.

Michelle flashed her tight-lipped smile and then mouthed "Later" to me.

I nodded and snuggled against Gemma again in the swaying chair. She downed the rest of her gin and tonic and promptly knifed the air with her finger for a refill.

Seb, the gracious host, hopped up. "There you go, G. How about you, Spazzy?" He swirled the contents in the pitcher.

I hitched a shoulder. "Sure. I don't need to go to my classes tomorrow."

"Tegan, have you been shopping yet for your Halloween costume?" Jenny grinned. "Only two weeks until the big day."

"I told you I'm not going as Princess Leia."

"But you promised."

"That was before I got a load of her outfit. Come to think of it, she wasn't wearing much at all."

"You saw the movie before agreeing. How could you forget?" Jenny joggled her head in a drunken fashion and slurred, "A promise is a promise."

"The only thing I remembered from seeing the movie when I was a kid were the furry things. Not a woman in a bikini chained to a hideous, slimy ogre."

"He's more like a slug from outer space with a toad face," Gemma corrected.

"You aren't selling it." I poked her in the ribs. Her eyes met mine, and I felt like I was swimming in a calming pool of green.

"I'm not letting you off the hook, Spazzy. You're the only one here who can pull off Leia, and all of us" —she motioned to the group, including April, who had been vague about her costume choice—"agreed to go as different *Star Wars* characters."

"Dude, I'm down with that, but not as Leia in *that* outfit."

"I'll do it," April said, and no one paid her heed, not even Jenny, until she added, "But Tiny T, you promised. It's not our fault you didn't know what you were talking about when you made the promise."

I could practically feel the death rays shooting out of my eyes at April. When we'd had the conversation, she'd confused *Star Trek* with *Star Wars*, and now she was acting like an expert on the George Lucas trilogy. Her motives were just as baffling as Darth Vader.

"She wasn't in her slave outfit in all three of the movies. Most of the time she's wearing a long white dress." Gemma took a nervous sip and edged away from me some as if startled or disappointed.

I squinted at the ceiling but couldn't conjure up the white dress in my memory from the most recent viewing a couple of weeks ago. Only the bikini registered.

———

HOURS LATER, Gemma and I stumbled into our dorm room. I had one arm around her shoulder, and she had one arm encircled around my waist.

"Here you go." Gemma sat me on my unmade bed, yanked off my shoes, pushed me down on the sheet, and tucked me in under my pink and white comforter. "Cozy?" She arched a ginger eyebrow.

"Snug as a bug." I tittered like a fool.

She stared down at me with an odd smile on her face. "I'm going to shower," she said with a sort of swallow.

"Righty-O, space captain." I sat up unsteadily to snap a salute, but only managed to slam the side of my hand into my eyeball.

As soon as the bathroom door shut, I chastised myself. "Righty-O, space captain?" I groaned and fell back onto my pillow, baffled by why I suddenly felt uncomfortable around Gemma. No, not uncomfortable, per se, but tongue-tied. Like I was trying too hard to be cute, funny, and charming.

Minutes later, Gem stepped out of the bathroom, dressed in a wifebeater and red pajama bottoms covered with ginormous white Ns. Her Irish skin had a pinkish hue, and the back of her shirt was drenched by her crimson locks. Gem's lips were red and full, making me tingle with jealousy.

Gemma swung open the battered door to our mini fridge and seized two Target brand water bottles. She held one aloft. "I think it'd be wise for you to drink all of this water before you fall asleep and then this one during the night. Or you might wake up in a tutu and hula hoop again."

I nodded, grabbed the remote to the stereo from the top of the fridge, which doubled as our nightstand, and flipped on the radio. "Fast Car" filled the silence in the room.

"How come you never talk about an ex?" I fluffed a pillow behind my back and then swigged some water.

Gem sat with her back against the wall, cradling her knees, facing me. "Not much to tell really." She avoided my eyes.

"*Au contraire*. I can tell by your avoidance you aren't playing fair." I lowered my head, trying to catch her eye.

"I'm not avoiding."

I slanted my head so it was nearly horizontal to the floor and stared into her eyes. "Yes. You. Are." I punctuated each word with a jab of the finger. "I know you better than anyone."

"Is that right?" Her tone was playful. "Even though we've only known each other a couple of months?"

"After living in a space smaller than a jail cell, it's true. So spill the beans right now, missy."

"Or what?"

"Or I'll…"

"That's what I thought. Empty threats will get you nowhere." She tsked, rubbing one index finger over her other, teacher-like.

"I'll s-show you an empty threat." I glanced around the room helplessly, my eyes not wanting to focus.

She chortled. "Yep! You showed me!"

I shook the water bottle at her. "Don't be so mean." My speech slurred and *so mean* came out *shhh-mean*.

Gem placed a hand on her tiny but perfect tits. "I'm

being mean? You're the one threatening me. Or trying to."

"Gemma!" I raked my blonde hair into a scrunchie, neglecting a large section in the back that hung limply, but I didn't have the energy or coordination to fix it. "Just tell me what I want to know."

"I'm sorry. What did you want to know again?" Her beguiling grin got to me in indescribable ways.

I lobbed a heart-shaped pillow at her head.

"That's the threat? A decorative pillow?" Nevertheless, she clutched it to her chest.

"No, that's not the threat. This is the threat." I bum-rushed her and straddled her on the bed, tickling her sides. "Tell me or I'll subject you to tickle torture."

"Teeg... stop!" She attempted to pull my arms away, but I escaped her fumbling hands.

"Or what?"

She hesitated for a moment. "I won't tell you what you want to know."

That captured my attention, and I put my hands in the air as if a cop commanded me to reach for the sky. "Okay, I'll be good. I promise." I sat on her bed with my back against the wall under her "Everything I know I learned from my dog" poster to still the spinning sensation. It was strange how my mind was trying to fight off the drunkenness as if knowing a golden opportunity awaited.

"Why do you want to know?"

"Why?" I put a hand on my chest. "Because you're

my roommate, but I feel... Sometimes, I feel like you purposely don't tell me certain things, and I don't want a barrier up between us. You're my best friend. Let me in."

Gem snorted. "Really? Emotional blackmail?"

I nudged her with my foot. "This isn't emotional blackmail!"

"Yes, it is."

I stabbed the air with a finger. "Take that back!"

"Or what?"

"Or I won't dress as Princess Leia." My tongue stumbled over Princess Leia, making me sound like I had a serious lisp.

Gemma chuckled, and it seemed forced. "Jenny and April are the ones insisting you dress as her, not me."

"What, you don't want me to?"

She shifted on the bed, remaining mute.

I needed to up my game, and only one thing came to mind. I forced her onto her back, climbed on top, and resumed tickling her mercilessly.

"Tegan, please," she shouted in a desperate manner. "Get off me!" She shoved with all her force, knocking me into the wall.

There was quiet in the room for a split second until Gemma blubbered, "I'm sorry. I didn't mean to..."

Simultaneously, I babbled, "Please, don't be mad. I'm just drunk. Please don't be mad at me." My brain and mouth were on different wavelengths, trying to figure out what spurred her to seriously wig out.

Gem helped me into a sitting position and tucked a lock of my hair behind my ear. "Are you okay?"

I nodded. "Are you mad?"

"I could never be mad at you." Her voice was softer and filled with regret.

I nervously ran my tongue over the gap in my front teeth.

She smiled weakly, glancing down at her freckled hands in her lap.

"Do you want to talk about it?" I pulled away. "I understand if you don't, but if you do, I'm here." I positioned a hand behind each of my ears and said, "Have ears, will listen."

She pulled a face. "I hate that poster."

Last week after a student attempted to kill himself, the mental health clinic had slathered posters with their new slogan that showed a cartoon guy with elephant-size ears all over campus. Really, that was the best the professionals could do when a student tried to off himself? Their idiocy put a buffer between the reason why the poster was needed and the jokes in my circle of friends. I couldn't resist peeling one off the back of a bathroom stall in the student union and taping it on my closet door. After the second day, our guests had added their own artistic flair. It was now covered with graffiti, my fave being: "What big ears you've got. Give me a peanut."

"Who in their right mind would go see a therapist, thinking he or she's half-human, half-animal?" I laughed in a mirthless way that clearly signaled my nerves were frayed by her out-of-character outburst.

"If you're in your right mind, do you really need a therapist?" she halfheartedly joked, lending insight that she also was at a loss to explain the weirdness.

Gem tugged on the cuff of her pajama bottoms, and I gnawed on a hangnail.

"Well, this is awkward," I said, finally trying to break the ice.

She nodded.

"You know you can tell me anything. I'm your friend above all else." What was she holding back? Was she a virgin? Never dated? Or did her flip-out mean something really bad had happened to her? Something that was best left unsaid?

"I know," she said without committing to divulging any personal details.

"What is it?" I rocked back and forth on the bed.

She turned her head in slow motion, a smile slowly tugging up the corners of her pink lips. "It's killing you, isn't it?"

"What?"

"That I have a secret." She no longer looked tortured, much to my relief.

"I knew it!" I clapped my hands together. "I knew you were keeping something from me."

"I don't remember the rule stating you had to know everything about me."

"Oh, it's a rule. I mean, it's like a Ten Commandments rule. Thou shall tell Tegan everything."

She laughed.

I shook her arm, jostling harder than I'd intended, causing her face to brush against my double D tits—the biggest reason why Jenny thought I was a shoo-in for the Princess Leia gig.

Gemma popped up immediately. "I'm so sorry."

"For what? I yanked you into me."

She rolled her lips, making them glisten.

I wondered what it would be like to kiss such soft-looking lips. Shoving that thought into my *what the fuck* mental file, I refocused on the matter at hand: Gemma. "I meant it earlier, when I said you could tell me anything and it wouldn't change a thing between us. Not one iota."

Gemma cowered back on the bed, supporting her upper body against the wall. "You can't make that promise."

"Yes, I can. I just did." I spit into the palm of my hand and stuck it out.

Her eyes widened.

"What? I hate the sight of blood and only ever make spit oaths."

"You're studying to be a nurse. How can you hate the sight of blood?"

My face burned. "My blood. I hate the sight of my own blood," I corrected.

"Oh, right."

She still didn't accept my spit oath. It was hard not to be slightly insulted, especially considering I hadn't made a spit oath since grade school.

"You didn't kill someone, right?" I joshed behind my now dried palm.

Her silence was unnerving. She drummed a finger against her lips, drawing my attention to them once again. Why was I obsessing about her mouth tonight? Something was seriously wrong with me, and I didn't think it was just the booze sloshing through my veins.

"What am I doing?" she mumbled to herself.

"Taking advantage of me."

Gem shot off the bed. "I'm doing no such thing. I'd never."

The color drained out of her face to the point even her lips were white.

I jumped up and moved to put my arms around her, but she stepped out of my grasp. "What's wrong?"

"I'd never take advantage of you. Never." She squared her shoulders.

"I didn't mean it that way. I meant, you were trying to distract me with questions since I'm drunk. Dude, I know you aren't a guy."

Her eyes darted to mine, the look of panic connecting directly to my heart, and I knew her secret right then and there.

I backpedaled two steps, putting my hands up to steady myself. "Oh," I whispered.

She ran a hand through her nearly dry hair. "Yeah, oh. Now you won't—"

I punctured the air with my palm. "Stop right there. I didn't mean it like that."

Gemma collapsed into a desk chair across the room. "How did you mean it, then?"

"I feel awful that I bullied you into telling me something you clearly didn't want me to know. I had no idea." Or did I?

"If you did or suspected, would you have reacted differently?" She hugged her arms under her breasts.

"Of course." I took four strides, knelt down, and laid my arms on her thighs. "It's no big deal. I don't care if you're gay. It doesn't change anything. I just wasn't expecting it. That's all. Honest."

"Right." She nodded.

I could tell she didn't believe a word I'd said. *And the award for "worst best roommate" goes to…*

"Seriously. It doesn't matter." I tapped her leg with a hand. "No matter what, you're my roomie." I followed up by squeezing her runner's thigh.

Gemma smothered a fake yawn. "I think it's time for bed."

"What? No way. I want to know about the girl." I smiled foolishly. "Now that the cat is out of the bag—no more reason for subterfuge."

She laughed despite her stiff posture. "You're so stubborn."

"You have no idea."

"Oh, I think I'm learning." Her eyes sparkled more than usual as she peered down at me. "But you only get one secret per day. You've reached your quota."

I glanced at the neon green digits on my clock radio. "It's 12:05."

"True. The day just started, so you have to wait until 12:05 *tomorrow* morning."

I whacked her arm. "You don't play fair."

"Says the emotional blackmailer." She got to her feet and yawned again, for real this time. "Seriously, I'm wrecked."

She had consumed way more alcohol than usual. We both had.

"Okay, safe for now. But I'm setting the alarm for 12:05 a.m. to find out the rest tomorrow."

Gemma stood in the middle of our twelve-by-twelve-foot dorm room, watching me with a neutral expression that seemed more put-on than normal. "Seriously, you're okay with this?"

I made a *pshaw* sound to seem more convincing. "Totally. You aren't the first gay person I've known."

"How can you say that if you didn't know I was gay until a few moments ago?"

I collapsed onto my bed and climbed under the covers. "I meant you aren't the first to come out to me. It happens…"

"All the time? What, lesbians flock to you like dykes to bikes?" She chuckled, settling into her bed.

"You'd be surprised. People love to confide in me.

You'll learn and surrender to me." Surrender? What did I mean by that? Her confession was nowhere along the lines of my best friend in high school telling me she had a crush on our English lit teacher and wanted to have his babies. All of the girls had a crush on Mr. Sweeney. Gemma's secret ranked among the ultimate —like CIA confidential.

Her quizzical brows seemed to be mulling over what I meant as well.

Even my alcohol-foozled mind clamped onto the obvious: I was blowing it. Gemma had just trusted me with a secret she had kept from everyone at Hill University, and here I was making light of it—or quite possibly she thought I was mocking her. But the fact she was a lesbian was slowly sinking in since I'd blotted out all the clues for weeks now. Why else would she prefer *Star Wars* over *Indiana Jones*? It had to be the bikini scene.

The knowledge that I was failing her and our friendship didn't mean I had a plan to fix it. I pulled the chain on the tiny lamp on the mini fridge. "Good night."

"Good night."

The curtains over Gem's bed weren't completely drawn, and I stared out into the star-speckled, inky night, pondering why I'd pushed Gemma so hard to reveal her secret. I was a busybody to a certain degree, but it was as if I had to uncover the truth no matter what.

My eyes wandered down and studied the back of her head, and I found myself wishing she wasn't facing the wall. Ages later, her breathing slowed, indicating she was drifting off. It wasn't until I heard the soft snuffling sound she made when deep in sleep that I allowed myself to settle for the night.

CHAPTER FIVE

I PRIED MY EYES OPEN AT 8:57 A.M. SO MUCH for making my nine o'clock class. I let out a puff of air, stirring loose strands of hair on my forehead. "At least it's Friday." I sat up to stretch and yawn.

Gemma's bed was made, and the room was eerily quiet. Was she in the bathroom? I didn't hear the shower. "Gem?" I called out. She didn't have an early class, so where could she be?

A jangle of keys outside the door partly answered the mystery.

"Good morning, sleepyhead." She placed two donuts with chocolate frosting and a plastic orange juice container on the bed next to me. "I thought you might need some motivation to get out of bed today. G&T Thursdays are hard on you."

Her tone was normal, but not once did she meet my eyes, and I couldn't put my finger as to why;

however, my pulse throbbed like something big had happened. Last night was foggy at best, and I sensed part of me thought it was best not to dredge up the memories. "My head is pounding," I said, feeling like the Cowardly Lion.

"Right." She opened her closet door to pull out her meds bucket that contained mostly vitamins. "Here ya go." She sprinkled two aspirin out of a bottle into my hand.

"Thanks," I mumbled and tossed the pills back with OJ. "So, you've already had breakfast downstairs?"

"Yeah. Got an early... meeting, er, group study session today."

Who would ever form a study session before noon on a Friday? Was Gem lying? That'd be a first.

"I should get going." She gave a slight wave as if she couldn't wait to leave the room.

"Wait, don't go," I said, and she paused at the foot of my bed, her back facing me. "What's wrong?"

"Nothing." She wiggled her fingers about. "Nothing's wrong."

I got to my feet and marched around to confront her. "Something is wrong. Tell me."

Gemma stared at her Doc Martins.

I lifted her chin with a finger. "Did I do something wrong?"

She shook her head, lips fastened shut.

"Gem?" I laid a hand on her shoulder.

57

She sighed, and her shoulders relaxed. "Do you remember much from last night?"

I blinked. Some memories of interrogating her about exes came into focus. Innocent tickling. Nothing serious, though, jumped to mind. "From the wood-pecker behind my eyes, I think I drank *way* too much." A sense of dread compelled me to stress the word "way" in case I'd done something so embarrassing she'd never forgive me. As my brother Glen would say, I was hedging my bets.

A faint smile appeared on her sweet face. "We both did."

"Do you feel okay? Hungover? Is that why you're acting strange?" I laid a hand on her forehead, which was radiating heat.

She hoisted one shoulder.

"There's more, though." I whacked my head to knock some sense into it, and regretted the action. "Oi!"

"Easy. No trips to Urgent Care today." She motioned for me to sit down. I patted the bed for her to join me. She did—even though her rigid upper body indicated it was the last thing she wanted to do.

"So, give it to me straight. What did I do last night?"

"Nothing. You did nothing last night."

"Was I supposed to do something? Is that why you're mad?" I stared at her, perplexed.

"I'm not mad. I'm just—look, it doesn't matter. You

clearly don't remember anything." She started to stand, but I forced her back down. From the flicker in her emerald eyes, it *clearly* mattered.

"Please. Put me out of my misery." I swiped a strand of red hair off her forehead.

"You really don't remember us talking last night? After we got home?" She lowered her head, looking me in the eye.

The fear in her imploring eyes sparked another fuzzy memory about a confession that started to come into sharp focus.

"You do remember." Her voice was barely above a whisper.

"Oh, Gem. I'm so sorry. I pushed you and pushed you. Can you forgive me?" I covered my heart with a palm.

"There's nothing to forgive." She sat up straight. "Look, I thought it over this morning, and if you want me to make a request to change roommates, I will."

"A new roommate request?" My pulse fluttered in the hollow of my throat. "I thought you said you weren't mad. Please, don't move out. I acted like an insensitive asshole, but does that warrant you leaving?"

"I'm not mad, but I know you didn't sign up to room with—"

I placed my finger on her lips. "Don't! Don't ever say it or think it. I would never do such a thing." I moved my hand to her cheek. "You'll always be my

Gemma. Last night doesn't change a thing. In fact, I think it'll bring us closer." I slung an arm around her shoulder and pulled her to me.

"Closer as friends?" She pulled away.

"Yeah, closer. No secrets. We should tell each other everything." I fiddled with the drawstrings on my pink polka dot pajama bottoms, not remembering when I put them on. It was typical of me to wake up after a booze fest to pee and then put on PJs before climbing back in bed.

"Everything?" Gemma laughed. "Not sure I could handle all of your secrets." She smiled, lessening the sting.

I waved her words away. "Don't forget. You promised to tell me about the girl. What's her name?"

"I thought you didn't remember much from last night." She shied away like a scared puppy.

"The important stuff is coming back to me." I thumped my forehead.

She glanced at her watch. "If I remember correctly, I still have a reprieve until a little after midnight. And I have to get going to… that meeting… er study group." She practically ran to the door.

"Coward," I shouted as she shut the door behind her. I laughed as I eyeballed the donuts. "Might as well not let these little gems go to waste." I ate the choco-latey goodness, licking my fingers, and then finished the OJ before hopping into the shower.

THE QUAD OUTSIDE of the student union was lined with trees ablaze with fall color, which popped vividly against the azure backdrop. I spied the back of Jenny's dishwater brown head as she rollerbladed through the crowd. I cupped my mouth with both hands and belted out, "Jenny!"

She didn't hear.

I ran after her, grabbing her shoulder when she hunched against a wall to support herself. "Jenny!" I shouted and lightly thwacked her shoulder since I now saw her headphones.

Jenny whirled around awkwardly, one leg flying out from underneath her and then the other. I put out both arms and wrapped her up against me, saving her from wiping out.

She smiled when she saw it was me. She slipped her headphones onto the back of her neck. "Hey, Tegan."

"Yesterday, you said only Gemma was steady. I just rescued your sorry ass."

"After causing me to lose my rollerblading groove. Doesn't count." She made a little cha-cha move, only to set into motion another wave of her legs slipping this way and that until stilling with great effort.

I laughed. "What are you listening to?"

She placed her headphones onto my ears. I gave a thumbs-up listening to "I Wanna Sex You Up" as she changed into sneakers she had pulled out of her navy and yellow Eddie Bauer backpack.

"You want to borrow the tape for when Josh is here?" She butted my shoulder, nearly causing me to fall to the ground. "Wowzer, a strong wind could knock you on your buttocks." She steadied me with her hands.

"That's not what my mom says."

"Pffft!" She waved me off. "Mother's don't know jack."

"You got that right." We started walking toward the entrance of the student union, her rollerblades dangling over her shoulder. "You done for the day?" I asked.

She nodded. "You?"

"Yep, just finished my history class." I put two hands in the air. "Free 'til Monday." I neglected to tell her that was the only class out of three today that I'd attended.

"Cool. What are you doing tonight?" She held the glass door open for me.

"Work, unfortunately." My shoulders sagged. "You?"

"April and I were thinking of Applebee's. Thought you and Gemma would like to go." She gestured to the line at Carl's Jr. tucked into the corner near the entrance of the student union. "Do you mind? I'm starving."

"Not at all. It's where I was heading."

She rapped her forehead with a finger and then placed it on mine. "Simpatico."

We slipped behind a handful of students in line, silently waiting.

Jenny ordered a Double Western Bacon Cheeseburger, large fries, and a Coke. I dittoed the order and handed her a ten-dollar bill. After divvying up the change, she shimmied through the crowd, carrying our tray across the food court before settling on an empty yellow plastic booth by the rear entrance that overlooked a small pond in the distance. For a Friday afternoon, the place was fairly busy but not packed. The energy of the area buzzed with the anticipation of the weekend.

"There you are." April scooted into the booth next to Jenny, nearly ramming Jenny against the wall.

At first I didn't notice anything, but when April smiled at something Jenny said—and it wasn't her bitchy smile—I experienced a lightbulb moment.

Jenny wasn't a beauty nor an ugly duckling. Her face was remarkably average, which could be a good thing if she ever ended up in a police lineup. Her muscular and squatty legs were a result of playing soccer since preschool.

April, on the other hand, had been homecoming queen her senior year (she usually inserted this into conversations whenever possible), meaning her tits and waistline rivaled a Barbie doll's.

If I had to guess between the two, Jenny was the

odds-on favorite for being a dyke. But the way April fluttered her eyes at Jenny and the way Jenny gobbled up the attention, they both were. Good Lord, was I surrounded by homos? Was that why my mother had a conniption when I was accepted at Hill University? Had my Bible-thumping mother known all along? She prided herself on knowing where all the undesirables lived within the country. Once my pilot father invited me to fly to New York City, but my mother pooh-poohed the idea before it had a chance to take off. Hell, Denver had been out of bounds for me, even though I went as often as I could without telling Mom.

I sipped my Coke through a red and yellow striped straw, forcing nervous laughter back into the pit of my stomach. Did Gemma know about Jenny and April? If she knew or if she suspected, then she knew I flat-out lied last night about knowing gays before. Jesus, I felt like a world-class rube. Gem, a girl from a small town in Nebraska, was proving way more worldly.

And what about Jenny's "simpatico" comment earlier? Was she implying I was like her in all ways? Even her carpet-munching ways?

"Earth to Tegan. Come in, Tegan." Jenny had her hands circled around her mouth, megaphone style.

"I'm sorry. What'd I miss?" I dipped a fry into a mixture of ketchup and mayo.

April smooshed her face upward when she eyed my own special sauce, but that didn't stop her from stealing two of my fries, sans the dip.

Jenny said, "I know you're working tonight, but what about brunch on Sunday with some of my softball buddies you haven't met yet?"

"Uh, sure." Was buddies code for lesbians? "What time?"

"Noon. Invite Gemma."

Yes, I should invite Gem. I could launch a mission of finding Gemma a respectable-looking girl to date.

Jenny pulled a Hill University visor out of her backpack and placed it on her head, letting her limp ponytail hang down her back. I scratched her name off the potential list of girlfriends for Gem. Gemma was sporty, and I suspected she'd like a girl on her arm who didn't scream dyke. Now that I was seeing the light about Jenny I was kicking myself for missing all the telltale signs people used to joke about back in high school. Visors. Air Jordans. Softball. Zero makeup. No one at my high school was out of the closet, but there were some pretty cruel rumors. I mostly ignored them, considering it was usually a football player who started it after being dumped.

Back to Gem, though, I wanted to find someone who wasn't overly perky but could be when need be. Someone good-looking with a sense of humor. Smart but friendly. Ambitious and kind. Damn, I needed to find her someone who was a lot like me.

Jenny motioned for April to stand so she could get out of the booth. "I have softball practice. See ya. Wouldn't wanna be ya."

April laughed too easily, and Jenny stroked a finger under her chin. I squirmed in my seat, wondering how many picked up on the lesbo vibe between the two. Would it be horrible if I stood up to announce I wasn't a lesbian?

After eyeing Jenny until she was out of sight, April flipped her attention back to me. "So, what's the deal with you and Josh? Is someone else turning your beautiful head?"

"What?" I nearly shouted in an *I just spied a ghost* kind of way. "No. No, of course not. I love Josh."

She narrowed her eyes. "But last night you said you didn't miss him. What's that about?" She crunched into one of Jenny's remaining fries.

I waved her off the trail, unsure what I feared she'd discover. The lesbian trail, maybe. Did she suspect about Gemma? "Drunk. Really, really drunk. Don't remember a thing I said."

"Okay," she said in a tone that implied she wasn't buying a word of my story but really didn't give a damn either way.

"In fact, I spoke to him this morning and tried to talk him into visiting. That's how much I miss him. He was my first thought when I woke up." Okay, he wasn't my first thought, but I did call him. Our conversation had been brief, but I had an urge to hear his voice, which had me somewhat baffled. "If he does, can Gemma crash in your room?" I stirred my Coke with the straw, making a mental note to call Josh back to invite him to visit.

That sparked her interest. "Of course," she purred like a vixen. "Every couple needs privacy."

"Are you sure it wouldn't interfere with... your weekend routine?"

April's face twisted in confusion and then cleared. "Oh, *that*. I'm sure one weekend would be fine. Who knows what will happen between the three of us."

Did that mean she suspected all along about Gemma? But then why was she so rude to Gemma, or was that how she flirted?

April took a sip from Jenny's Coke, batting her lashes at me not so innocently.

The impact of her leer made me queasy, and I rocketed out of my seat. "I have to get ready for work. Have fun at Applebee's tonight."

"Oh, I plan on it and then some afterward."

Ewwwwwwwww.

Not that I thought lesbian sex was disgusting, because I never thought about it, really. But now, it was hard to picture two of my friends going at it, especially when one of those friends was the plain-as-toast-with-no-butter Jenny. People in high school were constantly hooking up. But none of them with the same sex. Did that make me homophobic? Was that why I couldn't get the newsflash about Gemma out of my mind?

AFTER ONE IN THE MORNING, I finally finished my shift at the theater. Marc, the manager, dropped me off in front of my dorm on his way home, his habit whenever the two of us closed together. In order to save on gas money, I always walked to work. On the nights I closed with Heidi, Gemma staked out in the retro coffee shop next door so we could walk home together. It struck me that Gemma would make a great girlfriend for someone. I just needed to find that person, because in the couple of months I'd known Gem, she hadn't made any effort on the relationship front. She was too shy and sweet to make a move. Or had the girl she refused to talk about ripped her heart out?

Trudging up the stairs, I imagined what it would be like to kiss a girl. Surely their lips were softer. More plump, maybe. Josh spent the majority of his free time outside year round, and the boy had never heard of ChapStick. His rough lizard-like lips did absolutely nothing for me. My boyfriend from junior year had kissable lips—too bad others had agreed and sought them out. That man was a slut.

No light streamed through the quarter-inch crack at the bottom of our door. Was Gem out for the night? She hadn't mentioned any plans, but she never went to bed this early. Not on a Friday night. Gemma, a diehard *Cheers* fan, usually watched a rerun at twelve o'clock. *Cheers* followed by *Mash*, her second favorite, which incidentally was my father's favorite show.

Quietly, I edged into the dark room, waiting at the bathroom sink for a moment for my eyes to adjust. I was fairly certain there was a lump under Gemma's bedspread. I squinted to make out her beautiful red hair poking out from under the covers and cascading over the white pillowcase.

I sat on her bed. "Gemma?"

Nothing.

I bounced up and down on the mattress with great effort. She stirred when the bed lurched to the side, but she didn't wake.

I ran a finger through her hair. "Gemma? You awake?"

Gem rolled over and smiled broadly when she saw me. "Everything okay?"

"Yeah," I laughed foolishly. "It's well after 12:05."

She rubbed her eyes. "What?"

I scratched my temple. "You said you'd tell me about the girl."

Her eyes boggled. "You woke me up to talk about Kate?"

Kate. Yeah, the name was much too simple for someone like Gem. Gemma Mahoney was a strong name, which demanded a name equally strong. I'd always been proud of my first and middle names: Tegan Raye. Of course my last name, Ferber, made me cringe. Not that I was tossing my name in the hat for

Gem—that'd be crazy, right? I didn't know what was up with me lately. All these thoughts kept jumping in and out of my mind.

"Yes. Don't think falling asleep will get you out of your commitment. It's important to honor your pledge to me—to everyone." I knew I sounded like a nitwit, but I couldn't stop myself from going full steam ahead into the bullshit zone. I needed to know everything about this Kate chick to get at the heart of Gemma's problem. Not that being a lesbian was a problem. But being an unattached lesbian seemed lonely, and I only wanted Gem to be happy. I had to stifle a smile. I was in a relationship, and lately I'd been wondering why, considering we didn't live in the same state and Josh didn't really ignite passionate feelings. No matter. This was about Gem, not me. Maybe if I witnessed Gemma in a happy relationship, I'd work up the nerve to end things with Josh and find someone who made me happy.

She laughed. "What in the hell are you talking about?"

Not knowing the answer for sure, I pulled a bag of stale popcorn from my purse, one of the perks of working in the movie industry. "Want some?" She tried to reach for the bag, but I jerked it away, waving a finger. "Uh-uh. Only if you spill."

Gemma hoisted the covers off, laughing. "Fine, but I need some tea to wake up. Black and strong. I was sound asleep, ya know." She playfully rapped her knuckles against my forehead. Her skin was sleepy-warm.

"Deal. Make two cups. I need to wash off the movie theater stink." I collected my PJs and then my shower things from the floor of my closet.

When I exited the bathroom approximately seven minutes later, not that I was intentionally keeping track of my time away, Gemma stood outside the door with my yellow coffee mug. "Here. I added extra honey." Our fingers grazed during the handoff, sending a jolt all the way to my toes.

"Let's snuggle in your bed since your sheets are probably still warm." I motioned for her to follow.

During our late night talks, it wasn't unusual to huddle under the covers together. Our building had bricks inside and out and zero insulation. Even in the beginning of the semester, I froze my tits off. I climbed under her covers, still warm from her body, and Gemma settled at the foot of the bed with a quilt her mother and grandmother had made wrapped around her shoulders.

Gemma slouched against the wall, holding her mug in both hands. After three sips, she looked more alert and her hand descended into the popcorn bag.

I looked her in the eye. "Kate. Tell me everything."

"There really isn't much to tell. We didn't officially date. Just—"

"Midnight trysts?"

"Kinda. Her parents are really conservative."

"Are yours?" I whispered as if they could hear us conversing from Nebraska.

"Well, they're planning to vote for Bush again, but that's because they think Clinton's a pot-smoking hippie who doesn't know a thing about being president. Mom and Dad are hard to pin down, really." Her shoulders plummeted, and I could tell she'd put a lot of thought into figuring out her parents. Did she ever plan on telling them? I couldn't even imagine.

I thought for a moment and decided to dive in even further. "Did Kate's parents find out? About you two?"

Gem shook her head and then sipped some tea. "No. We were super careful. Like 'guarding atomic secrets' careful. To my knowledge, no one knew. The summer before our senior year, Kate stopped coming over and wouldn't take my calls. On the first day of school, I found out she was dating the quarterback."

"How long were you together?"

"Like I said, we weren't officially together." Her shoulders stiffened.

This Kate chick hurt her, of that I had no doubt. Why else would she keep distancing herself from the memory? "Okay, how long did you two have to guard your atomic secret?" I thought it best to stick to speaking in code and not mention the L-word. Love, not lesbian.

"Our junior year."

"An entire year and she just dumped you?"

"I guess you can call it that. We never said we were officially dating or exclusive, though."

"That bitch!" I smashed my hand down on the mattress.

Gemma smiled, and her eyes met mine briefly before shamefully zooming in on the popcorn.

"That must have hurt. Finding out that way and not being able to talk about it with anyone."

She nodded, and her inability to verbalize the pain made her suffering even more potent.

"I'm sorry. You deserve someone so much better than Kate." I shoveled in a handful of popcorn, utilizing the time to come up with an action plan. I swallowed the remaining pieces. "I think it's time to get you back on the horse."

"What?" She reached into the popcorn bag and placed several pieces into her mouth.

"To date a girl. Not all of them are bitches like Kate. Take me for example—"

Gemma's eyes grew three sizes too large, and her cheeks turned hellfire red as she gasped for air.

Did she think I implied I wanted to date her? No, she couldn't think that. But... "I didn't mean—"

Gemma waved me quiet as she cleared her throat free from all popcorn remnants. Finally, she wheezed. "Oh no. I'm not ready for that. Really." Maybe she picked up on my disappointment, because she said, "It's very sweet of you to offer—to find me a girl." She stumbled over the word girl but pressed on. "Right now, my focus is on school. Nothing else. No girls."

Somewhat relieved she understood my statement as an offer to find her someone to date and not me putting myself out there, I set my cup to the side to take Gem's hand in mine. "She really broke your heart, didn't she?"

Gemma studied our conjoined hands, and I didn't think she would actually confirm or deny. After wiggling her fingers free from my grasp, she looked at me with sincere and pleading eyes. "Uh, yeah, let's call it that."

I wanted to push her on the unusual answer, but something told me she wouldn't elaborate. Or did I not want to know the true meaning? Geez, finding out I was living with a lesbian was complicating the hell out of my life, not to mention my mind—like I was the one grappling with coming out of the closet, which was a ridiculous thought.

The silence was unnerving, and I uttered the first thing that came to mind at rapid-fire speed. "I spoke to Josh this afternoon. He's driving up next weekend to visit. He wanted to come for Halloween, but two of his buddies, who are twins, have to be here the weekend before for their sister's wedding. That way, he can split the gas money, and he won't have to drive alone."

"Really?" Her eyes widened to the size of flying saucers. "That's good. Yeah, that's good."

"April said you can crash at their place if you want."

"Of course."

"I know you aren't a huge fan of April's—"

She stopped me with a flick of her hand. "Don't worry about it. I'm sure you and Josh will want to be alone. I understand completely." She stretched her arms over her head and yawned. "I'm beat. Can I go to bed now that tonight's inquisition is over?" Her voice and smile didn't hold a lick of humor.

"Fine. Be that way," I pouted. "But just so you know, I don't give up easily." I crawled into my bed, snuggling under the covers and, for some reason, stuck my tongue out at her.

Gemma grabbed one of her T-shirts off the floor and threw it at me. "You better behave."

The playfulness had returned to her demeanor.

"Me, behave? Not in my DNA." I held the shirt in my arms, drifting off to sleep.

The last thing I heard was Gemma mumbling to herself, "You'll be the death of me."

CHAPTER SIX

Aᴌᴛʜᴏᴜɢʜ Gᴇᴍᴍᴀ ʜᴀᴅ ᴍᴀᴅᴇ ɪᴛ ᴄʟᴇᴀʀ ꜱʜᴇ wasn't looking for a girl, I was determined to find her a date.

At five minutes after noon, Gemma and I arrived at Denny's, one town over. I could barely contain my excitement to meet Jenny and her *buddies*. Fingers crossed one of them would be the perfect match for my redhead.

Jenny, Michelle, April, and two other girls sat at a table for ten.

"There you are!" Jenny waved us over and made the introductions. "This is Paula and Cissy."

Paula's horse face and buckteeth immediately ruled her out of the hat. Was she related to John Elway? Cissy, on the other hand, was stunning and way too girlie. I wasn't a lesbian expert, but I was willing to bet five bucks Cissy was as straight as they come, like me.

Not that I was super-girlie.

Crestfallen, I slid into a seat next to Gemma, with two empty seats to my right.

"The others will be here soon." Jenny retook her seat in the middle of Michelle and April.

"Where's Seb?" I asked Michelle.

"Probably in bed, where I left him. He deejayed the graveyard shift."

Jenny, playing host, announced, "Michelle and Seb both work at the college's radio station."

"Are you a DJ?" Cissy sipped her iced tea.

"No. I have a call-in show. Honing my headshrinker skills, so to speak. I also volunteer for the suicide hotline."

"How depressing." April's pinched face added to the effect.

Horse Face said "Good for you" at the same time, making April's statement even more awkward.

Michelle acknowledged Horse Face with a smile and didn't bat an eye in April's direction.

Jenny popped out of her seat, waving her arms as if directing an airplane in distress. "Over here!"

I turned to see two girls, one on crutches, walking toward us. The injured one didn't have a speck of makeup and was kinda cute in a sporty way. The other could have been April's twin.

"Here." I pulled out my seat for the girl on crutches, so she'd have to sit next to Gemma.

"Thanks." She sat down with effort, trying not to

jostle her bandaged ankle. At the last second before the leg made it successfully under the table, I spied nail polish, five different colors, on the exposed toes. Maybe that was a joke—like signing a cast.

Jenny introduced Rowena, the one on crutches, and Miranda, April's doppelgänger. There wasn't a chance in hell I'd even bother with Miranda. That left Rowena as my last hope. Aside from the questionable nail polish job and hideous name, I was pleased to have a contender for Gemma. Now it was time to put my matchmaking skills to the test. At least one of us could be in love—not that I wasn't, but Josh was so far away —and as they say, out of sight, out of mind.

The waitress came and took our order. Gemma and I both ordered French toast, and the rest got omelets of some type, except for April, who went for the chocolate chip pancakes. Did that mean she was in a good mood today? It was difficult to reconcile April and good mood.

Different conversations erupted around the table, and I spied Gemma sitting quietly, smiling but not contributing. This wouldn't do. Didn't she realize who she should set her sights on?

"Where are you from, Rowena?" I prodded the injured girl.

"Kansas."

"Really?" I bent over the table to see my roommate. "Gemma's from Nebraska. She's a Husker's fan."

Rowena turned to Gem and said, "Really? Our

teams play on November seventh and"—Rowena pulled back so Gemma could see her entire upper body and moved her neck with a flourish—"we're going to kick your ass. Rock chalk Jayhawk!"

Was she speaking English or in Kansas code? The blue and red bird wearing yellow sneakers on the front of her T-shirt led me to believe it was a Kansas thing.

If things were going to work between the two, I'd have to set Rowena straight about her sports loyalty. Even I, as Gemma's roommate, took an interest, and before this semester, I didn't give a flying fuck about any sport.

Instead of Gemma coming to her team's aide, she said, "What'd you do to your leg?"

Color dotted Rowena's cheeks in a not so flattering way. "I went to a Slip'N Slide party, where you had to make an entrance through the gate by sliding in. Let's just say it didn't go well."

Jenny overheard. "That's debatable. It didn't go well for you, but I for one won't forget it. It was hilarious, the way you confidently dove onto the banana yellow slide and didn't get halfway, spinning out of control and snapping your ankle." With her hand, she mined Rowena starting down the slide, getting out of control, and crashing and burning. "No one will ever forget you, Slip."

Rowena rolled her eyes but didn't appear overly offended by her hard-won nickname. "The good news is the cast came off last week. Now I just have to keep it wrapped and stay off it for one more week. I'm tired of watching these yahoos lose all their softball games."

I latched onto this nugget. "You play softball? Gemma *loves* softball." I leaned forward. "Don't ya?"

"Do you play?" she asked Gem in an *I don't give a rat's ass* voice.

"When I was a kid—not recently."

"Back in Nebraska, Gemma was a sportswriter." I nearly winked at Rowena so she'd pick up on the code —Gemma was a lesbian.

As if I was a foreign exchange student who didn't understand American customs, Rowena smiled at me and then turned to Gemma. "Is that so?"

Gemma hitched a shoulder, making it clear she wasn't enjoying the attention. Had she seen the nail polish job? Was that why she was playing so hard to get?

Cissy said something about last week's game, garnering Rowena's attention. Gemma glanced behind the girl's back and narrowed her eyes at me. I feigned innocence by smiling vapidly and batting my eyes. Gemma mouthed "Knock it off" and then playfully made a fist, miming she'd clock me. I had to laugh. The thought of Gemma ever hurting anyone was unthinkable. She winked at me, bringing a smile to my face. Why couldn't she be this playful with Rowena? If I were into chicks, I'd fall for Gem.

Two waitresses with trays interrupted and sorted everyone's meals. Out of the corner of my eye, I glimpsed Rowena probe her mouth with her thumb and forefinger to extract a wad of gum of the Big League Chew variety. Oh no, that wouldn't do. I was willing to overlook her clumsiness, since that was one of my fatal flaws, and she hadn't chosen her name. Her parents had stuck her with that. I didn't understand the nail polish, but again, I was willing to give her a pass until proven it was all her idea. But Big League Chew? Maybe it was a dyke thing or a softball quirk, if you could separate the two, but it was wrong. So, so, so wrong. She simply wasn't the girl for Gemma.

Jenny added two packets of white sugar to her coffee. "Ro, how is Fergs?"

The waitress was making the rounds, refilling most cups. Gemma requested another cup of tea in her soft but polite voice.

"Suffering with an epic hangover. Michelle, what'd you put in those Jell-O shots?"

Michelle waggled her brows. "Family secret."

"Damn, I wish I grew up in your family." Rowena stuffed her mouth with Mexican omelet, chewing with her mouth open. Not only did she need to learn the proper gum for a girl, she needed manners. This was not the way to win Gemma's heart; of that, I was sure.

Was this how lesbians identified themselves in public? Little things like Big League Chew, playing softball, eating with your mouth open? If that was the case, poor Gemma. I just couldn't see her with a girl ever. Not the tea-drinking Gemma.

"How long have you been with Fergs?" Michelle asked.

Rowena set down her coffee cup and tapped her chin with a finger. "Let's see; we met in high school. I was a junior, and he was a senior—so almost two years."

Fergs was a *he*? What about all the signs?

I needed to make sure I heard Rowena correctly. "Is Fergs his real name?" Sounded like an STD.

Maybe she picked up on this thought, because she replied coolly, "Yeah. His last name is Ferguson." Rowena continued eating and chatting with her softball buddies across the table, avoiding my eye. Obviously, she was done with me. Not that it mattered. I'd already determined she wouldn't do for Gemma. Rowena and Fergs deserved each other—hideous names and all.

Gemma caught my eye and stuck her tongue out at me. Everyone else was too busy inhaling their food and sharing bits and pieces about Michelle's party the night before to notice.

I shrugged.

By the time all of us had finished eating and shooting the shit, I came to the conclusion that only Jenny and April were into chicks and they were only making goo-goo eyes at each other. One word came to mind: yuck!

Finding Gemma a girlfriend wasn't going to be a simple task.

Never fear, I told myself. I wasn't the type to shy away from the monumental.

LUCKILY AFTER BRUNCH, Gemma had to bail to meet with a group for a sociology class project that was due tomorrow. She couldn't ream me on the way home, because we ended up chauffeuring April. Jenny and the gang had softball practice. Or was it a meeting? Hard to believe they could eat so much and then play. I'd be puking in a trash can.

Minutes after Gemma dashed out of the room with her backpack, Heidi called me to ask if I wouldn't mind helping out at the theater for a few hours since someone called out sick. Not wanting to but in need of the mighty dollar, I agreed.

By eight I returned to my dorm room, nearly smashing Gemma with the door. "I'm sorry."

She stepped away from the full-size mirror on the back of the door, waving me in.

"What are you doing?"

Gemma gripped a stack of index cards in her hand. "Practicing my speech for tomorrow."

"You have to give a speech? I thought it was a group project."

"We have to present our research to the class."

"Ugh. I hate speeches." I collapsed on my bed. "My

dogs are barking." I slipped my shoes off and wiggled my toes.

"Were you working? It's not on the calendar, or I would have met you."

"Heidi called me in at the last moment after Todd went home sick. Hungover is my guess." I massaged my right foot. "*Candy Man* opened on Friday, which means no more free showings of *A River Runs Through It*." Gemma and I had a fondness for the movie, even though she didn't think Brad Pitt was all that and a bag of chips, like I did. Now I knew why. I chuckled. Lesbians couldn't appreciate what was right in front of them. "What's your speech on?"

She flicked her hand. "It'd only bore you. Would you like a cup of tea? You look chilled to the bone."

"That'd be great." When I left this afternoon, it had been relatively warm, but boy did the temperature drop. Typical Colorado weather. "Tell me about your speech." I rested against the wall, my feet pointing toward the window and Gemma's bed. The light across the street filtered yellow rays into our room.

Gemma busied herself making tea. "Seriously, the speech is so boring. I wouldn't want to subject you to it."

"At least tell me what it's about."

"Did you see the movie *The Great Imposter*? It's an older film starring Tony Curtis."

I squinted at the ceiling. "That doesn't ring a bell."

"And you're in the movie industry." She tutted.

"Somehow my bosses overlooked this serious flaw on my resume."

She laughed, handing me a cup of tea.

"Thanks. What was the movie about?"

"It's about Ferdinand Waldo Demara, Jr. He was a con man. There's also a book about him called *The Great Imposter*." She settled on the bed, shoving a copy of last week's Sunday paper from her hometown, which her parents mailed every Monday, onto the floor. She took a cautious sip of the steaming tea.

"What'd he do? Rob banks?"

She shook her head. "No, he pretended to be people, like a surgeon. He actually operated on a few individuals."

I gasped. "And he wasn't a doctor?"

"Nope. He'd read medical manuals, but he had never been trained."

Curious, I probed. "What else did he pretend to be?"

"A prison warden, civil engineer, psychologist, professor, monk—"

I cut her off, laughing. "Why'd he pretend to be a monk? If I was going to con people, I'd have them think I was an actress or someone in the biz. Make them treat me like Hollywood royalty."

"People do weird things, like you pretending to be a matchmaker today at brunch. Who do you think you are, Hello, Dolly?"

Busted.

"I don't know what you're talking about." I avoided her eye.

"I think you do. 'Gemma *loves* softball,'" she mimicked me.

"I didn't emphasize love like that," I scoffed.

"Yes, you did." She repeated it with even more emphasis.

"Shut up! I didn't sound that way at all." I laughed, spilling some of my tea on my shirt. "Damn. I'm running out of clean clothes."

"Serves you right. I told you I'm not interested in dating just anyone. And FYI, not all softball players are gay. Living with a lesbian doesn't make you an expert. Promise me you'll stop." Her tone was overly playful, much to my relief.

I mimed zipping my lips shut and tossing away the key.

"That's not a promise. I need to hear you say the words."

I clamped my lips tightly together.

"Teeg," she coaxed.

"What words? Gemma loves softball?"

Gemma cocked her head the way she did when in the right. "Try again."

"Gemma loves the Cornhuskers."

"Still not the right words." She was smiling, and her eyes shone.

"Gemma loves con men... wait, I mean con women."

She groaned. "Why did I tell you my secret?"

"Because you *love* me."

The frivolity left her eyes, and she straightened her head. "Is that a fact?"

"I didn't mean it... not like that... like best friends."

Her confidence returned but not her smile. "You know, if you want to be anything like Demara, you're going to need a well thought out cover story and you'll have to stick with it. It'll save you from stumbling over your own tongue."

"Is that what you do?"

"What do you mean?"

"Pretending to be straight. Isn't that a con?"

Hurt flashed across her face, but she washed it away with a swipe of her hand and a sip of tea. "I don't pretend. People assume, and I don't correct them."

We sat silently, slurping our teas. The tension was killing me. "Practice your speech on me."

"Thanks, but—"

I motioned for her to zip it. "Please, I'd really like to know more about Demara. And clearly, I need to learn a few tricks of the trade to stop stepping in it."

That made her smile. "Okay, but don't expect too much. I think you need more help than my speech can offer." She followed that up with a heartfelt shake of the head.

CHAPTER SEVEN

A KNOCK SOUNDED ON THE DOOR, CAUSING ME to cringe. When I had invited Josh to visit, it was during a moment of weakness. I convinced myself I missed him and that once I saw him, old feelings would surge through me. Since placing that phone call, I realized guilt had guided my thoughts. Saying I didn't miss Josh at the G&T party, which seemed like a lifetime ago since learning about Gem, planted a seed of remorse. Lately, I'd spent more time thinking about finding a girl for Gemma and no time thinking about my own situation.

Maybe I missed the idea of having someone. Would it be possible when I opened the door and saw Josh in the flesh that I'd feel differently?

The person knocked again. "Tegan? You in there?"

"Here goes nothing," I mumbled on my way to the door.

"Jesus, I'm tired," he said as soon as I swung the door open. "Got any beer?"

I laughed, squeezing to the side to let him in. "That's the first thing you say?"

His smile revealed the dimple in his left cheek I had always found adorable. Josh placed his army-colored bag on the floor and enveloped me in his arms. "It's good to see you."

I melted against his firm chest. Maybe I did miss him.

"Got any beer?"

I backpedaled and slapped his arm. "No! But it's Friday night, and finding free beer in this town is pretty easy. First, you need to freshen up." I plugged my nose.

"Sorry. Slept through my alarm and didn't have time to shower before hitting the road." He surveyed the room. "Wow! Your room is huge compared to mine."

"You have to be joking." I scanned the room. "Gem and I are always bumping into each other."

He shook his head. "Nope. Everything's bigger in Texas, except the dorm rooms." He stretched his arms over his head. "Where is your roommate?"

"She's staying a few doors down."

He boosted an eyebrow. "Does that mean we have the place to ourselves all weekend?"

"It does." I tried to sound seductive but couldn't

muster the energy to pull it off like I did back in high school. Was the spark gone?

Not that he bothered to notice. Josh manhandled my arm. "You're lucky your dad splurged by getting you a room with a private bathroom. That's another thing that's different. I've been showering with other men."

"Really? Do you need to confess anything?" I joked.

The look of revulsion on his face stunned me. "I'm not sick in the head."

I put my hands up in mock surrender and stammered, "K-kidding."

Most of the boys back home would say *fag* and *faggot* during heated moments, but I hadn't thought about it too much. That was just talk—or so I thought. Was Josh homophobic?

The revulsion slid off his face. "Get naked." He tore off his Carhartt jacket and T-shirt and shucked his boots and jeans. All he had on were tube socks and tighty whities. He flexed his arms overhead like he was competing in a bodybuilding competition. "Like what you see?"

All I could process was Josh had been wearing cowboy boots. Was that a Texas thing? Along with his homophobia? However, we had never seriously discussed gays before, so maybe he'd always been homophobic. Only now he had the added flare of shit-kickers.

He morphed into a different muscleman pose. "I'm waiting. Or are you too overcome by my manliness?"

I chuckled. "Come on, chicken legs. Let's get you clean." I led him by the hand to the shower room. The phone rang, but Josh's engines were revving and there would be no stopping him now.

Before the water had a chance to get hot, Josh had me wrapped around his waist and up against the wall. I clutched his back with my eyes squeezed shut. He wasn't as large as my previous boyfriend, but he had a firmer grasp of what made a woman feel good, and when in the zone, he had an amazing ability to hold on until I was satisfied.

I fisted his hair as he penetrated deeper. I missed this part of the relationship.

WE EXITED the bathroom and entered the dorm room, both in our birthday suits since I'd neglected to procure towels.

"How do you like it here?" Josh asked.

"It's good." It hit me that we were acting like strangers now that the one thing that brought us closer was over. Maybe my friends back home had been right—it was better to make a clean break before leaving for college. Distance didn't always make the heart grow fonder, and from the blankness on his face, he was thinking the same.

Before I could ponder further, Gemma, Jenny, and April crashed into the room. I yelped and grabbed the comforter from my bed.

Josh hid his penis with both hands.

"Oh my God, I'm so sorry." Gemma shielded her eyes. "I called earlier to make sure no one was here."

"Oh, they're here all right." April zeroed in on Josh's hands. "In all their glory."

In the movies, Julia Roberts or someone would have had a snappy line to deflate the awkwardness from the situation, but all cleverness seeped out of my brain. "Do you need something?" I stammered, doing my best to pretend everything was normal.

"Forgot my wallet. It's okay. I don't need it." Gemma rounded toward the door and shoved the startled Jenny and grinning April into the hallway.

"Gem, wait." I snared her wallet from her desk and chucked it to her.

She nodded her thanks and slammed the door shut.

Josh burst into laughter, and I heaved a gut-wrenching sigh.

AFTER THE DEBACLE in the dorm room, I couldn't face Gemma, so I opted to drive across town for a party I had heard about from a guy in my nutrition class, knowing that the carless Gemma and crew wouldn't be there.

Josh had made friends at the party, and they invited us to tailgate before the game the following day. We woke up late and didn't have much time before making a mad dash to the stadium.

"Since when did you start liking football?" I asked after the tenth time he urged me to hurry once we had ditched my car, thinking it'd be easier to find them on foot.

"I've always liked football," he said in a voice that claimed he was manlier than most. Another product of living in the Lone Star State?

I bit my lip. No, he decidedly did not like football, but was it worth arguing over? We only had one day left before he needed to hit the road at the crack of dawn on Sunday.

"They're over there." He gestured for me to follow.

"Josh, my man." A guy named Derek chest-bumped my boyfriend, who until that moment, I'd never thought of as a chest-bumping kind of guy.

Another guy handed him a plastic cup. "Nectar of the gods."

I glanced around but didn't see anyone I knew, and Josh was too busy talking with his new buddies to notice I was standing all alone. Fuming, I meandered to the table and tent off to the side. At least there were burgers and brats.

"Tegan!" Jenny waved from across the parking lot. Gemma was at her side, along with Michelle and Seb. "Come on over!"

In a town the size of an ant colony, I knew it would be next to impossible not encountering anyone I knew. Still, I had hoped we could avoid happening upon the people who saw us naked right after fucking in the shower.

I caught Josh's eye and pantomimed if he wanted to join me and my friends. He held up a finger, laughing, and then gave his full attention to the guys he had met last night. My mind flitted to a night I'd had dinner with Josh and his parents; his mother had a bored glazed look the entire time, while his father didn't pay her a speck of attention. I shuddered and quickly crossed the lot to safety.

"What are you doing here?" Jenny thrust a beer into my hand.

"Thanks, but I'm driving," I said, pushing the can back at Jenny.

Gemma fished a Coke out of a cooler and popped the top for me.

"Thanks. Josh made some friends last night and insisted we tailgate with them today."

"Is that *the* Josh?" Michelle asked, squinting to get a better glimpse.

"In the flesh." Remembering what had happened the previous day, the heat rose to my cheeks.

Jenny sniggered until Gemma drilled her elbow into Jenny's side, bringing her in line.

"I guess he prefers hanging out with the boys." I slurped my drink, shrugging.

"No matter." Michelle ringed an arm around my neck. "You can hang with us."

All of them wore Hill University sweatshirts, except for Gemma, who stayed true to her Huskers. I tightened my coat. Besides the jock aspect of football, I wasn't a fan of a sport that involved being outside on a cold, windy day.

"Have a burger. It'll warm you up." Gemma motioned to the grill. Too bad she didn't have a brother, because I had no doubt he'd treat me better than my boyfriend, who was playing beer pong while I froze my ass off.

———

JOSH and I stumbled into the dorm room a little after two in the morning on Sunday. He had to leave in five hours to make it back to Lubbock before midnight.

He sat on the foot of my bed. "Help me with my boots."

I squatted at his feet. "Who helps you in Texas?" I yanked on his left boot with little success. I repositioned with my back to Josh and his leg between mine.

Josh steadied himself with his right hand on the wall. His left hand stroked my exposed backside. "I'm not usually this drunk, darling."

"For your information, when some dudes you don't really know or you likely won't ever see again challenge you to do keg stands, you don't have to rise to the challenge."

"I always rise to the occasion." His words held meaning I'd been blocking out of my mind all night after he ditched me to hang with the boys. From experience, his skills decreased drastically with each beer.

"You men are all the same."

"Not true. I kicked all their butts. Not one could match me. I think I drank at least half of that keg." He belched.

"Right. I'm so proud," I sneered and tugged on his other boot, having to put a leg on the bed to get enough oomph to pull the sucker off. Once it became free, I tumbled headfirst into the closet door.

Josh put his arms out, too inebriated to stand and properly help me off the ground. "You okay?" Without waiting for me to answer, he said, "Come here." He wore his *I'm ready to screw* smile.

Still seated on the floor, I looked at his smug grin, mussed hair from his cowboy hat (a new, and unwelcome, addition to his wardrobe since going to college), and red eyes. Reluctantly, I got to my feet with the intention of freshening up so he'd fall asleep waiting for me. "I need to shower first."

"No you don't. Come on." He managed to latch onto one of my arms, pulling me down on top of him.

His kiss was overly sloppy and wet, but mercifully short. Josh rolled on top of me, fumbling with his belt buckle. Even drunk, he managed to shuck his jeans and underwear at lightning speed, and his clumsy fingers worked on mine, dispensing them too easily for my liking. I rolled my head to the side. The sight of Gemma's empty bed made my heart lurch into my throat. Josh wedged a knee between my legs, his soldier coming to attention.

Having sex with Josh was the last thing I wanted to be doing at the moment, considering how miffed I was that he made me look like an ass in front of my friends. I wondered what Gemma was up to in Jenny's room. The thought of the three of them experimenting in bed flashed into my mind.

"Kiss me," Josh said. "It's like you're miles away."

I forced a smile and met his lips, imagining he was someone else.

But who?

The blurry image of the person I'd rather be kissing infiltrated my mind.

All that was discernable was red hair. Weird. I'd never dated a ginger before.

Before I could overthink it, Josh's arms gave out and he toppled onto me, his cock flickering at my entrance, causing my hole to tighten. At six-four and one hundred and seventy-five pounds, his useless, drunken body was too much on top of mine.

"You're squashing me." I jabbed my hip and arms upward, trying to make room.

"Sorry, darling. I'm a bit tired." He nuzzled his face

in the crook of my neck, still trying to gain access below.

I wanted to scream, "Stop calling me darling!" It was another unwelcome trait he had picked up recently, and I wondered whom he called darling in Lubbock. College had changed him—and not to my liking.

"I've missed you so much." His soft penetrating eyes reminded me of the man I used to know.

"Roll over onto your back," I said. "Let me help."

With Josh off me, I reached for his penis, taking it firmly into my hand.

He closed his eyes and groaned. "You feel so good."

I worked my hand rhythmically, and he clasped his hand over mine.

"I wish we weren't so far apart. God I miss you... this." He shuddered, and I realized he was about to come.

I frantically searched for a towel or something.

"Here." He handed me a white shirt. "I don't want to spoil your nice bedspread."

I smeared his come into the shirt, spreading the fabric to find a dry spot. That was when I realized what he'd handed to me. "Josh!"

He opened his beer-goggle eyes. "What's wrong?"

"You gave me one of Gemma's shirts!"

He looked at the shirt in my hands. "Oh. I thought it was yours. It was under your pillow."

"I can't believe you."

"How was I supposed to know? After you wash it, she won't be the wiser." He winked. "It'll be our secret."

"But—"

He placed a finger on my lips. "I have to get some sleep for the drive back."

I whacked his chest with a fist.

"Jesus, Tegan. You're acting like I killed someone. What's your problem? I drove over ten hours to see you, and you're busting my balls for handing you someone else's shirt. Why was the shirt under your pillow if it wasn't yours?" Some clarity glimmered in his eyes. Or was I imaging it?

"Don't change the subject." I shook a crusty finger at him.

He sighed. "Whatever. I'll buy her a new fucking shirt, okay? Can I get some sleep now?" His eyes shut, and I knew from his ragged breaths it wouldn't be long until he was sawing logs.

I swung off the bed, taking Gemma's shirt to the sink to rinse off Josh's spunk, but I couldn't bring myself to salvage it. There was no way I'd let Gem slip on any article of clothing that had been contaminated by Josh. Not with his semen seeped into the weave of the cotton. It seemed like an abomination. I'd buy her three new shirts to replace this one. I buried the shirt in the trash can in the bathroom and then hopped into the shower.

Afterward, I came out to find Josh dead to the

world on his back in the center of my bed—his arms spread out and feet hanging off the end as drool trickled from the corner of his mouth. I sighed and climbed into Gemma's bed, finally feeling at peace for the first time that night. I breathed deeply into her pillow, slightly alarmed by the impulse and confused by the comfort it provided.

"HOW WAS YOUR WEEKEND? Sleep okay in Jenny's room?" I asked Gemma when she returned to the room a little after eleven in the morning.

She jostled her neck back and forth. "Not too bad. Jenny had an air mattress for me."

"She's a sweetheart."

"The absolute best."

I swallowed.

"You?" she asked.

"Well, some have said I'm all that and a bag of chips." I put a hand on one hip, jutting it out like a 1940s actress on premier night.

Gemma pointed to my wall calendar taped next to my bedside. "You need a long black glove and a cigarette on a stick."

I studied Marlene Dietrich's image. "Yeah, right. I'll never be that glamorous."

"Not with that attitude." Gemma fell onto her bed.

"Gosh, I'm sorry. I totally forgot to make my bed. What did Josh think?"

I laughed. "Josh! He'd never notice if there was an undetonated atom bomb in the middle of the room. Besides, he passed out drunk in the middle of my bed, so I slept in yours. I hope you don't mind."

"Too much beer pong yesterday?" With a grin so wide it split her face in two, she hugged her pillow to her chest.

Confused about why she seemed so happy, I asked, "What'd you guys do last night?"

"Nothing much. Hung out, talked, and fell asleep watching *Saturday Night Live*."

"Funny?"

"Not bad." She shrugged. "Was it nice seeing Josh?" The confidence she had exuded moments ago slithered away.

I sat next to Gem on the bed, my legs crossed and my back against the window. "I don't know, really. It was weird. We hardly ever talk on the phone, and he's only written me one letter. And when I saw him in a cowboy hat and boots, I didn't know what to think. How did he change so much in three months? And have I changed?"

"He doesn't normally dress like that?"

"No way. I'd never date a hick—" I realized what I said and to whom. "Not that there's anything wrong with hicks. I just can't stand fake hicks; that's all." I chomped down on my bottom lip and released a puff of air.

She shoved her shoulder against mine. "Don't worry. No one in my family wears a cowboy hat. Boots, that's a whole different ball game."

"You look sexy in yours." My face shot up as if pierced with red-hot daggers.

"Not too hickish for your taste?" Again she prodded my shoulder.

"Not at all. If it ticks up your hotness factor, I say wear 'em."

"You think I'm hot?"

"Are you kidding me?" I squealed or screeched; it was hard to decipher. "With your red hair, emerald eyes, peaches and cream skin, and slender body?"

"So is that a yes or no?"

"Need an ego stroke today?"

"Doesn't everyone?"

"Okay. Then what about me?"

"You want me to stroke you?"

I laughed nervously. Had Gemma been drinking earlier? "My ego, ding-dong."

"Girls like you don't need ego stroking."

I crossed my arms. "What do you mean *girls like me?*"

"Girls who look like Elle Macpherson." She met my eyes, challenging me to disagree.

"Whatever!" I rubbed the back of my neck.

"Sore?"

"A little. I had a minor boot mishap last night and crashed into the closet door."

She widened her eyes. "You okay?"

"Yeah. Just tweaked my neck some."

She patted the bed. "Flip around. I'll rub it."

"You wouldn't mind? You have the best hands." A shiver ripped through my soul.

"So all the girls keep telling me."

I rolled my eyes. "One compliment about your boots, and now you have the self-esteem of Julia Roberts."

She dug her fingers into my neck meat. "Please, I look nothing like Julia Roberts."

"You have the red hair. That's more than I have." I started to sing Roy Orbison's "Pretty Woman."

She pulled my shoulders against her. "Don't be cruel."

"How is calling you *pretty* being cruel, might I ask?" I stared into her eyes, still leaning against her body.

"You're teasing me."

I crossed my heart with a finger. "I'm not teasing. Don't let your experience with Kate taint things."

Her expression and sigh held a sense of longing that excited and terrified me. I broke into Orbison's song again to overcome the nervous crackle in the air.

Gemma shoved me off her and resumed massaging my neck. "You're terrible."

I scouted over my shoulder to peek at her face again. "You don't really think that, do you?"

"Nah."

The longing still resided in the recesses of her irises.

"Gosh, I don't think I'm helping much. You seem tighter now than when I started." She jabbed her thumbs into my muscles.

"Don't give up. Not yet."

CHAPTER EIGHT

"I'VE TOLD YOU A MILLION TIMES, YOU DON'T have to wear the Princess Leia bikini outfit. Hell, you don't even have to be Princess Leia. There's always C-3PO." She gripped each of my shoulders with her hands and smiled. "You'd be covered from head to toe."

It was the night before Halloween, and Gemma and I were putting together the final touches of our costumes. Her Luke Skywalker outfit was a midnight blue bathrobe (Mervyn's didn't have a black one), a black glove for his fake hand, and a plastic light saber we had picked up in a toy shop. It flickered on and off even when the batteries were fully charged. The Luke costume seemed more appealing than donning a metal bikini.

I eyed the unworn gold bikini on my bed. "But I got the gold armband and chain for the Leia outfit."

"Okay, then..." Gemma rubbed the top of her head, one of the few signs of frustration she allowed herself to show. "You clearly want to wear the outfit"—she motioned to bits and pieces on the bed—"so tell me what the real issue is."

I sat heavily onto her desk chair, crossed my feet, and lowered my eyes to the carpet. "My scar."

"What scar?"

"On my back. I got it in high school when there was an accident—"

"An accident?" Her face screwed up in confusion.

"Kinda sorta. It's hard to explain, really." I flapped my arms about. It wasn't actually difficult to describe, but I never wanted to tell people what happened to avoid having it twisted into much more than it was. "It left a scar, and my mom said I was damage goods." I sighed. "I know it sounds crazy." I circled my finger around the side of my head in the universal cuckoo sign. "Since then, whenever I think about wearing a bikini, I flip out." I wrung my hands together.

"Okay. Have you thought about wearing a leotard under the bikini? A skin-colored one."

"That's brilliant!" I hopped off the seat, bouncing on my toes, clasping her hands, and waving our arms about in some kind of victory dance. "Come on!"

"Where?" She was grinning from ear to ear.

"Shopping for the leotard, of course. We'll have to go to Fort Collins." I placed a finger on her button nose. "And as a reward for your utter brilliance, I'm treating you to dinner."

"Ah, you don't have to take me to dinner. I'm just glad we finally came up with a solution so I don't have to listen to you whine anymore." Her broad smile was a pretty good indicator she wasn't all that annoyed with me.

"I don't whine."

She sucked her lips in, and I couldn't determine if it was for show or if she really was trying to curb a comment she'd regret.

"I don't whine," I repeated, my voice higher pitched.

"Of course you don't. Who would say such a thing?" She winked at me.

"Now that we got that settled, I'm taking you to dinner."

"Whatever you say, Tegan-the-non-whiner." She bowed like a knight from King Arthur's Round Table.

I rolled my eyes, choosing to ignore the nickname, which I hoped was the first and last time I'd hear it. "Great! It's a date." As soon as the word left my mouth, I panicked. "Er, I mean, it's a time for two friends to sit down in a restaurant and have dinner together, as friends."

"So just a friendly dinner between two friends," she mocked.

"Can we cram another 'friend' into the sentence?" I joked, hoping to bury the awkwardness.

"Hmmm…" She placed a finger to her lips, deep in thought. "How about: A dinner with two friends to discuss how awesome it is to be super-duper friendly and to have such a friendly time together, simply as friends?"

"You're a dork."

"I'm the dork? You're the one who freaked out when you said the word date." She placed a hand on my shoulder. "I know you're straight. No reason to go into panic mode, like you do, thinking I may hope for more."

I brushed her warm hand off my shoulder. "What do you mean *like I do*?"

She pointed to the brown sack on her desk. "Remember hyperventilating last week during midterms."

I thumped her shoulder harder than I intended. "Whatever. Are we going shopping and to dinner, or not?"

"By all means." She motioned for me to walk ahead.

———

THE WAITRESS in Chili's set down my chicken crispers and Gemma's burger. "Anything else?"

We both shook our heads.

"Want my corn?" I pointed to the small corn on the cob.

"Thanks!" She plucked it off my plate and placed it on her own. "So where's this scar?" Gemma bit into her burger. Grease and sauce trickled down the side of her hand, and she licked it.

I crossed my legs tightly and shifted in my seat. "On my back."

"Is it big or small?"

"Hard for me to say. I don't like to look at it.

"Did it hurt?"

I shrugged. "How about you? Got any scars?" I nibbled on a fry.

Gemma was kind enough not to push about my scar. "No. My life has been pretty boring so far."

"You make it sound like that's going to change soon. Do you have something to confess?"

She took another bite of her burger, and I waited for her to "clean up" the sauce again with her mouth, but she used a napkin this time. After swallowing, she said, "Not sure about how soon. But when I finish school, I want to move to one of the coasts. More sports teams to follow."

"And abandon the Husker's?" I feigned shock.

"Never." She raised both brows. "Once a fan, always a fan."

"Are you devoted to everyone in your life... or only sports teams?" I supported my weight on my forearms.

Gemma's eyes drifted momentarily to my cleavage. "Everyone? That I don't know, but I am pretty loyal."

"What about Kate? Do you two communicate at all?"

She shook her head.

"Do you ever hear about her?"

"Nah." She sat back in her seat. "Most of the news I receive from back home is about family and my parents' shop. Kate and her family keep to themselves, pretty much."

I sensed she was putting on a brave face, so I opted to change subjects. "What character will April be tomorrow night?"

"Who knows? Even Jenny has been kept in the dark, and I'd be the last person she'd tell."

"True. She hates your guts."

Gemma balled up her napkin and tossed it at me, laughing.

"I haven't been able to put my finger on why she dislikes you so much." I held onto her napkin so when Gemma took her next bite of burger, she'd have to lick her hand or wipe it on her jeans, and I was willing to bet she wouldn't choose the latter option.

"It's a mystery, but not one I care to solve."

"Yeah, probably best not to probe that too much. Who knows what you'd uncover—like she secretly has a crush on you and all she can think about is your lips —kissing them and feeling your tongue inside her mouth." I shifted in my seat again.

Gemma was in mid bite, but she froze, studying my face. Two or three seconds ticked by before she said, "I seriously doubt that." She licked her lips. "Besides, I'm not the type girls daydream about."

I chewed on my lower lip. Gemma took a massive bite of her burger, and the flood of sauce was a relief to see. It took several swipes of her tongue to get every last delicious drop. "Don't sell yourself short. I bet, right now, there's at least one girl crushing hard on you." I pointed a fry at her.

She laughed and then swiped my fry. "Who needs a girlfriend when they have a best friend like you?"

"TELL ME WHAT YOU WANT, Gem, and I'll do it." I lay on my side with her next to me under my bed covers.

She swiped a blonde lock off my forehead. "I can't."

"*Won't* is more like it." I pressed the tip of her perky nose with a fingertip.

"Pa-tay-to, po-tah-to," she mocked.

It annoyed me that she was mentioning potatoes. "I'm serious. Tell me. Do I have a chance?"

"With what?"

"With you?"

Gemma's face winced, and she sucked in a ragged breath. "That's never been the problem."

I closed my eyes, too afraid to see the truth as I asked, "What's been the problem?"

"You," she whispered.

"What's wrong with me?" I whispered back.

"You aren't into chicks," she said, which was so un-Gemma-like, and the statement gave me pause. Did she really just say that? Was this really happening?

"What if I wanted to try? With you?" I opened my eyes to see an easing in Gemma's frozen lips.

"What makes you think I'm willing to be your lesbian test case?"

I cupped her cheek. "I can see it in your eyes."

"Maybe."

"That's a start." I brushed my thumb over her lips. "Can I kiss you?"

She nodded.

I reciprocated the nod.

Neither of us moved.

I laughed. "We aren't making much progress."

"Not true, I think we are. I now know you like me." Her smile gave me the encouragement I needed.

I leaned in, and she met my lips halfway. At first, our lips smooshed against each other. It wasn't until I opened mine a crack that her warm tongue entered my mouth.

A moan escaped both of us.

Much to my delight, she deepened the kiss.

I could kiss her all night.

I wanted to kiss her all night.

Gemma rolled me onto my back, not breaking our lip-lock, and her hand roamed down my side. I didn't even care when it found my scar and then passed right on by.

"Yes, Gem. Yes."

Her hand slipped under my pale yellow Gap T-shirt, and her fingers migrated to my breasts. Her fingertips so soft, her kneading pleasant but urgent.

I fisted her hair, pulling her deeper into the kiss.

Gem's fingers trailed down my stomach, not stopping at the elastic band of my pajama bottoms. In one movement, her hand thrust under both the PJs and my panties and a finger split my wet pussy lips. She pulled her head up and peered into my eyes. "Can I make love to you?"

I bolted upright in bed, clawing at my shirt, and the wetness between my legs was intense. Tiny bubbles of excitement zinged through my body, confusing the hell out of me. But I craved her touch again. Each caress singed my skin and left her stamp on my body and soul.

"Tegan! Are you all right?" Gemma called from her bed.

Her bed?

I was in my bed, and she was across the room.

It'd been a dream.

Thank God. *I think.*

I looked across the room and saw the worry etched into her face. "Weird dream, that's all. I'm fine."

"You want me to come over there?" She started to lift the covers.

"No! No, it's fine. I'm fine. Stay put—I mean, stay warm under the covers." How would I explain the wetness on my sheet?

She recovered herself with her Husker's bedspread. "You sure you're okay? You look pale, like you've seen a ghost."

I lay back down on my back. "Really, I'm fine."

"Tell me about your dream," Gemma said. "Was it a scary one, or was it about Josh?" Gemma would never outright ask me if I had a sex dream.

I put a hand to my eyes, massaging them harder than was comfortable. "I can't seem to remember it."

I recalled every second of it and wanted to drift back into it, which horrified me even more. Or did it?

"Can you just talk to me?" I forced my eyes wide open.

"When my sister was a kid, she used to have night terrors. Oh man, you've never heard something so heartbreaking as a five-year-old screaming bloody murder because she was frightened for her life."

"What caused them?" I rolled my head to face her.

"Don't know."

"How did she overcome them?"

"Not sure. One night before bed I told her to dream of puppies. She hasn't had a bad dream since."

I tucked my pillow under my head, propping myself up. "You saved her."

"Nah." She waved a hand. "I just gave her a suggestion. She did the hard work."

In the dark, I could sense her blush.

"You're a beautiful person, on the inside and out."

"Weird dreams make you sentimental," she joked in a tone that indicated she was uncomfortable.

"Can you keep talking until I fall asleep? I need to hear your voice."

"Anything for you."

Gemma chattered on about her childhood. When she ran out of stories, she talked about the people in her hometown. Even mentioning two little old ladies who owned a craft store. Every once in a while, she made sure I was still awake, and when she saw my eyes peeled open, she'd start on a new topic. When she brought up her calculus class, I intervened.

"Gem?"

"Yeah?"

"Do you think I should break up with Josh?"

"Uh, not sure I should be the one making that decision. What do you think?"

I shrugged. "It was just so weird when he visited. I think the long distance—it's hard, ya know?"

She started to speak, hesitated, and then said, "Give it some thought. You said he isn't going home for Thanksgiving, right?"

"Right."

"So wait 'til winter break. See how it feels, and if it doesn't feel right, then you can make your decision. What's a few more weeks, really?"

I stared at the ceiling. "A few more weeks. That's a good way to think of it. Are you always this sensible?"

She ignored my question. "Besides how he acted when he visited, is there another reason why you want to end it?"

Oh God, did she know I had a racy dream about her? Did I call out her name? Cry out, "Oh, Gemma, I've wanted this for so long," and then moan?

"I don't know. I—it's hard to explain. Inside, I feel like something's wrong or different." I ran my fingers back and forth over my eyebrows, messing them up and righting the hairs again.

"I know what you mean."

"You do?" I could hear the shock in my question.

"Oddly, I do." She didn't explain, and I wasn't sure if I should push her to.

Neither of us said anything for what seemed like an eternity, and I thought she'd fallen back to sleep.

"Good night, Gemma," I whispered, thankful I was able to say her name.

"Night, Teeg."

She sounded wide-awake like me.

CHAPTER NINE

"TEGAN, YOU LOOK GREAT." MICHELLE, dressed as Obi-Wan "Ben" Kenobi, hugged me. Her gray beard scratched my cheek.

Jenny stepped back, appraising my outfit. "Um, I don't remember Leia wearing a bodysuit. What gives?"

I flushed, not wanting to explain about my scar.

Gemma came to my rescue. "Geez, Jenny. It's October in Colorado. You want Tegan to freeze to death?"

I squeezed Gem's hand and released it just as quickly. "Yeah, it's cold as shit in this basement. Cement walls, ya know. Your Hans Solo outfit looks a lot warmer than my gold bikini." It was actually sweltering in the basement with about forty people crammed into the space, dancing, talking, and drinking. Seb and Michelle had gone all out with the decorations, transforming the place into a creepy haunted house with dry ice for fog. Somehow they had smoke coming out of the punch bowl.

Sebastian, in a Chewie outfit rented from a shop, growled like the character, showing he supported my decision to wear the leotard, and then gave Jenny a menacing look.

"Thanks, Se—I mean, Chewie."

He howled, "You're welcome."

"Anyone seen April yet?" I asked.

"Nope. Not sure she's coming." Jenny's expression seemed troubled. "She's, uh, feeling left out."

"How?" I put a hand on my hip. "She was the one who didn't want to dress with the group and wouldn't tell us anything about her costume."

Jenny shrugged. "You know April, always got her panties in a bunch."

It was the first time I had heard Jenny say anything negative about anyone.

"Oh my God, you guys are a trip!" A girl I didn't know, wearing a slutty French maid outfit, approached. "I clearly didn't get the memo that this was a *Star Wars* Halloween party."

Jenny ogled her up and down. "I, for one, am glad you didn't."

The girl, much to my surprise, enjoyed the compliment. "In that case, care to dance?"

Jenny thrust her light saber at Gemma. "Hold this."

Seb and Michelle tailed them and started to jig as well.

Gemma and I stood off to the side, not speaking. Someone behind us was breathing heavily, and I flipped around and saw Darth Vader. Whoever was inside spent some serious coin—the getup could have been worn on the movie set, or it may have been worn in the movie. And the Vader-like breathing was spot-on. I always thought Vader would be taller, though.

"April?" I squeaked.

Darth Vader didn't confirm or deny. Its attention was on Jenny getting down with the maid.

Gemma inched closer to me, and I couldn't blame her. If it was April inside, she was more intimidating than ever. And Gem was dressed as Luke Skywalker— he and Vader didn't get along, even though they were father and son.

"You want to dance or something?" I asked.

Gem looked at the light sabers in her hands. "What should I do with these?"

"Hold onto them." I jerked my head to the heavy-breathing Vader. "We might need them."

Gemma laughed and led me onto the dance floor, her sabers lighting the way for us in the dark basement. Occasionally a strobe light flashed, but it didn't illuminate much of anything. Much to my relief, Michelle and Seb grooved with us. I pointed to Vader, and Michelle had to squint to see, but she nodded appreciatively. Chewie raised a paw and let out a terrifying roar. Jenny, too involved with the French maid, didn't notice.

Darth Vader whipped around, his cape snapping in a terrifying way, and left the room.

Gemma, Michelle, and I raised our eyebrows and turned to see if Jenny noticed. If she did, she didn't care. We all shrugged and continued dancing.

An hour later, while the four of us took a break from dancing, April appeared, wearing an *I Dream of Jeanie* outfit. She was all smiles—for April at least. "Did I miss anything?"

"Uh, nope," I said. Jenny and the maid were in the corner getting it on.

April's eyes landed on them briefly, not showing any emotion. "I need a beer. Anyone need anything?" She waited patiently.

"No thanks," Gemma and I said in unison.

When she was out of sight, I said, "What the fuck? Who was in the Darth Vader outfit?"

Michelle lit a cigarette. "We should have dressed as Scooby-Doo characters because this is one fucked up mystery."

Seb removed his mask and took a drag of Michelle's cigarette before putting the mask back on without saying a word.

Michelle laughed. "I love the strong, silent type." She discarded her cig and hustled her boyfriend back onto the floor, dancing provocatively. It gave me the creeps to see Obi-Wan "Ben" Kenobi seducing Chewie.

Gemma, like Seb, didn't say anything.

"You okay?" I asked.

She snapped out of her funk. "What? Oh, yeah."

"Do you want to leave?"

"No. Not unless you do." Her eyes were a bit bleary, and I wondered if the alcohol was kicking in.

"Do you want to dance?"

"Do you?"

Did I? From the looks of Michelle and Seb, they didn't want to create a foursome, and I wouldn't have my buffer. But standing in a dark corner with Gemma was making me nervous. April was across the room, chatting up Frankenstein, who was quite good-looking for a man brought back to life.

"Yeah, why not. Show me some of your Nebraskan moves." I wiggled my ass, and Gemma's jaw dropped, making me smile. "Leave those behind." I motioned to the light sabers.

Before we started dancing, April was already in a lip-lock with Frankenstein. "Wanna bet she and Frankie leave together?"

Gemma surveyed the couple. "I hate losing money."

"You hate losing, period." I wrapped my arms around her neck. "I'm a little tipsy." I felt compelled to give a reason as to why I was holding onto her.

"Could be the pre-party drinks you insisted on." She maneuvered me closer to her body.

"Yeah, I'm sure that's it." I rested my head on her shoulder.

A faster song came on, but I didn't let go of

Gemma's neck. Her arms squeezed me tighter. I glanced up and gazed into her eyes, which were even blearier than before. I stumbled, but Gem didn't let me fall.

"Thanks. The booze is really hitting me."

"Do you want to take a break?"

That was the last thing I wanted. I shook my head. "No, let's keep dancing. It's a party after all."

She smiled, and her arms continued to hold on tight. "Never fear. I won't let you fall."

"You're good to me."

"That's what best friends are for."

"Exactly." I rested my head on her shoulder again. "To hold onto each other." I almost added "forever."

SEASON ONE

THE FIRST TIME

CHAPTER ONE

"OH, MY GOSH! I'M SO SORRY!" I SLAMMED THE door of the dorm room and fled down the hallway, crashing through the gray metal door leading to the stairwell.

With hands on knees, I sucked in a deep breath. Then another.

"I just saw Gemma completely naked," I said to no one in particular since the landing was devoid of human life aside from me, Spazzy Tegan.

In an attempt to still the tornado of emotions churning inside, I theorized it probably wasn't all that unusual for college roommates to see each other in the flesh. Dorm rooms, after all, didn't provide many nooks and crannies to hide one's skin. Delicious creamy white skin—*Tegan, don't go there.*

A *but* blurred my logic. Not Gem's butt. The *but* that exposed the true heart of the matter. Gemma and

I had been extra careful when it came to nudity. I'd always been shy in this department because of a scar and other insecurities. As Mom was fond of saying, I was roomy in the hips. And Gem took shyness to a whole new level. Of course, there was more under the surface. For one, Gemma had recently confided to me she was a lesbian, and she was afraid she was forcing her sexuality on me. That didn't freak me out. Other stuff did, but I was doing my best to shove all of it below the surface. So much, in fact, if it took the form of an iceberg, it would slice through a ship three times the size of the *Titanic* upon impact, not hours afterward.

I sighed, resting my forehead against the cool stone wall of the stairwell, knowing I couldn't hole up here for the rest of the semester. It wasn't even February yet. The term was barely underway. And the reason I'd busted into the room in the first place was because I needed to snatch an assignment due—I glanced at my watch—in ten minutes.

I tiptoed back into the hallway. Outside the room, I raised a fist to knock on the door, willing my heart to stop hammering. Could Gemma hear it from inside the room? My mind flashed to the heart removal scene in *Indiana Jones and the Temple of Doom*. The weird chanting filled my ears. The victim prayed as his arms were locked into the odd metal contraption. The priest with the scary skull headdress reached not for the man's chest but mine. The thumping of the heart grew louder and louder, threatening to burst my eardrums.

I shook the image from my thoughts.

Ever so lightly, I rapped my knuckles on the wood.

Gemma, now clad in jeans and a hoodie, swung the door open. "Why'd you knock?" she said in her normal voice, although there was evidence of the beginnings of a blush.

"Sorry. I didn't want to..." I left the obvious unsaid.

"Don't you have class?" She didn't sound defensive, but her arms hugged her chest. Was she mad? Feeling violated?

"I forgot my nutrition paper, which is due... now." I tapped my watch, avoiding her eyes.

"Ah." She dragged out the word.

Was *ah* a word? Exclamation, perhaps? *That's right, Tegan. Keep thinking of stupid stuff to keep your mind off what happened.*

I grabbed the paper from my desk and stuffed it into my bag. "I'll see ya later."

"I'll try to keep my clothes on." She flashed a shy smile.

Did she know the effect she had on me? Her lips, soft and tempting pink.

"Yeah, me too." I opted to amscray—completely cowardly I admit—so I couldn't glimpse her reaction to that inane comment.

THAT NIGHT, after returning from the cafeteria, Gemma and I camped out on our respective beds, watching a *Roseanne* rerun. For the entire episode, neither of us spoke, which was highly unusual.

When the credits rolled, Gemma asked, "Do you want to talk about earlier?"

I nearly swallowed my tongue. Finally, I croaked out, "What about earlier?"

"When you barged into the room... after my shower. You've been weird since then." Her tone implied she hadn't been able to knock the incident from her mind either.

"Oh, that." I chewed on a hangnail, accidentally ripping it off and making my finger bleed. I hated the sight of my own blood. I tucked both hands under my butt to prevent more carnage, ignoring the fact there'd be a drop of blood on my sheets. It was time to wash them anyway. "It was no biggie. So, I saw you in the buff? Honestly, I'm surprised it hasn't happened before. Don't worry your pretty head about it." Why did I have to babble? And toss in *pretty head* to boot?

"I didn't convert you to women, then?" Nervous laughter burbled out of her like spurts of water from a leaky faucet.

"Uh..." How could I put into words what I'd felt when I saw Gem in her birthday suit and the thoughts that hadn't left my mind since?

"Kidding." She put her palms in the air.

"Did you want to see me naked? To get even?"

Gemma blinked.

Could I make this situation more awkward? Probably yes.

I stood, stretching my arms overhead. "I should go to the library."

Gemma glanced at the digital clock on the beat-up mini fridge next to her bedside.

Before she could question me further, I said, "I have a history test on Friday, and I'm so not prepared." I dragged out the word *so*.

"Okay. Do you want me to go with you?" Gemma glanced over her shoulder to peer out the window into the black night, concern registering in her hunched shoulders.

"I'll bring my whacking stick." My dad had purchased a massive flashlight he claimed would double as a weapon in a pinch. Even with it, I still hated the thought of wandering across the field to campus on a cold winter night. "Or, maybe I'll study in the cafeteria now that dinner service is over."

The worry in Gemma's shoulders lessened.

At least one of us felt more relaxed.

As if in tune with my troubled mind, she said, "I really was kidding."

I forced a confident smile. "I know, but if I did lean that way…"

Gem filled in the blanks. "I'd be your first choice?" Her teasing smile reflected in her eyes.

"Exactly!"

"We're cool, right?" Her face was sincere.

"Of course, we are. Besties don't fall apart over something so silly."

"Good." The relief in her eyes troubled me some.

I grabbed my backpack and vamoosed in a hurry for the third time in one day.

Downstairs, I reached into my bag and discovered I'd neglected to pack my history notebook and textbook. Unwilling to face Gemma again so soon, I doodled in my nutrition notebook until I deemed an adequate amount of time had elapsed for my ruse.

I was unsure, though, who I was desperately trying to fool.

CHAPTER TWO

"I'M GOING TO FAIL!" I COLLAPSED ONTO THE pillows on my bed, with arms flailed out.

Gemma, on her bed with her back against the wall near the window, peered over a copy of *Rubyfruit Jungle*. We were both in a women's studies class and had a paper on Rita May Brown's lesbian coming-of-age novel due in a week. Gemma's soft green eyes always calmed me. "No you won't, Teeg." I loved that nickname. Most called me Tiny T or TR, the initials of my first and middle name—Tegan Raye. Only Gemma called me Teeg. When possible, I avoided telling people my last name: Ferber. In grade school, the mean kids had called me Furball.

I grunted. Gemma always cheered me on, no matter what. We'd grown close over the past few months. During a weekly "gin and tonic Thursday" house party, which came into being after listening repeatedly to "Hey Jealousy" by the Gin Blossoms, one of our friends said, "You two belong together, like gin and tonic."

Jenny had added her two cents by saying, "Dude, you're so right. Gemma is totally the gin: quietly confident and dependable, and TR is the spazzy fizz."

Now, people referred to us as G&T. I wasn't thrilled that Jenny viewed me as the fizz, but it was hard to argue the point considering I could be high-strung on occasion. Or so people kept telling me.

On the portable speakers behind me, Whitney Houston belted out the line "And I will always love you." I spied Gemma peeking longingly in my direction. The first time I had noticed, it frightened me. Now, I coveted it. If only she would do it purposefully so I could address it.

"I haven't been to class in over a week, and tomorrow's our first test." I stared out our dorm room window, where snowflakes zipped across the murky sky. The soft yellow glow of the streetlight across the road didn't fit the stormy mood in our sleepy Colorado college town. The first of February had brought the biggest storm of the season.

Gemma tapped a pink highlighter against her leg in time with the next song on my mixed tape: "Under the Bridge" by The Red Hot Chili Peppers. Her charcoal gray Cornhuskers hoodie made me smile. I wasn't a sports person, but since meeting Gemma last August, when we'd both started our freshman year, I stayed abreast of all the football news. Hill University wasn't in Nebraska's division, but that didn't stop Gemma from knowing all the top players on all the teams of our small-time conference. In Keller, her hometown, she'd been the sportswriter for the high school paper. No matter what, Gemma was always Gemma—as her ubiquitous hoodie confirmed. Even though she was attending school in Colorado, she usually wore a shirt, hat, or sweatshirt proclaiming she was a Cornhusker through and through. Her parents even mailed the Sunday paper so Gemma could keep up with her beloved state and school.

"You always panic over exams, but then you rock them. Stay calm. Maybe you need a break. You've been cramming U.S. history into your brain since seven this morning." She set her book on the floor.

I sat up and rolled my neck from side to side. "Maybe."

We'd first met on the day we moved into our dorm room and discovered we'd be living together in the tiny twelve-by-twelve-foot space. Over a relatively short amount of time Gemma had become my best friend. My rock. My...

She patted the big N on her bright red Huskers bedspread, beckoning me. I complied.

"Here. Let me massage your neck." Her soft hands gripped my shoulders and kneaded the tension. "You'll be fine. You hardly attended class last semester for the first half of this course and got As on every test." Her fingers roamed down my back. "You're a nerd."

"*I'm* a nerd? I'm not the one who got an A-plus in Calc 101 last semester."

Her hands dug into my shoulder, pulling me back against perky breasts. Jasmine perfume wrapped around me like a hot towel straight from the dryer. "Don't be mean," she said.

"I'm not being mean." I swiveled my head to look into her eyes. Golden flecks glowed in her green irises. "I'm jealous. I had to take Math for Idiots and had several sessions on long division."

"It wasn't that bad. Struggling with math doesn't make you an idiot. You got As in all your classes last semester, even in math. Stop acting like you're a nitwit."

I shrugged, and she pushed me away to focus on my neck once again.

Moments later, she said, "Lie down so I can work on your back."

A surge of heat pulsed through my body as I did as I was told.

"Wait. Tug your shirt up a bit," Gemma instructed in a not-so-demanding way. This wasn't the first time she'd given me a backrub. That time hadn't elicited any alarm bells. Weeks later, however, I noticed a tingling sensation when her hands were on my bare skin. It wasn't until finals week last semester when I realized the throbbing sensation was sexual.

I obeyed and then settled on my stomach with my hands above my head like I was about to dive headfirst into the deep end of a pool. Gemma wended a finger down my back. Her fingertips lingered on my scar. "Is this from the accident?" She'd seen it before, of course, but never asked. Not many knew about what had happened, and Gemma knew how embarrassed I was by what I deemed a hideous scar. When it had happened, my mother joked I was damaged goods.

"Yeah," I croaked. When I was a junior in high school, I volunteered to help construct sets for the drama club. Some jock had to help us after getting busted for supergluing the locks on the principal's Ford Bronco. He had been showing off with a nail gun the carpenter left behind and shot it off multiple times into a part of the set. One of the nails crashed through the flimsy board and lodged into my back. Luckily, it missed any organs. The tiny scar made me self-conscious, though. To this day, I still hadn't worn a bikini.

She outlined the scar tissue with a finger. "It resembles a heart, kinda."

A powerful wave trembled down south. I tried to focus on something else but could only think that Gemma Mahoney, a woman who came from such a small town in Nebraska that when she uprooted they had to adjust the number on Keller's billboard from population 407 to 406, was straddling me. *Come on, Tegan. Get it together. You have a midterm tomorrow.* This was not the time to pursue the thoughts I'd been having for weeks.

Right before winter break I had a fantastic and vivid dream about kissing and more with Gemma. When I woke, flushed and embarrassed, I brushed it aside. It wasn't the first dream involving a girl, but it was the first with Gemma as the leading lady. Unlike those other dreams, I couldn't stop thinking about it. When she'd given me a backrub during finals week, I knew why I couldn't stop dwelling on the dream. I wanted her. Wanted her bad.

"Are you nervous for this weekend?" I asked in an attempt to distract myself. Gemma's parents were coming to visit, and she planned to tell them she was a lesbian.

She stopped rubbing my lower back. "Terrified."

En Vogue's song "Free Your Mind" started playing. "Why don't you play them this song and then break the news?" I said.

She laughed. "I can picture it. Mom. Dad. I'm black."

I chuckled and twisted my hip to nudge her. "You're such a dork!" We both grew quiet again. "Ya know, you don't have to tell them during this visit. You can wait until you're ready."

"I know, but it's such a shadow always looming over me. My parents are awesome, and it's 1993. Besides, who's to say I'll ever feel totally ready." Her fingers drummed up and down my back, letting loose hundreds of goose bumps.

I nodded. I tried to imagine telling my parents I wasn't a virgin. That would not go over well, let alone compounding it with saying I was gay. My parents, who lived forty-five minutes south of Denver, a much more liberal city than Gemma's entire state, would not be cool with it. I imagined Mother preaching Bible verses and dousing me with holy water to exorcise the evil lesbian spirits. My father wouldn't say anything. He never did. His silence was deafening and hurt the most.

Gemma's parents were sweet, although old-fashioned. Gemma was the first in the family to attend college. When I'd met her father, Cormac, one of the first things he asked was how my father tolerated me living so far away from home. I was only a two-hour drive away, half as far as Gemma's commute. Her mother, Ava, wore clothes I was certain she'd sewn herself. We were nearing the millennium, but her folks definitely weren't as hip as Gemma hoped. And part of me wondered if they had ever heard the term *lesbian* spoken aloud. The concept they most likely understood, but the word was probably never muttered in their home or town for that matter.

The image of Gemma naked flashed in my mind. Why'd I have to crash into the dorm room yesterday right when she'd dropped her towel?

Gemma didn't talk right away about her sexuality,

but after a "gin and tonic Thursday" party last October, she had confessed to me in private. The next morning, she was so embarrassed she couldn't look me in the eye and said she'd understand if I wanted a new roommate. I told her straight away I didn't have any issues with it. Actually... If only she knew, but how could she? I didn't until recently. Not until that dream coaxed the flowering of my lesbian seed.

"I'm sure they'll assume some bull dyke will get her hooks in me or something. It would be easier if I had a girlfriend to introduce them to."

We laughed nervously over the image.

"I have an idea." I wiggled out from under Gemma and sat down facing her on the tiny dorm bed. "Why don't you tell them I'm your girlfriend? They like me. That might make it easier for them." Was I being too obvious? Was I saying, "Gemma, I like you?" without really saying it? My mother always told me I loved to tap-dance around things instead of stating how I felt.

Gemma stared, wide-mouthed.

"Or n-not," I stuttered and searched for the fragments of my ego on the carpet, which desperately needed vacuuming.

"You would do that? For me?"

Relieved, I placed a hand on my chest and said, "Of course. Wouldn't you?"

She smiled awkwardly, and for the first time since meeting, I didn't know what one of her expressions meant.

"Do you think they'd believe us?" she asked.

I brushed some loose strands of red hair off her shoulder. Gemma hated when hair got anywhere near her face. It was either in a ponytail or glued down with tons of hairspray. "Maybe we should practice."

She squinted. "Practice being girlfriends? How?"

I avoided her eyes and watched the snow splatter the window. It was really coming down. Still not looking at Gemma, I said, "Maybe we should kiss."

"Kiss?"

"Well, what if they want proof or something?" I hitched up my shoulders. That sounded asinine, but I couldn't think of another way to get the ball rolling. Outright telling her I was attracted to her seemed too risky for me, Play-it-Safe Tegan.

"I doubt my parents will demand we kiss as proof."

"It will help us." I added, "With our roles, I mean." Did she hear the desperation in my voice? Ever since that dream, I had wanted to feel her lips on mine.

Gemma swirled away as if a ship struck by a tsunami. "Uh, I don't know."

"What? Am I not your type?" I tried to feign offense and not show how much the thought wounded my heart.

During one of our recent late-night talks, Gemma had shown me a photo of her high school girlfriend, who in my opinion was as plain as a baked potato with no toppings. Of course, that could be my jealousy speaking. The girl dumped Gemma and started dating the quarterback their senior year because she wanted a *normal* life. When Gemma had arrived last August, she was still heartbroken.

"Who wouldn't want to date you? You're blonde, blue-eyed, and not to mention gorgeous. And you have a sexy gap between your front teeth like Madonna." A blush infiltrated her face so easily, as if always there.

I was desperate to feel her lips on mine, but I feared Gemma would never make a move on a "straight" girl. *Tegan, stop playing it safe all the time.* "Come on. It's just a kiss. One measly kiss." I moved closer with each word. She didn't pull away.

Our lips met briefly, and Gemma bolted back. Her eyes told me she didn't want to stop but felt compelled to by our friendship. Every fiber of my body was pleading for more.

I grabbed her face with both hands, and our mouths met. Gemma kept her lips closed before hesitantly letting me in. I deepened the kiss. She responded. Her arms encircled me, and we kissed. Really kissed, not for practice but because we wanted to.

In my head, I kept chanting, "I'm kissing Gemma Mahoney!"

Her lips were much softer than the boys I'd kissed. And she didn't immediately stick her tongue in my mouth and drool like Mitch did in the eighth grade. At first, Gemma let me take control, but then she delicately took the lead. There was passion, but not the aggressive passion I was used to with Josh, my last boyfriend. This kiss was quickly becoming the kiss to which I would compare all others.

Gemma snapped her head back. "What are we doing?"

I wanted to rap my knuckles on her forehead and say, "I thought it was obvious." Instead I said, "Kissing. What's wrong? Don't you like it?"

"Yeah, of course I like it. But we shouldn't." Her voice was soft, and lust burned in her eyes.

"Have you thought about that? About *me* before?" I twirled the drawstring of her hoodie around a finger.

It was Gemma's turn to gaze at the snow outside. Her shoulders slumped like she had forgotten my birthday or something.

"Hey, it's okay. You don't have to answer."

"I want to. But..." She laced her fingers, pulled them apart, intertwined them, and ripped them apart again until she settled on frantically tapping her fingertips together in front of her rosy lips.

"But what?" I needed to hear her say it.

"You're straight. Remember?" She stared into my eyes. "You had a boyfriend until recently."

It was true. Josh, the boy I'd started dating my senior year of high school, was now going to school in Texas. When we'd seen each other over the holidays, I realized my feelings for him had evaporated.

"Just because I haven't slept with a woman, doesn't mean I'm straight. At least completely." I stared down at my No Fear T-shirt Gemma had given me, the non-jock, for Christmas as a joke. It proclaimed, "Second place is the first loser." Was it a sign that *this* was my last clean shirt today of all days? Have no fear? Go for it? Slowly, I raised my eyes to meet hers.

"Have you thought of sleeping with a woman before?" Gemma's pinched face prepared for disturbing news. Would it be horrible for her to find out I liked her?

"Yes," I said, averting my eyes again.

"You have?" Her voice faltered some.

I nodded.

"Who?"

You, ya moron.

I said, "There was this one girl in my drama class last semester who I thought about. She looked a lot like Demi Moore in *Ghost*. She even had the short hair."

"Did you ever kiss her or anything?"

I shook my head.

"Have you ever kissed a woman?" she pushed.

"You mean, besides you?" I cracked a small smile. "No."

She swallowed. Her hand sought mine. It was clammy, but I didn't mind.

"I've thought about you," I confessed.

Gemma blinked as if she had spotted a leprechaun. I didn't know what to think, but I'd come this far.

"Have you thought about me?" I asked.

The nod was so slight I wasn't sure if I imagined it. I quirked an eyebrow.

She cleared her throat. "Yes. Yes, I have."

The moment I'd hoped for on so many occasions was finally happening. It was like standing on a precipice before taking a fall, and the thought didn't scare me. Not completely.

"Teeg... are you sure?"

I responded with a kiss. For what seemed like a lifetime, we kissed. Finally I said, "God yes, I'm sure." *Sayonara, Play-it-Safe Tegan!*

Our hands sought the other in a tangled mess. I fisted her red hair. Gemma pulled me close, letting out a soft moan.

She pulled away from our lip-lock. "We should slow down."

"I know. It's our first time. We should savor it."

Gemma's eyes glowed with primal desire.

"But, I don't know if I can take it slow." I cupped her cheek. "Not with you looking at me like that."

Gemma cradled her hand over mine. "Like what?"

"Like you want to eat me."

"I do." She didn't bother playing coy.

There was no fighting it. Our bodies became entangled once again. Kissing. Pawing. Groping.

Gemma wrenched the collar of my T-shirt and trailed her tongue along my collarbone.

"I want you," I said.

A lust-filled groan escaped from her lips, and she

ripped my shirt over my head. I reciprocated, jerking her sweatshirt and T-shirt off as fast as humanly possible. The kiss had spurred an overpowering yearning, unleashing all the inhibitions forged by my parents and society. From Gemma's urgency in tearing off my shirt, I sensed she felt the same. Not knowing what to do next, I kissed her again.

Gemma took charge and pushed me gently onto the red comforter to climb on top of me. Her hand ran up and down my side. My fingers fumbled with her white lace bra, and I was shocked to learn how hard it was to unclip someone else's bra with one hand.

I laughed. "I was expecting a sports bra."

"I'm not that much of a jock. I do own normal bras."

I ran a finger along the lace. "Sexy." I reached around with both arms in another attempt to unhook it. "Seriously? Why can't I do this?"

"Let me do that for you." She sat up and slowly revealed perfect, tiny breasts. My glimpse of Gemma naked yesterday had happened so fast I didn't notice her tattoo. With one finger I stroked the butterfly above her left breast.

Gemma smiled shyly. "May I?" She gestured to my bra. I tilted up for her to undo the clasp. She slid the straps over my arms and dropped the bra onto the floor.

"You make it look so easy," I joked.

"I've practiced with my blowup doll."

"Really?" I squawked.

"No! I've been with Kate." Her sincere eyes grew wide, and a flash of fear shone in the yellow flecks.

"It's okay. I guessed you weren't a virgin." I winked to reassure her. "Neither am I."

We'd always avoided sharing that one detail during our talks. Sex was a forbidden topic in my household, and it was a difficult habit to break. I think Gemma's family was even more hush-hush. Whenever we watched a movie with a sex scene, she always turned three shades of red, and I sensed she wanted to cover her face and watch through the cracks of her fingers. The thought almost made me laugh. As soon as it became apparent we both wanted each other, our shyness flew out the window. Mostly.

Gemma bit her lower lip. "But never with a woman." She stated it as a fact.

"Nope."

She nodded knowingly.

I cupped her chin and said, "Please, I want you to make love to me."

The fright in her eyes flashed brightly and then dimmed. Her smile grew wide. Gemma leaned down and kissed the hollow of my throat. I let out a small gasp. She kissed and licked her way to my right breast. She flicked my nipple with her tongue, and a louder gasp escaped from me. My nipple grew hard, and Gemma bit it gently at first and then a little harder.

"Oh," I exhaled.

Gemma's mouth savored the other nipple.

It was driving me insane, and my hips curved upward. Gemma gazed into my eyes, and I mouthed, "Please." She started to make her way down, leaving a shimmery trail as her mouth and tongue descended.

Down and down she went.

The anticipation was driving me mad with an overwhelming yearning I'd never felt. Juices pooled in my panties.

"I feel like I'm about to burst." I ground my head into the pillow.

"I take it you want me to continue." She licked my belly right below my belly button until she reached the top of my jeans.

"Yes. God, yes."

Without any prodding, I raised my hips so she could wrench my jeans off. My panties went next. She gawked, bewildered, and I wondered if I should talk her through it. Then I remembered Gemma had done this before.

"Everything okay?" I asked when Gemma continued to stare.

"I never thought I'd see you. All of you." Her face lit up.

"Is it all you imagined?" I joshed.

She laughed. "You can say that." Her fingers softly raked my coarse hair. "And then some."

Gemma traced her finger along my slippery lips. She ran it up and down several times and then licked her finger all the while eying my reaction. I slowly exhaled. Before she did anything else, her delicate pink tongue wet her lips.

I couldn't peel my eyes off of her, not wanting to miss a moment.

Her head started to dip toward my pussy.

Gemma's mouth opened slowly.

And then her tongue was on me. Exploring. I fisted the sheets with both hands. She parted my lips, and a tingling sensation ripped through my body.

Gemma's eyes flickered to mine, questioning if she should continue.

I bobbed my head, too overcome with exhilaration to speak.

She winked at me, and her tongue entered.

An excited squeal slipped out.

She didn't venture too far. My hips started to gyrate, guiding her deeper inside. Her hands clamped onto my butt, and she moaned with fervor. That electrified my senses even more.

"More, please," I pleaded in a soft tone.

Gemma's eyes burst open with eagerness, and I nodded to confirm the request.

She replaced her tongue with a finger, ever so gingerly.

"Don't stop," I panted. "Whatever you do, don't stop."

She seemed to understand what I meant, and her

tongue concentrated on my clit while her finger plunged in and out.

"Oh my God." I writhed. Gemma added another finger inside. Her tongue circled my bud frantically, and I could tell she was trying to keep it in the right spot. Try as I might, I couldn't hold still.

"Oh... oh... oh..." I repeated over and over.

Gemma drove in deeper. I sat up, which flustered her, and she pulled her head away. I guided her mouth urgently back into position and flashed a supportive smile. She continued stimulating me with her tongue.

"Oh... I think I'm going to..." I couldn't say the last word. An orgasm coursed through me, pinging frantically against all my nerve endings.

Gemma started to steady her fingers.

"No, don't stop."

One deep thrust brought me back to the brink of bliss. My fingers gouged the flesh on her back. I wondered if it hurt her, but I couldn't stop myself.

My body shuddered once.

Twice.

After the third time, I collapsed back onto the bed.

Gemma left her stilled fingers inside me. Another jolt zagged its way through my body.

"That was—"

"Amazing," Gemma interjected. She propped her head onto a palm. Her lips and chin glistened.

"I've never..." I panted and stopped speaking.

"Josh never?"

"No. Never. Nothing like that."

"Not even?" She glanced down at my pussy.

"When he went down on me? No, he was always in a rush."

Gemma's guilty grin informed me she meant something else.

"Oh, you mean when I masturbate." I felt my cheeks speckle.

She nodded shyly, making me wonder if she ever said the word out loud. Our comfort level around each other was growing by leaps and bounds tonight.

"Again. Nothing like this."

"Really?" Her eyes grew with anticipation.

"What about you and Kate?"

"Oh, she never..." She swallowed. "She was never very comfortable with her feelings and desires." Gemma's eyes scampered to my side of the room and seemed lost in the pink rose pattern on my Laura Ashley comforter.

"All the time you dated, she never went down on you?"

Gemma shook her head.

"Fingered?"

A slight, self-conscious nod of the head indicated yes but not often.

"But you went down on her?"

"Of course. Many times." She reddened, realizing her error. Gemma wasn't the type to criticize anyone, not even a selfish lover.

I sucked my lips into my mouth as far as they would go to avoid telling Gemma what I thought about Kate. This wasn't the time.

"Has anyone gone down on you?"

Her silence was loud and clear.

"Trust me. It felt amazing." I greedily locked her mouth to mine. She seemed hesitant at first but quickly succumbed. "I like tasting me on your lips."

"I like the way you taste."

I tugged on her belt.

She slapped my hand away and then blanched about her knee-jerk reaction. "You don't have to," she said.

I laughed. "I know. I want to."

"Are you sure?" Her finger wandered down my nose and rested on my lips. "We don't have to rush. This is happening so fast. For a straight girl." She smiled, but I could see concern shimmer in her bright green eyes.

"Ha! If I'd only known how good lesbian sex was in high school. Trust me, I want to. Now." Before she could stop me, I flipped Gemma onto her back and tried to yank off her Guess jeans.

"Wait!"

I straddled her, enjoying the feel of her bare stomach on my pussy. "What's wrong? Don't you want me—?"

"It's not that. It's..." She let out an exasperated

sigh. "I don't want you to wake up tomorrow wondering how things got so out of hand."

I patted her wet chin. "Little late for that, don't ya think? Stop being the responsible one for once. I want to be inside you. To taste you. I want to make you feel like I did moments ago. Please, trust me. I want this. I want you. And I'm a woman. I'm sure I can figure out what goes where." I made a circle with my thumb and forefinger and then inserted my tongue in the middle. Humor was my go-to when against the wall.

She laughed. "That's not what I mean, and you know it." Gemma patted my hand on her midsection. "There's a lot to think about. I don't want to get hurt. And I don't want to ruin our friendship. Besides, you're the one who's always joking that you're Play-it-Safe Tegan."

I huffed. "Really? Now's the time you bring that up?"

"Simply pointing out the elephant in the room." She propped herself up on her elbows.

I shoved her back down. "What's the difference between you going down on me and me going down on you? How is that less threatening?" I raised both eyebrows and ground my wetness into her stomach, causing her to close her eyes and stifle a moan.

After she recovered, she said, "It's not less threatening, but..." She shrugged, unable to complete the thought.

"So I'm still straight since my tongue hasn't landed on your clit. Is that what you're thinking?"

"You're more straight than lesbian that way." She smiled to soften the blow.

I ignored the impulse to point out she wasn't that much more experienced on the lesbian front. That probably wasn't the best tactic to get her to relax. "How can I get this through your thick head? I like you. I want you." I biffed the side of her head.

Gemma's eyes softened. "I like you, too."

"Progress." I feigned high-fiving. "I want to show you how much I like you." I leaned down and kissed her. Gemma's resolve was wilting faster than a daisy in hundred-degree weather. My hand snaked under her jeans and massaged the warmth through her panties. "It seems not all of you agrees that we should stop."

"You aren't playing fair." She shifted under me.

"Neither are you." I nipped her earlobe and whispered, "Pretty please with a cherry on top? Your cherry?"

She captured my lips, deepening the kiss instantly.

I broke away. "So, can I?"

She nodded.

I cupped my ear. "What? I'm sorry. I didn't catch that."

She growled. "You win."

"Win what?" I licked a nipple.

"I want you. I don't know why I'm being difficult. I mean, here you are, a beautiful naked woman on top of me"—she trailed a finger down my back—"and I'm putting the brakes on. It's insane."

"It's not insane. It's you. Remember, you're the levelheaded one, and let's face it; sex is a lot of things but not levelheaded." I softened my tone. "I know how much Kate hurt you. But I need you to understand that I'm not Kate. I have no intention of using you and then ditching you for the quarterback. I promise."

"*Promise* promise?" The sincerity in her face implored the truth.

"*Promise* promise. I've imagined this"—I motioned to the tangled bedspread—"for a long time, Gem. Not just the sex, but being with you. I like you." I punctuated each word with a thrust of my head, and my double-Ds bobbled with each jerk. Gemma noticed but pretended she wasn't ogling my girls.

"Me, too. Many times." Her eyes found their way back to my boobs.

I jiggled my tits and said, "You like?"

Gemma reached for one, but I was too quick. "That's not how this is going to work. My turn."

"A taste, please, and then you can have your way with me," she pleaded.

"Ah, I didn't know you were a tits girl. I can definitely use that to my advantage." I smothered her face with them. Not that she minded. "Now, will you let me get on with it?" I growled playfully in her ear.

"You can be so dramatic." She laughed.

"You can be so stubborn." I planted a sloppy peck on her cheek.

Gemma pulled my mouth to hers. "Hopefully not too stubborn."

"Never." I peered into her eyes. "No matter what."

Her entire body turned to jelly.

I peppered her chest with kisses. When I took a nipple into my mouth, her body relaxed even more and then tensed with eagerness. I moved to the next nipple, while my hand roved its way down her side. Her skin was soft. Seductive.

My fingers found their way down below and slipped under the hem of her panties. Gemma was wet. Much wetter than I'd anticipated. While my mouth sucked on her nipple, my fingers explored her pussy lips.

Gemma let out a satisfied mewling sound, urging me on. She didn't resist this time when I motioned for her to lift up so I could remove her jeans and white satin panties.

"Your bra and panties match," I said, tickled pink.

"Of course. Why wouldn't they?" She arched an accusatory brow. "Liking sports doesn't make me an uncouth dyke."

I shook my head as if I'd been spinning. "Did you say the D-word?"

She fluttered her eyelids. "Maybe. My mind is elsewhere at the moment."

"Right." I licked my lips.

My tongue trailed down her stomach, stopping briefly for soft kisses. I could lose myself forever in her milky skin.

When I reached her soft mound of pubic hair, I laughed.

"What?" she asked breathlessly.

"The carpet matches the drapes. I've always wondered." I rubbed my face into the glorious ginger hairs.

"You could have asked." She inhaled when my finger penetrated her slightly.

"So much better finding out this way." I winked.

She smiled, pushing her head farther into the pillow.

My eyes feasted on the finger moving in and out of her. "I never thought I'd get the chance," I said in a voice barely above a whisper. "God you feel good." I closed my eyes briefly to focus on being inside Gemma. So warm, inviting, and tight. I pushed in farther.

Gemma murmured and elevated her hips off the bed.

I slipped another finger inside. Gemma responded by convulsing more. It was fascinating to witness how I made her feel. How I made her thrash about on the bed. My quietly confident and dependable Gemma wanted to be fucked. By me.

She was moving more frantically, and I knew she was getting close. I pumped my fingers harder. Leaning down, I took her bud in my mouth, and she let out the most satisfying sound I'd ever heard. Her taste was pungent and alluring. Nothing like I expected. Just one taste and I knew I would crave it always. Hunger after her.

As I circled her clit with my tongue, Gemma moaned louder and louder.

She never asked for more, but when I went in deeper, her intake of breath let me know she liked it. Deeper and deeper I went. Gemma's breathing intensified. My thirst to taste her increased. She was pouring into my mouth.

I couldn't believe I was going down on Gemma.

Fucking hell, it was marvelous.

I'd never thought sex could be this good. Now, I understood the fuss.

I never wanted this to be over.

Her body started to tremble, and she reached for my hand. I squeezed her fingers, letting her know how much this meant. Our gazes fixated on each other's, and I saw what I was feeling reflected in her eyes.

If only we could stay like this forever.

She smiled as if in tune with my thoughts.

Her back arched completely off the bed, and she grabbed a pillow again to squelch her scream. I went in farther and thrust my fingers upward. Her shriek intensified, even though it was scarcely perceptible. I wondered if she had half the pillow in her mouth to muffle her ecstasy. Her entire body shook.

When it finally ended, I settled next to her. Gemma still had the pillow over her face. Resting my head on top of her chest, my fingers played with her ginger pubic hair.

A giggle escaped from deep inside me.

Gemma lifted the corner of the pillow. "What?"

"I can't believe I'm lying naked with you and playing with your pubic hair."

"I wish this night would last forever," she said with a dreamy expression.

"Night? I wish this moment would." I kissed her chest.

"So, no regrets?" she asked with a concerned smile.

"Only that we didn't do this sooner. If I had to do it all over, I would have said this on the first day, 'Hi, my name is Tegan. Nice to meet you, Gemma. Take off all your clothes.'"

"You make it sound like a bank robbery."

"I feel like I've been robbed. Think of how many orgasms we could have had."

"Think of all the nights I could have fallen asleep in your arms."

I snuggled into her embrace. Gemma's "Everything I need to know I learned from my dog" poster hung on the wall at our feet. I'd never seen it from this vantage point before. My bed faced the opposite wall where I had plastered movie posters I scored from my part-time job at the theater across the street, including *Reservoir Dogs, Basic Instinct, Dracula, The Bodyguard,*

Scent of a Woman, A Few Good Men, and my absolute favorite: *A River Runs Through It.* A few of the posters curled up at one corner since some of the tape wouldn't stick on the cold bricks.

"What are you thinking?" Gemma asked.

"I was looking at your poster. I've never seen it from this angle. You?"

"How happy I am."

I popped my head up. "Yeah? How happy?"

"The happiest."

I teased her nipple with my finger. "What about now?"

"Even happier." Gemma closed her eyes.

My finger trekked down. She was still wet, and when I pressed her clit gently, Gemma groaned. When I quickly inserted my finger inside her, Gemma's eyes exploded.

"We have so much lost time to make up for." Without another word, I went down on her. Once again, she smothered her face with a pillow.

Afterward, I removed the pillow. "I never would have thought that my sweet, quiet roommate from Nebraska would be a screamer in bed."

"Do you think anyone can hear us?" she asked, half-pleased and half-concerned.

I laughed. "I'm sure we're not the first on this floor to fuck. Jenny and April have been making eyes at each other for weeks now in the cafe."

Gemma's eyes clouded over when I said the word *fuck*.

"Do you think they love each other?" she asked.

I shrugged. "Jenny for sure. But I have a feeling April's taking advantage of all the perks of college living, ya know? She's not the type to fall for someone and to start calling them *poopsie*."

"Oh." The word spoke volumes. Gemma wasn't the type to casually sleep with someone, and I suspected my comment about April taking advantage of having a female roommate probably planted an unpleasant thought in her heart. Did it remind her of Kate?

There was a pregnant pause. I lifted her chin with my finger to meet her eyes. "That's not what tonight was, okay? Remember, I *promised* promised."

Gemma's lips curled up. "That's right. You did."

"Listen to me. I am not April. I'm not Kate. I, Tegan Raye Ferber, like you, Gemma Mahoney. A lot." I kissed her forehead. "However, I wouldn't mind experimenting more with you and only you." I waggled my eyebrows.

"I think that can be accommodated." She pounced on me, letting me know she wanted to take charge of my body. It was fucking hot to see how much she wanted me and how comfortable she was around me and only me. I wanted to surrender to her, over and over.

"I love feeling your skin against mine."

She let out a little growl.

It was still a shock to watch her go down on me. Her red hair tickled my thighs. Her tongue went inside, and she opened her eyes, staring at me. The smoldering look in those emerald eyes told me everything I needed to know. She'd been in love with me this entire time. I smiled at her. I was falling for Gemma. I was falling for a woman.

I screamed as I came.

"WHAT TIME ARE we meeting your parents?"

Gemma pulled her comforter almost completely over our heads. The bed was narrow and I was practically on top of her, yet a frigid draft from the window blasted through and made me shiver. The howl of the wind announced the storm wasn't over by a long shot.

"You don't have to come."

"Do you not want me to?"

"It's not that. I don't want to put you in the middle."

I tapped my fingers on her chest. "Hey, I don't know where you were this evening, but we're in this together."

"Thanks." She nestled into my arms.

Whooping came from the hallway. "Woo-hoo! Classes are canceled tomorrow!"

"I guess you won't be taking that test tomorrow after all." Gemma giggled.

The real test would be with her parents on Saturday.

"Now I have the whole weekend to cram."

"Yeah."

"And we have the whole night to fu—make love." I nuzzled my face against her neck.

"You can say it."

"Fuck?"

"Yes. I know how much you love the word." She caressed my breast.

I squirmed. "Shit, I didn't know how much until tonight. Fuck, Gemma, I love fucking you."

Gemma stopped tickling me.

"I love it, too."

ON FRIDAY, we slept in past eleven, missing breakfast. Snuggling in bed, Gemma cradled me in her arms.

My stomach growled, sounding like the noise I imagined a bear's belly made after waking from hibernation.

"That was impressive," she joked.

"Be nice or I'll eat you."

She squeezed her arms tighter around me. "Promises, promises."

I laughed.

"We should get you something to eat, though, to keep up your strength."

I burrowed my head into the crook of her neck. "I don't want to leave this room."

She played with one of my blond ringlets. "Is it too early for pizza?"

I popped up. "It's never too early for pizza."

Gemma reached for the phone, not needing to look up the phone number.

When she was done, I said, "Are you inviting people over?"

She smiled knowingly. "Like you, I don't want to leave this room. Three pizzas should power us through."

"Through what?"

"A riveting game of chess." She arched a suggestive brow.

"I had something else in mind. Maybe naked Twister."

Gemma cupped one of my double-Ds. "Can you balance with these?"

"Somehow I manage, and they're really good at this." I smothered her face with my girls.

Gem, of course, didn't resist.

I supported my weight with both arms, hovering over Gem. "You're such a sucker for boobs."

"Only yours." She kneaded them with her hands.

"You better stop. The pizza will be here soon. Even though I'm new to the lesbian world, I think it's bad manners to answer the door while going down on a woman."

"Are you kidding me? Odds are good the delivery person will be a dude, and what guy doesn't have wet dreams about having a front row seat to lesbian goodness?"

I laughed. "You can be such a dork."

Gemma sucked my nipple into her mouth, rekindling my desire.

"Oh, Gemma," I moaned, tossing my head back.

A rustle outside the door captured our attention.

"That was fast," I said.

Gemma craned her neck. "I think it's one of our floormates."

Sure enough, the door across the hall slammed shut.

"Maybe I should hop in the shower." I sniffed my armpit. "All the lesbian goodness made me work up a sweat."

"I'll get in after you."

"Care to join me?"

Gemma rested on her elbows, soaking in my nakedness. "I would, but someone has to listen for the door."

I snapped my fingers. "Right. Be out in a jiff."

Under the hot water, I massaged shampoo in my hair, unable to stop thinking about last night. I had sex with Gemma. Finally.

My toes went cold, and the sensation crawled up my legs, overtaking my body despite the water temperature.

Oh my God. I had sex with a woman.

I was a lesbian now. Like, officially.

I breathed in and out of my mouth.

And we didn't practice safe sex.

Was there such a thing as a female condom?

Wait, Tegan. Gemma couldn't get me pregnant.

But could she transmit an STD?

She'd only been with Kate, though. Surely lesbian STDs weren't rampant in Keller, Nebraska.

Just great. Not only was I a lesbian, but I knew absolutely nothing about them. I was the worst lesbian on the planet.

The bathroom door opened. "Tegan, you okay?"

"Yeah," I said in an overly cheery voice.

"You sure? You've been in here awhile."

I cracked the shower door open. "Have I?"

"Over twenty minutes. The pizza is here." Her soft eyes surveyed my face.

Gemma was so kind, sweet, and comforting.

Not to mention fucking hot.

All the whirring thoughts dissipated like when the sun bursts through gray clouds, banishing raindrops.

"If the pizza's here, why aren't you getting wet with me?" I opened the door all the way.

"Is there any hot water left?" She put her hand under the spray.

"I'll keep you warm."

CHAPTER THREE

SATURDAY MORNING ARRIVED, AND GEMMA and I left our room for the cafeteria on the main floor. Per usual, we walked down the five flights of stairs. The two elevators took forever and also creaked and squawked, which gave the impression that at any second they would hurtle to the ground, not stopping until reaching China.

We made a beeline for the cereal dispensers and then filled several small glasses with orange juice and water.

"G&T!" April waved us over. Her smile was as fake as her bleach-blonde hair and tan.

We carried our trays and sat opposite our floor-mates. The place was nearly abandoned. Most didn't get out of bed for breakfast on Saturdays.

Jenny grinned foolishly. "We haven't seen you two in days. What's up?"

Gemma's eyes boggled, and her cheeks burned. Our newfound sexual confidence didn't extend beyond our room.

"Oh, I'm slammed with midterms and papers. Poor Gemma has been helping me study." I momentarily placed a hand on Gemma's thigh.

"That blows," Jenny said.

"Totally ruins the image I had of you, Tiny T. I'd thought for sure you'd be holed up for more entertaining reasons." April's suggestive wink and sneer were so crystal clear that people sitting five tables away would know their meaning. Once last semester, Gemma had to crash in April and Jenny's room when Josh visited. Ever since then, April had this image of me being a total slut. She turned to Gemma. "It totally fits *you*, though. You're always such a good helper bee." April licked the yogurt off her spoon.

Jenny jabbed an elbow in April's side. "What do you guys have planned this weekend?"

"Gemma's parents are coming tonight for dinner," I said.

"Again? Weren't they just here?" April directed the question to Gemma.

"Nah. It was *my* parents who visited," I lied. Jenny smiled knowingly. For some reason, April hated Gemma. Actually, she hated most people, but she was civil to me. I put up with her attitude, knowing that if I turned on her, she'd make our lives a living hell, especially Gemma's. I also put up with her since she was Jenny's roommate and I adored Jenny.

April narrowed her eyes. "Oh, that's right. Your mom's awesome." Her smile made me uncomfortable, and Gemma shifted in her seat as if she was defending her territory.

My mother, who in my opinion was not awesome, was an aerobics instructor and had shown up one weekend to lead a private class for me and my friends. Her motto was to sweat off the freshman fifteen, and when I'd gone home for Thanksgiving, my mother exclaimed, "Aren't you exercising at all?" I wondered what dear old Mom would think of my new exercise regimen.

"Gemma, are you going to the game tomorrow?" Jenny asked in an obvious attempt to change the subject.

"You bet."

Gemma and Jenny played on a coed intramural inner tube water polo team. Most of the games turned into a splash-fest.

"And will our best cheerleader be there?" Jenny said and then sipped her water.

"I wouldn't miss it for the world," I said.

April huffed and stood up abruptly. "Gotta run." When she walked by, she messed with my hair more flirtatiously than normal, making both Gemma and Jenny fidget. Did she suspect the real reason Gemma and I had been holed up in our room? Were we emitting some sort of sapphic vibes? She would be the last person in the world I'd ever confide in.

As soon as she was out of sight, I turned to Jenny. "What died and crawled up her ass?"

Jenny sighed. "She failed an astronomy test earlier this week and has been a total bitch since. Her mom won't keep paying for school if she brings home another F." Jenny shook her head like a weary boxer after ten rounds.

"If you need a break, you can come to dinner with us," I said. It wasn't until Gemma dropped her fork that I realized my mistake.

"Thanks." She stuck her chin out at Gemma. "I love your folks, but I have plans to see a movie. Next time, though. I promise."

If there is a next time after Gemma's bombshell.

"What movie?" I swallowed water in an attempt to still the thrumming in my throat.

"*Alive.*" Jenny scooped in a mouthful of Cheerios. There was nothing spectacular about her. As my mom would say, "She had a great face for radio."

"Good choice! Dress warm. When Gem and I saw it, I was shivering. Can you imagine your plane crashing in the Andes?"

Gemma wrapped a leg around mine. I peeked at her and saw her *don't worry; no one can see* look.

"And eating your teammates?" Gemma's mischievous smile didn't fit the conversation.

Jenny guzzled the remaining milk in her cereal bowl and stood to take her leave. "Later."

We both nodded.

When the coast was clear, I said, "I'm so sorry. I almost completely blew it."

Gemma laughed. "It would have made tonight even more awkward. Not sure I want to say I'm a lesbian and also have my parents infer I'm in a ménage à trois."

That made me giggle. I had no idea anyone from Gemma's town even knew the term.

Jenny wasn't shy about being a dyke and most suspected when meeting her. Even Gemma's hick parents knew with one glance that she was different from most other girls.

Gemma hadn't told any of our friends that she was gay. And of course I hadn't spilled the beans about my recent revelation. Not yet at least. I was famous for putting my foot in my mouth, so it was probably best to keep it under wraps for now.

"Come on. Let's get some studying done before tonight." Gemma stood.

"Is that what you call it?" I flashed a seductive smile.

She shook her head playfully and motioned for me to walk ahead of her in the hallway.

"Who would have thought studying would be so invigorating?"

Gemma drew in a deep breath. "Remember, you

actually have an exam on Monday." She opened the door to the stairwell.

"Yes, Mom. But all work and no play, makes Jill—"

In the deserted staircase, Gemma pushed me against the wall and kissed me hard.

"Thank God I got you as a roommate and not a bitch like April."

"Would you be kissing her instead?" She ran a finger down my shirt.

"No! Never." I pinched her ass for good measure.

"What do you think the hair thing meant?" She checked out our feet.

Gemma's jealousy struck me as cute. "Oh, probably trying to get to Jenny. You know April. Besides, I think she's overly sexual with most people so they'll notice her. Now, we'd best get upstairs and get our learn on." I patted her butt. "Scoot. Your parents will be here before we know it."

Gemma chewed her lower lip.

I tugged her arm, forcing her to face me. "Don't worry. I'll be right by your side. Everything will work out."

I hoped my face didn't show my true feelings. I was terrified. Scared out of my mind for Gemma. And for me.

"Come along, poopsie," I said.

GEMMA'S LESBIAN
PROCLAMATION

CHAPTER FOUR

THE HOSTESS LED THE WAY THROUGH A horde of sorority girls, most of whom looked like Shannen Doherty, Jennie Garth, or Tori Spelling of *Beverly Hills, 90210*. Thankfully, they were leaving Applebee's as we ventured farther and farther until the girl plastered a smile on her face and dramatically waved to the last booth near the bar, saying, "Here ya go, folks."

I scooted over, and Gemma squeezed in next to me. Ava, Gemma's mom, sat opposite me, and her husband, Cormac, took up the remaining two-thirds of the bench.

Before the hostess had time to scram, a waiter appeared and set down four waters. Talk about efficiency. "Would any of you like something to drink besides water?" he asked.

Gem and I chirped simultaneously, "Chocolate shake, please."

"Coffee, please," Ava said with a motherly smile.

"Diet Coke." Cormac glommed onto the menu with meaty fingers.

Once the waiter left, Ava straightened her back and propped her elbows on the table. "How are classes?"

"Fine," we both chorused. My voice was more enthusiastic than Gemma's.

"Gemma, are you feeling well? You're deathly white. Did you not sleep last night? You always look pale when you stay up late." Ava leaned over the table to feel her daughter's forehead with the back of her hand.

Neither of us got much sleep the previous night, and it wasn't because we were studying, unless you plunked our activities into the sexual education category.

"Pulling a lot of all-nighters?" Cormac asked.

I choked on my water, drawing their attention to me. Gemma bumped my leg under the table, and the amusement that danced in her eyes made me choke more.

"Put your arms up." Cormac demonstrated by reaching for the sky.

Gemma rolled her eyes. "Dad, she's choking. Not deaf."

"J-just s-swallowed wrong." I cleared my throat in an attempt to tamper the tickle. "I'm good."

The waiter arrived with our drinks.

Gemma held my shake and slipped the straw into my mouth. "It'll help your throat," she coaxed.

Ava eyed us with a curious squint.

Cormac tapped the menu to get the waiter's attention away from me, the spaz. "We'll start with spinach and artichoke dip along with mozzarella sticks. Those are your faves, right Gemma?"

Gemma nodded.

"Very good, sir." The waiter spun around.

"Tegan, your little fit reminded me of the time when Gemma's uncle Dermot decided to piss on a fire ant hill," Cormac said.

"How are you connecting the two, dear?" Ava asked with a knowing smile.

"What do you mean?" He seemed generally befuddled.

I'd learned long ago that Cormac's transitions into one of his tall tales never made sense. I suspected Ava knew that better than most, but she enjoyed goading him.

"Are you going to let me tell the story?" he asked.

"By all means. Don't let logic get in the way of a story." Ava motioned for him to continue.

Cormac playfully huffed, and Ava winked at me. I wished my parents enjoyed each other's company half as much as Gemma's parental units.

"Now where was I?" He rubbed his double chins for effect and then snapped his fingers. "That's right,

Dermot and the ants." He wiggled his butt on the seat. "Let's just say Dermot wasn't entirely sober when he came up with his scheme. So last Fourth of July, it was hotter than hot, which meant beer flowed like water. We were nowhere near a restroom, and Dermot had to go. Real bad. That was when he spotted the anthill."

"Dad!" Gemma tried to interject.

"Not you, too, Gemma. Hold on a second. The women in my family don't ever let me talk," Cormac said to me with as much sincerity as he could muster. "Oooh boy, those ants were hopping mad! And fast." He rubbed his palms together. "I can still remember him standing there with his jeans around his ankles—"

Gemma and her mom both sighed and shook their heads.

When Ava interrupted again, Gemma caught my eye and gave me the look—the one that said, "I'm going to do it, so prepare for the lesbian declaration." Fear clawed its way into my mind and body. Even though I'd been steeling myself all day, the impending bombshell seized my throat, almost rendering me incapable of breathing. Under the table, I focused on tightly twisting a napkin around my finger. This was Gemma's moment after all.

Mostly.

Did she still plan on telling them I was her girlfriend?

I tried to swallow the lump in my throat but failed.

Gemma didn't notice my panicked wheeze. And I

knew she wasn't stalling for time to gird her nerves. When Gemma set her mind to do something, she did it, by golly. I admired that, even though I was insanely jealous at times by her grit and how everything always seemed to work out. Like the time she had spaced on studying for a calculus test but aced it anyway.

Shit, Tegan. Was I hoping today would be a complete and total disaster? I chewed on my bottom lip. I was the worst girlfriend in the world, and it was only day three of our relationship.

Gemma cleared her throat.

Cormac ignored her completely, still playfully arguing with Ava. "Woman! Are you going to let me finish my story?"

"Oh, I know once you get going, nothing will stop you." Ava patted his cheek.

"Darn right." They shared a glance that made me squirm. Parents and sexual attraction—I never wanted to make the connection. Cormac turned back to us and continued as if he'd never been interrupted. I wondered how many times he'd told this story. "But the poor sucker couldn't get his boots off because it was so dang hot that summer and he had decided not to wear socks. The sweat superglued the boots right onto his feet. Dermot hopped around on one foot and then the other, desperately trying to yank off his boots while the entire time those suckers swarmed up and over like demons heading toward his—"

Gemma's tight smile didn't quiet her father.

She placed a hand on the sleeve of his navy L.L. Bean sweater. While Ava knitted her own sweaters, she admitted it would take knitting until the end of days to make sweaters large enough for Cormac. He thought the joke was hilarious. Me, I would have been pissed. After living with my mother for eighteen years, I was tired of snide comments about my weight. I was only a size six and well within a healthy weight according to my doctor. Not that Mom ever listened. Anything above a size zero was a complete and total failure in her mind.

"Dad, I want to tell you and—"

"The look on Dermot's face. We thought for sure he'd—"

Cormac stopped when the waiter approached with the appetizers.

"What do you say, ladies? Shall we all order the double-glazed baby back ribs?" Cormac raised his bushy and unwieldy eyebrows over his round wire-framed glasses.

Gemma and I nodded enthusiastically. Typically, when Gemma and I splurged by going to dinner, we shared an entrée, drank water, and skipped appetizers and desserts. The best thing about parents visiting was gorging on yummy, free food.

The waiter's interruption gave a moment's peace to settle my thundering heart. It was like I was the one coming out. If Gemma actually mentioned our new status as girlfriends, I guess I was doing just that. I dug my nails in my thigh. When I had concocted the girlfriend plan before we kissed for the first time, I hadn't been thinking of the consequences. My only thought had been to get Gemma's lips on mine.

Tegan, stop! Focus on something else before you have a full-blown panic attack.

My eyes found Gemma's dad. He took note and said, "Did you know that Gemma has met Bill Clinton in the flesh." He shifted in his seat again, and I remembered Gemma mentioning he had back problems. "You see back in Keller, everyone in town and visitors pop into our outdoors shop for all their hiking, fishing, and backpacking gear. But it's more than that. They come for their morning, afternoon, and what-the-heck cup of Joe in the small café nestled in the back. Ava runs it, and she makes the best cinnamon rolls."

Ava blushed.

He squeezed her hand. "It's because of her scrumptious rolls I got this gut." He patted his belly. "Even presidential hopefuls stop by during elections to sample one and to press the flesh with locals. That's how Gemma shook Bill Clinton's hand during the last election." Cormac nodded at his daughter.

BY THE TIME the waiter came to clear our dinner plates, Gemma was rubbing her forehead. I'd lost count of how many times she tried to get Cormac's attention. Secretly, I was pleased Cormac was such a storyteller.

When the waiter finished, Cormac said, "Did you read our letter last week about Grandma Mavis and her dog?" He locked eyes on me. "She took the dog to the vet because she was absolutely convinced he'd swallowed her wedding ring. When I caught wind they were going to operate on the poor creature, I had to confess that I took it to have it resized for—"

Gemma balled up her fists, snapped her eyes shut, and belted out, "I'm a lesbian!"

Several people near our booth craned or swiveled their necks to spot the source of the admission. Many stared slack-jawed. No one in sight moved or uttered a word. If this were a piece of art, it'd be titled *Gemma's Lesbian Proclamation.*

Thank God the sorority chicks had left, or this news would spread faster than a herpes outbreak.

The song "Don't Let the Sun Go Down on Me" played in the background, and I had to suppress a nervous giggle. I twirled a mood ring around my middle finger. It was blacker than black.

Cormac's surly frown faded, but the new expression was completely devoid of any emotion.

Ava tutted and picked up a stray fork. Slowly, she ran her thumb over the tines, and I wondered if she planned on stabbing herself in the chest to end her suffering. If it were my mother, I would be ducking, fearful she'd plunge it into my eyeball. I shuddered, imagining the sucking sound of her yanking out one of my peepers.

Gemma studied her father's blank demeanor and then her mother's determined face.

I wished for a magic carpet to sweep us away. The clamor around us sluggishly returned to the normal pitch. Except at our table.

Gemma's cheeks flushed, paled, and then flushed again. The silence at our table was excruciating, and I desperately tried to formulate a joke to ease the tension, but all I could get out was, "Ur..."

"Okay, sweetie," Ava said after several seconds had scratched by. She fidgeted with a loose thread on her turquoise sweater, and I wondered if she wanted to unravel it and start over from scratch.

"Okay?" Gemma's eyes narrowed as if trying to detect a trap of some sort with her mother's two words and conduct.

I was, too. I examined the petite schoolmarm frame to sense whether her use of the word *sweetie* was a ploy to lull Gemma into thinking everything was all right and then *POW!* Off she'd go to a straight conversion camp that zapped inmates for impure thoughts about people of the same sex.

Cormac rubbed his jawline, as if calculating the correct words for a verbal tightrope. "It's not such a huge shock, dumpling." His fingers tapped on his chin as he forced a supportive half smile that didn't look at all natural.

"What do you mean?" Gemma asked in a shaky voice.

"I think what your father's trying to say is we suspected, dear."

Both of them seemed sincere. My initial thought that this was a trap started to ebb.

"You thought I was gay?" Gemma's tone suggested she couldn't wrap her mind around their reaction.

I was flummoxed. This was the perfect outcome for the lesbian bombshell, and Gemma was upset that they weren't shocked. I wanted to shout, "What's wrong with you? Your parents aren't crying or dousing you with holy water. Chalk this up as a victory."

"There's nothing wrong with being a lesbian." Her father bobbed his head supportively.

I glommed onto the table with all ten digits to stop the room from swirling. What the fuck? All day I'd been preparing for different scenarios and thinking of things to say to comfort Gemma. Not once did I picture Cormac proclaiming there was nothing wrong with being a dyke. What was wrong with him? And why did everything always have to work out for Gemma? I wanted to be her savior for once. For her to cry on my shoulder. I cringed. What was wrong with me?

"Gemma, gay, straight, it doesn't matter." Her mom patted Gemma's hand. "Don't worry. Everything's going to be fine."

"Look at Aunt Ruth," Cormac threw in.

"What about Aunt Ruth?" Gemma asked.

Cormac raised his eyebrows, doing his best to force the meaning telepathically into Gemma's mind.

"Aunt Ruth is a lesbian?" Once again, there was a hush at the tables nearby.

"Of course. She and Aunt Hannah have been together for years."

"Hannah!" Gemma palmed the top of her head. Was she trying to keep her cranium from exploding?

"Your aunts are incestuous lesbians?" I blurted.

Cormac's boisterous out-of-character laugh snapped Gemma out of her funk.

"That's funny!" Cormac slapped his thigh. "Incestuous lesbians. Wait until I tell this story in the shop. I like you, Tegan."

I clapped both hands over my mouth, stifling my shock. Would he tell them about Gemma, too? My parents would probably never speak to me again if I told them, and there was no way in hell they'd confess to their friends and neighbors.

Gemma noticed I was struggling with the Ruth and Hannah connection. "They aren't related to each other or us. Everyone calls them Aunt Ruth and Aunt Hannah. They own Violets, a sewing and yarn shop."

"Oh," I said, now wondering if the word Violet was code for lesbian in Keller, Nebraska. Nothing was making sense.

"Does everyone know about them?" Gemma spun her head *Exorcist* style back to Cormac.

"Mostly. Really, I thought you knew. It's known, but not talked about."

Ava cleared her throat. "Not because there's anything wrong with it." She locked eyes on me. "It's how we are. If we don't talk about you, that means we accept and like you."

I nodded as if that made total sense. Inside, I was screaming and starting to wonder if I would ever understand anything after this dinner. The creepy theme song for *The Twilight Zone* invaded my mind, getting louder and louder. The *dee dee DEE dee* and then the bongo drums repeated over and over until Rod Sterling's voice announced, "You've entered the lesbian Twilight Zone."

CHAPTER FIVE

GEMMA AND I TRUDGED BACK INTO THE DORM, kicking off our snow-caked Doc Martens in the small entryway of our room. Her parents were staying at the Best Western across the street, and Gemma planned to have breakfast with them before they drove back home.

"Would you like a cup of tea?" she asked, rubbing her hands together and then blowing into them. Before I had a chance to respond, she was filling the teapot and flipping on the illegal hot plate. Smuggling in this possession was one of Gemma's rare rebellious acts, though she only used it for the teakettle because she was addicted. Once I'd asked why she didn't heat the tea water in the microwave, which was permitted by the university. She'd been aghast by the mere suggestion, and her squished-up face had proven I'd committed a tea sacrilege. I didn't understand, but I was a coffee gal who wasn't afraid to drink instant in a pinch. It wasn't until I met Gemma that I knew there was such a thing as loose leaf tea. She claimed larger tea leaves were better for the body. I wasn't a health nut, but slowly she was converting me to the soothing drink.

Still bundled up in coat, hat, and scarf, I sat down heavily on the Laura Ashley comforter I had begged my mother to buy.

"You okay, Teeg?" Gemma shucked her jacket and unwound her hand-knitted Cornhusker scarf, a Christmas gift from her grandmother last year.

I nodded while rubbing my tongue back and forth over the gap in my teeth, a nervous tick that drove my mother insane.

Gemma squatted in front of me and clasped both of my hands. "What's wrong? You're doing that tongue thing."

"I can't believe it," I mumbled.

"Believe what?"

"Ruth and Hannah…"

She laughed. "*I* can't believe it. All these years, I never knew I lived in one of the most progressive cities in the country." Gemma snatched the wool hat off my head. "You're turning beet red." Next, she shook my right arm and then my left out of the coat.

"And your parents didn't care. Not at all. They suspected even!"

She carefully draped the coat over a desk chair.

The kettle whistled, and Gemma busied herself making tea. She proffered my "Same shit different day" mug then and gripped her Nebraska one with both hands.

"Can you tell me why you're so upset?" Her voice wasn't accusatory, considering she was the one who had just come out to her parents and not me. Gemma never got around to telling them about us, which was a huge relief, I thought. She was curious. Maybe she was slightly concerned by my reaction to her parents taking the news much better than expected. Hopefully, she didn't have an inkling I had been secretly wishing the announcement would crash and burn a tad. I was tired of being the spazzy one all of the time. And now that it had gone so well with her folks, would she push me to tell mine?

"I'm in shock, I think."

Gemma nodded, giving me time to sort my thoughts, but it was hard to locate them, as if everything I thought I understood had shattered to bits and was waiting to be reassembled into logical patterns.

She unbuttoned her flannel shirt, revealing a Rugrats T-shirt given to her by her youngest sister for her nineteenth birthday. I loved this side of Gemma: sweet, sentimental, and playful. But right then, even her cuteness couldn't knock me out of my ill mood.

"Don't get mad, but I thought they'd take the news differently. Not disown you or anything, but not simply say, 'Hey, it's cool that you're a dyke.' What I witnessed tonight—it doesn't happen that way, not that I have any experience, but seriously, it's not how I imagined it. Not at all."

"They didn't say it that way." She laughed.

"No, they were even nicer about it. Accepted you completely without shedding a tear or preaching. Fuck, my mom has been pointing out for years how I'm different from all those around me. And not in a kind way. For her, being different is a sign of weakness." I motioned to my Carhartt jacket on the chair. "My mom knows more about fashion trends than I do. My Doc Martens, baby doll dresses, overalls, skorts—she buys everything for me. Individuality is not a word, but a curse."

Gemma wrapped an arm over my shoulders, nudging my head against her chest. "Are you scared to tell your folks?"

I clutched her T-shirt, strangling Tommy Pickles's image. "I don't see them ever accepting it. Accepting me. What I am. Never."

"But you thought the same about my parents." I knew she was trying to talk me off the ledge, but her hopeful tone and shoulder squeeze irritated me. She would never be able to understand what it was like growing up with my mother. When I was eight, I had needed glasses, but Mom had insisted I wear contacts. The memories of sitting in the optician's office for hours, tears streaming down my cheeks, my mother's lip snarl, and the poor lady trying to steady my hands as I failed over and over to place the lenses on my burning corneas were forever etched in my mind.

"Your parents are nothing like mine. Your parents aren't like any parents I've met. All of you live in a warped version of *The Waltons*."

Gemma's body tensed.

"I don't mean that in a bad way. I'm jealous. So fucking jealous."Gemma's tension slipped away as quickly as it appeared. She kissed my cheek. Quietly, we sipped tea, not speaking.

"I'm going to hop in the shower." No matter what, she showered every night before going to bed.

"Okay. I'm going to sit here and try to figure out this thing called life." I half-heartedly smiled.

Her eyes crinkled, and she bit her lower lip.

"Kidding. Go. Enjoy." I waved her toward the bathroom.

THE CREAK of the bathroom door alerted me that Gemma was done in the shower. She was normally quick, but it didn't seem possible that several seconds had whizzed by, let alone enough time for Gemma to shower. Was I trapped in a time warp?

I had to pee and bolted upright when Gemma shimmied into the room towel drying her hair. Before we kissed the night of the blizzard, she usually dressed before leaving the bathroom when I was around. But tonight, she was stark naked.

"Well, hello," I said lamely. I practically had to go on a hunger strike for weeks to convince my tightwad father to splurge for the dorm room with a private bathroom. Not once did I envision this perk.

"Hello." A confident smile and a seductive wink knocked all thoughts about what had transpired earlier at the restaurant out of my head. "Going somewhere?" she asked in a sexy tone.

"Pee."

Gemma chortled. "Don't let me stop you." She stepped back to give me space.

I couldn't peel my eyes from her bare skin, even though we'd spent the past several days in bed exploring each other's bodies. "I don't think I have to go anymore."

"Are you sure?" She sidled up next to me, and I inhaled the Irish Spring scent radiating from her skin.

"Yep."

Our lips met. All the muscles in my body relaxed. So did my bladder, almost. "Hold that thought." I placed a finger on her lips. "I really do have to go."

As soon as my butt hit the seat, the pee gushed out. "I can't believe it," I muttered.

"Can't believe what?" Gemma shouted from the other side of the door.

I finished my business, stepped out of the bathroom, and washed my hands at the sink by our closets before answering. Gemma stood behind me, still towel drying her hair.

"You. I can't believe *you*." I flipped around and squished her aquiline nose with a finger.

"What about me?" Her face inched closer to mine.

"Strutting out of the bathroom in your birthday suit."

"Considering everything that's happened this weekend, I decided why not? You don't like it?" she teased. "At least this time you aren't running out of the room screaming your head off."

I ignored her dig about the other day, considering I still felt foolish. "Like it? I love it. It's a new house rule."

During our first floor meeting back at the start of the academic year, the resident assistant had suggested we set house rules to help us ease into our new living situations. I'd laughed it off. Gemma had taken it seriously and forced me to sit down that night to craft the rules. She'd jotted all of them down on a pad of paper. When we'd finished, she even taped the final product onto her closet door.

Gemma grabbed a pen off her desk. "Shall I add it?"

"Maybe just make a mental note. We don't want visitors stripping down. Not all of them, at least."

"Ah, good point." She snapped the cap back into place.

"Not sure I could handle seeing April in all her fake

glory." Rumor had it she'd already had a boob job, which was her high school graduation gift from her mom, who was engaged to a plastic surgeon. I wasn't sure what bothered me more, that she'd gotten a boob job or that her mother's lover had sculpted April's new breasts. Yuckers!

Gemma's eyes transformed. "You over your shell shock, yet?"

"Not yet. But totally willing to table it for the night."

She crossed her arms. "And why's that?"

"Because my girlfriend is smoking hot and standing naked right in front of me." I tugged her arms apart, exposing perky breasts. I traced the outline of her butterfly tattoo.

"They're tiny," she whispered, and embarrassment crept into her voice and body language.

I circled a nipple with my finger, making it hard. "They're beautiful."

She closed her eyes, and I pushed her up against the closet door.

"Oh," she squealed.

"You like?" I didn't wait for her to speak. I captured her lips with mine. Her tongue forcefully pushed its way in. That was answer enough.

It was hard to believe that only days ago we hadn't ever kissed, let alone fucked. Now, we couldn't spend thirty minutes alone without getting it on.

I had her pinned against a poster I got for free from

the health clinic during orientation week. My mom was horrible at keeping track of records, and I had to get re-immunized before I could attend any classes. They were handing out posters that stated chlamydia wasn't a flower. A photo of a colorful bluish green mushroom-looking thing caught my eye. How could bacteria associated with an STD look so beautiful?

Gemma pulled away, panting. "You're thinking of the poster, aren't you?"

"Sorry, it's too funny considering you're naked—"

She rolled her eyes, not a trace of anger on her beautiful face. "You. Naked. Now."

I saluted her. "Yes, ma'am!"

After tearing my shirt off, Gemma reached around to unhook my bra and then gently kneaded my breasts. "I wish I had tits like these."

I stepped back to strip out of my jeans and panties. "What're you talking about? I'd kill for small boobs. You can sleep on your stomach. You have no idea how good you have it."

"It's overrated."

"Trust me, having a C cup in the seventh grade was not fun."

She nodded but continued to ogle my now double-D jugs.

"In the seventh grade, I was flat as a board, and it wasn't much fun when boys ran their hands down my back, checking to see if I was wearing a training bra," she said with a faint blush.

I nodded, recognizing her pain. "The grass is always greener." I cupped a breast. "You aren't flat now." My thumb and forefinger pinched her nipple.

A wicked smile appeared, and Gemma slipped a hand between my legs, separated my lips, fingered me gently, and then sucked the juices.

"Feeling frisky now that you got the lesbian monkey off your back?" I wiggled my eyebrows.

"Maybe. Or maybe it's the effect you have on me." Gemma lifted my chin with a slender finger.

I sucked her finger into my mouth.

Her eyes closed, and she moaned. "Kiss me."

"As you wish."

She elevated an eyebrow, acknowledging I'd quoted *The Princess Bride*, her favorite movie.

We locked lips and deepened the kiss instantly. Without stopping, Gemma guided me toward my bed. We clumsily toppled onto the comforter.

"Oomph," I uttered.

"You okay?" She brushed some strands of hair out of my mouth.

"Yeah. Grace has never been my strong suit."

"Really? I hadn't noticed."

I rolled my eyes. "I didn't choke at dinner."

"Yes, you did. You can choke on air."

"Cannot!"

"And fall down because of air." She splayed her fingers as if she intended to tick off more humiliating scenarios.

"Whatever!" I smothered her mouth with mine to quiet her.

She didn't complain and held my arms down with one hand above my head. Her other hand traced all the way down my left side, though I hoped she wouldn't touch the scar on my back. Her delicate touch issued a tingling sensation that made me whimper in yearning.

"Make love to me. Please, Gemma."

The kiss demonstrated Gemma's overwhelming desire. Her fingers parted my lips below, teasing and tempting. My hips gyrated as if I no longer had control over them because Gemma did. She had complete and wonderful control of my body.

She entered, and I stifled a squeal by fervently exploring her mouth with my tongue. It was as if I needed to devour her while she was inside me. A hunger to feel close on all levels.

I raised my hip against her crotch. "You're so wet."

"That's another effect you have on me." Gemma slowed her finger thrusting. Her emerald eyes smoldered. "I'm not the only one." Her finger dove in deep and stayed. "You like that?"

"Are you taunting me?"

"Moi?" Her finger slipped out, but the glint in Gemma's eyes said it was no accident. She fondled the lips and entrance, but didn't penetrate again.

It was driving me blissfully mad.

And it gave me an idea.

I snaked a hand down my own body, stopping

briefly to flick a nipple, before arriving at my magic spot.

"What are you doing?"

"Isn't it obvious?" I arched my eyebrows. "You were tormenting me. I decided to play the game. Do you want me to stop?" I continued to massage my clit.

"Depends. Do I get to play?"

"By all means."

I thought she'd touch herself. Instead, she hammered her fingers inside me, frantically slipping in and out. I doubled my efforts on my clit. Within moments, I was close. Gemma nudged my fingers to the side and took my throbbing bud into her mouth, circling her tongue right where I craved.

The scream that left my body released not only the sexual tension and satisfaction, but it wiped away all my fears about being with a woman. At that moment, I wanted to confess to everyone that I was in love.

In love with a girl.

And not just any girl, but with Gemma—the most caring, intelligent, sexy, and giving lover.

She glanced up. Her chin glistened, and the knowledge of how much she loved eating me out flipped my lust into overdrive.

I steered her head to mine, tasting me in her mouth, all the while rolling Gemma onto her back, nearly causing us to crash to the floor. Narrow dorm beds weren't designed for lesbian sex.

"I need to be inside you. To taste you," I said.

Gemma moaned when I slowly entered. Her warmth and wetness greeted my finger. I gazed into her eyes. "I don't know what you've done to me, but no one has ever made me feel this way." I bit her nipple. It responded, but the fragrance down below beckoned. My tongue trailed down her stomach. My teeth grazed her ginger hair, and then I landed right where I wanted.

She poured into my mouth. My fingers pumped in and out. Gemma's hips matched my desire, thrusting up and down. I caught a glimpse of Gemma smothering her face with a pillow.

It wouldn't take long now.

I wanted her to come. In my mouth. To flood my fingers. To scream at the top of her lungs. I cherished that I was the only one who made Gemma feel this good.

She came. Hard.

As her body writhed, I didn't let up, sensing she wasn't finished. Neither of us could ever get enough of the other. It seemed impossible that I'd ever tire of making love to the only person who knew me better than anyone else. The only person who ever made me feel beautiful and loved.

Gemma wasn't merely my friend or just my lover. Even *soul mate* didn't do justice to my emotions. Gemma meant everything to me, and I hoped she felt the same.

I tried to block out the memory of signs I'd seen on

the quad last week. The ones proclaiming things like "God made Adam and Eve, not Adam and Steve" and "God hates fags." Why couldn't everyone accept our love?

Even I had lingering doubts, not about my feelings but how others would perceive me. Sometimes I hated myself.

The jerk of her body brought me back, and I stilled my fingers and tongue before resting my head against her thigh.

She ran a hand through my hair, calming my turmoil. "I love the things you do to me."

"Not as much as I love doing them to you."

"That sounds like a challenge." She laughed.

"Maybe."

"And how do we prove who loves it more?"

I moved up and nestled into her arms. "Sixty-nine."

"Have you ever?" she asked.

"No. Honestly, all the boys in high school talked about it and blow jobs so much the idea alone made me ill. Josh loved to tell everyone the joke about Miss Piggy."

Gemma crinkled her brow.

"You haven't heard it?"

She shook her innocent head. "No."

I clamped my lips together, locking it inside. Gemma tapped my forehead playfully. I gathered she was still too spent to speak much.

"Okay. Why can't Miss Piggy count to seventy?"

Gemma hitched one shoulder.

"She gets a frog in her throat at sixty-nine."

"Wh—? Oh." Gemma's eyes told me she wasn't impressed.

"I know. Such a gross thought. Before you, I never thought I'd enjoy sex this much. It was okay with Josh, but I didn't ever initiate it or pine for intimacy. It was more like I knew it was expected, and it was best to get the deed out of the way each time."

She held me closer.

"Earlier, when your dad was talking about your uncle and how he was pissing on an anthill—I couldn't believe the words spilling out of his mouth. My parents would never ever talk about anything like that in front of me. I'll never be an adult in their eyes."

"I'm sorry. He can be a bit much sometimes." Her face tinged a lovely shade of rose. Even when embarrassed, Gemma was beautiful.

I placed a finger on her lips. "No. I enjoy Cormac's stories. I'd love for my parents to be more open. Not so repressed and distant. Your parents are an odd mix of traditional and modern. Your mom knits and sews most of her own clothes, and tonight I found out she buys her materials from two little old lesbians. How cool is that?"

She laughed. "I didn't know how cool my parents were until tonight."

"You're so lucky. Do you know what my parents would do if I told them?"

"What?" she asked in a serious tone.

"First, they'd yank me out of school. Second, they'd send me to a nunnery. Third, if the nunnery didn't cure me of my wicked ways, they'd disown me. I wouldn't be able to atone enough to get back into their good graces."

"Will they hate me?" Gemma frowned.

"Most definitely."

The hurt in her eyes reminded me to think before I spoke.

"I've gone and put my foot in it again, haven't I?"

A sexy gleam shown in her eyes. "'Your aunts are incestuous lesbians!'" she mimicked my high-pitched voice from earlier.

I buried my face into the crook of her arm. "I can't believe I said that. And to your parents!"

"Oh, Dad's going to tell that story until he dies. By Monday afternoon, it'll be all over Keller."

"Can I ask you something?"

She nodded, quirking a brow.

"Do you think if Kate knew about Hannah and Ruth, she still would have…?" I didn't know how to politely say "dumped you."

"Her family is ultraconservative, so I doubt she would have changed her mind. Dad jokes that one day the family will disappear and we'll hear about them twenty years from now, living among one of those wacko religious cults that preach about the Second Coming or something."

"Was Kate like that?"

"Yes and no."

Gemma didn't talk about Kate much, and I'd be lying if I said I wasn't dying to know more about the competition.

"Who initiated your first kiss?"

Gemma fluffed a pillow to prop up her head. "It just kinda happened, really. We were watching TV in my basement, and we always cuddled together on the couch—it's freezing down there—and one minute we were watching *Cheers* and the next we were smooching."

"Like the immaculate kiss," I joked.

"Don't let your mom hear that." Gemma pinned me with her faux parental expression.

"Trust me, I stifle myself around them."

"So you can control yourself, then?" Gemma squeezed me tightly, letting me know she was kidding.

"Hey!" I defended weakly.

"Don't be mad. I love your random outbursts and your twisted sense of humor." She gestured to my chlamydia poster. "And lately I've been benefiting from your lack of control. This weekend has been the highlight of my life... so far," she added to needle me. Or maybe as inspiration.

"Lack of control," I parroted. "I'll show you control."

I hovered over Gemma's breasts and rubbed my clit.

Her eyes widened. "This is your definition of restraint?"

"Not mine. Yours."

She blinked.

"You can't touch me. Not until I come."

She swallowed. "What if you beg me to help?"

"I won't." I smiled to soften the blow.

Gemma watched intently as I slid a finger inside, while my other hand still focused on my pulsating flower. Her rapid breaths urged me to quicken the pace.

Gemma stretched her hand down her body. I peeked over my shoulder and eyed her pleasuring herself. "Hey, control, remember?"

"You said I couldn't touch *you*. I was never in the equation."

"Leave it to you to think of that loophole." Continuing to hover over Gemma's breasts as I masturbated while she was also fucking herself was sending me into a tizzy. I wanted her tongue on me. I simultaneously inched and lowered closer and closer to her mouth.

The concentration on her face was my answer. Gemma knew what I wanted, and she was sticking to the rules that I'd put in place.

Fuck.

My goal was to torture her, and now I was the one being tortured. Delightfully so, but still.

Gemma came first. When her body rocked up and down, I fell off the focus wagon.

"Did you come?" she asked in a breathy voice.

"No, I was enjoying the show."

She beamed and motioned with a finger for me to come hither.

"You mean—?"

Gemma gripped my thighs and brought my cunt to her mouth. The mixture of her hot tongue and my longing brought me to a whole new level. Gemma, hearing my excited sigh, fervently brought me to the brink and beyond, and then back to the brink. She showed no signs of stopping, and my body and soul begged her to continue.

God I loved lesbian sex.

CHAPTER SIX

"You know, they say the tongue is the strongest muscle in the body," I said.

Gemma lay on her back with her eyes closed. She had one arm draped around me. "Are you saying you want more?"

I whacked her arm. "No. I'm saying I'm really impressed by your stamina. Your tongue must be the strongest in the world."

"I've never known it to fatigue," she teased. "What about yours with all that gabbing?"

"Oh please, one of us has to keep the conversation going. You're the strong silent type, and I'm not."

This made her smile, but she kept her eyes shut. "What about the heart?"

"What about it?"

"Wouldn't that be the strongest muscle? It pumps blood day and night."

"Maybe, but right now, I'm voting for the tongue. Your tongue."

"Did you know the tongue consists of eight muscles and unlike the muscles in the rest of the body, they don't develop around a bone? It's more like an elephant's trunk or the tentacle of an octopus."

"Ewww. An elephant's trunk? So not the image I want in my head right now." I buried my face in a pillow.

"What about an octopus tentacle?"

I slapped her taut stomach. "No! Don't be weird."

She tickled my side.

"Stop. I have to pee."

She didn't relent.

"If you don't stop, I'll pee on you," I warned.

"Okay, okay." She put her palms up in mock surrender. "Truce until you get back."

When I returned to bed, I noticed it was almost four in the morning. "Shit, look at the time."

Gemma didn't bother. She raised the comforter. "I'll try to behave and let you get some sleep."

"I'll sleep when I'm dead," I said, before climbing on top of Gemma. "Will your parents suspect anything if you fall asleep during breakfast?"

"Nah. Thanks for being there tonight, even though I never got around to telling them about us."

I waved her off. "It was going so well. Why bother?" I prayed she didn't notice my relief.

Gemma's eyes clouded over. "Will you ever tell your parents? About you?"

I bit my lower lip. "I haven't really put much thought into it. This is all so new." I felt horrible for lying. The thought of telling them had plagued me since the first time I dreamed of kissing Gemma.

She nodded. "I'm thinking of telling Jenny."

I shot up. "About us?"

Gemma's perplexing crooked smile unnerved me. "No. About me. It's not my place to out you or anyone."

"Oh… I didn't mean…" What *did* I mean?

"It's okay, Teeg. I know."

"You know what?"

"You aren't comfortable. Not yet, at least."

Her smugness rubbed me the wrong way. She'd only told her parents hours ago and now she was an expert on coming out? She was the better lesbian? More confident? I didn't like her implication, even though I'd barely poked my head out of the closet.

"What's wrong?" Gemma asked.

"Nothing. I think I'm just tired."

"Let's go to sleep, then." Gemma wrapped me in her arms, freeing my irritability, almost.

"Good night," I mumbled.

"Good night, sweetheart," Gemma said, completely oblivious to the turmoil surging through my mind.

The word sweetheart quelled my anger. She hadn't

meant anything by her comment, really. I was being Spazzy Tegan. Again.

"Gemma?" I stammered.

"Yes?"

"Would you still love me if I never told my parents?"

She opened her eyes and stared into mine. Our heads rested on the same pillow. "Tegan, there's nothing you can do that would make me love you any less." Gemma flicked a tear off my cheek. "No pressure from me. Ever."

"What if I never told anyone?" I whispered.

"No matter what, I'll always love and cherish you."

"Even if I never shout from the rooftops that I love you?"

She smiled. "I don't need recognition like that. The look in your eyes is enough." She rested a hand on my cheek, and I placed mine on hers.

"I love you, Gemma. I really do."

"I know. Your eyes tell me." She kissed me. "Go to sleep before you have another freak-out session."

Slowly, I started to drift into blissful sleep, until a thought struck me. Did my eyes tell everyone? I groaned. Play-it-Safe Tegan was rearing her head once more.

LESBIAN ON THE BRINK OF INSANITY

CHAPTER SEVEN

"GREAT MOVE, GEMMA!" I SCREAMED through cupped hands from where I sat on a metal bench in hopes she'd hear me over the clamor in the indoor pool. The perpetual shouting, splashing, and the ref's whistle during the intramural inner tube water polo match increased the thrill. If Gemma's team won today, they'd make the playoffs. There wasn't a trophy at stake, but Gemma always remained fiercely competitive.

"Never thought I'd hear anyone say that." April slid next to me. "That Gemma has great moves." She nudged my shoulder.

I stiffened, not that she bothered to notice.

"Who's winning?" she asked and then blew on her nails. During breakfast, Jenny had said April was meeting her mom for a spa day.

I refused to comment on her freshly painted fuchsia

nails. "We are, and it's almost—" The cheering from Gemma's team overpowered my voice. I jumped up and down and clapped like a fool at the Macy's Day Parade.

April remained seated but clapped. Or more like she pressed her palms together twice without making any noise. Jenny noticed April's presence and waved. April shifted on the bench, blocking Jenny from her sight. While Gemma helped Jenny out of the pool, I had to resist the urge to wallop the back of April's head to knock some sense into the bleach-blonde bitch. Would it kill her to try harder? Jenny was a wonderful person and deserved a roommate (and sometimes lover) who wasn't so catty.

"We won!" Gemma rushed up and threw her arms around me.

Jenny attempted to do the same to April but was stopped short with a scowl and protective hands blocking her face.

"Don't get me all wet!" April shouted, igniting flames of humiliation in Jenny's eyes and cheeks.

The three of us froze, unsure what to say or do to overcome the awkwardness that smashed all traces of jubilation from Jenny's face.

"What should we do to celebrate?" I asked with forced excitement, and I turned my back on April's buzzkill.

"Milkshakes!" Jenny shouted.

I marveled over her ability to let April's behavior

slide into oblivion. She probably had to or the emotional roller coaster would kill her.

"Yes!" Gemma joined her hands as if pleading for me to agree. I was the one with the car, after all.

"Milkshakes it is." I threw an arm around Jenny. "Great goal, Jen-Meister!" Gemma joined in, and the three of us hopped up and down as if the team had advanced to the gold-medal round in the Olympics, not a silly collegiate competition.

April backed away. "Sorry, but I have plans."

Gemma and I shared a worried glance. It wasn't a secret that April was a bitch, but did she have to go above and beyond when it came to Jenny?

"That's okay. Next time," Jenny said. She wrapped her arms around Gemma and me and whisked us toward the locker rooms. Was Jenny finally sick of April's bitchiness? One could only hope.

I scouted over my shoulder to witness April's pinched expression. When our eyes met, she quickly morphed her pained frown into a forced grin. I tried picturing April in twenty years but couldn't. She was so plastic it was nearly impossible to see her evolve. She'd always be this way: fake.

———

THE TOWN of Alfrid wasn't known to many outside the small community. When I'd started considering colleges, the big three: the University of Colorado,

Colorado State University, and the University of Denver quickly dominated all conversations with my mother. She treated the decision like all others in my life, as a popularity contest. For weeks she'd say, "So-and-so's kid is going to CU," or "Did you hear that Billy down the street is going to DU?" I hated it.

When I'd received a college brochure from Hill University in the mail advertising their nursing program, I knew that would be my choice. When my mother screeched, "You can't go there. No one's heard of it! It's imaginary!" I made sure come hell or high water I'd be accepted. I gambled by only applying to Hill, unbeknownst to my mother.

There was one flaw in my plan. Alfrid, situated on the Elbert River along the Colorado Front Range jammed between Boulder and Fort Collins, didn't have much to offer besides rundown frat and sorority houses, two pizza shops, Applebee's, the usual fast-food joints, and a strip mall that was so dilapidated it'd be best to board it up and let nature reclaim the space. I was a city girl, and Alfrid, in my book, barely qualified as a town. There was one gem, though, an ice cream shop reminiscent of the heyday of soda jerks and bobby soxers. Gemma said visiting was like making a quick trip home.

For me, it was a wild retro diner with the best milkshakes on the planet. Hands down.

The three of us squeezed around a table for two,

victorious that we'd scored seats at all. Several groups lingered by the door, hoping for a table.

"Paula! Cissy!" Jenny waved over her softball teammates, who'd just walked in. "What're you doing here?"

Cissy, dressed like a Barbie doll, crinkled her forehead as if determining whether Jenny was using voodoo to get her to divulge something top secret. "Getting ice cream. You?"

Jenny tossed an arm around Gem's shoulder. "Celebrating our big win."

Paula smiled at me. "Congrats!"

Her smile and tone set off alarm bells. "Uh, sports aren't my thing."

"That's not true," Jenny said, turning to Paula, whose toothy grin always reminded me of John Elway. "Tegan is the best cheerleader. Hands down."

Paula's grin bordered on desperate. I really needed to find a way to block my *I dig chicks* vibe. As far as I was concerned, only one girl made me feel this way.

"I expect to see you at our softball games this spring, then," Paula said in such a sweet, quite possibly pleading voice.

I tried coming up with the words to let the poor girl down easily, but Cissy came to my rescue. "Come on, Pauls. Michelle is waiting in the car."

Pauls? Was that a dyke thing? Luckily, my name was unisex, which in my mind made it impossible to shorten in a way to out my lesbianness. Was that a word? And if it was, did it mean the condition of being a lesbian? Stifling a laugh, I flicked my fingers as a way of saying goodbye.

The two of them made their way to order shakes to go.

Gemma licked a spoon, and a smidgeon of orange Creamsicle shake dribbled onto her chin. I imagined licking it off, starting with her chin and working my way over her naked body. Gemma playfully nudged my foot under the table. Maybe the naughty thought was inordinately transparent on my countenance.

"Would you like my cherry?" I dangled a juicy orb by its stem in Gemma's direction.

She tinged redder than the cherry and shook her head. I sensed she wasn't embarrassed, and I couldn't wait to get her home to find the source of the fire burning inside.

"I'll take that." Jenny plucked it from my fingers.

Gemma hitched up a shoulder, and I silently fumed. Jenny was the most unobservant person. Not that I wanted her to pick up on the vibe between Gemma and me, but to snatch my cherry? The nerve!

I dipped my finger into the whipped cream on top of my shake and noticed Gemma eyeing my finger as it entered my mouth. I moaned slightly and repeated the process more slowly. Gemma shifted in her chair, crossing her legs, and I had to resist the impulse to shout, "Fire in the hole!"

Her eyes boggled when I dangled my last whole

cherry in front of my mouth, batting it with my tongue before sucking it in all the way.

I relished the flavor and had no intention of swallowing anytime soon. Gemma arched an accusatory brow and wore a sexy grin that implied, *Wait 'til I get you home alone, you saucy little minx.* I could barely contain my excitement. I wanted to be ravaged by Gemma and closed my eyes to imagine the scenario.

"Jenny, when did you know you were a lesbian?" Gemma asked as breezily as someone inquiring about the weather.

I choked on the cherry.

Seriously choked.

Both Gemma and Jenny leapt into action and banged their fists against my back. Panic seized me as my air passage continued to constrict.

Jenny yanked both of my arms over my head. Gemma continued whacking my back. Wilbur, the ancient owner of The Soda Jerk, shoved his bulk through the line of people at the counter and asked, "Can she breathe?"

I wanted to shout, "No, dumbass!" but words failed my air-starved body. Instead, I continued to rasp unsuccessfully.

"Step aside," said a man who was a shoo-in for Harrison Ford's younger brother minus the scar on his chin. Before I knew what was happening, he hoisted me out of my seat, wrapped his arms around me, plunged his fists into my belly, and then thrust upward. Half a cherry shot out of my mouth and zipped across the room before plopping down in front of some classmates from my Principles of Nutrition course. Fantastic. News like this would spread like wildfire.

"Are you okay?" asked the younger version of Harrison. He squatted in front of me, after helping me retake my seat.

I nodded, trying to block out all the eyeballs on me. A table of sorority girls next to us whispered excitedly behind their hands.

"Can you breathe?" Harrison asked.

Gingerly, I inhaled.

"Good. Take it slow." He patted my knee. His blue flannel shirt made his indigo eyes pop. I wanted to run my fingers through his chestnut hair. God, this man was the definition of sexy. The hunk stood.

Confusion whirled through me. Did my reaction mean I was straight again? Or worse, a fence-sitting bisexual? No, it couldn't be. I was with Gemma—that made me a lesbian in my book.

"Thanks so much!" Gemma pumped his hand up and down.

"Can we buy you a shake?" Jenny asked, glancing at Wilbur, who bobbed his head in agreement as he hooked his thumbs around his suspenders and tugged them away from his plaid shirt.

"No need, ladies. Glad to be of service."

An employee behind the counter summoned

Wilbur, and he reluctantly left after giving me one final look-see to ensure I wasn't going to kick the bucket in his shop.

My rescuer peered down at me. "You're in my history class."

"I am?" I tried to control my fluttering lashes.

"U.S. History Since 1865?"

I nodded, unsure if my voice would hold out after the choking ordeal.

"You ready for tomorrow's test?" the dude asked as if he hadn't just saved my life.

"I hope so. You?"

"It's my least favorite subject." His forehead crinkled.

"If you ever need a study buddy, let me know. It's the least I can do." I covered my mouth to cough.

A grin overtook his face and eyes. "I might take you up on that. I'm Erik." He held out his palm.

I reached up to reciprocate. "Tegan."

Jenny cleared her throat. Erik and I still held the other's hand. His skin was warm and inviting, the grip strong.

Inviting? What was wrong with me? I wasn't attracted to men. Not anymore, or so I'd thought when I declared my love for Gemma. I was a one-person type of gal, and the special person in my life was standing right next to me, I chided myself. Now wasn't the time to ponder my reaction to Erik. Or aversion to Paula.

"I should be going," Erik said. "Glad you didn't die."

I giggled like a silly thirteen-year-old girl. "All thanks to you."

"See ya in class, Tegan." He emphasized my name.

When the coast was clear, Jenny started to sing, "Erik and Tegan sitting in a tree…"

Gemma stiffened. "We should get you home."

"I'm fine besides being utterly humiliated." I smiled weakly.

Gemma shuffled her feet before retaking a seat. "Are you sure?" Her tone softened.

"Yes, please. I've made enough of a scene." I winced and rubbed my neck.

"Does your throat hurt?" Jenny asked.

"A little."

Gemma leapt into action. "I'll get you a hot chocolate."

I squeezed her hand briefly when she passed.

Jenny made a few more comments about Erik, but I was able to nip it in the bud before Gemma returned with a hot chocolate overloaded with whipped cream and a cherry on top.

"Free of charge." Gemma waved to Wilbur. "Watch out for the cherry—the silent killer."

It was a good sign Gemma cracked a joke, considering the brief appearance of her green-eyed monster. I've always marveled over her ability to toss aside irrational thoughts when push came to shove.

I tossed the cherry into my shake glass and shoved it to the side. Jenny's drink was nearly gone. Gemma, who usually never left until she finished every drop, didn't touch her half-full glass. Okay, maybe her jealousy fit wasn't completely gone.

"You going to finish that?" Jenny motioned to Gemma's shake.

"Nah. Go for it."

Jenny didn't pick up on Gemma's negative aura, but I sure as hell did. Jealousy, with a dash of anger, was carved into her frown. What happened to the levelheaded Gemma everyone counted on, most of all me?

I needed to do some damage control with Gemma and stat. I tried to imagine how I'd react if she fluttered her lashes and giggled like a lovesick girl around someone else. I'd probably storm out of the joint. Gemma was cool as a cucumber, emphasis on cool at the moment and not in a good way.

Jenny cocked her head. "Why'd you ask that question earlier, Gemma?" Jenny fished the cherry out of my shake glass. Seriously, the woman had no clue.

Gemma cocked her head. "I'm sorry, but I can't remember the question after Tegan's near-death experience." Her attempt to laugh sounded more like a cat hacking up a hairball.

I suspected Gemma hadn't forgotten the question at all, but didn't want to send me over the edge again. Hopefully, that was another positive sign that she still cared for me. Or she was utterly humiliated to have me, the closeted one, as her girlfriend.

"When I knew I liked girls," Jenny refreshed her memory.

Gemma blushed, further transforming her face into an embarrassed eggplant. "I'm sorry. It's none of my business. I shouldn't have asked."

Jenny waved the thought away. "I don't mind."

Gemma relaxed. Jenny glanced in my direction and then Gemma's, and it was like I could see her mentally connecting the dots: Gemma's question, my nearly choking to death, and Gemma's brief fit of jealousy. Maybe Jenny wasn't as dumb as I'd thought. And did my eyes rat me out whenever I peeked in Gemma's direction?

This was bad. So very bad.

"In answer to your question, eleventh grade," Jenny said.

Gemma nodded in agreement.

"You, too." Jenny stated without an ounce of uncertainty.

Gemma nodded again. I half expected Jenny to demand when I knew, but she didn't. Neither gazed in my direction.

And that irked me.

Good grief, Tegan. Make up your neurotic mind.

A few minutes ago I'd almost died when Gemma waded into the lesbian danger zone for the second time this weekend, and now I was peeved that the two dykes out of the closet were ignoring me, the hidden one.

And then there was the Erik factor. I found him attractive. My mind wandered back to the confusion zone, pondering if I was lesbian, bisexual, or experimenting like April—that thought made me almost puke in my mouth.

What would Gemma think? God, I didn't want to hurt her. I'd promised I wasn't like Kate, who'd tossed Gemma aside for the high school quarterback. I wasn't, was I? Finding Erik attractive didn't convert me into a backstabbing bitch, right? And it didn't mean I was questioning. Curious, maybe. Shit, that didn't sound better. What was wrong with me?

Gemma and Jenny were silently studying me.

"I'm sorry. Did you say something?" I asked.

They both shook solemn heads.

"Then why are you staring at me like that?"

"Making sure you're okay," Gemma said.

"I'm fine, okay? I'm not a wild creature on exhibit at a zoo, so stop staring."

Hurt etched onto both of their faces. Why was I being such a jerk?

"I'm sorry. Maybe I should go home."

Jenny helped me stand, and Gemma wrapped a coat around me. "Want me to drive?" Jenny asked.

I nodded. They were being so kind and protective. I so didn't deserve it.

The ten-minute ride home was silent. We said

goodbye to Jenny in the lobby, although we lived on the same floor, and Gemma insisted that we take the elevator instead of trekking up five flights.

Once inside our room, she asked, "Would you like some tea or coffee?"

It was the first time she had offered to make me coffee with her illegal hot plate. It wasn't like she had offered me her kidney, but it kinda felt like it. She was being magnanimous, and I was being a shithead. A spoiled brat.

What was wrong with me? I wasn't taking it to April's extreme, but that didn't make it better or make it right. I sat on my bed.

"Gemma, I'm really sorry."

She quirked a curious ginger eyebrow. I loved it when she did that.

"Please don't be angry with me." I didn't say anything about Erik, the knight who had swooped in and saved my life. That was probably why I was drawn to him—not sexually, per se, but as a rescuer. Yeah, that was it. Was this an example of Florence Nightingale Syndrome? Falling for a caregiver? Gemma would know. Not that I would ask.

"Angry with you? For choking on a cherry?"

This made me howl with laughter. "Choking on a cherry!" I continued laughing. "In a way, you're right on the money. Such public declarations encouraged by Jenny did pop my lesbian cherry so to speak."

Gemma collapsed onto her bed, while I stayed put

on mine. I drew my knees to my chest. She wasn't finding any humor in the situation, and I couldn't blame her.

"It's just that..." I faltered. "All this. You. Me. It's all so new."

She bobbled her beautiful red head.

"I'm not saying I don't want to be with you."

Fear flashed in her yellow-green eyes. "Does it have anything to do with Er—?"

"No!" I put a palm up, shielding my eyes. "Please. Don't look at me that way. It has nothing to do with him. I'm overwhelmed. Is it all right if I don't tell anyone about us? For now?"

Confusion smashed the fear right out of her eyes. "Tell about us? Why do we have to tell anyone? I thought we settled this last night." Her words carried a hint of frustration.

Now it was my turn to tilt my head like a perplexed puppy dog. Not that I could see it personally, but I was fairly certain that was what I resembled.

"Isn't that the next step in your plan?" I asked in a tiny voice.

"Plan?" she echoed.

I rested a chin on my knees.

"Tegan, do you think I'm on some lesbian pronouncement crusade or something?"

Yes, I did, but from her pained expression the implication was hurtful. *And the award for worst girlfriend of the year goes to...* I needed to snap out of my funk.

"What? No. Of course not," I stammered.

"And wasn't it your idea to tell my parents we're dating?"

"I'm not talking about your parents. I couldn't give a rat's ass who in Keller knows who or what I am." Or at least I didn't think I cared. Word wouldn't travel all the way back here, would it?

"What you are?" She crossed her arms. "What are you?"

Never before had Gemma used a harsh tone with me.

"I don't know. Gay, straight, bi, asexual...? I don't know."

"I think we can rule out asexual." Her lips screwed up. She was trying to make me laugh, yet my insides churned.

I burst into tears and buried my face in my cradled arms.

Gemma was at my side in a flash. "Shhh. It's okay, Teeg." She rocked me. "I didn't mean to be an ass."

Great. Now Gemma thought she was at fault, when it was me who was to blame.

"It's not you. It's me."

Gemma pulled away after hearing the classic lines delivered in many breakups.

Fuck! Why couldn't I get anything straight!

"Hold me. Until I can pull myself and my thoughts together. Please."

She did, thank the Lord.

Wait. Could I fuck a girl and still believe in God?

Shit, shit, shit!

All this was too much. I stifled a yawn. Great. Would Gemma think I was bored?

The center of my chest was on fire.

How could I feel like my world was crashing down around me when I was in Gemma's arms? Sweet, wonderful, loving Gemma.

Why was my brain torturing me with all of these doubts when all I wanted was happiness?

Could we stay together without anyone finding out? If my mother even had an inkling...

"Tegan? Are you all right?"

I hadn't recognized the signs, but I'd started to hyperventilate. "H-he-he-he."

Gemma sprang into action. She grabbed an old brown paper bag she kept on hand after my first panic attack during midterms last semester.

"Here." She thrust it in front of my mouth. "Slow. Slower. Don't take deep breaths." She removed the bag from my mouth. "Breathe in through your nose. Hold it. One. Two. Three. Okay, let it out through pursed lips. Good job. Do it again." She gestured like she was conducting an orchestra.

My breathing stabilized. Gemma encircled me in her arms. "You okay?"

"Yeah, just tired." Tired of looking like a fool. A lesbian fool.

"You've had quite the day."

I nestled into her arms. "So have you. And now I'm ruining it."

"You aren't ruining anything."

"Please tell me you don't hate me." I clutched her arm.

"Shhh. I could never hate you. Slow your breathing down, sweetheart."

Sweetheart. I was still Gemma's sweetheart. A calm settled over me like I'd been submerged into a warm bath.

"I'm wiped out." My eyelids descended as the tea kettle whistled.

CHAPTER EIGHT

"FEELING BETTER?" GEMMA RUBBED MY BACK.

My eyes fluttered open but snapped shut again. "What time is it?"

"Five."

We were in my bed, under the covers. "Morning or night?"

"Night. You'd mentioned this morning you wanted to study some for your history test before bed."

I rubbed my eyes. "I hate school."

"No, you don't. You love learning. You hate tests." Gemma was still my enthusiastic cheerleader.

"And papers," I grumbled like a crabby child, regretting it instantly.

Gemma hopped out of bed and put the kettle on. "Coffee or tea?"

"Coffee. Strong."

"Gotcha."

I propped myself up against the wall with pillows cushioning my spine. "Gemma—"

"Not tonight, Teeg. Tonight you need to focus on studying."

Relief whooshed through me, but it didn't wipe away the guilt in my soul.

"Let me say one thing."

Gemma wheeled about, and her fragile smile gave assent.

"I love you," I said.

Her smile mutated into a shit-eating grin. "That's all that matters." She put a hand up to silence me. "For now. We can have a heart-to-heart once the dust settles."

The lesbian dust.

Why did I insist on adding *lesbian* to everything? So I liked Gemma? What was the big fucking deal? Gemma wasn't falling apart at the seams. She was making me coffee so I could study for an exam. For her, everything was normal.

She was normal.

I was the lesbian on the brink of insanity.

Gemma might have sensed the internal turmoil roiling through my mind. "Hey, what did I say? Not tonight."

"I didn't say anything," I pouted.

"Oh, I can see the debate waging in that beautiful

head of yours, and from the looks of it, you're losing." She circled a finger in front of my face.

"Kiss me."

"No." She backpedaled.

"Why?"

"Because you need to study, that's why." She smiled like the devil. A redheaded she-devil.

"All I want is one measly kiss." I lifted the covers for her to join me.

"Then why are you trying to get me into bed? Not going to happen."

"Gemma!" I squealed.

She plopped a notebook and text onto my lap. "Study." She followed that up by handing me a steaming cup of joe.

I was flabbergasted when she curled up on her bed with a macroeconomics book. Really? Macroeconomics was more appealing than sex? Sex with me?

Without peeking up from her book, she said, "Don't. Don't say it. Don't think it. Study. The quicker you settle down, the quicker you'll finish, and then I'll help you relax."

"I'm ready for the test now!" I tossed the study materials onto the floor.

She snatched up my notebook, flipped to the first page, and asked, "What's the era after the Civil War called?"

"Reconstruction."

"Correct, but everyone knows that. Who was the seventeenth president?"

"Uh…"

"I'll give you a hint. Who was the sixteenth president?"

"How is that a hint?"

"Log cabin." She scratched the tip of her nose. Was that supposed to be a clue?

"Lincoln." I dragged out the pronunciation.

"Correct. And when he was assassinated, who became president?"

"His vice president."

"And his name?" She eyed me with a smugness I found sexy and annoying in equal measure.

"Give me the book." I let out a puff of air.

"I'll make you a deal. I'll help you study and each time you get a question right, you'll get a kiss. A peck, no tongue. Not until I think you're ready for the exam."

"And then we can get naked?"

She tugged on her earlobe and smiled. "And then we can get naked."

I raked my hair back and twisted a black scrunchie around the unruly blonde mess while she got cozy at the foot of my bed. "Before we start, I need some music." I grabbed the stereo remote and hit play. "Once" by Pearl Jam blared over the speakers. After I adjusted the volume, I cracked my neck, shook out my arms, and gave Gemma my complete attention.

"Bring it."

Gemma grilled me with questions. If I didn't know the answer, which was most of the time, she offered an explanation. When I nailed one, she leaned over and gave me a peck on the cheek, hand, collarbone, shoulder, or wrist. Never on my lips.

It was erotic as hell.

"How do you know so much about American history?" I asked.

"My AP teacher in high school was meaner than a pit bull." She shrugged. "And once I learn something, it sticks." She tapped her noggin.

We made it through the notes, and I thought the cramming session was done, but she still gripped the notebook.

"Aren't we done?" I ran a finger down her bare arm.

"Not yet." She flipped to the first page and peppered me again with questions. Now, I was answering almost everything correctly. Her quick pecks morphed into lingering kisses.

"Final page," she said. "Each time you get a question right, one of us will take off an article of clothing. First me, then you." She motioned with her hand that we'd repeat this until finished.

Now she was talking.

Neither of us had much on to begin with. Gemma must have undressed me when I'd fallen asleep earlier. She was always taking care of me.

I got the first question right. Gemma took off her

gray Husker's T-shirt. Next, I removed my flannel pajama bottoms. The third I got wrong, but she gave me a kiss as a consolation prize. When I deepened the kiss, Gemma pulled away, waggling a teacher-like finger in my face.

Intense desire raged through me. Was it possible to climax solely from anticipation?

Gemma's simple but sexy black bra was next.

After another correct response, she helped me ease off my *Edward Scissorhands* T-shirt. The slow and delicate way she relished the act sent a jolt through my hot zone. Her fingers traced circles on my skin, avoiding my nipples, even though they begged for her attention. Down south was pleading as well, but we both held back.

Who'd break first? It was a game now, and there wouldn't be a loser.

The next question was easy peasy, and I helped Gemma remove her Umbro shorts. All she had left were black panties. I was still wearing mine and a bra. Days ago, both of us would have been beyond self-conscious in this state. Now, we were completely comfortable.

Why had I doubted this earlier today? Or since *it* had happened?

This was the most natural thing in the world.

It was love. Did it matter that it was *girl* love?

Gemma's breasts hitched up with each intake of

breath. She didn't bother asking me another question. Her sexual desire dared me to act.

Our eyes locked. Gemma's eyes smoldered. My skin tingled.

"You're beautiful, Gemma."

Still, neither of us made a move.

"Am I forgiven?" I asked.

"You were never in trouble with me. Tegan, I'd never push you to make any declarations. I wanted to tell my parents because they're not just my parents; they're my best friends. And here, besides you, Jenny is my best bud. I feel alone..." A tear glistened on her cheek as it snaked toward her chin, where it elongated, before plummeting onto the sheet.

I cupped her face where the tear track mark still shimmered. "Why didn't you tell me?"

"I really didn't realize it until I told them. Now, I feel at peace. I want you to feel this sense of tranquility, but I know it's too soon. I've known since high school." She placed a hand over mine, which still rested on her face. "I'll always be here for you and will never push you."

"What if I need a push?"

"I'll cheer for you, but only you will know what you need. You have to tell me what you need."

Never before had I experienced such true love for and from another person.

"I need you," I said.

"You have me."

Our lips passionately collided. My tongue searched for her truth.

I toppled on top of Gemma, never stopping the kiss.

We deepened it.

"I could kiss you forever," I said.

She pulled my lips back to her hungry mouth.

Our fingers traveled up and down the other's body. Each touch magnified the electrical pulses in my heart and soul. Was it wrong that I wanted to devour Gemma? Her body? Her mind? And her love?

She consumed me, and I wanted to consume her.

Right then, Gemma's hand slipped under my panties and entered me.

My breath caught, but Gemma didn't hesitate. She was learning my signs. Her mouth wandered to my neck. Nipping and licking my earlobe.

I raked her back. She let out a satisfied groan and gazed into my eyes. Down below, she intensified her efforts.

A splash of wetness welcomed each thrust.

All the while Gemma plunged in and out, she didn't take her eyes off mine. I blinked excessively but was determined to stay focused. I needed to see her watch me come.

I was close to bursting.

"Stay with me," she pleaded.

I palmed her cheek.

My back arched. A vibration spread from the epicenter of our love and rocked both of our worlds.

Neither of us could tear our eyes off the other.

Lights flashed. My eyes tried to close, but I steadied them the best I could as I trembled.

"Kiss me while I come." I pulled her to my greedy lips.

Within moments, I broke apart to cry out in rapture. Sexual bliss. So basic and primal. Vital.

Gemma didn't stop. She slipped my panties off and went down on me, taking my throbbing clit into her mouth. Her fingers slowed but still softly penetrated.

I writhed and fisted the sheet.

A second orgasm began to surface. "Slow. I want to savor every second." The sensation overtaking my body was as if I was bobbing in an ocean, waiting for the next crashing wave, and instead of being afraid, I couldn't wait for the rapture. For Gemma to bring me home.

Her tongue lapped my bud sensually.

It was as if I was fated to holler Gemma's name. Every aspect of my life collided into hers, forever entwining our souls.

"Oh… Gemma… I love you."

She dove in as far as she could.

"Yes!" I bolted up and cradled her head with both hands. She'd opened the door, and I gushed into her mouth. My head lolled all the way back.

Gemma stilled everything as the eruption raged.

I collapsed onto the bed. Gemma rested her head on my thigh. Her eyes sparkled with passion and exhaustion.

For the second time today, my eyes couldn't stay open. I flashed a tired smile, and my lids drifted together.

The last thing I remember was Gemma's words, "I love you, too, sweetheart."

CHAPTER NINE

ON THE WAY TO MY HISTORY CLASS, I SPIED Michelle, Jenny's best friend from their high school days. She and her boyfriend, Seb, cohosted our weekly G&T get-togethers.

Seeing me she waved exuberantly, making her thick brown curls dance. "Hey! Where are you off to with such a serious look on your face?"

"History test," I said, doing my best to quiet the unease in the pit of my belly.

Michelle clamped a hand on my shoulder. "Easy. You'll be fine."

"I hope so. Gemma helped me cram."

She took a step back, placing a finger on her chin. "There's something different about you."

"No there isn't!" I squawked.

Michelle nodded her head as if I'd confessed to

robbing a bank. "I knew it!" She leaned closer. "You met someone, didn't you?"

"While studying for a history test?" I forced my voice not to betray the truth behind the words. I'd known Gemma for many months now, but lately it seemed each moment spent with her or even thinking about us, I uncovered another layer of the depth of her feelings for me and mine for the bewitching redhead.

"You didn't study all day and night. A little birdy told me about a certain incident yesterday. A knight. A damsel in distress. Schoolgirl giggling." Michelle waggled her brows.

I wanted to throttle the clueless Jenny. The last thing I needed was a rumor about Erik. "Please. I wasn't in distress. Only choking."

Michelle's boisterous laughter seemed to emanate from her toes. "What's your definition of distress? Choking counts in my book."

Waving her off the Erik scent, I said, "I need to go. See ya on Thursday."

"Bring your new beau," Michelle hollered after me.

I glanced over my shoulder but curbed the desire to say, "I have been, but I didn't know it at the time." Instead, I shook my fist at her.

She mimed shooting me with an arrow like she was Cupid.

I retreated inside the building, furtively scouting the lobby for Erik. The last thing I needed was another run-in with him with Michelle right outside. She was worse than a bloodhound when it came to relationship stuff. If I wasn't ready to come out, keeping my feelings for Gemma a secret wouldn't be easy.

I SAT in the back row, jubilantly scribbling the final short answer for the history test. I was certain I had aced the multiple-choice section as well as the mini-essay. I had hypothesized if Lincoln had not been assassinated, he would have been impeached. At first, I was stumped in my writing until an image of Gemma flashed in my mind. I smiled remembering her glistening eyes and could practically hear her reciting word for word how Andrew Johnson, who was impeached, followed Lincoln's plan for Reconstruction. Thank God she'd had a bitch of a teacher in high school, who'd crammed all those useless facts into her gorgeous head.

I waltzed to the front of the classroom and slapped the bubble sheet and blue book onto the pile.

"Feeling pretty good about it, Miss Ferber?" Dr. Kendrick asked. He actually wore a tweed jacket with elbow patches, and his resemblance to Vice President Al Gore was uncanny.

I smiled confidently. "Sure am."

His pinched face conveyed "I'll be the judge of that."

About half of the students had already completed

the test. Usually, I was one of the last to finish. Erik was on the opposite side of the room, on his way to turn in his exam. He caught my eye and winked. I gave a two-finger wave, ensuring no one saw.

When I emerged from the classroom, someone shouted, "Teeg!"

I searched for Gemma and spotted her bursting from the stairwell. I waved.

"How'd you do?" asked a sultry voice behind me. I flipped around and nearly swooned when I locked eyes on Harrison. I mean Erik.

"O-okay," I stammered. "You?"

"Not as good as you apparently." He appraised my boobs, nodding his head as if his gawking at my tits was actually a compliment.

Gemma approached. "How'd it go?" She nodded at Erik but didn't pay him much attention. Not that he could tear his eyes from my chest to notice the slight.

"Nailed it!" I high-fived her. Erik raised his hand and, even though I wanted to ignore him, I slapped my palm against his. Mom always said manners first. He tried to squeeze my hand, but I yanked away and crossed my arms over my apparently too tight turtle-neck sweater.

"We should celebrate," Gemma said.

Erik nodded. Did he think he was now one of us? Saving my life had gained him entry into the Tegan-Gemma inner circle? Put that way, it kinda did. There'd be no Tegan without him.

"How 'bout Friday? Drinks on me?" he asked.

I toyed with the idea. I wasn't interested in getting involved with Erik. Could I handle him staring at my boobs for free drinks? Gemma pursed her lips. Could Gemma handle it? Her thinning, bloodless lips said not a chance in hell.

"What do you say?" He wrapped an arm around both of us.

Was he envisioning a threesome? Now he was really pushing his luck.

"Maybe. I'll need to check my schedule." I couldn't meet his eye and instead gawped at his massive Air Jordans. Did that mean...?

"Well, let me know if you can pencil me in." He widened his eyes suggestively before strutting off like a peacock.

"He's interesting," Gemma said, putting him down not in words but in tone.

"The dude couldn't keep his eyes off my tits like every other guy I talk to. Why are men such pigs? Saving my life yesterday doesn't give him the right to blatantly ogle me." I looped my arm through hers and whisked us away from the crowd gathering outside the classroom. "The only one I want leering at my chest is you," I whispered in Gemma's ear.

"I don't leer!" she forcefully whispered back.

"Yes, you do." I shoved the glass door open and immediately shielded my eyes. Sunrays bounced off the mounds of snow. Gemma slid her Oakley sunglasses from the top of her head firmly into place, which simultaneously freed her flowing red locks. I pulled my Target brand shades out of my bag.

I crinkled my nose at the dirty mounds of gray snow lining the sidewalk. "How long until this mess melts?"

"The roads and sidewalks are clear, but the massive piles—not for weeks."

"I hate snow days after a storm. Such an unsightly mess."

"Want to know where it's still pristine?"

I squeezed her arm.

"Walt's Hill."

"Yes!" I squealed. "Why didn't I think of that?"

Walt's Hill, named after the university's founder, was a mile or so from campus, and it'd become a sledding hotspot.

"Let's go this way." I gestured to the empty soccer field, where only a few had trudged through the foot of snow. "I want you to myself."

Gemma stopped in her tracks. "Full disclosure. Jenny will be there. Have you recovered from the—?"

"Do you think Jenny suspects?" If she did, why'd she tell Michelle about Erik? Or did Michelle hear from another little bird? Alfrid was crawling with gossips.

"About us?"

I nodded.

"Not positive, but she'd have to be an idiot not to."

"Are you saying I wasn't smooth?" I bumped her shoulder.

"By smooth do you mean nearly dying when the word *lesbian* popped up in conversation?"

"Whatever."

"I don't think Jenny would ever say anything, though. That's not her style."

Gemma was right, but the thought still made my stomach cartwheel.

"There's more."

I raised my eyebrows.

"She invited a girl she has a crush on."

"Not April?" My voice was three decibels higher than normal.

Gemma shook her head.

"Bernice."

"God, what a hideous name." I clapped a hand over my mouth.

Gemma laughed. "She goes by Bernie."

"That's a helluva lot better. What happened with April?"

"Nothing, I guess. Jenny said they fooled around some, but there was no future."

We laughed.

"All this time, I never suspected Jenny was so levelheaded. Thank God she'd finally come to her senses." I peeked at Gemma. "When did you find this out?"

"About which? The sledding or Bernie?"

"Both. You know I love gossip." Just like everyone else in this sleepy town.

"This morning."

"This will be like a double date, then."

"Kinda," Gemma stammered. "Only we'll know, though. We can stop off at our room, change, grab lunch, and get our sleds. We're meeting them at the top at 2:30." She glanced at her watch. "That gives us an hour and a half."

As soon as we entered the room, I pinned Gemma against the door and kissed her hard. "Thank you for helping me study."

"If that's my reward, I'll help you study for all your tests." She twirled a blond lock around her fingers.

"That was a teensy taste. This is your reward. Let's skip lunch." I stripped out of my clothes and lay on the bed with my legs spread wide. "Come and get it."

Gemma's eyes bulged, and she squinted at her watch again.

"Did you really check the time?" I asked, slipping my hand between my legs, skating a finger over my pussy lips. "Here I am, served up on a silver platter, practically, and you're calculating if we have enough time."

"Uh..."

"Stop being so logical. Now strip!" I commanded.

She dutifully complied and climbed on top of me, straddling one of my thighs. "At least not all of you is logical. You're already slick." I reached down and teased a finger inside. "So warm and inviting."

Gemma's lips took possession of mine, kissing me with a new level of passion. The type that conveyed she wanted to dominate me. It flipped my lid, in a good way. I rolled on top of her, pumping my fingers harder inside.

"Hey, I thought this was my reward." Gemma's closed eyes and satisfied moan muted her complaint.

I tweaked her nipple, sucking it into my mouth. "Are you complaining about being fucked? You're already in hot water for the watch thing. Don't push it." I moseyed to her other nipple and gave it the same treatment.

"Or what?" She groaned as my lips started their trek down her toned stomach.

"I may never let you out of this bed." I flicked her bud with the tip of my tongue.

"Yes. I'm complaining. Really complaining. This has to stop."

I stilled my fingers and pulled my mouth away from her.

Gemma's head popped up. "What are you doing?"

"You asked me to stop." I rolled my wet lips. "Such a shame, because I love the way you taste."

Gemma yanked my head back to her twat, pleading in her action.

"That's what I thought," I said.

I fucked her until she screamed into her pillow, not once but three times.

"SHOOT. WE NEED TO HURRY." Gemma sighed regretfully. It was a little after two. "Where'd the time go?"

"I don't know. It seems to stop when I'm fucking you." I smacked my lips smeared with Gemma's secret sauce.

I would have been perfectly fine staying in bed the rest of the afternoon, but Gemma was never one to let anyone down.

We dressed in snow pants and warm ski sweaters in record time.

Minutes later, we were trudging up the hill behind our dorm, which was located at the far end of campus. Hundreds of boot marks marred the winding trail.

I dropped a glove, and Gemma leaned down to retrieve it.

"Thanks!" I pulled her arm. "Come on. I'm excited to meet Jenny's chica." Oddly, I wasn't wigging out. Maybe I was getting the hang of lesbian dating. *Dating*. "Gemma!" I exclaimed.

She spun around. "What'd you drop now?"

"Not that. I realized we haven't been on a date yet." I palm slapped my forehead.

"What? We've gone to dinner and movies."

"Yes, but that was as friends. We haven't been on an official date yet. Not since we kissed and then some." I paused, straightened my sweater, and snatched my sunglasses off. "Gemma, would you go on a date with me this Friday?"

"What about drinks with Erik?" she teased.

"Erik who?" I feigned surveying the immediate area. "I want to take my girl out. If she'll let me."

Gemma smiled but didn't speak.

"Is that a yes or a no?"

Still she waited.

"I see I have to do this the hard way." I started to get on one knee.

"What are you doing? You'll get all wet."

"I was going to propose a date, and I like it when you get me all wet."

Gemma laughed and pulled me up into her arms.

A copse of pine trees and quiet on the trail emboldened me, and I leaned in for a kiss.

"Well, well, well. What do we have here?" April rounded the corner and sidled next to us followed by Jenny and a black girl I'd never seen.

I stepped away from Gem.

"Tegan slipped," Gemma quickly tried to cover our *faux pas* of kissing in public.

"That's not what I saw." April eyed both of us with her *I caught you* smirk. "Unless she fell into your mouth."

Play-it-Safe Tegan wouldn't have been so careless.

Maybe I shouldn't bottle her up all the time to avoid moments like this? And why was April here at all? Gemma hadn't warned me that buzzkill was tagging along.

"Tegan, are you okay?" Jenny winked at me, but her voice was filled with concern. "You aren't hurt, are you?" She raised my arms to evaluate the imagined damage.

"I'm fine. I think Gemma rescued me in the nick of time." I wiggled my arms out of Jenny's and brushed some snow off my knee.

"This is Bernie." Jenny motioned to the woman who was the spitting image of Denise Huxtable. No wonder Jenny had tossed bitchy April overboard. Bernie was all that and a bag of chips.

"Berns, this is Tegan." Jenny dug her elbow into my side. "She's somewhat clumsy, so be careful." She waved to Gem. "And this is Gemma. Everyone refers to them as G&T."

We all shook hands.

"Tegan, if you're okay, let's roll. Walt's Hill beckons." Jenny widened her eyes.

"I'm as ready as I'll ever be."

Gemma's eyes bored into mine as if telepathically asking, "Are you sure this is okay? You won't choke, hyperventilate, or freak out?"

I steeled my nerves and nodded.

"Aw, you're such a trooper!" Jenny regarded the

group. "Last one to the top is a loser." She was already running by the time she finished.

Gemma dashed off. "Not a chance!"

"Such a child!" April shouted with a hand cupped around her mouth.

Bernie and I sized the other up as if determining whether or not to join the childish chase. "Come on!" I sprinted to the best of my ability. Running in snow boots while toting a bright red sled was not easy.

I was the last of the four but well ahead of April, who took her sweet-ass time, much to Jenny's and Gemma's annoyance. The top of the hill was packed per usual.

"You can't get enough of me, can you?" asked a male voice.

I sensed Gemma's grinding teeth without having to scan her face.

I slowly pivoted to confront Erik. "It seems I can't get *rid* of you." I poked his hard chest with a finger.

He smiled, ignoring another brush-off. Boys and their egos. Of course, hunky men like Erik probably didn't hear no very often. A Raiders baseball hat denied me a glimpse of his blue eyes.

"Join me for the ride of your life?" He elevated his fancy sled that put my plastic saucer to shame. "It's lightning fast."

"I think you're barking up the wrong tree." April inserted herself between us.

Erik tilted his head with vacant eyes. "Hi, I'm

Erik." He put a hand out. April took it. Then he craned his neck. "What about it, Tegan? You game?"

Every ounce of reason screamed for me to say no. But I had a glimmer of hope that if I went with Erik, April would somehow magically forget that she saw me swapping spit with Gemma. Play-it-Safe Tegan kicked into hyperdrive.

"Uh, sure." I wheeled about to Gemma and mouthed, "I'm sorry," before saying, "Can you hold this for me?" I handed her my sled.

Gemma took it without saying a word and didn't look at me. Jenny squared her shoulders and angrily cocked her head.

"All right. Let's go." Erik sat on the sled and gestured for me to sit in front of him. I did. He pushed off and leaned into me, holding me with one arm. His day-old scruff grazed my cheek. Could he smell Gemma's juices on my face?

I screamed. Erik hadn't lied. We shot down the hill, and the image of Clark Griswold in *Christmas Vacation* on his greased sled shooting down the mountain flashed before my mind.

It didn't matter if Gemma wanted to kill me. I was going to die, anyway.

I gripped the sides of the sled and belted out, "We're going to crash!"

We did. The sled slipped out from under us. Erik and I flew into the air and bounced down another ten or fifteen feet before grinding to a halt.

Erik laughed while he had me pinned on the ground underneath him. Neither of us moved. I wasn't positive why Erik remained still, but I was running an internal check to determine if certain parts of my body were irreparably damaged.

"Tegan!" Jenny and Gemma both shouted as they pulled up next to us.

Erik still didn't let me up. He brushed some snow off my face and appraised me with a wicked glint in his eye that reminded me of the one my ex, Josh, had worn right before we had sex. I guessed Erik's next step and wiggled out from under him before he could kiss me.

"Are you crazy?" I shouted at Erik, stamping my boots in the snow.

"I warned you." He got to his feet and brushed off his jacket and jeans. "Are you okay?"

"Yeah, no thanks to you."

"Don't be mad. Come on. It was fun. Admit it."

I glowered at him.

"Okay. I'm sorry. Let's do it again. I promise not to scare you." He put two gloved palms in the air.

I shook my head.

April magically appeared. "I'll go!"

Erik assessed her fake boobs and then nodded. "Sure." The two of them started the climb back up to the top.

"Are you okay?" Jenny asked.

I peeked at Gemma, who was silently fuming. I

wanted to say, "No, I'm in deep shit." Instead I nodded, willing my eyes not to overflow.

"Bernie has your sled at the top."

"Thanks, Jenny."

I tried to say something to Gemma, but she turned her back on me.

RELATIONSHIP LIMBO

CHAPTER TEN

FRIDAY MORNING IN THE CAFETERIA, APRIL and I sat alone at a table.

"Hey, have you seen Gemma lately?" I tried to sound perky but kept my eyes downcast, absently stirring my Lucky Charms with a spoon.

Last night, for the first time since we had moved into our dorm room, Gem didn't return.

"Uh-oh, trouble in G5?" April's fake smile made me squirm. She was the last person I wanted sympathy or relationship advice from. While peeling a banana, she continued, "Jenny stayed at Bernie's apartment off campus. Maybe Gemma joined them." She chomped into her banana, gnawing on it slowly, before adding the kicker. "You know, Tiny T, I think both Jenny and Gemma have jungle fever. Leave it to Jenny to find the only black lesbian attending Hill University."

I didn't reply to her racist comment out of fear of

confirming Gem and I were an item. Or had been before the Walt's Hill fiasco. Besides, that was the last image I needed running through my head. Shit, did Gemma have pictures of me and Erik running through her tortured mind? I abandoned my Lucky Charms and fresh fruit, untouched. For two days, I'd only been able to eat half a banana. My mom would be so proud of the inevitable pounds that were sure to melt off.

"I have class," I said, standing.

"Good luck finding your roomie." April winked conspiratorially as she waved a cheery hand. I wanted to shove her fingers where the sun didn't shine.

Trudging to class, I pondered my breakup with Josh over the holidays. It had been sad, but it hadn't torn me up inside and I hadn't missed one meal. As far as I knew, Gemma and I hadn't broken up, but how could I be in a relationship with someone who wouldn't talk to me? Since the sledding episode, she'd only said the following words to me: please, thank you, excuse me, and no thanks. Her forced politeness was like a swift kick to the gut each and every time. I would have preferred if she'd let me have it. Told me what she thought so we could begin to work our way through it. Not pretend that we were nothing more than friendly acquaintances who said, "No thanks," when I asked if she'd like to talk.

In the grand scheme of things, my relationship woes didn't amount to a hill of beans, as my mother would say. She'd remind me of all the children starving in Africa or some mumbo jumbo like that to snap me out of my self-pity funk. But right then, the only thing that mattered was the fact Gemma hadn't said two words to me in four days. Being in relationship limbo was killing me.

And now I had to get through three classes before I could launch a "find Gemma" mission.

I GLANCED at my hot pink Baby-G watch my mother had given me for Christmas. Ten minutes remained in my U.S. history class, and then I would be free to start the weekend. Yeah, right. I was physically and emotionally drained. That didn't stop the professor from droning on about Grover Cleveland's presidency. Like any of the thirty students in the room cared, least of all me.

All I could think of was Gemma and how she absolutely refused to hear any explanation concerning the incident on Walt's Hill.

Before Erik had tried to kiss me, Gemma and I planned on going on our first official date this evening, but I couldn't get her to confirm or deny if she was still interested, not simply in the date but in me. Most of the time, she was absent from our room. When Gem was around, she swayed her head as the songs "November Rain," "End of the Road," "Black," and "Nothing Compares 2 U" streamed through her headphones. I could only hear snippets of the songs and was sick to death of them. How could she still stand them?

"Tegan." Someone nudged my arm.

I scouted over my shoulder.

"Class is over. What'd you do, fall asleep?" Erik waved to the remaining handful of students fleeing the room.

I wish. Sleep was MIA, like my appetite and Gemma.

Not that I wanted to confide that to Erik, who seemed to forget he was in the doghouse after nearly killing me sledding Monday afternoon. "I must have."

He rattled a box of conversation hearts. "Want one?"

I shook my head.

"Sure you do." He handed me a yellow one that read: *Miss you*. Maybe I should leave it on Gemma's pillow to get the ball rolling. Or would she construe it as a guilt trip or desperate ploy? I tightened a fist around the heart, saying a silent prayer for Gemma to come back to me and then popped it in my mouth.

"Did you check your calendar?" Erik asked with a brazen grin.

"What?" I didn't trust Erik one bit and feared my body language was loud and clear. Mom also preached I should fake being nice since it was sinful to hurt someone's feelings. She didn't have any issues hurting mine, though.

"Drinks tonight. To celebrate surviving the first test. Only two more to go this semester."

"Oh, that. I don't think I can. Gemma—"

"She can come. Our house is having a party. In fact, invite your whole floor if you want." He tossed his long arms across the seats next to him, causing his biceps to flex, put his foot up on the back of my seat, and fixed his sapphire eyes on mine. His hair was slightly tousled as if he'd been wearing a hat earlier. Then I spied the headphones around his neck, and my mind drifted out of the room. Was Gemma listening to yet another breakup song?

"House?" I managed to say when I saw Erik's quizzical expression.

"Frat house." He cocked his head in the universal *of course* way.

Erik was a frat boy. Another black mark against him.

"I'll be sure to spread the word. Which frat?"

He rattled off the name of the most notorious Greek house on campus. The one that had been threatened to be disbanded last year, but at the last moment, several prominent men had swooped in and saved it. Decades ago, they were members, and they'd sworn to the president of the university that they would personally ensure no more monkey business would happen. Not that anyone believed it, but the men had also made huge donations to the university.

He rose and patted my head like I was a puppy. "See ya tonight."

I rolled my eyes after he left. "Treat me like a dog." I huffed under my breath.

I was the last one in the room when the lights switched off. I waved my arms over my head to trigger the motion detector to switch the fluorescent lights back on. It wasn't instant, and the creepy flickering sound of the electrical current surging through the three-foot tubes under the cracked plastic covers was reminiscent of the noise made in horror flicks right before a psychopath chops off someone's head with a chainsaw.

I bolted from the room.

It was still relatively early on Friday afternoon. Now that Gemma and Jenny were MIA, I had limited options for entertainment. I could head back to the dorm room and study for my nutrition test on Tuesday or head to the cafeteria for lunch in hopes that Gemma and Jenny were there. They still had to eat, and I knew for a fact that Gemma was low on funds. Cormac wouldn't deposit her monthly allowance until the fifteenth. It was only the twelfth of February.

I decided to kill two birds with one stone and hauled my text and notebook to the cafeteria. If I had to, I'd sit through the remaining lunch service and stay put through the dinner hours, ready to pounce on Gemma.

The thought of pouncing on Gemma elicited a

completely different notion of jumping Gemma into my sex-crazed mind. At the moment, though, I'd settle for holding hands. I missed the little things the most. The way she smelled. The cute snuffling noise she made in my ear when asleep. The—

"Tell me what fantasy is going on in that beautiful head of yours because the expression on your face is too delicious for words."

I wanted to peel my eyes open and see Gemma sitting across the table. I implored to the relationship gods for it to be my sweet girl, even though it wasn't her voice. Maybe she had caught a cold or something.

It was April. So much for pleading with the universe.

"Sorry to disappoint. Cramming nutrition crap into my brain." I tapped my open textbook with a mechanical pencil.

"Trust me, TR, you could never disappoint me." She flashed a seductive smile to accompany her innuendo. Ever since she'd stumbled upon Gemma and me kissing, she'd gone into overdrive being excessively sexual. Or was she trying to get into my head? She had to suspect that Gemma was avoiding me after the Walt's Hill debacle.

I repressed a shudder. "Where's Jenny?" I hoped my voice didn't sound too desperate.

She shrugged. "Chem lab, maybe."

Jenny wasn't taking chemistry this semester.

"Have you seen Gemma?"

April twirled overcooked spaghetti around her fork. Or tried to at least. "You still haven't heard from your girlfriend?" She batted her eyes to soften the blow. It didn't, and her grin relished the knowledge.

"Wait." I palm slapped my forehead. "She has econ," I lied. Gemma had that class on Tuesdays and Thursdays.

"She's pretty smart, isn't she?" April gobbled a crusty slice of garlic bread.

"The smartest." And kindest, but I didn't verbalize that to April. She wouldn't see that as a positive.

April's face glowed, and I followed her eyes to the cafeteria entrance. Jenny and Gemma finally made an appearance at 2:08 p.m., twenty-two minutes before the place stopped serving lunch slop so they could prepare for the dinner rush.

They hesitated, but then Gemma strolled up to our table and set her backpack down next to me. "Can you watch this?"

Overjoyed that she had said four words to me, I enthusiastically nodded as if she'd asked me to babysit a puppy.

Jenny placed her bag next to April, who in turn grunted her ascent, even though Jenny hadn't asked.

I counted the minutes it took for Gemma to round up her food and beverage. She returned with two limp slivers of pepperoni pizza, a small salad dripping with blue cheese, and Pepsi.

"So, Gemma, I thought you were in Econ. Are you

actually ditching?" April nudged my foot under the table.

Gemma peeked at me before addressing April. "We had a test. I finished early."

Gemma had covered for me. Surely that meant she still loved me. Or she didn't want to get into it with April, her nemesis. *Please, God, let it be the former.*

"Gem's a test-taking machine," Jenny added. Did that mean Jenny wasn't angry with me anymore, either? She slurped a spaghetti noodle into her mouth, painting watery marinara all over her chin and upper lip.

Gemma and I laughed. April crinkled her nose but stayed uncharacteristically quiet. The shift in power seemed to be leaning in Jenny's corner, making me nervous.

"Where's the token student?" April wasn't the type who'd go quietly into the night.

Jenny's sucked air into her mouth. "Bernie was valedictorian of her school."

"That's good. I'm not a fan of affirmative action—robs the deserving, you know." April sipped her diet Pepsi angelically through a straw as if she'd announced we were expecting rain later that afternoon.

"Gemma was valedictorian as well," I said in hopes of stalling World War III between the two for another day.

"What's the plan tonight?" April asked, resting her head on a palm.

"Uh," was my not-so-brilliant reply. Were Gemma and I still on for a date? Or had she protected me from April's wrath out of habit, not love?

Gemma and Jenny exchanged a meaningful look. "Bernie's roommates are having a few people over tonight," Jenny tossed out.

"I'm surprised you aren't sick of Bernie yet. You typically go through women like toilet paper." April's squared shoulders counteracted all happy-go-lucky vibes at the table, and we were already coasting on fumes.

"You're invited, of course." Maybe Jenny sensed April was on the warpath and was trying to defuse the situation before blowing all of us up.

Gemma's left leg twitched next to mine under the table, making it clear that Bernie hadn't invited April.

"No thanks. Tegan and I have plans, isn't that right?" April sweetly smiled to mask the obvious fib.

"We do?" I squeaked.

"Wait, I thought we had plans." Gemma rushed to my rescue again.

I bobbed my head. "That's right. We do." I smiled absently at April across the table. "I'm sorry. I totally spaced." I bumped my knee into Gemma's under the table, hoping she'd deduce my reason for laying it on thick: to avoid April's wrath. Gem didn't pull her knee away. Another minor victory.

"That's okay. There's always tomorrow." April

wadded up her paper napkin and threw it onto her plate.

"*Groundhog Day* is playing across the street," I told Gemma. "They were screening it last night after work for the employees, but I wanted to wait to see it with you."

Gemma smiled. Weeks ago we'd seen a preview of the movie, and Gemma, the über Bill Murray fan, said she couldn't wait to see it.

"So, Gemma, does that mean you're skipping Bernie's party?" April asked.

Gemma nodded as she forked a mouthful of iceberg lettuce drenched in dressing.

"I have class." April rose but kept her eyes glued to mine. "Don't do anything I wouldn't do."

"Oh, before you go. Erik's frat is having a party. He told me to spread the word," I said.

April smiled. "That's right. He told me when we were sledding. I'll gather the troops from the floor." Hovering over the table, she pinned me with icy blue eyes. "Is Erik fair game?"

"W-what?" I stuttered.

"He's fine, but I wouldn't make a play without your permission, of course, since it's obvious he digs you." She stretched out a finger and motioned to me and then herself. "You and I need to stick together." She jerked her head toward Jenny and Gemma. "No one else will take care of us."

I ignored most of what she said. "Oh, of course you

can make a play. I'm so not interested in Erik." I waved like that was the most ridiculous notion in the world.

"You sure? He's absolutely gorgeous and built." April pushed another nail in, and out of the corner of my eye, I saw Gemma squirming in her seat. "And he told me how he saved your life while everyone else stood by and watched helplessly."

I came to their defense. "They tried to help—"

Her bitter laughter cut me off. "Tried." April flickered her eyes toward the guilty parties. "Useless actions are just that. Useless."

None of us spoke. Jenny's face screamed her rage. Gemma's burned with shame.

"I'll take your silence as answer enough. Erik will be mine by the end of the night." She strutted out of the cafeteria with determination in each twist of her round caboose.

"I'm pretty sure she's not buying that I tripped on Walt's Hill and you rescued me," I said. I fought off the tightening sensation in my chest. "Ten bucks she tells Erik."

Gemma's nose crinkled. Why'd I mention him specifically?

"Don't worry about April," Jenny said as if she was a mafia don.

"What are ya going to do? Tell her to shut it or she'll swim with the fishes?" I tried to force a smile.

"I know people." Jenny cracked her knuckles.

I believed her for a second.

Gemma started laughing first, and I joined in, relieved that I wasn't the pariah of the group. At least not at the moment. One reason to be thankful for April.

"April's all talk, Tiny T. Don't worry." Jenny tilted her head to peer into my eyes. "I'll set her straight."

"How are things with Bernie?" I made goo-goo eyes.

She burned redder than a Coca Cola can.

"That good, huh?"

Gemma kicked my leg under the table.

"Well, I'm off." Jenny waved and winked at us, seeming taller. Was it Bernie's influence, or did kicking April to the curb unburden her shoulders?

There was an awkward silence between Gemma and me.

"So, I'm in the doghouse?" I said.

Gemma sighed. "No, not really." She shifted in her seat. "I thought you needed space."

"That was the last thing I wanted this week."

"What did you want?" She picked at her pizza crust.

"You. To be with you."

"Not Erik?"

"I don't like Erik!" I crossed my arms. "Sheesh!"

Gemma flinched and monitored those nearby. No one seemed to notice my outburst.

I nudged her leg under the table. "I promise, promise I don't like Erik, okay? Not like that."

Gemma stared at me, not giving any indication if my avowal was satisfactory.

"You still want to do dinner and a movie tonight?" I needed to hear from Gemma's mouth that everything was okay—or at least on the road to being okay.

"Of course, but I'm low on funds." She stared at her salad. Lately, she'd been talking about getting a part-time job to pay for an apartment in Denver this summer.

"I asked you on the date, so I'm paying."

"Is that how it works?" she joshed.

"For tonight at least. I picked up a couple of extra shifts this week, and the movie's free. One of the perks of my job."

"Are they hiring?" She sat up straighter.

"I can ask Marc on my next shift."

She nodded her thanks.

"Can we talk?"

"Sure, but first I have a meeting with one of my profs. Meet you in the room in an hour?" She flung her Eddie Bauer backpack over her left shoulder.

Before she stood, I put a hand on her arm. "Thank you."

Gemma studied me and then smiled. "Relax, please. I don't want to have to worry about you having one of your famous panic attacks." Her tone was teasing, but her eyes showed her true frame of mind—she still cared.

CHAPTER ELEVEN

NINETY-SIX MINUTES LATER AND NO GEMMA. I was on the verge of a full-fledged fit. Maybe I had misread Gemma's eyes. She didn't really care—not in the way I wanted. Gemma, being Gemma, would always care about a friend in her life. But did she still love me the way I loved her? Did she still want to be with me? Kiss me? Feel my body against hers?

I frantically paced the room, and each time I passed the window, I squinted in hopes I'd see Gemma returning, even though our window overlooked the parking lot not the classroom buildings. Logic and fear didn't go hand in hand, apparently.

The jingle of keys outside the door made me panic. I perched on the edge of my desk in hopes I looked unruffled. There was no way I wanted Gemma to know I was on the precipice of losing it because she took thirty-eight minutes longer than she'd said she would.

I snatched a magazine with a woman in a bikini on the cover off the shelf next to me and casually flipped through the glossy pages.

Gemma entered with flushed cheeks and out of breath. "I'm so sorry. My professor was a bit of a windbag."

I peeked at my watch. "Hmmm… oh, wow, look at the time. I had no idea it was so late." I kept my eyes glued to the magazine.

She tilted her head to read the cover. "Really? You had no idea that I'm more than thirty minutes late?"

I shook my head. "None."

Gemma tugged the magazine from my hands. "When did you start reading my *Sports Illustrated*?"

"Since they started showing chicks in bikinis," I said lamely.

"They've been doing that since the sixties." Gemma put a finger on her chin. "Let me guess. You were pacing until you heard me in the hallway."

I gripped the edges of the desk with my hands and leaned away from her cuteness. "I was not." It took effort to sound indignant.

Gemma stepped closer. "Really?"

"Really." I leaned back some more and crossed my arms.

She wedged herself between my legs. "Teeg?"

"Oh, all right. I may have been pacing."

"I knew it. That's why I ran all the way here." With a jerk of her head, she motioned me into her arms.

"I'm pathetic," I said into her chest.

Gemma patted the back of my head. "No, you aren't. You're adorable, actually."

"If you think I'm adorable, why have you been avoiding me all week?"

"Like I said earlier, I was giving you space. Bernie—"

"What's Bernie got to do with this?" I muttered into her sweater.

"Bernie suggested giving you some space—to see if you missed me." Gemma's self-assured tone was starting to wilt.

"So all this was a test or twisted game of some sort?" And I wasn't happy she openly discussed our relationship with an outsider. What happened to her pronouncement that she'd never out me? Then I remembered that April, Jenny, and Bernie saw me kissing Gemma. If April wasn't buying the *I tripped* story, there was no way the out-and-proud Jenny and Bernie would. My recklessness outed me. Me? Play-it-Safe Tegan. Mom would be so proud—not about this scenario, but about me taking a chance. Not that I would ever tell her about Gemma. Oh, the irony.

Gemma lifted my chin to gaze into my eyes. "I didn't mean it to be that way. I'm sorry."

I wanted to shove her off me. Tell her to go to hell for making me worry needlessly because Bernie said it'd be best that way. What the fuck did Bernie know?

She was only two years older. That didn't make her Oprah.

But Gemma's sincere eyes and soft lips compelled me to kiss her.

And I did.

Gemma didn't hold back and met my lips with a ferocious desire.

I frantically yanked her sweater and shirt off, carelessly dropping the articles onto the carpet. She reciprocated with mine. Her sports bra was next, and her nipple responded enthusiastically when I sucked it into my mouth.

"You weren't expecting to get naked today, where you?" I asked.

"What makes you think that?"

"Your sports bra. Usually, you have on something with a tad more pizzazz." I traced my finger around her right areola.

"Maybe. Maybe not." Gemma cupped my breast with a greedy hand, squeezing it harder than normal. The pain was more than worth it.

"Jeans off, now," I commanded. Gemma complied, and I shucked my Diesel jeans like a high school boy on prom night. I pushed her onto my bed, climbed on top, and lay there.

"What's wrong?" she asked.

"Nothing. Nothing at all. This is what I missed most these past few days—feeling your body heat. Your smell. The comfort of being near you."

Gemma wrapped her arms around me. "I missed it, too."

I pulled my head out of the crook of her neck to glare into her eyes. "Don't listen to Bernie anymore. Next time, talk to me." I tapped her forehead as I spoke each word.

She gave a salute. "Yes, ma'am."

"Damn right." I giggled.

"And no more sledding with Erik."

I put a hand out. "Deal."

"Any other matters we need to discuss?" she asked businesslike.

"Kiss me."

Oh God did she. Make-up sex wasn't an unknown concept to me, but I didn't really comprehend the big deal. If this kiss was any indication of the lust that was in store for me—holy fucking ja-moly!

Gemma rolled me over and nuzzled my neck and hair. She inhaled deeply. "I love the smell of your shampoo."

"Pantene gets you hot?"

"You. You get me hot, Tegan." She playfully nipped my earlobe and then tugged on my Yin and Yang earring with her mouth.

"Which are you?"

"What?" Gemma pulled away from my neck.

"Yin or Yang?"

"Please. I'm yang. You, my nervous nelly, are yin."

"I am not."

"Do we need to go over all the panic attacks, choking fits, pacing in the room when I'm running late?" She outlined my nipple with her nose.

"Whatever," I said in a breathy voice.

Her tongue explored my breast but never landed on my nipple, even though it was bursting for attention.

Gemma moved to my right breast but squeezed the left nipple between her thumb and forefinger.

"Harder," I pleaded.

She did.

The simple act set me ablaze.

With a glance, Gemma acknowledged she understood my desire, but a ray of sunlight burst through the window, highlighting a mischievous glimmer in her green eyes as if she was saying, "Wait. It'll be worth it."

I knew it would be, and yet I craved her inside me. Was desperate for it, really.

Gemma skated a hand down from my breast to the slight mound of hair and then back up. My hands instinctively tried to guide hers to the hot zone.

She laughed. "Behave. If you can't, I'll tie your hands up."

There was no way she would ever do such a thing. Would she? The thought revved my libido.

"I dare you," I countered.

Gemma quirked a determined eyebrow. "You really want me to?"

"I really do."

Without a word, she popped up, grabbed two silk scarves from my closet, and tied one hand to the metal bedpost and then the other. She tugged on each to ensure I couldn't easily escape.

Her plotting wasn't done, and she wandered over to her desk to retrieve a turkey feather her father had sent in the mail as a formal invitation to Thanksgiving last year. Gemma straddled me; her red bush tickled my belly.

She set to work, tracing random designs on my bare skin with the feather. She ran it over my entire body, even the bottoms of my feet, which was surprisingly sensual. I closed my eyes. Within moments, I was writhing underneath her, but Gemma was enjoying herself too much to rush.

Right when I thought I'd die from anticipation, she tossed the feather to the side to explore my neck, earlobes, breasts, collarbone, and shoulders with her tongue. I ground my pelvis against her, but she ignored my pleas.

This was foreplay kicked into high gear.

"You're driving me crazy." I raised my head to see her.

Gemma stared at my pussy. "I know. I like it."

A spurt of hot juice coated my thigh. "I may come without you."

"I don't think you will." Her tone oozed with confidence. "And if you do, you'll have to be punished."

I was mad with desire.

Gemma flipped around and faced my feet, still straddling my pussy. Leaning all the way over, she licked my thigh and worked down, giving each toe proper attention. Her creamy white ass was right there, and I couldn't touch it. I wanted to nibble on each cheek and seriously contemplated breaking free from the silk restraints, even if I had to tear the bedpost in two.

Maybe Gemma sensed this. She sat up and regarded me over her shoulder, smiling like a woman in complete control. "You aren't thinking of breaking free, are you?"

I slowly shook my head.

"Good girl." She kept watch of me, while her fingers glided over the top of my slick lips.

Slowly, she parted them. I sucked in a breath.

"You like?" she asked.

"Very much."

"How much?"

"Let me show you."

Gemma crinkled her brow. I was able to motion with a finger that I wanted her to sit on my face.

"Ah, I see."

I silently observed as she mulled over the idea. Seriously, what was there to think about?

She grinned at my impatience. Then she inched closer to where I wanted her. I was able to get a taste, but then she pulled away. "How much do you want it?"

"Fuck, Gemma, I want you."

"Convince me."

I sighed.

Gemma inserted a finger, and I let out a shudder.

"Words won't help me right now. I can only show you."

Gemma smiled and slipped another finger inside me.

"Please." I closed my eyes. "Please, please, please," I chanted.

Gemma slowly lowered onto my eager mouth. When she landed, my tongue was ready, and from the wetness that greeted me, I realized how much Gemma had enjoyed torturing me. It was a wonder that neither of us had orgasmed.

My tongue darted inside. Gemma moaned and buried her face in my pussy.

"Fucking hell, Gemma. This is so hot." I lapped at her clit. She filled my mouth, but I wanted more. Needed more. I doubled my efforts and was rewarded with a deluge of nectar.

Our bodies trembled, yet neither of us slowed down. My legs started to shake. Gemma groaned. I loved how excited she got when making me come. My needs were always of utmost importance.

She took my sex into her mouth and drove her fingers in hard and deep.

I shook all over. It energized me, and I circled Gem's clit with vigor. I wanted us to come together. I knew I was close, but I tried to hold off. It wasn't easy with the way she was hammering me down below.

A forceful squirt filled my mouth. It was only a matter of moments for her. Gemma's legs quivered.

The orgasm hit me hard. Coming at the same time heightened the emotions.

"Jesus," I screamed.

Gemma collapsed on top of me.

My body jerked again. "Fuck, we need to fight more. Make-up sex fucking rocks."

"Who said we're done?" Gemma licked my sensitive clit, knowing to go slow.

Our thrashing had loosened my constraints, and I slipped both hands out. I placed them on her delectable ass, dug my head into my pillow, and said, "Don't stop. Please don't stop."

Gemma didn't.

It was getting dark out.

I rolled onto my side and lazily ran a finger over Gemma's breasts. "Where do you want to go for dinner?"

Gemma, eyes closed, pushed her head farther into the pillow. "We don't have to go anywhere. I'm fine having dinner downstairs."

I slapped her taut belly.

Her eyes popped open. "What was that for?"

"We are not dining in the cafeteria on our first date!"

"Easy, princess." Her happy-go-lucky smile soothed me.

I resumed running a finger over her bare skin. "Sorry, I didn't mean to overreact. But I want you to know this isn't a fling. Whether you like it or not, we're in a relationship." I tugged her earlobe with my lips.

"If you want to leave the room, you may want to refrain from doing that."

"Doing what?" I licked her lobe and neck.

"Yes, that. Or we won't leave bed until Monday."

The idea was tempting. So very tempting.

I straddled her. "What if I do this?" I rubbed my clit against hers.

"Now you're talking. Or moving." Gemma's eyes closed, and her breathing intensified.

My plan had been to torment her, but shit it was too good to stop. So I didn't. Soon enough, Gemma pulled a pillow over her head. She was close, as was I.

Gemma came first, and I pulled away.

"No, don't stop until you come," she commanded with her head still covered. "Please."

I nudged the pillow out of the way. "Don't worry. I'm not a martyr."

Her eyes widened when she realized my intention. I lowered onto her mouth, and my head flopped back when her tongue slid over my engorged sex.

It didn't take long at all, but Gemma held me in place, with two firm hands on my thighs, eagerly bringing me to another brink.

A second wave of rapture crashed through my body. I leaned back on two hands and belted out, "Oh fuck!"

I rolled off, and Gemma cradled me in her arms.

"God, I love you," I whispered. "The things you make me want to do."

She nuzzled her nose against my cheek. "I love you, Tegan Raye."

"Now, tell me. Where can I take you to dinner?"

Gemma laughed. "You're like a dog with a bone."

"You still haven't answered me. We are going on a date tonight. I'll give you twenty minutes to power nap, and then we're hitting the showers."

"I like the sound of that."

"Separately or we won't leave. Our relationship is moving out of the confines of this room. Watch out world; here we come!" I spread my arms out wide, embracing the idea.

Gemma shook her head. "Can't say you aren't passionate."

"Passionate and madly in love. Now where would you like to go?"

"Taco Bell."

"Taco Bell?" I shrieked.

Nonplussed, she said, "Yes. You asked, and I answered." She shrugged.

"We can't go to Taco Bell on our first date. It's unheard of."

"Why can't we? I'm craving Mexican, and that's the closest we have in Alfrid. Besides, who says we have to have a fancy meal on our first date? Why can't we go to Taco Bell? It's your favorite joint in town, considering all the late night runs we make. What's the difference really between the Bell and Applebee's?"

"I never suggested Applebee's."

"There's not a whole lot in Alfrid."

I tapped her forehead. "I have a car. We can go to a real city for dinner. We have options."

"That's not the option I want," she teased.

"You aren't playing fair." I sighed. "I'll consider if you promise you aren't suggesting Taco Bell because I'm paying."

I could tell by her determined eyes she wouldn't budge on Taco Bell nor would she flat out lie to me. I had to admire that, even if it drove me bonkers.

"What if we got it to go and drove to the top of Lover's Rock?" she tossed out.

"Lover's Rock?" I narrowed my eyes.

"Oh, Signal Rock. Bernie told me that's the nickname students gave it."

Hmmmph. I was tired of this Bernie chick, but I pushed that aside. "So it'd be kinda like a picnic." I was warming to the idea.

"Yes! Isn't that more romantic, sweetheart?"

"I think I can live with that. Barely."

She hopped up. "No need for a power nap. Three burrito supremes will give me all the energy I need."

I groaned. This wasn't how I imagined our first date.

Gemma noticed. "Come on. Let's shove aside the romantic notions of our parents and live how we want. Embrace love our way."

"Well, when you put it that way, I could murder five tacos. I haven't eaten all week."

CHAPTER TWELVE

"WHAT TIME DOES THE MOVIE START?" GEMMA asked and then bit into a burrito.

We sat in my car overlooking the town of Alfrid. Lights speckled the view, but the paltry number was unimpressive, yet I was drawn to the vastness down below. So much open space that hadn't been conquered.

"There's one at seven and the second showing at quarter to ten." I crunched into a taco. Little scraps of meat and cheese fell onto the wrapper in my lap. "You know, this is better than I thought." Aside from the Taco Bell stink, which was like no other smell on the planet, but I kept that too myself.

"I told you." Gemma added hot sauce to her third burrito. She motioned to the bag. "Don't forget your Mexican pizza."

"Not that, you goof. This. Sitting here with you."

"You approve then. An hour ago, that wasn't the case." She nudged my arm with an elbow.

My beat-up Honda Accord was a hand-me-down from my mother. It was more than half my age, but it still ran well. At the moment, the powerful heater was my favorite feature.

"I'm tired of winter." I wiped off the fog on my side of the windshield and side window with the sleeve of my Carhartt.

"Do you know why kids come here?"

"To Lover's Rock?" I attempted to sound sexy.

From the gleam in Gemma's eyes, I'd succeeded.

"Yes."

"Bernie's name is pretty much self-explanatory," I said.

"I think I'm missing the point entirely." Gemma balled up the empty burrito wrapper and tossed it into the white paper bag at her feet.

I finished chewing the last bit of my third taco and washed it down with Dr. Pepper. "Do I need to explain it to you?"

She nodded. "But I'm a visual learner."

"What about hands-on?" I ran a finger down her cheek.

"Even better."

I leaned over and kissed her. It didn't take long for us to shed our jackets so we could really get it on.

"Is this helping you understand?" I whispered into her ear.

"Oh, yes. But just in case, don't stop."

"I have no intention of stopping. We're the only ones crazy enough to be up here this time of year."

I slid my hand under Gemma's shirt and cupped her breast. Not satisfied, I wiggled underneath her bra and squeezed a nipple. She let out a satisfied gasp. Emboldened, I unzipped her jeans. Gemma nodded and reached down to grab the lever to lower her seat. My hand slipped under the hem of her panties.

"You're so wet." I pumped my hand some more. "I want to taste you."

Gemma lifted up, and I lowered her jeans and panties enough.

She clasped onto my head with both hands. When I took her swollen sex into my mouth, she moaned. The center console provided a tricky obstacle, but my desire aided my upper body to contort in ways I didn't know it could.

I peeked at her. I loved how her expression screwed up when in sexual bliss.

It was getting extremely warm in the car, and the windows were completely fogged.

"I'm about to…"

A tapping on my window made me jump three inches, and I hit my knees on the steering wheel as I popped up from her crotch.

Gemma grabbed her coat and tossed it onto her lap. Her seat bolted upright, forcing her to sit ramrod straight.

I turned to the window, swiped the condensation with my arms, and saw a police officer with a flashlight. He motioned for me to roll down the window.

I had to resist the urge to slam my right foot on the gas pedal. Instead, I clutched the knob and rolled down my window halfway.

"Good evening," the male police officer said.

"Hi," I yelped out.

The man leaned to the side and flashed the light into Gemma's face. "What the...?"

"Is something wrong, Officer?" Gemma asked in a serene voice.

The cop shouted over his shoulder, "It's two girls."

A second cop approached and asked, "Are you okay?"

The voice was feminine.

"Uh, yes, we were talking," I said as sincerely as possible.

"It's pretty cold out for sitting in your car and talking." The male cop rubbed his chin, trying to process what he'd seen. His eyes noted Gemma's jacket. Did they spy the sliver of skin showing?

The female officer pinned me with a sympathetic stare as if she was trying to communicate with me telepathically. "Which one?" she asked.

"Which one...?" I hoped she'd fill in the blank.

"Who's nursing a broken heart?"

Oh. Now I understood the game. "I a-am," I intentionally butchered the response and grabbed a napkin to dab my dry eyes.

"If you ask me, he's not worth it, sugar," she said.

The male cop scrutinized me and then his partner, shaking his head. "What are you two talking about?"

My rescuer ignored him. "You'll have to forgive my partner. A confirmed bachelor with no sisters. He doesn't understand women." She winked at me. "Go on home and talk there, okay?"

"Of course. I'm sorry."

"Why are you letting them go?" The man put his hand on the side mirror as if he was going to stop the car. "I'm not buying they were only talking. Check out all the condensation. The residents are tired of kids coming up here..." He paused and studied us again, and I was fairly certain he couldn't figure out what we were doing. I covered my wet chin with my palm. "And they're in a tow-away zone," he added.

"Come on, Warren. She's had a hard enough night."

"What do you mean?"

She whispered in his ear, loud enough for me to hear. "She got dumped by her boyfriend, and she's in the family way," she added for good measure. Or I hoped she did. Did I look pregnant? Taco Bell gut.

Officer Warren stepped back and mouthed, "Oh." Without saying another word, he marched back to his patrol car.

The female cop, whose name tag read Rodriguez,

leaned down and poked her head through the small opening of the window. "Be careful. Next time I may not be here to save your asses." She motioned to Gemma's lap. "Zip up." She smiled more to herself and shook her head. "Sometimes I miss college."

After she retreated to the patrol car, I put the car into drive and pulled out overzealously. The car fishtailed on the frozen pavement.

"Easy, Tegan. Don't get a ticket now."

I eased off the gas pedal.

My hand shook on the gearshift. Gemma placed hers on top and gave it a squeeze.

"That could have been bad," I said.

Seven minutes later, we were in the parking lot of the movie theater. Neither of us had said a word since the Signal Rock bust.

Gemma contemplated me with a furrowed brow. "You okay?"

I started to shake.

Gemma rubbed my back. "It's okay, Teeg. Nothing happened."

"Nothing happened!" Snot flew from my nose. "I can't believe it." I covered my eyes and leaned over the steering wheel. Now my body was nearly convulsing.

"Don't cry. Please don't cry."

I leaned back into the driver's seat. "I'm not crying."

Gemma adjusted in the car seat to see my face. "You're laughing?"

"Of course I'm laughing. Can you believe it? Officer Warren knocking on the window while I was going down on you." I blotted my eyes with a Taco Bell napkin that reeked of burrito supreme. "And you. I couldn't believe you. With your pants down and calm as a cucumber asking, 'Is something wrong, Officer?' How were you so calm?"

"I don't know. The question popped out." Gemma didn't laugh with me, and I wondered if she thought I was losing my mind or on the verge of a different type of panic attack.

"Don't worry, Gem. Really, I'm okay. Are you?"

She shrugged. "Nothing like that has ever happened to me. I've never even had a speeding ticket."

"Never?" I'd had two, and my mom was always nagging me about the points on my license.

"It helps not having a car." She grinned.

"Did you drive much back home?" I rested my head against my seat. The silly shock was starting to wear off, and the hammering in my chest and head was subsiding. Jesus, what would I have done if Officer Warren called my parents or something? I tried to focus on Gemma.

"Loads. I've been driving since I was fourteen."

"Fourteen!"

"Small towns have different rules."

"How'd you even reach the pedals?"

"I'm not that short. You make it sound like I was a child."

"You *were* a child!"

Gemma laughed. "You sound like your mom."

"Gemma! That's the meanest thing you've ever said to me." I slapped her thigh harder than I intended. She was right, which made it worse.

She put a hand on my thigh, and I pushed it off.

"Oh come on. Don't be mad about that. I was joshing."

I wasn't that hurt, but the thought of another round of make-up sex was enticing, so I continued the charade.

"Tegan. I can tell you aren't mad."

"Oh really? How?"

"You aren't biting your lower lip like you're trying to hold in a nasty comment."

"You mean so I won't sound like my mom?"

"I never said that." She put both palms in the air. "Never."

"But you thought it." I leveled my eyes on hers.

"Nope. Never. You're the one who always jumps to that conclusion. I utilized a common phrase—no malice intended. I promise, promise."

I clamped down on my lower lip.

Gemma let out a rush of air. "I kinda like it when you bite your lower lip. It really shows off that sexy gap between your teeth—makes me hot."

That mollified me some. "Maybe you should pick more fights with me so I do it."

"You mean like you're doing now." She leaned against the passenger door to apprise me head-on.

I tried to keep up the charade but couldn't. Gemma looked so cocky with her arms crossed over her breasts along with the slight tilt of her gorgeous red head. "Okay, you win." I pulled her head to mine.

A knock on the window scared the shit out of me.

"Not again," I growled and rolled down the window to give the intruder a piece of my mind. "What now?" I shouted out the window.

"Whoa!" Jenny backed up a step. "What's got your panties in a bunch?"

"Jenny, what are you doing here?"

"Seeing a movie. What about you two? Are you here to see a movie or make out?" Jenny teased.

"What about the party?"

"Lame so we scrammed."

Gemma got out of the car, and I did likewise.

"What movie?" Gemma asked.

"*Sommersby*. Bernie has the hots for Jodie Foster."

Gemma nodded in a way that implied, "Who doesn't?"

"What about you two?"

"*Groundhog Day*." Gemma opened the theater door and motioned for Jenny and me to go ahead.

"Oh, that's right!" Jenny bonked her head with a hand. "How's your first date going?"

"How do Taco Bell, Signal Rock, almost getting arrested, and fighting in the car stack up?"

"Dude, that's epic. A first date you'll never forget!" Jenny waved to get Bernie's attention. She had her arms laden with sodas, a large popcorn, and Reese's Peanut Butter Cups. A woman after my own heart. Maybe this Bernie wasn't so bad after all.

Gemma hopped in line. "Wait for me, Gem."

"Gem—that's cute," Bernie said. She nodded to Gemma as a hello. "Let's go, Jenny. I don't want to miss the previews."

They made their way into theater one. Over her shoulder, Jenny shouted, "Meet up with us after your movie."

I gave a thumbs-up without thinking.

Gemma was almost to the front of the line when I butted in. My coworker spotted me and motioned me to the side. I tugged on Gemma's jacket and whispered, "I got the hook-up."

She grinned. Not only was our movie free, but so were the snacks. Even though this might be the cheapest first date in history, I had a feeling I'd remember it for other reasons.

Walking to the theater, I giggled.

As if in tune with my thoughts, Gemma whispered in my ear, "Is something wrong, Officer?"

I bent over, laughing.

People around us gave us space.

Gemma motioned for me to walk ahead. We settled into our seats in the back row in the far corner.

I laid my head on her shoulder. "This was the best date ever, mostly."

"Every day with you is an adventure, Teeg."

UNDER LOCK AND KEY

CHAPTER THIRTEEN

GEMMA STEERED ME TO THE SIDE OF THE swanky restaurant's entrance. "You okay?"

"Yeah? Why?" Catching my reflection in the mirror, I fluffed my blonde locks and ran a finger over my teeth to wipe off a lipstick smear.

She cocked her head so it was nearly horizontal to the ground, her beautiful red hair tumbling over a shoulder. "You know why. This is our first double date and"—her head lurched upright, and she lowered her gaze to her simple black heels—"you have a habit of freaking out."

"Sheesh. No need to plant any unnecessary thoughts into my fragile and immature mind." I crossed my arms over my chest, accidentally pushing the girls upward and putting more pressure on my dress, which was doing its best to contain the goods.

Gem put up two palms, one holding a black purse. "Don't be mad, please."

I laughed and hooked my arm through hers, much to Gem's surprise. "You're sweet. Really. But this isn't a blind double date or something. It's dinner with Jenny and Bernie—our only lesbian friends. And in case you missed it, we drove by the Denver zoo a few minutes ago." I jerked my head to the north. "We're two hours from Alfrid. The odds of us running into anyone from school are pretty much nil in downtown Denver. Besides, I haven't had a freak-out episode for over two months." I stabbed two fingers in the air to emphasize the accomplishment. "Give me some credit."

Gemma patted my arm. "If you say so. Just in case though, I brought a first aid kit from the Red Cross class I recently finished." She rattled her purse.

"It's insulting that you took a first aid class because of me." I folded my arms over my chest again.

"I didn't take it solely for you. Knowing first aid makes me a better citizen." Gemma avoided my eyes completely.

"And it has nothing to do with the fact that when I choked on a cherry, Erik gave me the Heimlich while you sat there helpless?"

"What are the odds of that happening again?" Her smile confirmed she thought the odds were quite high that something would happen to me.

A couple pranced by in their evening wear, giving us a wide berth. My crossed arms and tapping foot probably didn't emit a happy-go-lucky vibe.

"Come on. Let's get inside." Gemma opened the door and ushered me inside with the wave of her arm.

"Can I see this magical first aid kit?" I whispered as I swished by her.

"Why?"

We stood off to the side while the hostess dealt with the couple in front of us. "I just want to see it."

Gemma clutched her bag with both hands, shaking her head as if my simply touching it would jinx its healing power.

"Gemma!" I managed to unzip the bag, even though Gem didn't relinquish it completely. The kit was much larger than I anticipated, taking up much of the space in her purse. I rifled through it. "A snake bite kit? Jesus."

She shrugged. "It's best to be prepared."

"Aren't you a good Girl Scout? You really think I'm that much of a spaz that I need a personal caregiver?"

The hostess motioned us forward. I advanced three steps, and one of my heels snagged on the fringe of the entryway rug. "Whoa," I said as I tried to gain purchase in my four-inch heels. I tottered on the ridiculously high death traps and stumbled into the hostess stand in front of a wall-to-wall fish tank with the most exotic and colorful specimens I'd ever seen in person. Who owned this joint? Jacques Cousteau? The stand didn't impede my progress, and if it wasn't for Gemma grabbing my arm at the last second, I would have face-planted into the glass. Should I make fish faces on the glass in an attempt to make it seem like I intended to get up close and personal?

"You okay?" asked the hostess dressed in a slim black dress. She steadied the teetering podium with one hand, straightening her dress with the other.

"What?" I eluded Gemma's helping hand. "Yeah, I'm fine." I fixed the skirt of my teal dress, the one I had worn to homecoming senior year, and remembered how it had flown upward in the kerfuffle and revealed my red lace date panties. "We have a reservation," I said in an authoritative tone.

Gemma smothered her mouth with a palm, but jiggling shoulders provided solid proof of laughter.

"Of course. What's your name?" The hostess smiled as if this was my first time in a fancy-schmancy place wearing high heels.

"Tegan," I replied with a touch a haughtiness. I cranked my head to the side to avoid staring at the poor lobsters in the crowded tank crammed next to the spacious fish tank, which housed much smaller creatures in comparison to the crustaceans. How many lobsters would survive the night?

"I think the reservation is under Bernice Sparks." Gemma stepped to my side, flashing the smile she used when trying to defuse a situation. Was she anxious I would snap at the hostess, or did she note my unease about the lobsters? A few weeks ago, I had cried when a man at Red Lobster playfully asked if he could personally scoop out his meal. I wasn't a vegetarian but did have a strict rule about not seeing a creature alive moments before it arrived on a plate.

The woman trailed a finger down the reservation book. "Ah, here you are. The other two haven't arrived yet. Would you like to wait in the bar or at the table?"

"We'll wait at the table." Gemma smiled sweetly.

"Of course." She snatched two menus. "Follow me, please." She gave me the once-over as if asking whether or not I could make it to the table without wiping out. Maybe she thought I needed hunky men to whisk me to the table in a litter, Cleopatra-style. I did my best to wipe away her insinuation with a fuck-you smile.

We took our seats, and Gemma accosted me when the coast was clear. "You okay?"

"Do you ever feel like a robot? Always asking if I'm okay?" I pressed her knee under the table to take the sting out of my comment.

"You'd think the nurse-in-training"—she pointed to me—"would be the one taking care of me. Not the other way around."

I stuck my tongue out at her.

"Don't pull that muscle. You'll need it tonight." She joggled a ginger eyebrow.

"Only if you're lucky."

"Lucky? I can count on one hand the number of days you've been able to keep your hands off me since our first official date in February. What's today?" She mimicked counting the days. "The second to last day in April."

"Keep talking and the only action you'll get in the foreseeable future will involve sitting naked on top of the washing machine during the spin cycle."

Gem bolted out of her chair. "Bernie! Jenny! So glad you made it." Her face and neck matched the color of her hair.

Bernie took the seat to my left, her gaze absorbing Gemma's embarrassment and the fake determination in my eyes. "Trouble in paradise?"

"There won't be any trouble, will there, Gem?" I rested my chin on intertwined hands, batting my eyelashes.

Gemma mimed zipping her mouth shut and throwing away the key.

Bernie pivoted in her chair to face her girlfriend of a few months. "I think we just missed the drama."

"Threat was more like it." The redness leached out of Gemma's skin as she slid into the seat next to me. Bernie's presence had this weird way of calming people. Everyone but me. There was something about Bernie that reminded me of my best friend since preschool—who'd stabbed me in the back on prom night during my junior year. The entire world thought Darla was perfect—that she even shat diamonds that smelled of roses. For as long as I could remember, my mom would constantly say, "Why can't you be like Darling Darla?" Darling Darla—pul-lease. More like Darla Barfla.

Bernie clapped her hands together. "Oh, it's barely after six, and there's already been one threat. I love the drama involved with women-only relationships. Keeps me on my toes."

A waiter, in black slacks, starched-white button-up, and tie, approached. "Would you like to start off with a bottle of wine, ladies?"

I was about to decline when Bernie piped up. "That would be lovely." She perused the wine list and mumbled some French-sounding words, but the only one I understood was merlot.

"Very good." The man ducked his head, but not a hair moved. Someone should give him the heads up to lay off the Dippity-Do hair gel.

"What happens when he cards us?" I whispered behind my hand to Bernie.

"He won't; trust me. Besides, I'm twenty-one. I'll say the bottle is for me if he causes a stink, but he won't." She winked Darla-like.

My eyes roved over the other diners in the upscale steak and seafood joint. All the men clad in suits and ties and the women in dresses. The only girl who wasn't in a dress was Jenny, but she at least wore expensive-looking trousers and a periwinkle silk shirt that highlighted curves I hadn't noticed before.

The waiter returned with a bottle and proceeded to uncork the wine. He splashed a small serving into Bernie's glass. She took an even smaller nip, nodding her approval. He topped off the glass and then served the rest of us.

"Would you like to hear tonight's specials?" he asked, both hands behind his back.

I stared with one eye closed, waiting for him to shout, "Let me see your driver's license!"

But he didn't.

Gemma nudged my foot under the table, and I wondered if I gawked like I was waiting to be punched in the face. I blinked several times, trying to squelch the unease of breaking the law.

"Please," Bernie purred, and he responded with a grin.

He appeared to be picturing Bernie, dressed in a sleeveless black dress with a diamond pendant perched above ample cleavage, like he wanted to eat her for dessert after his shift. It was hard not to laugh, since it seemed clear we were on dates. This wasn't the type of place to catch up with classmates on a Thursday night. Maybe he hadn't received the memo that girls could date girls.

He prattled off three dishes, one of which was lobster. Gemma stroked my thigh, giving me her *it's okay* smile.

"I'll be back in a few minutes to take your order."

"Please do." Bernie clearly enjoyed his ravenous

smile and leering eyes. I'd wager the dude couldn't say how many others sat at the table. The only one he had eyes for was the older woman in our group. Of course, Bernie, a dead ringer for Lisa Bonet, had that effect on most. Another irrational reason not to like her. Understanding the way my hackles rose around Bernie was nonsensical didn't actually rectify the problem. Bernie had always been kind and open to me, yet I couldn't swat away the unease when in her presence.

Jenny shook her head, rolling her eyes in that exaggerated way that connoted pride, not anger. She'd developed this look soon after meeting Bernie. If it were me, I'd probably be miffed if Gemma blatantly toyed with a waiter, man or woman. And the way Gemma had reacted when I'd gone sledding with Erik —it was easy to surmise my attraction to men would be a ginormous issue for her, which was why I kept this secret submerged inside. Luckily my interactions with Erik had been restricted to quick conversations after history class away from Gemma's glare. He wasn't such a bad guy, after I got past his bluster. And now that April had her hooks in him, his full-court press had eased, allowing us to evolve into the friend zone.

Was it normal for Bernie to openly flirt with men? We did score a bottle of wine, so I wasn't going to raise any objections. Besides, she wasn't my girl. However, if she burned Jenny, Bernie would hear an earful from me. Contending with Darla most of my life was good practice.

I eyeballed Gemma in her emerald dress she had purchased with her mother two weekends ago for this occasion. Gem's mom had put two and two together well before her daughter informed her we were a couple, and she'd accepted me right away. Gemma confided her mother was tickled pink to make the drive for a girl's weekend to purchase a dress for her eldest daughter. I hadn't bothered notifying my mom about the big night out for the simple fact that I couldn't disclose to her my date was a woman, hence why I recycled my homecoming dress.

Gem had kept the purchase under lock and key, so I wouldn't snoop and spoil the surprise. I had been convinced she'd wear pants and a blouse like Jenny since I'd never seen Gemma in a dress. When she had stepped out of the bathroom earlier, I couldn't believe my eyes. It was the first time I'd seen her without any clothing or article affiliated with the Cornhuskers.

The four of us had planned this night as the last hoorah before final's week to celebrate the end of freshman year, except for Bernie who was entering her fourth and final year in the fall.

Bernie raised her glass. "A toast, ladies. To surviving your first year! All that's left is passing your finals."

We clinked glasses, and I took a cautious sip of wine. I had to drive us back to Alfrid after seeing *Les*

Mis. Bernie's dad had scored us free box seat tickets and arranged for a limo to pick us up outside the restaurant.

"So, Tegan, what'd you threaten Gemma with?" Jenny's crooked smile showed amusement.

"Not much. Just no sex." I peered across the table at Jenny, whose jaw dangled open.

"Ouch!" Jenny snapped her fingers.

"Oh, don't withhold sex. Make her work for it. Have you read the novel *Exit to Eden*?" Bernie shifted in her seat, crossing her right leg and revealing a provocative slit up the side that had escaped my attention when she'd approached the table. Where did she think she was? On the TV show *Melrose Place*?

I tapped newly manicured nails against the side of my wineglass. "*Exit to Eden*? No, that doesn't ring a bell."

Bernie leaned close. "Are you into exploring? Sexually, that is?"

Um, I was dating a woman, or had she not noticed?

"In what way?" I asked, trying to control my snippiness. Why did Bernie remind me so much of Darla? Was it their *I'm older and know everything so pay attention, rube* airs?

"You know. Dominatrix. Submissives. Sex slaves." She rattled each off while waving a flippant hand in the air as if this was normal dinnertime banter. "I'll lend you my copy."

The overly-gelled waiter appeared with his lecherous grin firmly affixed. "Are you ready to order?"

Gem, true to her Nebraskan roots, ordered a sixteen-ounce rib eye. I got the coconut-crusted fried tiger shrimp. Jenny selected fish and chips, which I was sure was listed on the kid's menu. Bernie put us all to shame by requesting the Chilean sea bass with a miso glaze.

"May I recommend a Chablis for the sea bass?" The waiter held his pen expectantly to add the item to the ticket.

"Ooooh... yes!" Bernie fluttered her lashes.

"Very good." The dude left without making drink recommendations for the rest of us. What went with fish and chips and fried shrimp, though? Beer?

"He seems to like you." I smiled innocently.

"Jimmie? He's harmless." She shrugged off my insinuation.

"You know him?" My voice cracked.

"I come here often with my parents," she confessed with a hint of embarrassment, clueing me in that she wasn't always in charge. I tried picturing Scott Baio's head on her shoulders á la *Bernice in Charge*.

"Bern's dad is the governor's chief of staff," Jenny tossed out as she buttered a piece of bread. "We had lunch with him earlier today."

Bernie scratched the back of her neck, staring down into her drink. Did Miss Perfect have family troubles like the rest of us? Did her parents aim too high for Little Miss Sophistication?

"Do you plan to go into politics?" Gemma placed a hand on my inner thigh, making my skin tingle. Bernie was right about one thing. I shouldn't withhold sex. I slipped my hand into Gem's, enjoying the way she laced her fingers through mine.

"Good question. I'm applying to law schools, but I'm thinking I'll follow in Mom's footsteps. Be a judge."

A politician and a judge for parents. No wonder she knew everything. How had she ended up at Hill University and not Harvard? Surely a story there, but Gemma's nails digging into my palm made it clear tonight wasn't the night to ask. Bernie was picking up the check after all. When she invited us, she had been crystal clear this evening was her treat. I'd never seen a musical before. My family was the bowling alley type, and the closest Gem got to Broadway were high school productions she had reviewed for the local paper because no one else would write about them. Jenny, shocking the hell out of me, loved the theater, and she and her mother had had season tickets since Jenny was a seventh grader. One thing college had taught me so far was not to judge a book by its cover. More and more, I realized the need to reprogram my brain. Of course, it might take a thousand reminders when around Bernie.

"You won't mind lending me your copy of *Exit to*

Eden? I'm curious." I glommed onto my wineglass for liquid courage.

Gemma cleared her throat.

Bernie straightened in her chair. "I'll pop by tomorrow. It'll be a fun, not to mention an incredibly sexy, diversion for when you need a break from cramming for finals."

Jenny elbowed Gem. "You don't know what you're in for." She followed that with a suggestive wink.

THE FOLLOWING DAY, I popped into the library to buy a study guide provided by my professor at the copy center. While I found it slightly absurd the material cost a buck—seriously, was the prof that hard up for dough?—and questioned the legality, I sincerely enjoyed learning about nutrition.

The center was in the basement, in the heart of the fiction classified by the Dewey Decimal System. After my transaction, I found myself wandering through the aisles, browsing the spines of books. While I didn't want to admit it, my eyes were seeking the novel Bernie had suggested. Something about Eden. Had Mr. Dewey broken out erotica when devising his classification?

A computer sat in the corner. I plopped into one of the desk chairs, wiggled the mouse to wake the computer, and typed Eden into the search bar.

"Holy moly," I whispered. There were hundreds of references including the word Eden. Clearly, I had to simplify the search, but I couldn't will my fingers to tap the pertinent keys to spell *porn*. No, *erotica*.

I peeked over my right shoulder. Then my left. Assured that I had the dimly lit corner in the basement to myself, with one eye closed, my right index finger hunted and pecked the correct letters on the keyboard. After submitting the new request, I held my breath, fearful alarms would blare and someone over the loud speaker would shout, "Alert! Alert! A student is looking for porn!"

More titles appeared on the screen, but a cursory glance made it clear I still wasn't successful.

I sighed.

"Having trouble?"

I whipped my head around and nearly fell out of my chair when my eyes laser locked onto Bernie's as they squinted to see the results of my search.

Placing a hand on my heart, I whispered, "You scared the shit out of me." Casually, I clicked on the new search option with the mouse, erasing my previous efforts.

Bernie perched on the edge of the desk, sitting much too close for my liking. She rooted in her mom-like purse. "I was on my way over to drop this off." Bernie fanned the pages of the book, miming it was scorching hot, before dropping it into my lap.

I snatched it up. Low and behold, I now had my

greedy paws on the book I'd been trying to find in the library as if Hill University had been founded by Dr. Ruth. "Thanks."

"Doing research?" she asked.

"What? No. Why?"

She tilted her head, her forehead furrowing in confusion.

I realized she wasn't referring to the novel she'd lent me, but was questioning why I was searching titles on the computer. "Oh, that. Not really. I lost my history textbook, and I was hoping the library had a copy. No such luck," I fibbed.

"That sucks and right before finals. What class are you in?" She leaned back on the heels of her hands, giving me a different view of her curves.

I averted my eyes to my lap. "US."

"I took Western Civ, but I may know someone in your class. You want me to make a few calls?" Her body sprung upright, her cleavage practically smooshed into my face.

"Nah." I waved, scooting my chair back. "I have my notes. I think I can manage. Thanks, though."

She took a notebook out of her bag and scrawled her digits on a blank page. Ripping the page out, she said, "If you change your mind, give me a call. Call me whenever." Bernie stared at me intently as if expecting me to say something. When I didn't, she stood. "I better get going. My study group only has a room for a couple of hours."

I nodded, wondering why she was acting weird. "I should get home. Good luck with finals."

She leaned down and hugged me. "You, too."

Bernie disappeared into the room off to the right, and I ducked behind a stack of books. "What a freak?" *Says the girl searching for erotica in the library.*

CHAPTER FOURTEEN

IT WAS FIVE MINUTES AFTER NOON ON THE first Saturday in May, but Gemma and I still lazed in bed, snuggled under her thick Husker's bedspread. Madonna's "Vogue" played on the radio.

"I wish we had room service." With the tip of my nose, I outlined the butterfly tattoo on Gem's breast.

"Tell me what you want, and I'll sneak it out of the cafeteria." She started to get up, but I yanked her back under the covers.

"No! Stay and keep me warm. I hate that they turned off the heat in the building just because it's springtime."

She laughed. "It's supposed to be seventy today. Although it's probably only in the forties now, and the brick walls don't help with insulation. If you put your footie pajamas on, you'd be toasty warm. Nothing says sexy like footie jammies." She poked my side.

"I'd rather use you."

"Use me?" Gemma's brows waggled.

"You know what I mean."

"I don't." She rolled on top of me and plucked some hair off my cheek. "Explain it to me."

"Can I show you instead?" I rested a finger on her lips.

She playfully bit it and growled. "What if I want to be the one to use you?" She widened her lovely Irish green eyes.

I spread out my arms and went limp under her naked body. "I'm your prisoner. Do with me what you will."

Her knee separated my legs. "I see you've been doing your *Exit to Eden* homework, given to you by Mistress Bernie."

I lifted my head off the pillow to see her face clearly. "Really? You're bringing up Bernie right now?"

Gemma gazed into my eyes, somewhat shocked by my tone. "Why do you dislike her?"

"I don't dislike her." I scoffed.

Gem nestled my chin with her hand. "Teeg."

I couldn't or wouldn't explain that Bernie reminded me of Darla. The hurt still blazed inside. Besides, Gem would point out I was acting irrationally, which I'd already recognized.

"I don't like how she makes me feel. Like a hayseed right off the farm."

I avoided Gem's thoughtful eyes, a feat considering

her face was front and center. I'd witnessed on more than one occasion how Bernie had a soothing effect on everyone else.

"Shouldn't *I* feel like the hayseed? I'm the one from a small town. You grew up in a suburb of Denver," she joked, but the smile fell off her face when she met my teary eyes. "Oh, Tegan, I'm sorry. I didn't mean anything. Please don't cry."

I blotted my eyes with the sheet. "I know. I'm not upset with you."

She cradled me in her arms. "I wish you'd stop putting so much pressure on yourself. No one expects anything from you."

I snorted. "Thanks."

"That came out wrong. I mean all I want from you is for you to be yourself."

"This is me. I'm Spazzy Tegan." I giggled and burbled through the tears.

"I, for one, love Spazzy Tegan." She kissed my forehead. "Even when wiping out in a fancy restaurant." She sang the restaurant line from Sinead O'Conner's song "Nothing Compares 2 U."

"No, not that song. Not after you listened to it on repeat after the Walt Hill debacle."

"But it's a good song. Don't let that ruin it for you." She smiled weakly, understanding she was on thin ice for once. It had taken several weeks for her to fully apologize for overreacting to the Erik situation, and I'd done everything to prevent reigniting her jealousy. Her fear of being left for a man again skated under the surface. I squished my eyes shut. That conversation was for a different day.

"Do you wish I was more like Bernie?"

Gemma flinched. "W-what?"

"Do you wish I was more sophisticated? Shit, even Jenny, the Frisbee golf fanatic, has season tickets to the theater. Until Thursday, I'd never stepped foot inside a theater that didn't sell popcorn."

Gemma propped her head up on her elbow. "And you think that matters to me?" She traced circles on my chest.

Hi, I'm Tegan, and I constantly need confirmation from my girlfriend.

"I'm nothing like your mother. When I say I don't have any expectations of you, I mean it. I don't expect you to graduate at the top of your class. I don't expect you to become filthy rich. I don't expect you to exceed in all aspects of life."

"Ha! She doesn't expect the best from me. She thinks I'm going to fall flat on my face. Mom's banking on that."

"Which is one of the reasons you push yourself to be perfect. I don't want perfect. All I want is to be with you, warts and all."

"I don't have any war—"

Gemma captured my lips with hers, simultaneously silencing my neurotic mind and kindling my sex drive.

"On your stomach," she commanded, taking charge

of the opportunity. "You need a massage. You're stiff as a board and might break in half in the slightest breeze."

"Yes," I whimpered and did as instructed, suppressing a smile. There were some perks to being a nervous Nellie when it came to being Gem's girlfriend.

Gemma kneaded my shoulders with her strong hands. "You want to know something about Bernie?"

I suppressed a groan, enjoying her hands on me.

"Her parents think she's going through a phase and that once she graduates, she'll find a nice young man and settle down."

"She's halfway there with Jenny."

Gemma spanked my bare butt. "Don't make me punish you." Her voice was devoid of a real threat.

"You wouldn't dare!" I said, wondering if I'd like it. I had only leafed through some of the pages in Bernie's book. I had so much to learn in the sexual exploration field.

Gemma's body lowered onto mine, erect nipples gouging my back. She peppered my shoulders with kisses and then, out of the blue, bit my neck hard, but not so hard I didn't like it. Gemma raked my side with her nails.

My breath involuntarily hitched. "That's my punishment? I like it."

Gemma took note and sunk her teeth into my neck again, almost vampire-like. Would there be a mark? That'd be a first, but the thought wasn't upsetting.

Shit, I never understood the fascination with vampire stories, but if any of the books described this sinful joy, sign me the fuck up. Except for the actual ingesting blood—ewww.

"Kiss me," she said with more force than expected.

I swiveled my neck as much as my muscles allowed to meet her request. She nibbled on my lip before her tongue forced its way in, staking claim. Right when I thought she had sated her desire, she upped the passion and force. Her hand separated me below, and Gemma slid inside. I wasn't expecting her to penetrate so soon, but my body tightened around the invasion.

She hammered in and out, breathing heavily. Having the majority of her weight on top of my backside as she fucked me from behind with a fury I hadn't experienced before brought me to a whole new level of sexual frenzy.

"Gemma, I'm so close—"

She slowed her fingers.

"What are you doing?"

"Slowing things down."

"Why?" I tried to suck her fingers deep inside me so I wouldn't lose the sensation.

"Because I like making love to you and we have all day."

She was sweet, no doubt, but at the moment I didn't want sweet Gemma. I wanted to be fucked. Hard.

"Please, don't stop. Not now."

She chuckled in my ear. "Are you begging?"

I looked over my shoulder. "Do I have to?"

Her eyes sparkled. "It might help your cause." She kissed my cheek innocently, as if unaware of my frustration.

I growled. "Please, don't stop. I want you to fuck me."

"Hmmm, methinks I have the upper hand." She laid her head down on my back.

"Upper hand?"

Oddly, the stalling made me want her more, and I sensed my face and tone plainly showed she indeed possessed the winning poker hand.

Sure enough, she picked up on it—she'd have to be a moron not to. "What am I going to do with you?" she asked.

I shook my head, laughing. "I've been telling you what I want. Do I need to get on my knees and beg?"

She blinked, unsure. "I'd never—"

Not letting her finish, I shimmied out from underneath, flopped onto the carpet, and placed my hands together. "Please, I want you to make me come."

Gemma swung her legs over the side of the bed, glorious red bush and cha-cha spread before me. She tried maneuvering me back onto the mattress, but I honed in on the shimmering border of her pussy. The effort caused my tongue to slide out, swiping my lips. I wanted a taste. Fuck, I wanted more than that. And from the glistening proof, so did she. "I think I have a new idea." I gestured to her engorged sex in dire need of attention.

Gemma slowly panned downward, widening her legs. "You like what you see?"

"Oh, yes, I do."

"Then you can't have it." She fastened her legs shut, but her voice was losing its edge.

Oh fuck no. It was time to turn the tables on Gemma's teasing antics.

I shook my head and then wrenched her legs apart. Gem didn't push my mouth away, instead she gripped my head with both hands. "You naughty, naughty girl."

I might have been naughty, but I was also on cloud nine. From Gemma's tensed muscles and moans, she was right there with me.

My tongue dove in, wanting to explore her love channel, inside and out. I stretched my tongue as far as it would go, swirling as if licking a lollypop. Gemma's lollypop.

I glimpsed Gem, head slumping back as far as humanly possible, supporting her upper body with locked arms behind her, carroty mane almost reaching the sheets.

I dove in once more, before replacing my tongue with two eager fingers, pumping slowly, burrowing inside her warmth. Gemma's muscles tightened around me, giving my mouth free rein to skim over her lips.

"Jesus," she muttered.

I jerked my head back, enjoying the view from the floor. "Tell me what you want?"

"I think you're doing it. And then some."

"And then some? You asked for it." I added another finger.

Gemma's eyes popped open and just as quickly glued shut. "Harder."

I pounded her pussy while circling her clit with the pad of my thumb. Somehow, Gemma's head dipped even further back. "Are you doubled-jointed?"

"Hmmm…"

I laughed over the inability to answer a simple question. "You like this?"

"Oh, yes. Bravo."

"What if I stopped?"

Her head whipped up. "No!"

"You did it to me." I slowed my fingers but couldn't bring myself to remove them. Not completely.

"It was wrong of me."

"How wrong?"

"So very, very wrong."

"And?" I increased the tempo again.

"And I plan on making it up to you," she panted.

"And?" I asked again.

"As soon as I can, I will."

"Promise."

"Promise, promise," she squeaked out, barely able to speak.

"You better." Not waiting for a reply, my tongue flicked her clit, and then I sucked it into my mouth.

Gemma let loose a squeal, and I realized she wouldn't be able to muffle her orgasm with a pillow like usual. That revved my raging hormones.

My fingers continued to pump while I stimulated her clit.

Her breathing intensified.

I doubled my efforts.

Gemma's body quivered. Wanting to take her to the orgasm cliff and beyond, I plunged another finger inside, and she said, "Oh, fuck me!"

Her wish was my command. Never before had I inserted four fingers, and with the way Gemma's body responded, I wanted to kick myself for not doing so sooner. She gushed over my hand. Her juddering thighs vibrated my cheeks.

"Fuck, fuck, fuck," she repeated.

It took me a second to comprehend goody-two-shoes Gemma was chanting my favorite word when it came to sex. Shit, this experience was transforming into the screw of a lifetime.

"Oh... I'm coming..." And then she let it out. The scream I'd been dying to hear ever since our first time. It was even better than I imagined. Ironically, she came right when Slash's guitar blared the opening cords to "Sweet Child o' Mine," hopefully drowning out her shriek from others' ears. It was for me and only me. I could have died right then, with a hand inside Gemma and my mouth lapping up her juices, making me the happiest corpse in the world.

Gemma's shaking started to subside, and she held my head in place. I knew before I gave her clit one last flick that she was beyond stimulated, but I couldn't resist. Her body twitched, and she clasped my head tighter, emitting another groan and then, "Jesus, Tegan!"

"That was the first time I heard you scream," I mumbled into her pussy as I inhaled the heady just-fucked scent.

She collapsed onto the bed. "That was unbelievable."

I hopped off the floor, stretching my cramped legs and back. "It was. The fuck of the semester."

"So far, but we aren't done." She tugged me down on top of her. "I promised, promised, remember."

"Don't you need some recovery time?" I cupped her flushed cheek, proud of my efforts.

"Hogwash. I'm not a dude." She hurled me on my back, immediately delving inside. Foreplay wasn't necessary at the moment.

"Thank God for that. Kiss me."

I loved the way Gemma kissed. The emotions expressed with her mouth on mine, her tongue stoking a flame inside only she could ignite.

She drew away, grinning. "The question remains: can you handle four fingers?"

"I'm willing to give it a good old-fashioned college try."

Gem eased in a third finger, allowing for time to adjust.

"More."

She hesitated before easing a pinky finger inside, carefully moving in and out.

"You feel good. All of you." I kissed her again. "Don't stop."

Gemma drilled harder.

My back arched.

"More. More. More!"

"Fingers or harder?" she asked with determined eyes.

"Harder. Go in deep." I closed my eyes in anticipation.

It was like she wanted to reach all the way to my heart to give it a squeeze. My cooch welcomed each thrust, and I was close to exploding.

"Whatever you do, don't stop," I begged.

Someone knocked on the door of our dorm room.

I shook my head and whispered for Gemma to continue.

"Tegan!" my mother hollered from the other side.

Gemma and I froze. She still had all four fingers buried inside me, unmoving.

"Tegan! I hear you in there. What racket are you listening to, young lady? Let me in." Mom whacked the door.

"What's she doing here?" I whispered. It wasn't like her to show up unannounced.

Gemma's face went white as a ghost.

"Don't move. Maybe she'll go away." I'd already been denied one orgasm earlier and was so close now. *Fuck it to hell.*

Gemma's horrified grimace communicated *You can't be serious.* She tried to pull out, but I encircled her wrist, keeping her right where I wanted, and shook my head. "Stay. You feel so good," I quietly pleaded.

"Tegan Raye Ferber! You let me in right now!"

That was the straw that broke Gemma's back, and she freed her fingers before I could say, "Boo!"

Mom—the ultimate buzzkill.

"Just a minute," I chirped as if I hadn't heard her previous rapping on the door. I spun to Gemma. "Quick, light some incense and hop in the shower. Give me five minutes before coming out."

A flash of red scrambled, following my directions. I slipped into PJ bottoms and a crumpled T-shirt that reeked of cigarettes and stale beer from last night's impromptu gin and tonic party that had taken place on Friday instead of our typical Thursday drink-a-thons.

"Mom, what are you doing here?" I said when I swung the door open and gave an exaggerated yawn worthy of an Oscar.

"Were you still in bed?" She tsked. "It's almost one in the *afternoon*." She stressed "afternoon" as if I didn't know it was daytime. Mom shoved past me and shook her head at the carnage in the room. The clothes I'd torn off Gemma and vice versa when we had stumbled into the room at two in the morning were strewn over the carpet, which hadn't been vacuumed for months. Gem and I had fucked like rabbits on and off all morning like we did most weekends, and considering Mom had interrupted our recent caper, I feared the aroma of lesbian sex clung in the air.

She crinkled her nose. "How can you live like this?"

I shrugged and hugged my arms against my tits.

"Get dressed, missy. We're going to lunch."

Her commanding hand gesture annoyed the hell out of me. "What? I have plans with Gemma and some friends."

She took a step back, giving me an eyeful of her *aerobics instructor skinny* body. "What? You don't have time to spend with the woman who brought you into this world on Mother's Day?"

"Mother's Day is a week from Sunday!" I pitched my hands in the air. She'd finally done it. Lost her damn mind. It had only been a matter of time, and she chosen this day to do it.

Gemma walked in wearing jeans and a Nebraska T-shirt. A towel was twisted around her head, and the scent of soap wafted into the room. "Hello, Mrs. Ferber. This is a lovely surprise." Her smile genuine.

"At least someone is happy to see me." Mom leveled disappointed eyes at me.

Gemma shuffled awkwardly. "I should get going."

"What? No. We had plans." I blocked the exit.

"This is how you treat me when I surprise you for Mother's Day? For future reference, surprising me on Mother's Day is your job, not mine." Mom waggled a finger in my face.

"It's not Mother's Day! I've never missed one yet, and you can't change the day on a whim and expect everyone to fall in line."

She bared her teeth in an attempt to smile.

I didn't budge.

Gemma eyed me and then my mother with a pained expression, giving the impression she wished she had Star Trek powers and could beam out of the room.

Mom wheeled to Gemma and asked in a syrupy voice, "Would you like to join us for lunch?"

"I wouldn't want to intrude on this *special* day." She tripped over the word *special*, not that Mom acknowledged it. She was a pro at pretending. Most crazy people were.

I wanted to scream, but couldn't blame Gemma completely. Mom and I had placed her on shaky ground right in the midst of a Ferber family feud.

"It's no intrusion. Besides it's the only way I'll get my daughter to spend Mother's Day with me."

I chomped down on my bottom lip and counted to ten. "I need to shower before we leave."

Mom motioned for me to go ahead.

Again, I stifled a retort. This was my place. Not hers. Besides, Daddy was the one who paid the bills. The majority of them, at least. Half of the aerobics classes my mom taught were at the community center, and she didn't receive any compensation. Mom's real contribution to the family was to ground our self-esteems to a pulp. My older brother had skipped the most recent Thanksgiving, Christmas, and New Year's to be with his girlfriend in New Hampshire. Glen had busted his butt all four years in high school to receive an academic scholarship. Leave it to my brother to plan for the future, and now he was a free man, while Mom could pop into my life whenever she desired.

If Gemma wasn't alone with my mother, I would have stayed in the shower the remainder of the day. I was fairly certain the bathroom door was sturdy enough to withstand an attack even from my freakishly super-fit mom.

I left the safety of the bathroom to discover Gemma and Mom laughing. When they saw me, both immediately clammed up.

"What's so funny?" I asked, trying not to sound bitter.

"Oh, nothing," Gemma said with a sense of caution.

"I was just enlightening Gemma about the time

you peed your pants during the Christmas play." Mom chortled.

Gemma's thin-lipped smile got my hackles up.

"I was five!"

"I remember it like it was yesterday. The wet spot just grew and grew." With her hands, Mom mimicked the expanding wetness and then slapped her knee. "I even got it on VHS. Next time, I'll bring it." Mom prodded Gemma in the side.

"You will not!" I flipped on the hair dryer to drown out her rebuttal.

To her credit, Gemma squirmed in the desk chair as if about to be electrocuted.

Mom perched on the edge of my bed while Gemma straddled my desk chair, arms draping over the plastic backrest. Only six inches separated them, and from Gemma's locked jaw I sensed my redhead was bursting to bolt. Mother patted Gemma's knee and signaled for her to bring it in for what I assumed was another humiliating episode from my childhood.

Seconds later, Mom bent over laughing and Gemma peeked to see if I was watching. I caught her eye, and she smiled apologetically as she pretended, hopefully, to enjoy the joke.

I raked my hair back into a scrunchie and said, "Are you two ready?"

Gemma leaped up as if a rattler had latched onto her creamy ass. That made me laugh. Mom laughed along with me even though I was certain she had no idea what was so funny.

"Where are we going?" I asked.

"Bennigan's," Mom said.

"That's an hour—"

Gemma pinched the back of my arm to silence my protest.

"Don't blame me. You insisted on moving to this tiny hamlet with only an Applebee's. I can't stand Applebee's."

I didn't see much difference between the two restaurants, but what the fuck? My Saturday was already ruined. Why not waste two hours trapped in a car with my mother. *Kill me now, Lord.*

We stepped into the eerily quiet dorm lobby, and the female resident assistant manning the front desk flinched when she locked eyes on my mother.

"Mom, how'd you get upstairs?" I asked.

"Oh, Broom Hilda finally saw it my way." The play on the pronunciation of Brunhilda got her derision across. "Can you imagine she tried to tell me I needed your permission to go upstairs? That would have ruined the surprise. And needing my daughter's permission? That'll be the day." She tutted.

Gemma and I shared a *good grief* look, and I made a mental note to apologize for my mom's behavior, a habit I'd hoped to leave behind when I left the nest. Glen had the right idea—move far away and never come back. Never ever.

In the lot out front of the dorm, Mom motioned to her Ford abandoned haphazardly in the loading zone. It was a step better than her taking the space designated for handicapped motorists, which I had personally witnessed more times than I cared to admit. Oddly, for a fitness nut, she always scoped out and claimed the primo parking spots.

Jenny and Bernie approached the building's entrance, and my heart nearly lurched out of my body when I spied their conjoined hands. Jenny must have registered my freak-out face because she dropped Bernie's hand lightning fast.

"Mrs. Ferber. How are you?" Jenny plastered on the smile she reserved for parents and professors.

"I'm well." Mom glommed onto her purse that hung over her left shoulder as if we were in a seedy New York neighborhood. "Who's this?" She got a load of Bernie, who wore her jean jacket unbuttoned, showing off a white cotton T-shirt with *Pussy Pride* scrawled in permanent black marker. Inwardly, I groaned. Gemma and I casually took a step away from our friends.

"This is… a classmate, Bernie," Jenny said, her eyes darting from me to my mom and back again.

Bernie stuck her mitt out, and Mom hesitated one moment too long to shake. I could see pain in Bernie's eyes. She probably expected to be shunned by strangers in this mostly white town, but by a friend's mom? Bernie remained mum and uttered, "Nice to meet you, Mrs. Ferber." Her clipped words made it clear she was being polite for my sake.

"The pleasure is all mine." Mom had recovered her fakeness. "We're going to lunch. Would you girls like to join us?"

Gemma and I now stood behind my mom, and we exchanged a *What the hell?* look.

"That's so sweet of you. But we have a study session," Jenny said much too quickly. I added two more names to my apology list. I wasn't sure if my mom was being a snob because of Bernie's race or sexual identity. More than likely, both factored into the equation. For a brief spell during my sophomore year of high school, I had dated a Hispanic boy named Cirilo. My mother had thought it hilarious to call him Cilantro behind his back.

"Good for you. Tegan was still in bed just minutes ago. Goodness knows what kind of grades she'll bring home this semester. Anything lower than a B minus and she'll be moving back home for good." She laughed as if that had been the plan all along. Send me to college for a year and watch me crash and burn.

If this was the rule, I had never heard of it. Not that I was in any danger. The lowest grade I was expecting this semester was an A minus.

Jenny and Bernie excused themselves, and I glanced over my shoulder and mouthed sorry. Bernie accepted it graciously with a flick of her hand. Jenny's eyes locked on the back of my mom's head, and I imagined she was pretending to be a sniper. Mom better hope Jenny and the resident assistant didn't stumble upon her in a dark alley.

I sighed. Good old Mom, always making an impression. How in the world did my father put up with it?

Gemma eased us into a safe conversation during the car ride, which revolved mostly around *The Joy Luck Club*. Mom's book club had read Amy Tan's novel last month, which she had raved about on the phone when we spoke during one of our scheduled weekly calls. Every Wednesday night at eight, I called collect to check in. Knowing Gemma, she'd probably overheard our conversation and realized this would be an excellent icebreaker. My redhead was ever so diplomatic.

I added *thank Gemma later tonight* to my mental check sheet of damage control. My lips curled up, and I was sure my cheeks turned red-hot thinking of the way or ways I'd thank Gemma. I pretended to fix my hair in the side mirror to hide that I was aflame with desire.

Gemma politely grilled Mom with questions from the back seat of the Taurus station wagon, which I affectionately called The Jelly Bean on Wheels. I sat shotgun and wished I actually had one. Not for the first time. Earlier mom had been rude—no, downright vulgar to Bernie—and yet most people only saw the person she pretended to be. I bet she never made a disparaging remark during book club, but if I brought any of the characters over for dinner, I'd get an earful afterward.

WE PULLED into Bennigan's parking lot, and I sprinted from the car. "I have to pee," I said over my shoulder. I didn't, but I desperately needed a moment to get my shit together to be able to sit down for a meal with my mother without plunging a dull knife into her chest. Or mine.

Gemma waltzed into the bathroom as I splashed cold water on my face. She leaned against the counter. "You can do this. One lunch and then home."

"How do you do it?" I asked.

"What?"

"Be nice to everyone. You saw how she treated Bernie." I dabbed my face with a rough paper towel, blotting away the water and guilt for my secret thoughts about Bernie. "And listening to her talk about *The Joy Luck Club*—her empathy. Please. When the Gulf War started two years ago, do you know what she said?"

Gemma shook her head.

"Let's bomb the hell out of the little brown people and show them who's boss."

Gemma hugged her chest and peered down at her feet.

I peeked in the mirror, assessing my colorless face. Pinching my cheeks to add a healthy pink, I flipped around to Gemma and said, "Happy face on. Let's eat."

Gemma motioned with her hand for me to walk ahead.

"Coward." I grazed her cheek with a finger on my way out of the restroom.

Mom sat at a four-person booth along the back wall with a clear view of the front door, her usual preference. She always acted like she was constantly embroiled in the board game Risk, vying for ways to conquer territories, or in her case, people. My parents were solidly middle class. This suited my father, an airline pilot. Mom, the aerobics instructor, didn't crave money—just respect and admiration.

"There you two are. I thought you'd fallen in, Tegan," she joked and was about to launch into what I assumed was another mortifying childhood story.

"What shall we order?" I scooped up the menu and started listing possibilities. "Chicken tenders, ribs, fish and chips, the Monte Cristo—"

Mom banged a fist on the table like a judge silencing a courtroom. "Absolutely not. A sandwich drenched in batter, fried, and then coated with powdered sugar. Not only will it kill you, but it's disgusting. I recommend the grilled chicken salad."

I nodded, pretending to agree.

The waitress, dressed in a green Bennigan's polo and acid-washed jeans from the 80s, arrived. "You ready to order?" Her bubbly personality practically fizzed onto the floor as she popped her gum.

I tilted my head for Mom to go first. "Grilled chicken salad."

I nudged Gemma's leg, and she requested the French dip. I hadn't seen that on the menu and nearly changed my mind.

Bubbles rounded to me, her mouth forming an airhead O. "The Monte Cristo, please." I handed the book-like menu to the waitress.

Mom straightened her spine. "She'll have the grilled chicken salad."

"No, I won't. The Monte Cristo."

Bubbles furrowed her pale brow and sought my mother's clarification. "So the Monte Cristo or salad?"

"Monte Cristo." I locked eyes with Bubbles.

Mother took a deep breath and then shrugged.

The waitress dashed for safety.

"A moment on the lips—"

"Forever on the hips." I smiled sweetly. "I know."

"I was going to say your tits." She motioned to my double-Ds. Even before she became obsessed with exercise, Mom hadn't been large. Since becoming a Jane Fonda wannabe, she didn't have any tits at all, and most never saw her washboard stomach. It was her chest, or lack of one, that stood out, so to speak, and I gathered from all the cracks she made about my breasts, it irked the woman. Was this why I was so neurotic all the time? To avoid upsetting my mom even when she wasn't present?

Mom innocently gulped her water.

Under the table, Gemma placed a hand on my knee. "I haven't seen Mr. Ferber since moving-in day. How is he?"

Mom's face clouded over momentarily until the fakeness seeped back in. "He's good. Flying everywhere. With two kids in college now… well, you know." She pursed her lips, and it felt like her most honest reaction of the day so far.

Were my parents in trouble financially? We'd never had a lot of money, but we'd never had to worry about money either. At least I didn't think we did. Did Glen guess this? Was that why he'd worked so hard for a scholarship? All along I thought he just wanted to escape my mother's grasp. Not that there was a lot of fighting in our house, partly because my father was gone most days of the week and everyone else, including Mom, had lives outside of the house.

Gemma bobbed her head, seeming much wiser than her nineteen years.

"How's Glen?" I asked.

"He's not coming home for summer." She stated the news as if she were reporting the local high school football scores.

Glen's determination to stay away vexed Mom, considering the lengths she went to portraying her mother-of-the-century image—the perfect mom whose kids didn't appreciate everything she did for them. I had heard it enough times during my nineteen years.

"I got an internship in Denver this summer," I added fuel to the fire.

However, it brought a smile to her face. Denver was only a forty-five-minute commute. "Where?"

"At a hospital."

"You'll be changing bedpans all summer?" The glee on her face was off-putting.

"It'll be a good experience for me," I spoke to my lap.

"Does this internship pay?" she asked. Glen and I weren't expected to chip in on bills, but we had to pay for our own fun, and we both had started working during high school.

I shook my head. "It's only a few hours a week and will look good on my resume. But I have another movie theater job lined up for the summer—also in Denver."

"My, you will be busy." She smacked her lips.

"Gemma got an internship with the football team."

Mom asked Gemma, "In Denver?"

"Yes."

"On the coaching staff?" It was hard to decipher if she was kidding or clueless. Maybe it was a glimmer of hope that she wasn't as old-fashioned as I thought.

Gemma laughed. "I wish. I'll be a gopher in the marketing department. I'll probably spend my summer fetching coffees."

Mom drummed her fingers on the tabletop. "Everyone has to start somewhere. At least you won't be cleaning shit." She stopped and then asked, "Where will you be living?"

This was the thorny subject I'd hope to push off for a couple more weeks. Gem and I had reserved an apartment for the summer, but we weren't moving until June first. I had planned to divulge the news to Mom on June second.

"Two other girls will be in Denver, so the four of us got an apartment just outside of the city." There was no way I was going to tell her Jenny and Bernie were the other girls. I leaned back for the waitress to set down my infamous sandwich. The fried bread, jam, and powdered sugar made my mouth water.

Mom hesitated until the server left. "All four of you will be in one apartment. That should be interesting." Again she sipped her water and said under her breath, "It's better that way." She forked some salad into her mouth. My usually energetic mother looked frail and alone. It was as if I was getting a glimpse of my mother twenty years from now. I shuddered.

Gemma and I both heard her, but when I glanced at Gemma she gave a quick shake of the head. Probably right. This lunch was fraught with enough tension. I didn't need to rock a boat that'd already sprung several leaks.

"How big is the apartment? I'm assuming you two are ready to have rooms of your own after living on top of each other for the past nine months."

Gemma choked on her water, and I had to force my jaw upward with my hand.

"Uh, it's much more spacious than what we're used to. It'll seem like a mansion." A two-bedroom mansion. Even though it was outside of Denver, Gem and I couldn't afford a larger place. Besides, we wanted to continue sleeping in the same bed—hopefully one larger than the ones in our dorm.

Gemma's relieved sigh settled the guilt whirling inside for lying by omission.

We ate in silence, fortunately. My sandwich was much better than I envisioned, especially because I'd ordered it to piss off my mother. Powdered sugar on a sandwich—weird. After one bite I was singing a different song to the tune of *Holy jamoly this is scrumptious and sinful*. And I'd been on a roll when it came to sin. Another thing I had no intention of confessing to my Bible-thumping mother.

After Gemma demolished her French dip, she excused herself to use the restroom. I ogled her tight ass out of the corner of my eye. Maybe I should start running if it means I'd get an ass like that. Of course, Gem said she liked my curves, and Mom loved to point out I had curves coming out the ying-yang. Should I share about all the hours Gemma spent caressing, kissing, and licking my curves, especially my ta-tas?

Mom cleared her throat. Did she catch me checking out Gem's ass or guess the commentary running through my lesbian sex-crazed mind?

I peeked at her face, but she had her eyes trained on the water glass she cleaved with both hands. "Are you good friends with Jenny?"

"Yeah, she's great." It was easy to guess where this conversation was heading, but I thought if I tried being extra positive, I could head her off the scent.

"I don't think she's good for you."

I squared my shoulders but managed to say cheerily, "Why's that?"

"You know why." She leveled her frosty blue eyes on mine.

"Not sure I do." I innocently slanted my head, giving my best puppy dog impression.

Mom leaned over the table and whispered, "She's a lesbian."

"How do you know?" I spoke softly.

"It's obvious."

"How?"

"Oh, please." She waved her hand. "I've protected you so there's no way you'd notice when it comes to these types, but most people can tell with one look."

It took everything I had not to explode into laughter. Moments ago, I had been checking out my girlfriend's ass right under her nose.

"Associating with people like that isn't good. Especially in the long run. People might confuse you—"

"They'll think I'm a lesbian." Oh man, it felt good to say it, even though I was only messing with her.

She put a finger on her lips. "Shush!"

Gemma approached the table and hesitated. She'd make an excellent people barometer. One whiff and she had a good sense of the situation. Cautiously she retook her seat, leaving more space between us than previously. Her return nipped the conversation in the bud, but it played over and over in my mind during the rest of the meal.

CHAPTER FIFTEEN

THE CAR RIDE BACK PASSED ALMOST IN complete silence. Observing Mom's body hunched over the steering wheel and the way I sat in my seat with my back to her, Gemma didn't engage either of us in idle conversation. Occasionally, I regarded the side mirror and spied Gemma's complacent face taking in the scenery. Once, she caught me staring and winked so only I could see. Her daring move emboldened me, and I slipped my right hand along the side of my chair and wiggled my fingertips to get her attention. Gemma rested her head against the back of my seat and gave my hand a quick squeeze.

Mom dropped us off in front of the dorms. Her eyes gaped like they were a million miles away. I sensed I was missing something. A smidgeon of remorse forced me to stand outside and wave like an idiot until she was out of sight.

"You okay?" Gemma bumped my shoulder when it was safe.

"I don't know. That was really weird." I continued to stare at the road where her car had once been. She was heading toward the center of town, not the highway. Why?

A frown marred Gemma's face. This made the sick feeling in my gut churn into full-blown worry.

"What?" I asked.

Gemma gazed at the storm clouds over the foothills. "I think she's extremely unhappy."

"My dad travels a lot," I said as if trying to pinpoint the source of unhappiness. "And I'm not at home anymore."

"That could be it." She about-faced on her heel to go inside.

I trailed her inside the lobby. "Do you think it's something more?"

"No idea. I've only interacted with her a few times. But to show up insisting it was Mother's Day—that's bizarre."

"What's your gut say?"

Gemma avoided answering by saying, "Speaking of guts. How's your stomach handling the fried powdered sugar and jam goodness? Thanks for offering a bite— oh wait, you didn't."

"Me? You knew I wanted some of your French dip and you scarfed it down before I could say a word."

"How was I supposed to know you wanted some?"

"I want everything of yours. Haven't I made that clear?" I scanned her face to see if she caught I was only partly teasing. Her knowing smile was enough confirmation.

We made it to the stairwell and our footsteps cast unsettling echoes.

"Sorry about not sharing, but what was I supposed to do? No one was talking. I'm the quiet one, remember?" Gemma jerked a thumb at her chest, emphasizing the point. "I had no choice but to scarf the sandwich."

"When I'm around my mother, I'm not myself—"

Gemma butted in. "No, you aren't. You're filled to the brim with anger and resentment. It's not good, and it's awkward to be around."

"Am I that bad?" I reached for the handrail and pirouetted to see her face two steps below.

"Yes." Her honesty stung, but I couldn't lay blame.

I then dared to ask the question I already knew the answer to but prayed I was wrong. "Do you think my mom picks up on it?" I rested my head against the cement wall in the stairwell.

"Was that rhetorical?"

I sighed.

"Put it this way. The waitress picked up on it, and she's not exactly rocket scientist material."

I scratched at a fleck of peeling paint. "It's not that I want to hurt my mom's feelings. Most of the time, I don't know how to act because she can be so

combative and rude. Like the comment about my tits."
I jiggled the girls.

Gemma hopped up one step and put a hand on my shoulder. "I know. But maybe you can try a little harder to not let her get to you. At the end of the day, she'll always be your mom. It's up to the two of you to decide what type of relationship you want: friendly or combative. Or hell, somewhere in the middle would be better than all-out war."

"Why are you always so wise?" Of course, family situations were easier for Gemma. Her parents accepted her completely. The way they'd reacted to Gemma coming out was proof Gem's family was the opposite of mine.

"Some of us were born this way." She ducked in time, preventing my hand from walloping her head. "Ha! Too slow."

"I'll show you slow. The last one to the room has to do the other's laundry for a month." I shot up the remaining two flights with Gemma hot on my heels. Somehow, she reached the exit first, blocking me. "You cheated!" I accused.

"How?" She bent over to catch her breath. "You set the rules and took off without waiting for us both to start at the same time. *You*, my dear, cheated."

The stairwell was deserted on the fifth floor. Most residents on our floor used the elevator; however, I was convinced the contraption was on its last leg and I preferred the exercise. "Come here." I tugged the collar of her shirt to pull Gemma into a kiss, while at the same time backing her against the wall. It was the type of kiss that said in less than three minutes we would be naked and fucking.

The door creaked. "Well, well, well... you two can't keep your hands off each other, can you?" April's gravelly tone assaulted my ears.

This was the second time April had stumbled upon us kissing. The first time on Walt's Hill caused me, Play-it-Safe Tegan, to go into a full-fledged panic, and I nearly wrecked my relationship. But I was getting used to the idea of people knowing about Gem and me. Mostly.

I squared my shoulders and was about to say, "Jealous?" but then Erik appeared around the door with an odd expression. Mostly shock, but there was another emotion underlying the disbelief. I couldn't put my finger on it, though.

"You see, Erik. That's what I mean. You've been barking up the wrong tree this whole time." April tsked. "You'd think you two would be more discreet. What will everyone think?" April scouted over one shoulder and scrutinized the stairwell. "Safe, this time. But what about the next?"

April wasn't entirely innocent when it came to liaisons with women. Although, I was fairly certain her fling with Jenny was more for the experience, not love or desire to be with a girl. Of course, I would never out her publicly. That went against my lesbian code.

Without April taking note, Gemma moved to shield me. "Hi, Erik. How are you?" She acted like they were buds, which I assumed was for my benefit. An attempt to ease the awkwardness from the situation. I saw Erik in class, but I'd been intentionally keeping him away from Gem. April monopolizing his time helped immensely.

"G-good," he stammered. "You?"

"Not bad."

"Let's go, Erik. I think we've seen enough." April led him by the hand as they descended the stairs.

Erik rubbernecked over his shoulder. His eyes moved to Gemma and then to me. "See ya in class, Tegan." He bowed his head slightly, giving the impression of a man walking to his own execution.

I hustled Gemma into the deserted hallway and whispered, "What's with today? All the weirdness?"

"You okay?"

Inside our room, I let loose. "Gemma! Stop asking me that every time we get busted." I crossed my arms and leaned against the closet doors. "It wasn't the best timing, but it was bound to happen, really."

"Why's that?" she asked.

"Because I can't keep my hands off you." I swept her into my arms with too much force, and when we collided, we both let out a rush of air. My head conked against the door. "Sorry." I rubbed the soreness.

"I don't mind." She scraped a blonde strand off my cheek. "The bruises are well worth it."

"You make it sound like I abuse you." I laughed.

"You're kinda hard on both of us. How's your head?"

"Luckily, I have a thick skull. Now, where were we this morning before being so rudely interrupted?"

A sinful hunger glowed in Gemma's eyes. "I don't remember the exact position, but I believe you were on the bed."

I moved toward the bed and flopped down on top of my floral bedspread. "Like this?" I tipped my head to the side to see her reaction.

Gemma put a forefinger over her mouth, examining my position. "Not quite. If memory serves correctly, you were naked."

"Right." I sat up and shed my shirt.

"Getting warmer," Gemma said.

"I'm sure you are." I winked. "It'd be faster if you helped."

"And miss the show? No way." Gemma hauled a desk chair to the middle of the room.

"So that's how it's going to be?" I rose and approached.

"Now who's stalling?" Gemma waggled a finger.

I batted her hand to the side and mounted her lap.

"Seems like it'll be hard to strip while sitting down." She fondled my ass.

I leaned into her chest. "This has been such a strange day."

"It really has. What can I do to make you feel better?"

"A cup of tea would be nice."

She beamed. "Of course." Gemma summoned me to stand.

I kicked off my sneakers and climbed under my bed covers. I loved that Gemma didn't mind my drastic mood change one bit. If I was in her shoes, I may have been slightly perturbed by the sudden switch from raging hormones to making tea, but Gem was like no other person I'd ever met. She really cared about me.

"Gemma?"

"Yeah?" She had her back to me.

"I really do love you."

She swiveled her head and studied me over her shoulder. "I know."

This made me laugh. "I love that about you."

Gemma added honey and then handed over a mug. "What?"

"Your quiet confidence."

"Only you see it fully."

"That's why I love it." I sipped the chamomile tea. "You're turning me into a tea fiend."

Her brow crinkled. "I'm not sure the words *tea* and *fiend* go hand in hand."

"Only you would say such a thing. But shit, this stuff is like crack. Before I met you, I could count on one hand how many cups of tea I'd ever had."

Gemma clutched a mug with both hands and held

it under her chin, savoring the sweet steam. "What do you think today was about?"

"I've been wracking my brain, trying to figure it out. My mom is an oddball, but to show up unannounced insisting we celebrate Mother's Day a week early is more than strange. It's like she needed confirmation of some type. That we're still a family or I'm still her daughter."

The phone rang.

"Don't answer that!" I said, a peculiar sense of dread settling in the pit of my stomach.

Gemma shrugged. She wasn't a phone person and her parents usually called every Monday night. "More than likely it's Jenny," she said.

The phone continued to trill. On the seventh ring the answering machine clicked on. It was then I realized the blinking light indicating we had messages.

The message Gemma and I had crafted our first day blared. I narrated the majority of it, but Gem had surprised me when she piped in to say her own name. Now, her sweet voice sounded so young, and it was hard to imagine that happened nine months ago. She'd transformed from the quiet small-town girl into a confident woman—the woman I loved.

Last August seemed so long ago, but in the grand scheme of things, it was a drop in the bucket. But my first year of college had changed me more than my previous eighteen years.

Months ago, I didn't know love like this existed. I

thought couples mostly existed out of the fear of being alone. That was why I'd dated Josh. Everyone else had a relationship or wanted one, so I kept him around.

As I sipped Gemma's tea, I understood the depth of love. The desire to be near the person. Did my parents experience this type of love? My father was hardly home, and Mom kept herself insanely busy. Was my absence from home triggering the crazy in my mother? Or was something else happening?

The machine beeped, but the caller didn't leave a message.

One minute later, the phone rang again.

Gemma raised a worried brow over her mug. "I think we should answer."

She didn't move a muscle until I gave a quick nod. The dread intensified.

"Hello?" Gemma's voice was friendly, but strong as if expecting terrible news. "Just a second." She covered the phone with a palm and whispered it was Glen.

My brother never called me at school, and I hadn't spoken to him since last summer. We wrote letters once in a blue moon, but calling long distance was way too expensive for our budgets.

I motioned for the receiver. "Hi, Glen."

"Tegan. Have you heard from Mom?" The fact that he didn't start with typical phone pleasantries made my stomach somersault.

"Yeah, today. What's up?"

"Are you sitting down?"

I looked to make sure, even though I'd been propped up in bed for some time. "Yes, why?"

"How did Mom sound when you spoke?" he fished.

"We went to lunch together. She was... well, like Mom."

Glen was silent. I was the impulsive one; Glen the thinker.

"Glen! What's going on?" I twirled the phone cord around a finger.

"Dad's worried. She left the house on Friday and hasn't been home."

"Friday? And you're just calling me now?"

"He didn't call me until this morning."

"Why didn't he call me?" And then I remembered I'd been out most of the afternoon. The messages on the machine were probably from him.

"He's been trying." My usually aloof brother sounded exasperated.

"Okay, what's got your panties in a bunch?" I tried to sound lighthearted, but it was difficult with the lump the size of a plum in my throat.

"Dad told Mom he wants a divorce," he said with forced calm.

"W-what?" I stuttered. "That's why she showed up here insisting it was Mother's Day." I rolled my eyes. Mom would never declare she needed help—she'd find a way to seek it without verbalizing it.

Gemma sat down, concern etched into her ashen face.

"Mother's Day? Isn't that next month?" Glen asked.

"It's a week from tomorrow. You better put a card in the mail." I gasped for breath. "Why did Daddy ask for a divorce?" I tried to keep my voice even, but I was freaking out inside.

Glen remained quiet for a bit and then sighed. "Dad was pretty tight-lipped about that part. He said it was for the best."

"I know she's difficult… but divorce?"

"Hey, it's the nineties. We're lucky they didn't divorce when we were kids. We never had to shuffle back and forth between houses." My older brother was doing his best to put a positive spin on things for my sake. Maybe for his own as well. "Did Mom say where she was going when she left?" Panic underlined his words.

"You don't think—?" I gripped Gem's hand, trying to comprehend how my usually frigid mother would fall to pieces.

"Of course not! Reel in the crazy, Tegan. Dad—we—just want to make sure she's okay." His tone was firm.

I eyed the ceiling. "You know, after she dropped us off, she drove toward the center of town. Maybe she went to a hotel."

"Us?" He sounded curious.

"My roommate joined us."

"Oh." He seemed disappointed it wasn't a boy. Little did he know.

"I can go to the hotels. See if she's staying in one."

"Would you?" His forced calm returned. "I'll call Dad. Call him as soon as you know anything." Glen hung up.

By the time I'd filled Gemma in, the phone rang again.

"Hi, ladybug," Dad said.

"Hi, Daddy." I didn't know what else to say.

"Glen said you had lunch with Mom today."

I filled him in on the details.

He sighed. "Promise me if you find her, you'll call right away. It's probably best if you don't approach her, though. She's angry with me, and I don't want her taking it out on you. Just look for her car in the parking lot."

The shit must have really hit the fan when he asked for a divorce.

"O-kay," I stammered.

"I'm sorry to put you and Glen in the middle." His voice was more than exhausted.

"It's okay," I said without thinking. It wouldn't be okay for my father. He'd always gone above and beyond to keep their marital issues private. Whenever Mom tried to drag one of us into things, he put the kibosh on it.

We said our goodbyes, and I braced myself for operation "Find Mom."

"You want me to go with you?" Gemma stood, not waiting for an answer.

I didn't move.

Gemma squatted and cradled my hand. "You can stay here. I'll look for her. I know her car—what do you call it, The Jelly Bean?"

My gaze ping-ponged around the room. Gemma's collected voice sounded like it came from a different planet. One where everything made sense, and at the moment nothing in my life made much sense.

"They're getting divorced." I remembered the hell my best friend in elementary school went through when her parents divorced. The custody battle. Traveling back and forth on weekends and holidays. Surely it wouldn't be as bad as that now that Glen and I were adults.

"I know, sweetheart." She patted my thigh. "If you want to stay here, Jenny and I can search for your mom."

I shook my head. "No, I think I should go."

"Alone?"

"God, no. Come on. Let's go find her."

CAPTIVES OF LOVE

CHAPTER SIXTEEN

MOTHER'S DAY ARRIVED. THE REAL ONE. I hadn't seen Mom since learning of the impending divorce. However, we had made arrangements for the celebration on the phone a few days ago. Neither of us mentioned that we'd already celebrated a pseudo holiday, and we didn't broach the D subject. I wasn't even sure Mom was aware I knew, although she slyly inserted that Daddy wouldn't be around much. That was how she'd put it. Maybe that was her code for "Your father and I are getting divorced."

When Gemma and I had discovered her car at the Best Western near the university, I called Dad as instructed. He must have convinced her to come home, because when I called for our typical Wednesday night chat, she answered on the second ring, per usual.

"You ready for Mother's Day part two?" Gemma snuggled against my naked chest.

"Honestly?" I wrapped her up in my arms, nearly smothering her with my tits.

"Yeah," she mumbled happily.

"I'm dreading it. I wish you could go with me. Provide a protective layer."

She sighed and readjusted her head on my chest to peer into my eyes. "I wish I could."

Gem's parents and baby sister were arriving in a few hours. I'd yet to meet her sister.

"I'll be there in spirit." With her finger, she drew a heart on my chest.

"I know. And I'm sorry I won't be able to meet your baby sis, Bridget."

"Next time. She wants to meet you."

"Does she know about us?" I made sure my voice didn't betray any sense of panic.

"Nope. Just that we're buddies. Not sure my parents mentioned anything to her, and I know I haven't. She's only thirteen."

"Ah, too young to corrupt." I kissed the top of her forehead.

"Way too young."

"What age is appropriate to blab you're gay?"

Gem buttressed her chin on a bent elbow. "Good question. I think someone your age."

I twisted my hip bone into her stomach. "Are you implying I'm old?"

"Nope. But I have no issues corrupting you." Gemma manipulated a nipple with her tongue.

"In that case, corrupt away."

"Not sure I like that phrasing. Like I changed you." She snaked a hand down my side and back up again, setting all my nerve endings ablaze. I couldn't remember the last time we had slept in pajamas. Nakedness helped with our ritualistic early morning romps. Who in the fuck needed an alarm clock to get going in the morning when sharing a bed with a hot redhead? It was barely after seven in the morning, and both of us were wide-awake, raring to go.

"You want to quibble, right now, about my phrasing?" I pushed my head into the feather pillow.

"What thoughts should I focus on?" She sucked my furrowed nipple into her mouth, hardening it.

"Nothing. No bad thoughts should be coursing through your brain with my nipple in your mouth." My breath hitched.

"Duly noted. Do impure thoughts count as bad thoughts?" She peppered the base of my throat with soft kisses.

"What do you think?" An electric current zinged throughout my body.

"You're the one making up the rules." She nipped my earlobe.

I brought her lips to mine. "Enough chitchat. Get to work," I added playfully, waggling my eyebrows.

Gemma kissed me.

My hands roamed down her spine, landing on her ass. I cupped both cheeks with my palms, yanking her into my love zone.

Gem emitted a hungry groan.

I responded by pulling her even closer as if trying to merge both our pussies permanently. Her wetness slickened my thigh, forcing a primal reaction to spur our grinding pace all the while deepening our kiss.

"Sometimes it almost hurts to crave you this much. Like I'm going to die without your touch," I said.

Gemma's upper body hovered over mine. "I know what you mean. I can't imagine spending one night away from you." She continued to stroke her clit against mine. "I'm not looking forward to spending two weeks apart after finals."

"Let's make love like it's our last time." The words burbled out before I had time to contemplate the meaning.

She smiled wanly, in tune with the inner panic roiling through my mind. "It won't be, but I like the idea." Gemma recaptured my mouth, and I melted into the kiss and moment. Somehow, Gem's efforts made it feel like our first kiss all over again, recapturing my heart and soul.

She intensified her efforts with more aggression than normal, as if staking her claim forever. Her teeth sank into my bottom lip, tugging slightly. The sensation reverberated throughout my body.

"I love how you make me feel," I panted.

Gem repositioned, straddling my midsection, her ginger hairs tickling my stomach. Her emerald eyes feasted on my nakedness, devouring every inch. It was as if I could see the thoughts flashing through that wonderful brain of hers. The intensity in her face may have scared others, but I loved it when Gemma dominated me with her desire. Claimed my body for her pleasure. Giving her pleasure doubled mine. From the ardor in her eyes, I had a feeling this time I'd triple it.

Slowly, Gemma's mouth inched lower and concentrated on the area below my belly button and above my pubic hair, leaving a wet zigzagging trail on my skin. Her tongue didn't have a set pattern, but no matter. It wasn't the method that was driving me mad with yearning. It was the gorgeous woman asserting her right on my body.

My woman.

I loved the sound of that, even if only said in my head.

I reached for her head, curling my fingers into her red hair. "Oh, Gem," I moaned.

She continued kissing and licking as she made her way to my pussy. My nerve endings weren't on fire. They were beyond bursting. Her teeth grazed my pubic hair, and my legs instantly widened further in preparation. Without speaking, we both moved up on the bed so Gemma would have the room she needed to fuck me. We'd done this dance many times over the past few months, and it never seemed rehearsed. Always fresh. New. Exciting.

"I love eating your pussy." She pushed her face into the wetness as if showering in my love.

Each word caused my sex to beat as if making music only for Gemma's ears.

The burgeoning longing down below surged with each lick. She knew I wanted her mouth on me. Her tongue to part my lips, dip inside, and then focus on my clit. Gemma inclined her head down again, her tongue poking out, and then she stopped, a whisker separating us.

"How long can you wait?" she asked.

I shuddered and pleaded with my eyes.

"I'm sorry. I didn't catch that."

I smiled. "You love to torture me."

She nuzzled her nose into my sex, inhaling deeply, and then withdrew. "It does something to me. Knowing how much you want me. I can smell your desire." She laid her ear on my pussy. "Can hear the throbbing." A finger strolled over my inner thigh. "See the gooseflesh."

I chomped down on my lower lip. "You're killing me, Gemma. Killing me."

"I know, sweetheart. I know." She poked my hipbone with a finger. "And I love it."

"I love you. You have no idea how much."

"Not sure about that. Remember, your eyes speak directly to my heart."

"And my pussy?"

"Ah, your pussy. Holds me captive." Her head lowered and once again she paused briefly a hairsbreadth from bliss. "If only we had all day, I'd stay here for another hour under your control."

I guided her head to where I wanted her, and without a complaint, Gemma's tongue set to work.

AFTERWARD, Gemma hopped in the shower. She was meeting her parents for brunch in a little over an hour. Her family was registered at the Best Western, where my mom had stayed for two days before returning after my father vacated the house.

While Gemma prepared for her day, I hid under the bed covers in hopes of skipping Mother's Day. Not an option, but it was a comforting thought, however fleeting. The plan was to drive to my folks'—or rather mom's house since Dad informed me he'd moved out —and have a late lunch with my mother before making the drive back. I had a final Monday afternoon, luckily, or I would have been guilted into staying the night. The mere idea made me convulse.

Dad was flying today, and he'd confided to Glen, who then told me that he made arrangements to stay with a friend when grounded, giving Mom her space while they worked out their next step. Glen was convinced divorce was inevitable. I think Dad was as well. The only one in denial was Mom, but that was typical. I had a feeling she secretly hoped they could remain married but stay far apart from each other. It wasn't that she still wanted to be with him. I was pretty sure she wouldn't want to be slapped with the divorcee label. That equated to failure, and she hated failing. Labels suited the black and white thinkers of the world.

"You better get in the shower." Gemma towel dried her hair at the foot of the bed.

I hefted the comforter off and gathered my shower kit from the closet floor. "I'm soooo not looking forward to today."

Gemma stepped aside, wisely not saying a word. I'd been whining since she mentioned it was time for us to get out of bed to prepare for the day. I wasn't proud of the fact, and even though it wasn't fair to Gem, I wasn't able to curb my childishness.

I stopped at the bathroom door. Gemma had followed the four steps to the sink to blow dry her hair. "Hop in with me." I yanked her arm.

"I just got out." She tried to worm free.

"I know, but I need you."

Gemma furrowed her brows, but her lips curled up at the sides. "I don't want to be late."

"You won't. Besides, I can't see my mom without someone washing my backside properly."

"Oh really? This seems like a new rule." She playfully ran a finger down the sheet of house rules taped to the closet door. "It's not here."

I undid the belt of her robe and licked my lips. "It should be. It's a prudent one, if you ask me. Dirty backsides are a scourge in society."

Gemma crossed her arms over her perky breasts.

I fluttered my eyelashes, knowing she was a complete sucker when I did that. "You know you'll give in, so stop wasting time."

"*I'm* wasting time?" She rapped her chest with a finger. "You moped in bed while I showered."

I waved her off. "Come on. Get wet with me."

"I'm only washing your backside. No monkey business. You promise?"

"Aye, aye, Captain." I saluted.

The shower was tiny but spotless. We stepped under the stream of hot water, and within seconds, I was morphing into my normal self. Showers had always been my miracle drug. Gemma lathered my hair for me.

"That feels good," I murmured with my eyes shut.

Her fingertips massaged my scalp, and each probe chipped away at the tension in my body.

Gem rinsed the shampoo and mixed in a healthy dose of conditioner, leaving it be to do its job.

Gemma doused the bath sponge with Japanese cherry blossom shower gel and started with my backside, ensuring not to miss a spot. Then she spun me around and delicately sponged my front, including under each breast. Squatting, she cleaned one leg then the other. Before taking care of my pussy, she skimmed her tongue along the lips, landing for a split second on my clit. I stretched both hands out, using the slippery tiled walls to hold myself up.

The water cascaded down my body onto her wet red locks, plastering several clumps to the side of her face. Gemma gazed up, and I wondered if she was calculating if she could fuck me again and still make it on time for brunch.

I smiled sadly. "I know. You have to go."

Her body slowly snaked up mine, eliciting excitement that would be crushed in a matter of seconds. Gemma ringed an arm around me, whisking me into an *I'm so sorry* embrace.

Or so I thought.

Her kiss suggested she was only beginning. It wasn't until she shoved me up against the wall that I realized Gemma planned to rock my world. Her knee separated my legs, and her fingers parted my lips.

Her lips clamped down on mine, while her fingers entered my pussy with force.

"I thought you didn't have time." I closed my eyes and rested my head against the cold, wet tile.

"I hate that I can't be there for you today. Maybe this will help you power through." Gemma made her way down. She didn't linger on either nipple, but they craved attention. I pinched one between the pads of my thumb and forefinger. Time was short, and I wanted to prove I was a team player.

Gemma increased the depth and intensity of her hammering, and when her tongue circled my sex, a jolt made the tiny hairs on my body boing. One hand abandoned my nipple and slipped down to hold Gemma's head in place. I moved the shower nozzle so it wouldn't rain down into her mouth. I couldn't have her drown while eating me out.

"Oh my God!" I said.

No words came from Gemma, but passion screamed through her actions.

"Oh, don't stop!" I fisted her wet hair. "Oh, God, don't stop."

Gemma's tongue was in sync with my body, and within moments, the pre-orgasm lightshow flickered behind my eyelids. Her fingers expertly dove in and hit the spot that took me from pre-orgasm to full-on coming. Gemma pressed her tongue against my clit, initiating a seismic tremor.

"Jesus!" I screamed, praying the water drowned out the commotion.

A powerful aftershock almost as strong as the original quake slammed through me. Gemma kissed me hard on the mouth.

"I can't get enough of you." I nestled my wet cheek against hers.

Gemma sighed contentedly before withdrawing and

swiveling the showerhead to rinse her face in the now lukewarm water. "To be continued." She winked.

I nodded, unable to speak or move.

"Drive safe, okay?" she said.

I nodded again. Gemma gave me a peck on the cheek and then departed. My body collapsed against the wall. By the time I stepped out of the shower to dry off, the front door quietly shut.

"I love you, Gemma," I whispered, hopeful she sensed the words through the brick walls. It was as if I was consumed with the thought that she had to know the intensity of my feelings. Was this a result of my unfulfilling family situation or the relentless need to prove my worth?

She'd given me more than enough courage to power through the day. How I had ended up with someone like Gemma was a complete mystery, and I had to resist the urge to pinch myself to see if I was dreaming. In my topsy-turvy world, no one else compared to Gem. Of that, I was absolutely sure.

It took less than ten minutes to get ready, settling on a skort and Gap V-neck shirt. Although, knowing my mom, I should have spent more time fixing my hair, makeup, and selecting an outfit. I feared Mom's barbed words, but I had promised Glen on the phone last night not to let her needle me today of all days.

Behave was today's key word.

Before heading out, I popped into the cafeteria for a quick bite. I could be, so I'm told, cranky when hungry, and I figured that would wreck my chances of curbing snide comments my mother brought out of me.

Unfortunately, the Lucky Charms had run out. Was that an omen?

Shoving the thought out of my head, I settled on Frosted Flakes. At the juice counter, I filled a small glass with OJ.

"TR!" Jenny hip checked me, splashing some of the orange juice on my hand. "Ooops, sorry."

I wiped the back of my hand with a napkin. "You're chipper."

"It's a beautiful day."

"Yeah, that's it. You're the type to stop and smell the roses, right?"

I carried my tray to a table, Jenny in tow.

Taking a seat across from Jenny, I added, "It has nothing to do with a certain someone?"

She grinned. "Maybe." Jenny leaned over the table. "Bernie is amazing."

"It's good to see you happy."

"It feels good to be happy." Jenny shoveled in a scoop of Cheerios, munching loudly.

"What happened to the world being your oyster? Not settling down?" I teased.

"Phooey." She waved a hand, her expression turning serious. She swallowed some water. "You know, back in high school, I never thought I would find someone like Berns. I figured someone like me would always be single."

I wondered what she meant but didn't have the time to skim too deep below the surface. "Is that why you didn't date much then?"

"Maybe." Jenny looked toward the ceiling, her mouth slightly agape, showing her perfectly white teeth. "Actually, yes. Besides, I thought love was for chumps and always ended in heartache." Her facial expression softened. "You going to your mom's?"

I nodded.

"And your dad?" she asked.

"Flying."

Jenny shook her head. "Dude, I don't envy you. Or your mom. I'd be crushed if Bernie left me."

The sadness mingled with fear in her eyes made me wonder what would happen if she and Bernie split up. "It's a bit early to be talking about that," I said over the rim of my glass.

"You're right. Besides, why would Berns dump me?" Jenny thumped her chest.

I had been talking about my folks' situation, but I didn't correct her. "Only a fool would."

"Like April." Jenny straightened in her chair. "April fools." She busted into laughter. "Get it?" she asked when I barely smiled.

"Yep. You're a riot, Jen-Meister."

"Don't I know it?"

Not knowing what to say, I scooped in a large serving of cereal. Jenny's eyes fell to the table as if troubled. "You okay?" I asked.

Jenny glanced up, a smile firmly in place. "Yeppers. Just missing Bernie."

I laughed. "Geez, you two make me sick."

"Don't be jealous of our love."

While her smile lacked confidence, I was fairly certain she was being real. I couldn't help but think Jenny was on the path for a world of pain. Not even taking in my opinion of Bernie, there was no denying the fact she was two years ahead of us. Unless she went to law school at Hill, Jenny only had one year left with the Amazing Bernie. I repeated the nickname in my mind in a carnival announcer voice.

I rose from my seat, while downing the rest of my juice. "I've got to run. Have fun today."

"Hey, we're thinking of having people over tonight. If you're back in time, you and Gemma should come over."

"At Bernie's?"

"Where else?"

Did Bernie know Jenny was inviting people over? "Yeah, that sounds good. Maybe."

CHAPTER SEVENTEEN

IN THE DORM PARKING LOT, I GLANCED TO THE sky. Nothing but blue and, according to the weather forecast on the radio, it'd be seventy-five degrees. Hopefully that meant we'd eat outside on the back deck.

"Tegan!"

I wheeled about and spied Erik charging for me like a bull running through the streets of Spain. He had a goofy grin on his face, easing up before bowling me over.

"Hi." I took a half step back.

"This place is deserted." He waved to the nearly abandoned lot. "It's nice to see a friendly face."

"Aren't you having lunch or dinner with your mom?" I clenched my purse like a shield.

"What? Oh." His face clouded over, and he gaped at the foothills. "My mom died when I was five."

Open mouth, insert foot, Tegan.

"I'm so sorry, Erik." I placed a hand on his arm.

His face fell, transforming him into a lost little boy, not the cocky six-three frattie who seconds before had exuded happiness.

"Are you going to your mom's, then?" He fidgeted with the sleeves of a long sleeve shirt wrapped around his waist.

"I am."

His shoulders drooped. "Okay. Well, it was nice bumping into you." He put a palm up and started to walk away.

He wore cargo shorts, and it was the first time I got a good look at his toned calves. I'd never noticed until now how good some men looked in such shorts. Or maybe it was just him.

"Erik!" I called out.

He stopped and pivoted, head over his shoulder.

"Would you like to come with me?" I smiled in encouragement. Maybe bringing Erik home would distract my mother and force her into behaving.

"Really?" His lips curved upward.

I waved him back. "Come on, or we'll be late."

A grin spread across his face, lifting his shoulders back to his self-possessed nature. "I get to pick the music!"

I had to laugh. "No rap. I hate rap."

He saluted crisply as if he'd been a marine in a former life.

"You have that down."

"My dad's a major general in the marines." His voice lost some of its hilarity.

No mom and a marine as a father. Poor Erik.

We climbed into my Honda. Seconds after turning the key in the ignition, Erik fiddled with the radio. He landed on a station playing "Jump" by Kris Kross.

I quirked an eyebrow. "I thought I said no rap."

He rolled his eyes. "Dude, this is hip-hop." Erik placed a hand on my shoulder. "You're lucky I'm here to teach you about the important things in life."

"Whatever." I brushed his hand off.

Before we hit the highway, the catchy beat and chorus won me over. We both sang along, and at one point, I forgot I was driving and stabbed both hands in the air, bouncing up and down in my seat.

"Hey, lady. Be careful." Erik laughed as he gripped the steering wheel.

"Can't ever hit anything in this state." I gestured to the open fields.

"What? There's an innocent cow right over the ridge."

I had to squint to see it.

"In India, killing a cow is a crime," he continued.

"Really?" My eyebrows bunched. "Why?"

"They're a sacred animal." He shrugged. "Baby Got Back" started. "Oooooh... I love this one." He scooted up in his seat to show me his backside as he wiggled his ass, belting out the lyrics and nearly bonking his head on the dashboard.

I soon found out he knew the words to the next three songs: "Mr. Wendell," "Achy Breaky Heart," and "Rhythm is a Dancer."

He leaned back in his seat when "Stay" by Shakespears Sister streamed through the speaker. "How long have you and Gemma been together?"

My fingers clawed the steering wheel. "A few months now, but you can't say anything about that today." My voice came out harsh.

He put both palms up. "Don't worry. I know the protocol."

"Protocol?" I peeked out of the corner of my eye.

"My sister is gay. Our dad can never know." He flipped the lid on and off the ashtray on the console.

So that was why he didn't react with revulsion when April outed us in the stairwell.

"If it doesn't work out with Gemma, my sister is single." He socked my shoulder with his fist. "She's hot."

"Erik!" I whacked his thigh. "You can't say your sister is hot."

He laughed. "Why not? All of my buddies have been telling me that since I was twelve. She's four years older."

"If she's so hot, why is she single?" I tried punching holes in his claim.

"Not many potential girlfriends like that she's still

in the closet. She lives in New York. It's so different there and being gay isn't such a big deal, but I think she's so terrified of what will happen if Dad finds out. She's determined to keep it under wraps even when she doesn't have to. Dad never visits her."

I nodded, understanding her fear, but not willing to share this tidbit with Erik, who I hadn't spent much time with except for casual conversations after class. I steered us to a safer topic instead. "Is that where you're from? New York?"

"Nope. We lived with my grandparents in Kansas."

Erik fingered the buttons on the radio. After failing to find any decent songs, he lowered the volume.

"Who was the first person you told? That you're gay?" he asked, clearly missing my intention not to discuss my comfort level about being gay.

"Gemma." I stared at the straight road ahead.

"I figured. Who else?"

"No one, really."

"Then how did April know?" He wrenched his head to face me.

"She saw us kissing. That day on Walt's Hill."

"April outed you, then?" His voice was a mix of shock and annoyance. "She talks about you a lot. Like talks about you as if she's crushing hard."

"Great. Just what I need. A psycho bitch with loose lips."

"If I were you, I'd stay away. She's not even that great of a lay."

"Erik!" I laughed and swatted his thigh. "I can't believe you said that."

"Well, it's true. She acts like a cat on the prowl, and then in bed... she just doesn't... nothing happens." He tossed his hands in the air. "It's weird considering the act she puts on."

"What do you mean nothing happens? You didn't sleep with her?"

"No, I have. Many times. But on her end, nothing. Not even a moan. Or whimper."

"She's never come? Is that what you mean?"

"Yeah. And I don't think she's even gotten close. I even... you know..." He inspected his laced fingers in his lap.

"You went down on her and still nothing?"

He shrugged.

"And you think it's all her?" I needled. "Maybe you need a lesson or two about female oral sex."

"You offering to let me watch you and Gem?" His leer made me squirm.

"No!"

"Just kidding. And for the record, I've never had a complaint before." He glared at me defiantly.

I pondered his words. "No moans. Any sense of a build-up?"

"A little in the beginning. And then frustration—that's when she starts yelling."

"Yelling what?"

"Things like *not there, here*—*no harder. Stay focused. You're losing me. Is that all?*"

I mouthed, "Wow."

"It's the worst, so like I said, stay away. Unless you have the biggest ego in the world—though even then it'd be pushed to the limit. Luckily, I'm able to brush it off." He grinned ear to ear.

He was such a dude, only concerned about getting his jollies. Then again, why bring up April's inability to orgasm? Maybe he was struggling and hoped my being a female would provide the insight he needed. I imagined he couldn't discuss this with his frat brothers— they'd be cruel with their comments and nicknames like Not Erect Erik.

"Have you used your fingers while, ya know, going down on her?"

He rounded his head to gawk at me. "Lesbians don't have the market on fingering and eating out a chick. Besides, she kinda told me"—he cleared his throat—"Jenny failed as well."

"Huh. That's weird. Men or women can't get her to come." Was this sweet justice for such a bitch?

"Will you continue to see her after finals?" I asked.

"Not sure."

"I can't believe you!" I slowed down to let a car get in front of me.

"What?"

"Why would you continue seeing a woman like April?"

"Seriously? Come on. I'm a guy, and I have needs."

"But you're using her." I didn't know why I was defending the likes of April.

"She wants to be used."

"I'm going to pretend I didn't hear that." I jabbed his side with a finger. "How do you know she hasn't been trained to be used? God, you're such a guy!"

He squirmed in his seat. "Not all of us lucked out and got a sexy roommate like Gemma."

"You think Gemma's sexy?" I glanced over my shoulder to merge into the left lane and pass a semi.

"Uh, yeah. You don't?"

"Of course, I do. She's so shy I just thought she always flew under the radar."

"And I'm the asshole? You obviously don't appreciate your girl. Maybe I'll hook her up with my sister."

"Don't even think of it!" My temper flared.

"Easy, Tegan. I was only kidding."

I exited I-25 onto I-76 toward Grand Junction. "That's the second time you mentioned hooking up your sister. Are you worried about her?"

Erik fumbled with the shirt tied around his waist. "I just want her to be happy. When Mom died she stepped into that role. She's always been responsible, and I'd like her to think of herself for once."

It was surprising to hear him speak openly. "I'm sure she'll find someone. So will you."

"Hey now, I have a fuck buddy. That's all I need."

"Ever?"

The lines in his forehead crinkled. "Time will tell. I'm not looking right now."

I navigated the car through the hogback. "Almost there. Remember. Don't say a peep about Gemma. Oh, I probably should mention that my dad recently asked my mom for a divorce, but my mom doesn't know I know that." I laughed. "Maybe I should have brought that up when I invited you."

"You think?" He raised his eyebrows. "This should be interesting."

"That's my life."

"You okay?"

"I—" My voice faltered. "I really don't know."

"Mom! I'm home!" I ushered Erik through the front room and into the kitchen, where I typically found her. She'd made such a big deal on the phone about how she wanted to make lunch for us and not go to a restaurant. She probably didn't want me to order another Monte Cristo or some other fried food.

"On the deck," she shouted.

I spied mom in an apron, prepping the grill—Dad's usual job, not just on Mother's Day.

"You ready?" I asked Erik right before we stepped outside.

"Showtime!" he responded with more vim than I

would have been able to muster knowing the potential shit storm.

Mom's smile enlarged when her eyes landed on Erik. "Well, who do we have here?"

"Mom, I'd like you to meet one of my *friends* from school. Erik, this is my mom."

He put his hand out to shake, but Mom dismissed it and enveloped him in her arms, holding him closer than her usual way. Was my frigid mother showing her vulnerability?

After they parted, Mom cocked her head and said, "Has anyone ever said you look like Harrison Ford? Only younger?"

I nearly gagged on my tongue.

He nodded. "I've heard. Minus the lightsaber, of course."

My eyes drifted downward, causing my heart to cringe with disgust.

"Would anyone like a glass of wine?" Mom reached for her drink from the black wrought iron table under the oak tree.

"When did you start drinking? And it's only one in the afternoon." I stared slack-jawed.

She waved off my shock. "Don't mind her, Erik. Would you like a glass?" Her face was flushed, and I wondered if she was on her first glass. I hadn't contemplated this glitch since it'd never happened before. Mom was difficult to manage sober. What in the hell would she be like drunk?

Erik shifted on his feet. "Uh, sure."

"Or would you prefer a beer?" she asked.

"You drink beer as well? And offering alcohol to underage drinkers?" I leaned on the deck railing to combat the swirling sensation of vertigo as the vibrant blue sky and tree leaves twirled around my head.

She rolled her eyes, suggesting I was acting like a drama queen. "Your father left some. Erik might as well have it." Her squared shoulders made it clear Dad wasn't welcome here. Not anymore.

Was that the closest she'd get to admitting they were divorcing?

"Beer sounds great." Erik moved closer to me. Had he observed my body swaying as if I was about to tumble?

"Tegan?" Mom asked.

"I'm driving." I gritted my teeth, not that she bothered to pay heed.

Mom disappeared in the house to fetch a bottle of Dad's Heineken for Erik.

"It's okay." Erik caressed my back. "This is normal. She just needs time and patience."

I nodded, not comforted at all by his words or touch. I expected her to be weirder than normal, but drunk—never in a million years. Was the drinking a result of the impending divorce, or was I witnessing a trend that'd been building up behind closed doors? Was that why my father had taken such a drastic step?

"I figured you wouldn't mind drinking out of the

bottle. Rick always drank out of a glass, but you seem like a real man." Mom thrust the bottle into Erik's hand.

"This is great. Much better than out of a red Solo cup." Erik prodded my side.

Mom tittered. I was fairly certain she had never had a beer from a Solo cup and missed the reference to flat beer at frat parties.

Erik glugged a quarter of the bottle while mom guzzled down red wine like it was Welch's grape juice. Maybe I should have accepted some liquid courage. Not that we were the type of family who drank together. Dad would have an occasional beer. Glen and I never sampled alcohol in front of them, even though both of us had been imbibing since high school. That was how Ferbers did most things—in secret. Did my bible-thumping mother realize her hypocrisy was elevating to a whole new level? Getting snockered in front of her daughter?

"How are you with meat?" Mom asked Erik.

"Excuse me?" his cheeks actually tinged.

"I splurged and got steaks. Out of habit, I purchased three." She glanced away briefly, dabbing an eye. "Want to man the grill for us?" She placed tongs in his hand, not giving him a chance to deny the honor.

Erik banged the tongs to his forehead. "Yes, ma'am. It'd be an honor." He about-faced to tackle the grill.

I changed the radio station on the portable when the sixties song "It's My Party" blared. The last thing I wanted was for my mother to burst into tears.

Mom tugged my arm and motioned for me to lean in. "Are you two—?"

I put a palm up. "Just friends. His mom died when he was five, so he had nowhere to go today."

Mom's eyes softened. "Poor dear."

We both peered in his direction.

"Nice ass," she said.

I backpedaled, not able to banish the smile from my face. "How much wine have you had?" I shook my head, amused and terrified.

"Not enough." To prove her point, she took another slug.

Remembering this was Mother's Day, I clamped down on my bottom lip. "Have you heard from Glen?"

"He called this morning." She stared across the fenceless backyard at the slope of the hill dotted with pine trees and scrub brush. On the far side of the field stood houses, but from this vantage point, there weren't any signs of human habitation. My parents had always loved the privacy out here, but how did it make her feel now? Alone? Scared? Vulnerable?

Would they sell the house? I grew up here. I sighed. There were so many unanswered questions hanging over our heads.

Mom cleared her throat. "You hungry?" She

motioned to the side table laden with healthy finger food.

I snagged a carrot stick.

She dunked broccoli into some kind of healthy-looking dip. "How's it coming along, Erik?" Mom called out.

"Good. Do you like your meat still mooing or dead?"

"In the middle."

"Tegan?" He orbited the tongs in the air.

"Deader than dead."

"Burnt. Got it. I prefer if I turn my head, my steak has enough life left to eat my salad." He laughed at his own joke.

I crinkled my nose.

Mom chuckled. "That's how a real man should eat steak. Rick wouldn't touch a steak until it was blacker than charcoal. Such a waste of money."

I jammed another carrot into my mouth, annoyed by her parting shot at Dad. Was she dropping all these clues about her feelings toward Dad so I would confront her? Force her to own up about the state of her marriage?

Erik moved a filet mignon, presumably mine, to the center. Some fat sizzled, and the fire's fingers engulfed the beef.

"Oh, I like all the char." I took a step closer to Erik.

He jostled my arm. "Promise to try a bite of mine. I

know I can convert you." His eyes were tinged with desire, tripping an alarm in my head.

I stepped back. "I'm thirsty. Anyone need a refill?"

Mom's arm darted in the air.

Erik held the green bottle in the light to measure the amount left. "Sure. Thanks!"

In the kitchen, I leaned against the counter, chastising myself for getting into this situation. All I had to do was walk away and leave Erik in the parking lot. Instead, I brought him along, and we were bonding as friends. At least I considered him a friend, nothing more. That look implied he wanted the whole shebang. Dammit! Not that I could blame him since April was such a dud in the sack. How, though, would I explain this to Gemma? Did I have to? Things had been so good with us the past couple of months. After finals, Erik and I probably wouldn't have any classes together. Why rock the boat now?

"My wineglass isn't going to fill itself." Mom had entered the kitchen without my noticing. She opened the fridge and extracted a salad she'd prepared ahead of time and three different types of dressing.

I filled her glass less than halfway.

"Who are you? The wine gestapo?" She signaled with her hand for me to top her drink. "Don't forget Erik's beer." She bumped the screen door with her bum and toted the salad and dressing to the table outside.

I snatched a diet Dr. Pepper from the door in the fridge and fished in one of the drawers for a Heineken.

"Here you go, *dude*." I thrust the bottle into Erik's hand, careful to avoid making contact with his skin.

"Thanks, *dude*." He mopped his brow with his arm.

I couldn't stop a smile, acknowledging his mocking of my pronunciation of dude. "Hot?"

"So people keep telling me." He winked.

"Whatever, dude. Are you visiting your sister this summer?" I lifted an eyebrow, hoping he caught my meaning.

"Touchy!" He waved the tongs in his face as if fanning flames. "To answer your question, I'm staying with her this summer. I got an internship in the Big Apple."

"Really? Where?"

"A bank. I'm a business major." Erik lifted my steak off the grill and set it on the plate with the other two. "Dinner is served, ladies."

The three of us sat at the table under the oak tree.

Erik divvied the steaks. "Here ya go, Tegan. One piece of charred meat. Such a shame."

Mom handed the salad bowl to Erik and then handed me a ceramic dish that contained baked potatoes wrapped in aluminum foil.

Before I had a chance to slice into my steak, Mom said, "Shall we say grace?" She put her palms out for both of us to hold.

I forcefully sucked in air. Even drunk she insisted on saying grace. Wasn't that some type of sacrilege?

"May I?" Erik came to the rescue. Mom nodded and bowed her head. Erik followed suit. "God, we thank you for this food. For rest and home and all things good. For wind and rain and sun above. But most of all for those we love." He squeezed my hand.

Mom looked up. "Lovely, Erik."

He inclined his head while buttering his baked potato.

"Oh, the sour cream!" Mom hurtled out of her seat and trotted inside.

"I'm sorry about that," I whispered.

"What?" Erik chugged his beer.

"The grace thing."

"He waved it off. My grandparents are the same way."

"Here ya go." Mom set a tub of sour cream next to Erik.

"Would you like salt and pepper?" Mom handed the shakers to him.

"Thank you, Mrs.—Tegan's Mom." He turned cherry red and pivoted in my direction. "Tegan, I don't know your last name."

"Ferber," Mom supplied and then added, "But please call me Sally."

Erik turned to Mom and then back to me. "Ferber? Really?"

"Don't say it." I pierced the air with my steak knife.

"What?" he grinned foolishly.

"Furball."

He chortled.

Damn, I'd walked right into the Furball trap.

Erik placed a hand over his heart. "I would never say such a thing."

"Yeah, right. What's your last name?"

For the first time since meeting Erik, aside from when I asked about his mom, his swagger melted. "Nope. Not telling."

I eyeballed my mother, whose glassy expression showed she was barely keeping up with the conversation, but a hint of a smile suggested she liked the chemistry between Erik and me. I wanted to make it clear there wasn't a chance in hell, but it'd be a shame to burst her bubble on Mother's Day.

"Come on." I playfully rolled my eyes at Erik. "It can't be much worse than Furball."

"Oh, please. You had it easy." He lobbed a crouton into his mouth, chewing aggressively.

I pinned him with a *confess all* stare. "You can trust me."

"Nice try." He dangled his arms over the back of the chair. "I got your number."

I waggled a finger in his face. "You saved my life. That means we're bonded. You have to tell me." His refusal to disclose his name piqued my curiosity.

"Saved your life?" Mom butted in.

"The first time I met Tegan, she was choking."

"Choking?" Mom's eyes widened. "On what?"

Erik turned his head to me. "On what?"

"A cherry."

"And you saved her?" Mom continued.

Erik mimed giving me the Heimlich.

"You're a hero! A handsome hero," Mom spoke to me, causing my face to go up in flames.

I slurped my Dr. Pepper, avoiding her eyes.

Erik severed a piece of steak. Peeking up from his plate, he asked, "Is that how it works?"

"What?" I realized he'd circled back to my argument. "Yes. I should know my rescuer's last name," I said with as much conviction as I could muster, afraid I'd tip my hat. I really wanted to know I wasn't the only one with a humiliating last name.

He pointed his fork with a piece of steak speared by the tines at me. "If I tell you, it has to stay between us. Not even Ge—"

"Of course. Of course," I rushed to interject.

He mouthed, "Sorry," set his fork down, and rested his forearms on the table. "Cockshott."

"Erik Cockshott," I snorted, covering my mouth and snickering. "And I thought I had it bad."

"Careful, Furball. Your true colors are showing."

"Only a Cockshott would notice."

I amended my earlier nickname from Not Erect Erik to No Cock Cockshott.

"I think it's a fine name," Mother added her two cents.

Erik's scrunched face said differently.

"No seriously. Younger generations have ruined certain words. Back in the good old days, cock referred to a man strutting around like a cockerel—not you know..." Fortunately she left the rest unsaid, but she made a rather crude gesture in the pelvic region. My mother, the religious nut, had lost her marbles, and Erik had a front row seat. Mom perked up. "And you can't say queer or gay anymore. Those used to be normal words." She held her wineglass and took an exuberant swig before cradling the glass to her cheek. "Queer meant odd, and gay was happy. But no," she stage-whispered, "the perverts had to steal them."

I swallowed, and Erik stared down at his plate. I couldn't decipher if he was curbing a smile or wanting to defend his sister's honor.

"And pussy." She nearly jumped out of her seat, splashing some wine into her lap. "That used to refer to cats. Tegan had a pussycat that she adored when she was little. She insisted on calling it Pussy, even though the cat's name was Ginger."

Erik laughed so hard he had to cover his mouth with a napkin.

Mom joined him, bobbing her head up and down. "Really. She did. And do you want to know something really funny?" She leaned toward him.

Erik eyed me with a look of horror, but he couldn't help himself. "What?"

"When Tegan was three, she asked me for a spoon.

I thought she wanted it to dig in the backyard or something, so I never questioned. I just handed one over.

"Then one day I wandered into the laundry room and saw Tegan shoveling cat food into her mouth with that spoon. I asked what she was doing, and she responded, 'Eating Pussy's food' like it was perfectly natural."

"So that's when it started." Erik snorted like a pig. "And with a ginger!" He slapped his thigh.

"It is." Mom grunted.

I kicked Erik hard in the shin under the table.

He rolled his shoulders, shaking it off.

"My daughter. The pussy lover. Not that I can say that anymore. The perverts steal everything."

Erik coughed "Still fits" into his hand.

Oblivious to his antics, Mom said, "But I'm sure it was Tegan's cat food obsession that started it all. Just look at her tits, not to mention her breeder's hips. She'll make some man very happy." Mom gazed at Erik as if waiting for him to get down on one knee and ask me to marry him.

Aghast, I sputtered, "Mother!"

"Of that, I have no doubt." Erik arched his eyebrows, daring me to challenge him in front of my mother, the pervert hater.

I stared helplessly at both of them.

AROUND ELEVEN THAT NIGHT, I parked the Honda in the parking lot two dorms down from where I lived. I had never intended to stay so long at my mom's, but the afternoon and evening rushed by before I noticed it was almost nine. Mom veered close to gabbing about more embarrassing stories, but the wine seemed to seize her tongue, and I was able to keep her out of most of the conversations with Erik. Overall, it was a pleasant evening under the moonlight.

Both of us got out of the car.

Erik leaned on the trunk. "Thanks for letting me tag along today. It meant a lot."

"Not sure I'll ever recover."

"Your mom is a trip. Is she always that bad or only when drunk?" He buttoned up his flannel shirt. The temperature outside was rapidly dropping.

"She's always a challenge, and this was the first time I've seen her drunk."

"Does it worry you?" He motioned for me to sit on the trunk.

I waved off the idea, not having the energy to dissect my mother's mind-set. "Too cold. Besides, I better get back."

"I'll walk you."

"It's okay. I usually park in this lot. I'm used to it. What dorm is yours?"

"My marine father would have me shot by a firing

squad if I ever let a woman walk home alone after dark. Besides, I'm heading that way to Anders Hall."

"Chivalry isn't dead." I rubbed my bare arms.

"Not in my world." He peeled his long sleeve shirt off and handed it to me.

I put it on, the fabric still warm from his body heat.

"Come on. Let's get you warm." He bent his arm out for me to loop my hand through.

I did.

"I really appreciate you coming today. God only knows how much worse it would have been if it was just the two of us."

"Your mom is angry. There's no doubt about that. Are you close with your dad?" He steered us around a group of drunk boys who were clearly ready for the semester to be over.

"Not really. This past week I've talked to him on the phone more than I have since leaving home. He's a pilot," I explained.

"My dad is the same. Never around."

"Dads—what can you do?" I said in hopes to obliterate the awkwardness.

We reached the entrance of my dorm.

"Here we are. Thanks for walking me."

"Hey now. I said I'd walk you home." He pried the glass door open. "That means to your room."

"Oh, okay." Knowing Gemma would be home, my mind filled with ideas of ditching him before reaching the door. "You really don't have to, though. It's late."

He waved me off. "It's the least I can do. You saved me from spending another Mother's Day alone." Sadness tinged his words, ruining my chance of ditching him.

Each step closer to Gemma echoed in my head.

An oblivious Erik continued the march to my impending doom.

When we reached my floor, I whispered, "Shhh. Quiet hours have started."

He nodded in a way that suggested he understood the true meaning.

Outside the door, I reached into my purse to retrieve the key.

Before the door opened, Gemma said, "I've been worried sick. I tried calling, but no one answered."

"Oh, we were outside most of the time. I didn't even think..."

Gemma stiffened when Erik and I came into view.

"Erik walked me home in the dark," I rushed to explain.

"Now that you're safe and sound, I'll go." He must have perceived my sagging shoulders and the daggers shooting out of Gemma's eyes.

I staggered around and said, "Thanks so much, Erik." I put my hand out to shake for some absurd reason.

He shook it. "Tegan." He nodded to Gem and then regarded me. "See ya at the history final on Wednesday."

The darkness in the hallway swallowed him as I shut the door.

"Seriously, Tegan." Jenny hovered behind Gemma. "Didn't you learn from the Walt's Hill fiasco?"

Gemma stared, stone-faced, not giving me a glimpse if I was in the doghouse or not.

Bernie sat on Gemma's bed.

"What are you two doing here?" I set my purse on the desk, pretending nothing out of the ordinary had happened.

"Gemma called us freaking out since she expected you hours ago." Jenny leaned against the closet door.

"I'm sorry, Gem. I should have called. But my mom was such a mess I couldn't leave."

Gemma remained quiet.

"Please. Don't be this way. It was nothing."

"What was nothing?" she asked.

"Erik. He, uh, joined me at my mom's."

"You took Erik to your mother's?" Gemma's eyes matched the shock in her tone.

"I didn't plan it. It just happened."

Bernie and Jenny exchanged an *oh brother* look.

"It was nothing." I scanned Gem's eyes. "Can we talk? In private?" I whispered uselessly in the cramped room.

"I think I need some space," Gemma said.

"What does that mean?"

Gemma didn't respond. "Can I crash with you?" She waited for Bernie's answer.

"Of course." Bernie stood but studied me with sympathetic eyes.

Gem grabbed her backpack and tossed in some clothes.

"Gem, wait. I can explain," I cried.

"That may be true, but it doesn't change how I feel right now. And I think it's best I leave before saying or doing something I regret."

I tugged her arm. "Please, don't do this. You're blowing this way out of proportion."

Gemma stared down at my hand on her arm. Seconds crawled by before she twisted her head and said to Jenny and Bernie, "Can you give me a second?"

Both exited quietly.

Relief whooshed through me, until Gemma returned her face to mine. Her eyes brimmed with anger and hurt. She stood near the doorway with her arms folded over her chest. "So?"

"That's how you want to start this conversation?" I shook my head.

"How do you want to start?" Her arms tightened as if preparing for an onslaught.

"Civilly. First, ask Jenny and Bernie to leave. It's weird having them right outside the door while we talk. And we need to talk."

"Bernie lives off campus. If they leave, I won't have a ride."

"Gemma! You're jumping to some really horrible scenarios without giving me the benefit of the doubt."

I groaned. "Listen. After we talk, if you still want to spend the night apart, I'll drive you to Bernie's."

Her crinkled brow conveyed, *Yeah right*.

"I promise, promise. But I need you to hear me out, beginning to end."

The resolve in her eyes lessened. Not as much as I would have liked, but at the moment I'd take what I could get.

She stuck her head out into the hallway, whispered some words, and then shut the door. "First term of the agreement met."

If I wasn't livid with the beautiful redhead, I would have laughed. Even when she was being annoying on purpose, I wanted to rip her clothes off.

"Thank you." I collapsed onto my bed and patted the spot next to me. "Would you like to sit down?"

She moved a chair into the middle of the room and sat, straddling the back.

Neither of us said a word.

"Well?" She hefted her shoulders. "Shouldn't you be pleading your case?"

"You act like I murdered someone."

She kneaded her face with a palm, a trace of a tear forming in the corner of one eye. Was it an angry or sad tear?

"Why do you fly off the handle every time you see me with Erik? He's a friend. Nothing more."

She jolted up in the chair ramrod straight. "You don't think I have any reason to suspect his motives?"

Her stiff posture and inability to meet my eyes suggested she didn't trust my motives either.

"Do you want to know why I invited him to my mother's today?"

"Not really," she mumbled more to herself.

"I ran into him in the parking lot and asked him why he wasn't celebrating with his mother. Boy did I feel like an ass when Erik told me his mom died when he was a kid."

Gem's shoulders sagged some.

"You should have seen him. So lost. I couldn't let him walk away."

She bobbed her head. "Okay, but can you look me in the eye and tell me that was the only reason you invited him?"

"No, I can't."

She popped off the chair like a champagne cork. "I knew it!"

I shot off the bed. "You knew what?"

"You like Erik! All along, you've liked Erik!" She paced toward the door and back to the center of the room, rubbing a hand on top of her head.

"For the love of God, stop!" I screamed at the top of my lungs.

It worked. She froze mid-stride.

"Sit down," I gestured to the chair, and Gemma complied.

I squatted next to her and clasped both of her hands. "I don't know how to explain this to you so you'll understand, but finding other people attractive doesn't mean I'll act on that attraction. You hang out with Bernie all the time. Do you think she's pretty?"

"Sh-she's Jenny's girlfriend," Gemma stuttered.

"I'm aware. That's not the point. Do you think she's pretty?" I peered into her emerald eyes.

Gemma started to shake her head but conceded the point with a shrug.

"Would you ever put the moves on Bernie?"

"Of course not," she spat out.

"Don't get mad. I never thought you would. Not once have I ever accused you of such a thing, and not once have I said you can't hang out with arguably one of the most beautiful girls on campus."

Gemma glanced away.

"I admit I think Erik is attractive. Very attractive."

She sucked in a ragged breath. "The first day we met, you admitted you had a thing for Harrison Ford, even a look-alike."

"How do you remember that?"

Her smile wasn't reassuring. "Hard to forget."

My thighs burned from squatting, an exercise I'd hated in gym class and still didn't like. Realizing Gemma's angry spurt had dissipated for the moment, I retook my seat on the bed.

"Meeting Erik has thrown you for a loop."

"True," I said.

She flinched.

"But not for the reasons you think."

"What do I think?"

I snorted. "That I want to fuck Erik." There wasn't a need to sugarcoat the huge effing pink elephant in the room.

"Do you?" she whispered with her eyes downcast.

"No. I don't. I find my attraction to Erik confusing. When I hooked up with you, I was convinced I was a lesbian. No doubt in my mind from the moment we kissed. I was perfectly content with that knowledge. But then Erik happened. He's made me question some things, not my love for you or my desire to be with you, because nothing and I mean *nothing* will change that. But my identity. I don't want to be bisexual."

"Then don't."

I covered my mouth, stung by her blunt reaction. "If it was that easy, I'd do it. Don't you realize how much this has been killing me? How I feel like a failure? Like I'm letting you down?" My nose burned, a good indicator it was only a matter of seconds before the waterworks released. "I don't want to hurt you." My body heaved up and down, racked with sobs.

Gemma flew to my side, wrapping her strong arms around me. "Shhh, please don't cry. I hate seeing you cry." She rocked me back and forth, whispering, "I'm sorry."

"I hate crying."

She laughed. Really laughed. "For someone who hates crying, you sure do cry a lot."

I laughed with her, shooting snot out of my nose. I

used my sleeve to wipe it away, realizing too late that I still wore Erik's shirt. Luckily, Gem didn't seem to notice.

"Don't let Erik see that," she said but then added, "Or maybe he should."

We both grew silent as the awkwardness of my confession and her reaction seeped back into both of our minds.

"Do you still want me to drive you to Bernie's?"

She rested her head against mine. "I don't know." She stared at her hands in her lap. "No, I'm okay for now."

CHAPTER EIGHTEEN

AFTER TURNING IN MY HISTORY FINAL, THE last one I had to take, I should have been bubbling over with excitement or at least cracking a smile. But I didn't.

"Tegan!"

I whirled around in the hallway, finding myself in Erik's arms. "The semester is over!" He picked me up off the ground, crushing me against his chest.

I grunted.

He plunked me down. "Aren't you excited for summer?"

Dreading it was more like it. "I guess so." I hitched a pathetic shoulder.

He steered us away from a handful of students exiting the building and chattering about getting trashed to celebrate. "What's wrong?"

"Nothing." I hugged my stomach.

He hooked a thumb toward his chest. "Hey, it's me. Not some douchebag."

I actually laughed. Erik may not be a douchebag, but he was the source of my turmoil. Partly, at least. "Who told ya you aren't a douchebag?"

He smiled. "All the women in my life, except for April." He laughed. "But it's best to treat her like opposite day. Whatever she says, I translate it to make it good."

I rolled my eyes. "In the doghouse?"

He rolled back onto his heels, sticking his thumbs into the belt loops of his cargo shorts. "Maybe. You?"

"Absolutely."

He jerked his head for me to follow him outside. The sun blazed overhead. "Take a seat." He shoved me onto a bench on the path along the side of the building.

"Manhandling girls isn't exactly chivalrous." I rubbed my arms where he'd gripped me.

"Not opening up to a friend doesn't make you best friend material."

I sighed. "Gemma's having a hard time accepting me."

Erik slid onto the seat next to me, resting one arm along the top plank. "As a lesbian? That makes zero sense." He formed an O with his right hand.

"Sometimes I wonder about you. As a bisexual."

"You're bi?" His normally masculine voice cracked like a boy going through puberty.

"Don't get too excited. The only person I want is Gem."

He waved me off. "I know that. I just didn't know the whole... situation."

"It's not something I shout from the rooftops."

Erik nodded his head, simultaneously rubbing the two-day growth of beard on his chin. "Is she mad about the other night?"

I snorted. "You could say that."

"She thinks you like me?"

"Other way around, Cockschott." I scooted closer to the metal armrest.

He stuck his tongue out but didn't bite on my weak diversion attempt. "Ah. She's worried I like you."

I bit down on my tongue to stop the words "Don't you?" from leaving my addled brain.

"Give her some time. Maybe the three of us should go to dinner—" I started to object, but he mimed with his hand for me to shut it. "Not as a date or something. Once she gets to know me, she won't be able to hate me."

I laughed. "God, you have such an ego."

He flashed a crooked smile. "I can't help it if people love me."

I'd settle for Gemma loving me. Hell, even liking me at the moment would make things a heck of a lot better.

Erik glanced at his watch. "I've got to run." He rose, his shadow giving me a chill. "Seriously, Gem will come around. No one in their right mind would let you get away."

"Thanks."

"I'll stop by later to say goodbye." He patted my head as he spoke.

Before I could tell him that was a bad idea, he dashed off.

THE END of the semester gin and tonic party had arrived, and all I could do was stew in the corner on one of the couches in the basement. No one looked in my direction, and for that, I was truly grateful. I felt like Hester Prynne, except with a scarlet B for *bisexual* scratched into my forehead.

"Mind if I join you?" Bernie didn't wait for an answer and plopped down right in the middle of the three-cushion couch.

Seriously, the woman really did think she was Oprah. What irked me the most was that she was the only one trying to ease the situation. Jenny was firmly on Gemma's side.

"How you doing?" she asked with her face turned to mine.

"Fine, thanks."

"Is that why you're hiding in the corner?" She motioned to the drinkers across the room. A hazy cloud of smoke hung overhead.

"I'm not hiding." I hugged the couch pillow to my chest.

Her smile suggested I was being childish but she thought it was cute. "It's okay, you know."

"What's okay?"

"Being bisexual." Her voice was much too loud for my liking.

I put a finger to my lips.

Again, she flashed me that condescending smile that rubbed me the wrong way. Bernie cast her gaze over everyone in the room. "Everyone here is drunker than drunk. Don't worry."

I wanted to scream. Who did this chick think she was? If I wanted to worry, I would, thank you very much. Jesus, I was more neurotic than I thought.

She leaned closer, laying a hand on my thigh. "I felt the same way, at first."

Dammit. Now I was curious. Was Bernie bisexual? But then, of course she was. Bernie was everything to everyone all the time.

"It's not easy, I know. But it doesn't have to be hard, either."

She had me for a moment and then lost me by spouting Yoda-like advice.

Bernie nodded as if in tune with my confusion. "Gemma loves you more than I thought possible. Most people don't ever experience that kind of love."

"Don't you think I know that?" I tore a string off my shirt.

She didn't back off. The woman had more chutzpah than anyone I had ever met.

"I don't doubt that. What I'm saying is don't push her away trying to figure things out on your own. Talk to her."

"I tried that. Do you know what she said when I told her I hated being bisexual?"

"What?"

"That I should just stop. Like I can turn off the bi switch in my head."

Bernie chewed her bottom lip, the first sign she didn't know what to say.

"It's hard to get that out of my head." I circled a finger around my temple.

"I know. That's the problem with heated moments; snap judgments escape even from the most supportive people."

"So I should just forget she said it?"

"Not sure that's possible. But this would be a terrible world if no one received a second chance."

I closed my eyes. "Why do you talk like that?"

She laughed. "Like what?"

"Like you're a mix of Buddha, God, and Oprah."

"Ah, you're a straight shooter. I like that." She shoved my shoulder.

She liked that. Of course she did! Because she's Bernie, everyone's friend and therapist.

She squeezed my leg. "I want to be your friend, Tegan. I know you have a lot going on and think you're all alone. You aren't if you don't want to be. Even if you don't let me in, let Gemma in. She's beating herself up." With that, she stood and rejoined the party.

Gemma approached slowly, as if she were Marie Antoinette on the way to the guillotine. I couldn't decide what made me sadder: her slumped shoulders or the fear that churned in her emerald eyes, turning them a dirty shade of jade.

"May I sit?"

"Of course." I motioned to the cushion next to me.

Unlike Bernie, she sat on the cushion on the far side of the couch, facing forward.

I repositioned, now resting my back against the arm, and crossed my legs to face Gemma. Not completely at ease, I still gripped the pillow with both arms. Was I expecting her to rip my heart out or something while hoping the pillow would protect my chest cavity against all odds?

"How are you?" she asked.

I had to give her credit for taking the first step. It was more than I had done since that night.

I shrugged. "You?"

"Miserable." Her voice was barely above a whisper.

"Me, too."

"You have no idea how sorry I am. I never should have said what I did." She spun her head briefly toward me, but her neck jerked forward as if on a spring.

"I shouldn't have put you in that position," I said, flinching over the ridiculous sentiment. It was like we were in a board meeting, not two lovers trying to find middle ground. The past few days, we'd coexisted in our room. If I had to choose one word to define our interactions, it'd be *frosty*. However, the frenzy of finals drove us, and now that we had both completed our last exam, our relationship issue reared its ugly head.

Gemma nodded noncommittally.

"What do you want? From me?"

She swiped both palms on her jeans. I couldn't detect if she hadn't been expecting my bluntness or if she didn't know how to answer. Like she didn't know how to say, "I love you, but this whole bisexuality thing is much more than I bargained for."

"I want you. That's all."

I laughed and nudged her thigh with my foot. "You have me as long as you want me."

Gemma's head swiveled. "What does that mean?"

Great! I'd upset her again. "It means I want to be with you."

"But why did you put it that way? 'As long as I want you?'"

"Uh, I don't know. You kinda wigged out when I proclaimed I was bi."

"Exactly!" She punctuated the statement with a forceful *I Dream of Jeanie* nod, except she wasn't granting me a wish.

"So does that mean it's... it's...?" I couldn't say the rest.

"How could you ever forgive me?" Her eyes dropped to the couch cushions.

"Forgive you?"

"I completely discounted your feelings when you opened up. I had no idea how much you'd been struggling, and then when you let me in, I... Why would you want to be with me?"

"That's why you're so nervous? Why you won't look at me?"

She shrugged, still not making eye contact.

"Jesus, Gemma. It hurt, of course, but if I walked away from the most loving person because of one harsh statement, I'd be a fool. People—even ones in love—hurt each other." I nearly laughed, realizing I was speaking Bernie-like. "Besides, how many times have you forgiven or overlooked one of my many spastic moments?"

She smiled, lifting the cloud from her aura. "I wouldn't even know how to calculate the incidents. A sliding scale, maybe." She massaged her chin.

I nudged her thigh harder with my foot. "Gemma!"

"I mean, do panic attacks count? Choking incidents? Outbursts?" She was on a roll, ticking off each category with a finger.

"Pouting around my mother," I added.

"Yes! Now you're understanding my conundrum.

How do I factor in all your spaziness?" She slipped her hand under my jeans, stroking my calf.

I closed my eyes. "I missed your touch. Whenever denied, I realize how much your touch calms and excites me."

"Excites?" Her rapid breath was encouraging.

"Very much so."

Gemma surveyed the room. There were a few diehard drinkers left, and none of them gave two shits about us hidden in the corner.

"Shouldn't we talk more?" she asked.

"We can if you'd like. Or you can take me home. We have one night left until you go on vacation. I would like to create some memories to replay over the next two weeks."

Gemma rose, put her hand out, and said, "Come."

"Oh, God. I want to. Come all night long."

Gemma grasped my hand tighter. While we were among friends, not all of them knew we'd moved into relationship status; however, how most didn't guess was beyond me. Bernie caught my eye, giving me an *atta girl* nod. It annoyed and pleased me in equal measure. Maybe she wasn't like Darla.

Our dorm was across the street, and many of the students had already fled for summer break.

"Race you," Gemma shouted over her shoulder.

She dashed off, leaving me in the dust. Her playfulness indicated she didn't have a care in the world. It was then that I realized I would love to trade places.

Tomorrow, her folks and sister were picking her up for their annual summer holiday in Yellowstone and Grand Teton National Park. I was heading home to my mom's for two weeks until I could move into my first apartment.

An apartment I was sharing with Gemma. Even though things had been strained, neither of us mentioned cancelling the plan. However, the ink had dried on the contract and the first and last month's rent had been paid.

We were moving in together.

It hit me. Yes, we'd been roommates since I started college, but a computer system had paired us together. I had signed a summer lease on the apartment and then a year-long lease starting in the fall. It would mark officially moving in with my girlfriend and leaving dorm-life behind.

Gemma stopped on the other side of the street and stood with her head cocked, analyzing me.

Her red locks framed her soft, creamy skin like a painting in a museum.

Neither of us moved or said a thing.

She smiled her typical *What are you thinking now?* smile.

Her beauty bowled me over, and my knees wobbled.

She placed her hands around her mouth, megaphone style, and bellowed, "What are you waiting for?"

Her words drifted over asphalt, causing my breath to hitch.

"You!" I said.

"Do I need to come get you?" She panned up and down the street, not a soul in sight this late at night.

"No. Stay there. I like the view."

She laughed, shaking her head. "You always keep me on my toes. One moment you're ready to go; the next, you're planting your feet, refusing to budge."

"It's part of my charm!"

"If you say so." Her smile agreed, even if her words were meant to tease. She hooked her thumbs into her belt loops, and she started to whistle the theme song from *The Bridge over the River Kwai*—a movie about war prisoners in a Japanese war camp.

"Nice choice," I yelled across the road.

"I thought it fitting."

"Are you my captive?"

"Have been since day one. I just didn't know it."

"What if I'm your captive? Have been since day one?"

"Even better, then. We're both prisoners."

"Love prisoners," I corrected. It was insanely freeing to share my feelings for all to hear, even if the street was empty.

"Come on. Let's go home," she coaxed me to join her.

I stepped off the curb.

She waved her arms and shouted something, but I couldn't hear her over someone's screaming.

I was forced to the ground, whacking my head hard against the asphalt. Out of the corner of my eye, a bicycle wheel spun.

Gemma ran across the street. "Tegan! Are you okay?"

I looked into her face as it blurred and went dark.

ABOUT THE AUTHOR

TB Markinson is an American who's recently returned to the US after a seven-year stint in the UK and Ireland. When she isn't writing, she's traveling the world, watching sports on the telly, visiting pubs in New England, or reading. Not necessarily in that order.

Her novels have hit Amazon bestseller lists for lesbian fiction and lesbian romance. For a full listing of TB's novels, please visit her Amazon page.

Feel free to visit TB's website to say hello. On the *Lesbians Who Write* weekly podcast, she and Clare Lydon dish about the good, the bad, and the ugly of writing. TB also runs I Heart Lesfic, a place for authors and fans of lesfic to come together to celebrate and chat about lesbian fiction.

Want to learn more about TB. Hop over to her *About* page on her website for the juicy bits. Okay, it won't be all that titillating, but you'll find out more.

Made in the USA
Las Vegas, NV
15 September 2023